KT-462-170

# THE LAST ROMAN: TRIUMPH

Sixth century Byzantium. The Emperor Justinian is determined to reunite the whole of the Roman Empire and his best general, Flavius Belisarius, is poised to invade Italy. Flavius and his men march north unopposed until the local senators of Naples refuse to surrender and a bloody assault ensues. Rome, hearing of the fate of Naples, yields the city to Flavius, but before long the Goths arrive and stage a brutal attack which Flavius's army only just survives. Besieged and mired in a cesspit of corruption, Byzantium's greatest general must navigate a world rife with deceit and brutality where only the most cut-throat survive.

# THE LAST ROMAN: TRIUMPH

*by*

Jack Ludlow

**Magna Large Print Books**
Long Preston, North Yorkshire,
BD23 4ND, England.

British Library Cataloguing in Publication Data.

A catalogue record of this book is
available from the British Library

ISBN  978-0-7505-4368-2

First published in Great Britain by Allison & Busby in 2015

Copyright © 2015 by David Donachie (writing as Jack Ludlow)

Cover illustration © Nik Keevil by arrangement with
Arcangel Images

The moral right of the author is hereby asserted in accordance with
the Copyright, Designs and Patents Act, 1988.

Published in Large Print 2017 by arrangement with
Allison & Busby Ltd.

Magna Large Print is an imprint of Library Magna Books Ltd.

Printed and bound in Great Britain by
T.J. (International) Ltd., Cornwall, PL28 8RW

*Dedicated to the*
*'Famiglia Bruschini'*

*Paul and Mark have fed me well*
*for over 35 years at*
*Pasta Brown.*
*The next generation:*
*Harry, Anthony, Natalie and Georgia,*
*I know, will keep up the tradition.*

# CHAPTER ONE

The state of the world looked promising for the Roman Emperor Justinian in the Year of Our Lord 536. Sicily was Goth free and wholly pacified, while Sardinia and Corsica were firmly in the right hands. If there were continuing rumblings of discontent in the reconquered provinces of North Africa that was a region requiring to be pacified rather than fought for. Victory had also just been achieved over the Ostrogoths in Illyricum, securing the Adriatic coast all the way north to the River Timavo, the border with Italy proper.

The reconquest of the remainder of the Western Roman Empire was now deemed to be possible, this being an ambition Justinian had long harboured, one he had craved even before his elevation to the purple. Waiting in Sicily, Constantinople's most successful military commander and the *magister militum per Orientem*, Flavius Belisarius, was instructed to cross the Straits of Messina and begin the conquest of the mainland.

The army he commanded seemed far too small for such an undertaking, many less than that he had led when he defeated the Vandals of North Africa, yet the message from Justinian was blunt. With trouble an ever-present danger on the eastern border with Persia there were no more troops to be had: the man he trusted to lead his

9

invading army must make do with what he possessed.

To Flavius Belisarius numbers mattered less than experience added to discipline, and those he led had those qualities in abundance. The bulk of his forces had fought under him for many years now, some since his days as an untried commander on the Persian frontier. In addition he could deploy six thousand men from the imperial army under the patrician general Constantinus, who would act as his second in command.

That body included a large force of German *foederati*, fighters from beyond the Danube and the Rhine who lived for combat and would be used as shock troops. Constantinus also brought to the army substantial contingents of other mercenaries; Isaurian infantry as well as Hun and Moorish cavalry, but the backbone of the host Flavius ordered aboard the ships that would carry them to Italy proper lay in his own *comitatus*, personal troops attached to their general and fiercely loyal to his person, consisting mainly of heavy cavalry. These were soldiers he had personally raised and trained who could be deployed as mounted archers as well as spearmen.

The unfortified port of Rhegium, his first objective, observed from the deck of his command galley, looked somnolent rather than a city under imminent threat. To the north, directly opposite Messina, his army, under the watchful eye of his *domesticus*, Solomon, was disembarking across a pebble beach that made such an enterprise slow, uncomfortable and at risk from enemy interference. Yet from what he had seen sailing south it was going to be carried out unopposed.

The only road to and from the capital of Calabria was coastal and visible; Ebrimuth, the nobleman in command of the Goths, who must have had orders to oppose any landing, showed no sign of moving his troops to give battle, this in a situation where he could not be in ignorance of the movements of an enemy fleet large enough to transport some twelve thousand men as well as their horses. The coast of Sicily was visible to the naked eye.

The faint possibility existed that Ebrimuth was moving to a confrontation out of sight, yet that would mean a march along goat trails, through the mountains that stood at the back of Rhegium, which would be exhausting to the men he led. Still, the prospect had to be guarded against and patrols had been sent out to cover the paths out of the mountains that led to his landing beach and that, Flavius now reasoned, was where he needed to be.

The order given, the calls roared out and the oars of the galley dipped as the great mainsail holding them steady was raised: the wind that had brought them swiftly south was not there to make the return. As the vessel began to move Flavius kept looking at the port city he needed to capture. The reports he had told of a force too large to be left at his rear even if in its composition and numbers it was very inferior to his own. He was deep in contemplation of the ramifications of this when the voice from the lookout sounded an alert.

'Boat setting out from the harbour and there are armed men aboard. Goths, by their armour.'

'Size?' demanded the sailing master; he also had the job of controlling the fighting if his vessel was drawn into battle.

'Small, ten oars.'

'General?'

'I am not a sailor,' Flavius responded after a pause. 'It falls to you to decide what threat they pose.'

The man was rendered nervous by that response; the finest general the empire possessed, the Victor of Carthage and a man reckoned to be a close personal companion of the Emperor, was leaving a decision to him and to be wrong did not bear thinking about. He went to the side and raised a hand to shield his eyes, not only from the sun but also the glare reflected off the sea and it was quite a while before he gave his opinion.

'If they seek to board us I can't see them succeeding with such numbers.'

At a nod from Flavius the master had the oars raised on one side, which brought the galley round in a wide arc, all sticks dipped once more close with the mainland shore. More commands had half of them withdrawn while the rowers who abandoned their sticks quickly equipped themselves as fighters, donning armour and eventually lining up on deck, some with bows and others bearing spears.

Flavius could see the figure on the opposite prow now, standing in a way that sought to display boldness, a gleaming war helmet on his head and a white decorated cloak whipping in the breeze, while behind him stood a file of warriors also with spears, which had him call for a shield of his own.

Low numbers could mean many things and one of them might be an attempt on his life from a man ready to die to achieve it. The Goths would know by the standard on the mast who was on the enemy vessel. He might also surmise that to remove the head of an army was to atrophy its limbs and render it ineffective.

'Take station behind me, Father.'

Photius, his stepson, said this with a gravity way beyond his years, stepping forward to cover Flavius with his body and shield.

'If we stand side by side how will they know which of us is the desirable target?'

About to protest, the boy hesitated, then smiled, aware that he was being treated to a jest; how could anyone see Flavius Belisarius, who had stature and presence to spare, a man in his prime, set against a very obvious youth hardly old enough to have a beard.

'Could it be Ebrimuth, *magister?*' said Procopius quietly. Flavius answered his secretary, now stood behind him, with a nod, which prompted a firm opinion. 'He cannot be coming to issue a threat, can he?'

'Is what you are suggesting not too much to hope for?'

'Rhegium has no walls, for all we know he has fewer troops than we were led to expect and with a father-in-law like Theodahad, Ebrimuth cannot feel utterly secure.'

'King Theodahad might be marching south with a powerful Goth army as we speak, so this may be a ploy.'

Procopius brushed that aside. 'It's a long way

from Ravenna, *magister*, over two hundred leagues. If Ebrimuth is going to parley he best be prepared to have it last for many weeks.'

As ever, the pace of matters at sea allowed much time to think, especially as on a distinct swell, the smaller craft was making slow progress. After long consideration and with the putative enemy now in plain sight, Flavius requested that the master heave to and prepare to receive an honoured guest. Thus most of the oars disappeared, only those right fore and aft still in the water to hold the ship steady.

The armed men were rearranged in a fashion more fit for an inspection than fighting, while the gangway in the side of the galley was removed, the ladder that permitted entry from a much lower deck dropped into position.

'Hail, Flavius Belisarius, *magister* of Byzantium, from *Kindin* Ebrimuth.'

The cry from the prow, given in guttural Latin from a senior Goth noble by his title, was accompanied by a Roman chest-beating salute, this as the spears of his escort shot forward on extended arms, signifying no sign of aggression from the military commander and governor of Rhegium.

Much as Flavius disliked being referred to as a Byzantine, he had to acknowledge that even within his own ranks it had now become common currency. To him the name smacked too much of Greece and, like his father before him, he was proud to be called a Roman, seeing in that polity and its achievements a set of values to which he could adhere.

Greeks, who massively made up the largest

14

contingent in the imperial heartlands had, to his mind, few values at all, which in more temperate moments he would acknowledge as unfair; Romans and their Italian allies had been just as corrupt and febrile long before they ceased to hold a majority in the empire, a fact to bear in mind now he was landed on their shore.

'Do you come to parley for terms?' he demanded.

'I come to talk.'

If the two statements sounded as if they meant the same thing it was clear they did not, at least to the Goth, which intrigued Flavius. 'Then I bid you come aboard, *Kindin.*'

With the oars on the other galley shipped, a line was sent flying from one to the other, that followed by a thicker rope strong enough to bear the weight of bringing them together. Peaceful intent was underlined by the way the armed men of Ebrimuth's vessel laid down their weapons on the deck and took a secure grip on said cable, hauling until the two vessels lay side by side, resting on hastily dropped fenders, this as chairs were brought out on which the principles could sit.

Ebrimuth came aboard alone, skipping up the ladder onto the higher deck with an agility that underlined his youth, Flavius being treated to another old-fashioned Roman salute, which gave him a moment to take in the man's physical attributes. The Goth nobleman was barrel-chested and somewhat short in the leg, which gave his whole being an odd appearance. With his large upper body he should have been tall; with his lack of leg, and they were trunk-like, he was not.

15

The removal of his helmet revealed a well-scarred face, which indicated either a hearty warrior or an unlucky fighter, for the Goths were a fractious race who were inclined to internal squabbling, unwilling to let anything seen as an insult pass, when what counted as such could be as little as a churlish sideways glance. Fighting among themselves was as endemic as doing collective battle with their borderland enemies.

They occupied the heart of the old Roman Empire and had absorbed many of its ways, yet living in harmony with each other was not one of them. Nothing proved that more than the events which had taken place since the death of Theodoric the Great, a potentate who had not only pacified and ruled his fellow and troublesome Goths, but had done so in a way that won the approval of the native Italians as well, allowing them freedom to practise their form of Catholic worship, never seeking to impose his own Arian rites.

More importantly, Theodoric had, by his lack of greed for titles, kept content more than one Eastern emperor over a long and peaceful reign, never claiming any rank not granted to him, especially not imperial status for himself, an act which would have forced a martial response from Constantinople. For decades the two halves of the old Roman patrimony had lived in harmony and that had continued, if never quite as smoothly, under his daughter Amalasuintha, mother and regent to Theodoric's grandson and heir, the boy Athalaric.

How many times had Flavius and Justinian discussed the tortured situation in Italy over the last ten years since the death of Theodoric, always with an eye on opportunities; Amalasuintha seeking to hold at bay ambitious nobles, not least her cousin Theodahad while that same relative flirted, for his own personal gain in land and money, with Constantinople.

If Theodahad was a thorn in her flesh he was not the sole one: Amalasuintha had wanted her son educated as a Roman but the powerful nobles who surrounded her court demanded their future king be raised a Goth and in overseeing his upbringing they had completely debauched the youngster. The death of Athalaric, a mere sixteen summers old, reputedly following on from a too heavy drinking bout, left his mother exposed.

She had married Theodahad in an attempt to shore up her position. Her reward had been for her new spouse to stand aside while she was first incarcerated and then murdered by those same jealous nobles who had corrupted her son. The question occupying Flavius's mind now was simple: how would Ebrimuth, married to Theodahad's daughter, feel in such a fevered polity; safe or at risk?

'Your great reputation precedes you, Flavius Belisarius.'

The reply was as diplomatic as the Goth opening. 'As would yours, Ebrimuth, had God granted you those opportunities he has graciously gifted to me. Shall we sit?'

The two chairs had been set facing each other in the middle of the deck and these the principles now occupied, exchanging the very necessary pleasantries that always precede the nub of a negotiation, questions of family, of children and of the health of the imperial couple, for it was well known that Justinian did not rule entirely alone but was a man who relied heavily on his wife Theodora.

'He should get to the point,' Photius whispered, his tone irritated. 'It is a waste of time to indulge this barbarian.'

Procopius, standing with him and just out of earshot of the main conversation, smiled at the natural impatience of youth as Photius added to his complaint.

'We need to fight him and annihilate him, not chatter like fishwives.'

'And if we are not obliged to fight?'

Photius looked hard at his stepfather's secretary who, having given the young man a quizzical but silent response, returned his gaze to the two leaders, they having now moved on to more germane matters.

'I know you do not lead a force enough for conquest, *magister* Belisarius. Sicily is not lacking in those who keep us informed.'

'It is large enough for my immediate needs.'

'Even weakened by the garrisons you have been required to leave behind?'

'Thanks to the way you Goths have treated with the locals, that does not require great numbers. The Sicilians are happy to be back under the rule of a proper Roman Emperor. Is it not just as important that you examine the forces you lead? Few Goths, a dearth of cavalry–'

That got a wave at the coast and the narrow strip of land between the sea and the mountains.

'Hardly necessary in such terrain.'

Flavius masked any response; that was nonsense and both men knew it yet it did induce a thought. Had Ebrimuth, knowing what was coming and sure that the men he termed Byzantines would land north of Rhegium, constructed a defensive barrier to stop any advance on the city? The narrow littoral certainly leant itself to that as a tactic and it would impose a check on his aims. It was a fleeting reflection and one he dismissed; there was too much traffic between Sicily and Italy for such a set of works to be kept a secret.

'You may find that assumption to be fatal.'

'What is your aim, *magister*?'

'First to secure Rhegium, then the conquest of Italy and the reunification on behalf of Justinian of the twin parts of the empire. To do that I must march north and take Ravenna.'

The question had clearly been posed with no great expectation of an answer; that Ebrimuth got one so defined surprised him, so much so that he could not react, allowing Flavius to continue.

'Of course, I have no desire to be held up so far south in a fight I cannot lose. So I will offer you terms, *Kindin*. You and your personal followers can abandon Rhegium by treaty, taking with you your weapons, possessions and your families and we will not hinder your departure. Should you stay and seek to defend a city without one rampart to its name I cannot answer for what the outcome may be.'

'Even a man so renowned for his compassion?'

'I grant you I do not like to see a city sacked and blood uselessly sacrificed but there are times when it becomes impossible to control men forced to fight and risk death for that which is indefensible. Rhegium is a rich prize and you cannot say what the temptation to plunder will do to discipline.'

'You are asking me to ride back to Ravenna and tell my King that I did not even try to defend my city?'

'At least you will ride back.'

'And what do you think would be his response?'

'Theodahad knows Rhegium is impossible to defend. I have a superior army in terms of quality and numbers. With another army on the coast of Illyricum to threaten him he will not be hurrying to your aid, even to save his own daughter from falling into our hands.'

'An assumption.'

'A reasonable one. It is also reasonable to assume that if he allowed the marriage, you might not be his favourite courtier. Fathers can be harsh on the spouses chosen by their daughters.'

That checked the Goth and he lacked the skill to hide it; he had indeed married for love, in the face of parental disapproval from Theodahad, which only served to drive home that when it came to events surrounding the court of the Ostrogoth Kingdom of Italy there were, as far as Constantinople was concerned, few secrets.

Flavius Belisarius did not have to allude directly to the fact that Ebrimuth might have his head removed for his failure to defend Rhegium even if he survived any attempt to hold the port city in the first place. Certainly Theodahad's daughter would weep in either event but her father would have the sons of their union and, childless himself, that would present him with the basis of a dynasty, something dear to the heart of any ruler.

'A possible solution presents itself, *Kindin*.' That got narrowed eyes and a suspicious look, which to Flavius was unconvincing. 'It is in the nature of our Emperor to be compassionate to those of his enemies caught on the horns of a dilemma such as yours.'

'Which is?'

'To offer them sanctuary.'

Ebrimuth looked down then at his lap, which left Flavius to contemplate the top of his blond-haired head. He waited long enough to allow what he had just said to sink in before continuing.

'If you think Rome was once magnificent you have yet to see Constantinople. The city has a wealth almost too hard to encompass, even for me. I also serve a man who hates war–'

'Hard to believe given the number he has engaged in.'

'Many times we have been obliged to defend ourselves and we have a right to seek to recover territory long held by our predecessors, but I doubt you have any notion of the offers made to Theodahad over many years to bring such a return about.'

Ebrimuth's father-in-law was slippery as an eel and it was no secret he had flirted with Justinian when Athalaric had been the heir to the Theodoric throne. More recently he had agreed to sell his kingdom to Justinian in return for title to the old imperial estates of Italy, a source of massive and steady wealth, reneging at the last moment, it was thought for fear of his nobles. It was the breaking of that undertaking which had provided the justification for the present invasion.

'What was offered to him?' Ebrimuth asked, seeking to feign a degree of indifference, as if to imply the question was posed out of mere curiosity.

'Patrician rank as long as he renounced his Arianism. Land and a position in the administration of the empire, a place in the imperial armies for those of his followers who came with him.'

Flavius waited for Ebrimuth to be drawn out; he waited in vain. 'I would not be in any way astonished if Justinian offered the same to any high-ranking Goth nobleman wishing to eschew war in favour of peace.'

'Is Rhegium worth it?'

'It is to me and I am favoured by the fact that Justinian is open to my advice.'

The question that followed was posed in a near whisper. 'And you would be willing to advance such a proposal to him?'

'It would not please me, Ebrimuth, even on such a short acquaintance, to see your head stuck on a pike, wherever that might reside.'

'I must consult my closest followers.'

Flavius was tempted to say that most of them must have come out in that boat with him. The person he needed to talk to was his wife, which induced a sad feeling. He too needed to talk to his wife, but not on a subject even remotely facing this Goth. It was as well Ebrimuth stayed silent and contemplative; if he had not he might have sensed the sudden turmoil such thoughts

22

created in the mind of the man with whom he was negotiating.

Finally he spoke, standing as he did so. 'You will have your reply with the dawn, *magister.*'

Ebrimuth spun round to reboard his vessel with the same agility as he had shown when coming aboard. The lines were cast off and the single sail raised on the smaller boat as it swung round to head back to Rhegium on the wind. Photius was quick to approach his stepfather, to whom he was more loyal than to his transgressive mother. He had heard the last part of the exchange and wanted to know what the outcome would be.

'We must lose men to another garrison, Photius.'

'You are sure he will accept?'

'Of course he will, boy,' Flavius replied, with a gentle slap on the back. 'It's what he came for.'

'Procopius, you knew!'

The secretary, tall and gangling, just smiled again, which on such an aesthetic countenance smacked of condescension. 'I was tempted to wager with you, Photius, but taking ripe fruit from a child is too easy.'

'I am not a child!'

'No,' Flavius said with some force, aiming a sharp glance at a too sarcastic Procopius. 'You are a man and one I am proud of. Now let us get back to the landing beach and prepare to march north.'

The sailing master had been awaiting the order and with his rowers back on their oars, no longer in armour but dressed in nothing but loin cloths, he called out the required commands that got his galley moving. Flavius walked to the prow to take advantage of the cooling breeze as well as to think.

'Do you think Justinian will agree?' Photius asked Procopius.

'I do. The *magister* would be unlikely to make such an offer unless it had been previously discussed.' As the youngster nodded, Procopius added in a sour tone, 'Not that the Emperor is incapable of denying such an arrangement if it suits his purpose on the day.'

## CHAPTER TWO

There was nothing to trouble the army on the march north, this being a part of the world unused to war. The various towns which Flavius approached, lacking walls and faced with overwhelming force, quickly surrendered. In the present conqueror they found a man who had long ago set his stamp on what his troops were allowed to do in recently taken territory – no despoliation, anything acquired paid for, women treated with respect – and he had been known to hang transgressors in the past if his strictures were ignored.

His army, and that included his senior commanders, had been subjected to the same speech before they departed Sicily, one he had assailed them with on previous campaigns, a special emphasis being addressed to the newly joined troops under Constantinus. The land they were going to was being brought back to its rightful ownership, that of the true Roman Emperor. The people they would encounter, Goths and their allies apart, were not to be treated as enemies but responsibilities, and just in case anyone harboured doubts, there were sound reasons for kindness.

Required to move at speed and not favoured by numbers, they comprised a host that was in search of a quick result. They also had to be fed and there was no time for foraging or forced extraction of supplies. Captured cities would pay tribute to the new rulers and that money would be used to purchase what they needed, with word flying ahead to tell other cities they had nothing to fear.

Plunder would come in time but it would be taken from the Goths not the Italians. Two Isaurians who did not heed the message paid with their lives for their transgression, the army marching past the tree that held the two swinging corpses to drive home the point. That second-in-command Constantinus did not agree with either policy of the Belisarian reaction was plain if unspoken. It was also ignored.

The army sought as much as possible to stay near the coast and in touch with the accompanying fleet, not always possible as the old Roman road moved inland. Even if it was not in perfect repair everywhere, there was still enough of the old pavé to permit fast travel and with no enemy close by – Ebrimuth had assured Flavius that the main Goth army was still in Ravenna – it was possible to eschew caution in favour of progress.

There was no need for a cavalry screen. The only people out ahead were his own surveyors and foresters, the former selecting campsites, into which the soldiers following behind would find lines and markers laid out within which to raise their tents. The foresters would have spent the day gathering timber on which the army could cook the supplies that came in the commissary waggons bringing up the rear.

Naturally there was a section set aside for the commanders, usually in the centre of the encampment and on a slight mound and it was here that Flavius Belisarius would entertain his closest advisors and share with them his thoughts, always taking a chance to drive home his message that if this was conquest it came with duties.

As for what lay behind the day's march, anything pertaining to that fell to Procopius and Solomon his *domesticus*. With a substantial number of clerks to aid him, the general's faithful secretary and *assessor*, with his sharp legal mind, was required to produce a quick summary of the nature of the provinces once ruled from Rome.

That included titles to land, expected annual yields, population numbers broken down by sex and age, resources such as iron, tin and salt, all of which, once passed by the commander, would be sent back to Constantinople so that Justinian should know the value of his conquests. Solomon was expert at supply, it being no easy task to feed a host the size of that his master led and to him fell the task of purchasing food.

If it was a progress not a march, that ended abruptly when they came to Naples, which not only had sound and formidable walls but a Goth garrison, albeit one few in number. As his fleet sailed into the huge bay, Flavius sent word that they were to press as close as they could to the

Neapolitan sea wall but to stay out of range of any ballistae, which would be equipped to fire inflammables, deadly to ships. The aim was not for the fleet to fight but to let the citizens see that, with an army outside the land walls, they were cut off from supply.

Next he sent word to the city demanding the surrender of the garrison and also asking for the presence of someone to represent the indigent population, the notables who ran the city, men with whom he could parley. The Goths who made up the garrison did not even deign to reply but in due course a trio of Neapolitan negotiators were brought to his tent, one filled with his senior officers in full battle equipment.

To get there these worthies had been obliged to make their way between two long files of heavily armed soldiers. That message of strength driven home, Flavius was as charming as he could be, inviting them to sit and take wine, talking of matters unrelated to that which needed to be discussed. In reality he was seeking to gauge who might be willing to aid him and who might resist any blandishments he made, for he could not hope for common agreement. Naples, like any other great polity, would have factions in its ruling elite and the strongest of those would prevail.

Having set the genial mood to these stony-faced envoys, his first serious question was quite abruptly produced. 'The Goths occupy the fort, I take it?'

'I would not be willing to divulge their numbers,' was the rather sour response from one of the envoys, a pinch-faced fellow named as Asclepiodotus.

'I do not recall asking, but by your reply I can deduce they do not have the bodies needed to fully man the city walls.'

Asclepiodotus looked annoyed then, as much with himself as with this general who had caught him off guard, only to have to turn and face the next speaker, the second in command of the army, Constantinus, who naturally had the right to speak on such matters.

'Thus, should you wish to resist, it must be with the aid of the citizenry, who will struggle to stand against trained soldiers.'

Another notable, named Stephanus, responded to that. 'You did not ask us here to issue threats but to discuss terms. I believe it is first the habit of any putative conqueror to tempt with concessions?'

Flavius and Procopius, also present, exchanged a swift but discreet glance, followed by an almost imperceptible nod from the general. This Stephanus, quick to mention concessions, might be a weak link in what was, at first glance, not a trio willing to accede to demands that really did not have to be stated: open the gates, let us enter and we will take care of the garrison holding the fort.

The third envoy, Pastor, glared at Stephanus, obviously irritated by the tone of his question. 'Are we here for crumbs? It is for Flavius Belisarius to plead with us, we who make terms, not he!'

'You seek to impress us with display,' added Asclepiodotus, his manner offhand as he ran his eyes over the assembled officers, 'but it takes no great ability to count your own numbers.'

'I have what I need, Asclepiodotus.'

'To defeat the Ostrogoths? How many Roman armies thinking themselves superior have left their bones on a battlefield fighting against barbarians?'

'Perhaps I do not need to fight. My ships blockade your harbour and my soldiers control the countryside.'

'Your coming is no mystery,' Pastor said, the implication obvious: food had been stockpiled in case of a siege.

'I will put aside modesty and assume you know of me,' Flavius responded, his voice still lacking in any sign of irritation. 'Therefore you will know that with open gates you have nothing to fear from me and the men I lead. Lock them against me and the matter is altered.'

'We are but representatives of a larger body, General,' Stephanus interjected, cutting across his pinched-faced companions who looked set to provide a rude and possibly impertinent answer. 'We have a senate at our backs to which we must report what you say.'

The other two grunted and nodded in a way that seemed to convey that the soft words of the man addressing them meant little.

'That I appreciate. What I offer to you is no blood wasted for that which is inevitable, including your Goths if they are practical, set against much death and destruction of what is a pearl of a city and one the Emperor would be both happy and grateful to embrace.'

If the talking continued it did not do so to very much purpose. None of these men, Stephanus included, made any meaningful proposals, repeating the need to consult while Flavius could only repeat his mixture of blandishments and mild threats. Time ran into the sand and the trio departed, each with a gift from their host of some object of value given to him on the way from Rhegium by a less belligerent city.

Flavius waited till his tent emptied, leaving himself and Procopius alone, his secretary being the man with whom he could share his most intimate thoughts. 'The Stephanus fellow seems the least ill-disposed.'

That got an emphatic nod. 'I will seek to get word to him of the rewards he can expect for advancing our cause. I take it I am allowed to be generous?'

Flavius agreed to the bribe but made no enquiry as to how that would be undertaken; it was the sort of nefarious activities at which Procopius excelled. Not for the first time he was inclined to draw a comparison of this man to Justinian and their twin talents for intrigue.

Ever willing to call the Emperor a friend, Flavius could recall too many occasions, long before his rise to his imperial estate, when Justinian had embroiled him in deep conspiracies, never at any time being entirely inclusive in what he was seeking to achieve. It was by those means he had got his childless uncle raised to the purple, his own elevation thus brought about as night follows day.

Yet there was a difference between the two; he trusted Procopius absolutely to act on his behalf and had never had a moment's doubt that such would be the case, a care that extended even to his troubled private life and that was where comparison faltered. Justinian was too much the weathervane for true reliance, blown off course by his own whims as well as the machinations of the equally devious and tough-minded Theodora.

That thought brought him back to his own marital complications, which were never far from the surface of his considerations. His wife Antonina, left behind in Sicily, had, while in Carthage, formed an unsuitable attraction to their adopted *sort*, Flavius's godson Theodosius, something to which he had been blind while occupied fighting the Vandals. Procopius, more in sorrow than prompted by any other emotion, had informed him of what possibilities he had failed himself to see.

If he had harboured any residual doubts they had been challenged by one of Antonina's own attendants, a slave girl called Macedonia. She had stated as fact that which Procopius had only really hinted at. When he challenged his wife with the information given to him by a person well placed to observe, she had merely dismissed it as irrelevant and a lie.

Theodosius and Antonina were both in Sicily and with his fleet rejoined and in regular contact with the island he had sent Photius to find out if he still had cause for concern, something his position barred him from personally investigating. The young man's return had not brought comfort; Antonina was, it seemed, behaving like a lovesick adolescent and this with a man twenty years her junior.

31

Of course, no one would have spoken of such matters in his presence but Photius was seen differently, a youth to be ribbed with sly asides and barely disguised jokes as well as one able to see with his own eyes. Having reported what had been imparted to him, the more salacious jests tempered, the young man gave Flavius a look that he had employed before, one that seemed to ask why his stepfather did not just dispose of them both.

Flavius could not explain, for to do so made him sound even more of a potential dupe, quite beside the fact that such an act would be mortal sin enough as to render him an outcast. Strong in his faith and dedicated to honourable behaviour, he could not repudiate a woman whom he had married, taking solemn vows as he did so, even if her reported conduct broke his heart.

But there was another reason and that impacted on his career as a soldier as well as the campaign in which he was now engaged, one he was sure required him to lead in order to be successful. If that was immodest for Flavius it was based on a sound appreciation of the qualities of the man who stood to replace him.

Constantinus was a good general but for Flavius he was too eager a conqueror. Even in Illyria, where he had successfully campaigned in a land which was firmly the territory of his emperor, he had apparently treated the local population as if they were an extension of his enemy, allowing his troops the freedom to despoil as they saw fit.

Antonina was also a bosom and long-time companion of the Empress Theodora, indeed it was she who had brought them into intimate contact within the imperial palace. Having, he suspected, manoeuvred them into marriage – Flavius was honest enough to admit to being willingly seduced by a woman for whom he still had a deep affection – Theodora had insisted Antonina accompany Flavius on his North African campaign.

Unsure of why that should be it had taken Procopius to alert him to a depressing fact and one not in dispute. His wife was writing to Theodora relating anything her husband uttered that would be taken as disrespectful to both Justinian and herself. When he thought on that he was brought to the blush by some of the jests he had made, sure they would never be reported to someone ever on guard for treachery.

Theodora resented his friendship with her husband, which preceded her own connection. Flavius Belisarius could plead till the stars fell from the sky that he had no ambition other than to serve a man to whom he owed a debt and he considered a friend, as well as an empire to which he had dedicated his life. It would be in vain.

The Empress, risen from such a humble background – she had been a singer, an excitingly daring dancer and perhaps more besides – had raw nerves when it came to her class allied to her position. She knew there were people who would be only too willing to rip her into small pieces, and saw disloyalty and threats to imperial security everywhere.

That applied very much to a man in whom Justinian was willing to confide, had been too often alone with and had proved to be a superbly successful soldier, a set of credentials that in the past had led to imperial usurpation. Added to that, Flavius Belisarius was popular with the people, cheered wherever he went in his consular year. How could he not hanker for more?

'How went the parley?' Photius asked, once more admitted to his stepfather's command tent.

'In the balance I would say.'

The trio of worthies had been back three times and so far nothing had been concluded, each time the excuse of consultation being advanced to continue delay. Flavius knew that was only partly true; they were really waiting to see if the Goths of Ravenna were going to come to their aid.

'And if they do not?'

'Then it depends, Photius, on only one factor. Do the notables of Naples think we can win in Italy or do they expect us to be defeated by Theodahad, in which case surrendering to us would be a very precarious move indeed, for there would be retribution on a scale of which only the Goths are capable. Perhaps we shall get a better indication tomorrow when they have promised to return with a definitive answer.'

Flavius put an arm round the shoulder of the youngster, still looking troubled by the inform- ation he had brought from Sicily. 'Enough of this, come join me on my nightly stroll.'

It was a habit of Flavius, when circumstances permitted, to walk the lines of the encampment before his men bedded down for the night. If they called out to him he would answer, if they seemed inclined to talk he would indulge them, and if one or two yelled out a demeaning joke, that would invoke genuine laughter.

Flavius was ever aware that leading an army was personal; these men might in truth be fighting for Constantinople but they would only do so effectively if they were also fighting for him.

It was a lone envoy that came the following dawn. Stephanus, shown to the general's tent by Solomon, carried with him a list of demands so comprehensive and challenging that he was genuinely embarrassed to deliver them. Questioned, he admitted that the list had been drawn up at the insistence of his two fellow negotiators, Asclepiodotus and Pastor, who held the greatest sway in the senate and the city. It was telling these two had not dared to consider delivering them alongside Stephanus, no doubt fearing for their heads.

Having played a careful hand, Flavius had kept his overriding purpose well hidden. The city he needed to take possession of was not Naples but Rome. To do that he must get to the city before Theodahad reinforced it to such a degree that a siege would be difficult, if not impossible – the Eternal City, well defended, was too huge a task for an army of the size he led.

Naples mattered only in that, like Rhegium, he could not leave it behind and hostile on what was his line of communication and his possible line of retreat in case of failure. Outside a very tight circle of senior commanders such an eventuality was never discussed, but it would be a poor general who did not consider the possibility. Every one of his inferior commanders had been just as circumspect as he, but they too would keep it in mind, the object in falling back being to keep the army intact so as to fight another day.

'Stephanus, I feel you have been honourable in this.'

'I seek only that which is best for my city, *magister.*'

'Tell me, if I accede to these demands will that get me what I want?'

The envoy, a plump and prosperous-looking individual with greying curls and rounded cheeks had the good grace to look embarrassed, which prompted Flavius to look kindly upon him.

'I bid you go back to your council of notables and tell them I agree.'

Flavius looked at the list once more so did not see the surprise on the face of Stephanus. He was being told that he would be required to pay a huge indemnity in talents of gold; that his soldiers could not enter the city and he could only do so by invitation, while the Goths in the fortress would be given the option to remain or depart unharmed, added to which his fleet must return to Sicily, this to be verified by a Neapolitan escort vessel.

'*Magister,* I–'

Flavius held up his hand to stop the clearly un-comfortable envoy, who even with his plump cheeks seemed to suddenly age, so concerned was his expression, which underlined what Flavius supposed: accept these demands and more would follow.

'You are an honest man, Stephanus and I sus-pect that you are singular in that regard, but tell your fellow citizens this. My design on their city is one in which I seek to secure my own safety and that of my men. I have no wish to fight to attain that but if I must I will, and do not let them think their walls will be enough to protect them. I bid them consider this. Naples is not the first fortified place to defy the kind of men I lead, so I suggest they consider the fate of those which did so in the past.'

Stephanus tried to speak but he could not find the words to respond; he merely bowed low and left. Flavius followed him out of the tent and looked south to where the great volcano of Vesuvius smoked from its cone, that sending out a larger belch of sulphur, which seemed to him, as he crossed himself, to be a harbinger of something awful.

'Solomon, a call to my officers, if you please, to assemble here so we can finalise the plans for the assault on Naples.'

'They will not surrender?' Photius asked.

'No. They think they can keep us talking and to no purpose.'

As was supposed, the acceptance of such conditions did not satisfy the likes of Pastor and Asclepiodotus or the factions they led; such men had made up their minds to resist from the very beginning, fearing the Goths more than Flavius Belisarius. Put upon Stephanus was again the unfortunate bearer of this news, at which point Flavius gave him the option of staying within the Byzantine camp or returning to Naples. Dignified as ever, he chose to go home.

# CHAPTER THREE

The first aggressive act was the cutting of the aqueduct, but it was imparted to Flavius by a sympathetic citizen that there were too many wells in the city for this to be totally effective. Time being of the essence – with winter coming the place of safety lay within the walls of Rome – Flavius could not depend on starvation to bring about a surrender, which meant a costly assault on the well-maintained walls, repulsed by Goths aided by armed Neapolitans.

He lacked the men with the skills required to construct a siege tower or the luxury of time to do so, which meant yet more assaults by ladder and that faced all the options open to defenders outside mere arrows and spears, which included rocks dropped onto the heads of those climbing.

Even worse, if the location of the attack was anticipated they had time to move into place their ballistae, which meant a barrage of stones faced just to get to the base, where they would be subjected to great urns of boiling oil, this tipped over the battlements to scald the skin. Flavius was losing men and that he could ill afford.

To take a city like Naples required a force at least three times the size of that available, one that could so threaten a single section as to leave another part of the parapet short on defence. Flavius was everywhere, both in these attacks and afterwards, to reassure and cajole but in his heart he knew that some coup would be needed to bring on success, that or a change of heart within the city.

Accompanied by Photius and a personal escort, he spent every passive moment inspecting the defences, seeking some as yet unseen flaw. It was his stepson who clambered up a supporting pillar to stand on the undamaged side of the broken aqueduct, his call for his stepfather to join him one Flavius was reluctant to ignore; he would never concede agility even to one so young. Once alongside Photius, they splashed down the gentle slope of the waterway to the point where it had been broken, the water falling into a line of barrels set below.

On the other side of the gap the arched roof that prevented evaporation was still intact and defenders had used the rubble from the destruction to block access, creating a wall of fragmented stone that seemed impassable. Had Photius asked to be allowed to jump the gap permission would have been refused; he did not. The youngster just ran and leapt, leaving Flavius with his heart in his mouth, his anxiety made worse when the lad landed badly and had to roll to avoid a fall backwards.

He then stood up and grinned to reassure his stepfather, the shout of admonition Photius acknowledged with a backwards wave as he closed with the blockage and began to claw at the un-mortised stones, in his efforts managing to create a small opening, one that he began to enlarge. In this he seemed to be succeeding, at which point his stepfather called softly that he should cease his furious scrabbling.

Flavius was not up to the leap achieved by Photius; he had to clamber down one side and up the other, this time followed by his guards, issuing instructions when on the sloping surface that the attack on the masonry should be carried out with quiet care. Two things were obvious apart from what was before him, the most evident being one he had already recognised: silence, which denoted the lack of any guards on the inner side. The second was that they were far enough from the city walls to be able to work unobserved, hidden by what remained of the arched canopy of the aqueduct.

Stones were being removed gently now and it was obvious the construction had been haphazard, relying on depth rather than mortar or the skilful interlocking of dry stonework that was really required. It took a long time to get a result but the sudden feeling of cold air on the face told a now filthy and dust-covered Photius that they had made a breakthrough.

'Enough,' Flavius commanded. 'Replace that last rock and rebuild something behind it to cut out any light.'

'We will be coming back?'

'Most certainly, but this needs to be thought through.'

'If we do assault by this route I ask to be given command.'

It was pure inspiration that made Flavius ask if his stepson spoke Goth, it was the shake of the head that allowed him to decline the request and he was not about to say that which was as yet only an idea; if what he had in mind went wrong, it was a route to certain death.

To acknowledge it was open to severe risk was an understatement and that became more obvious as he worked out in detail what needed to be done. Flavius knew the men to whom he allotted this task would have to make the attempt during the hours of darkness and they needed to get to the end of what would be an unlit tunnel and one that could not be reconnoitred in advance.

If there was a strong body of defenders at the point where it crossed over the city wall they would only discover that with contact. If not, and once inside, they would need to keep going until they came across a wide enough conduit to provide an exit, something like a side channel that fed a set of baths. They would likely be close to the centre of a densely inhabited city in which the natives were hostile.

The Isaurians, four hundred in number, were chosen to mount the raid, they being a body of fighters he knew were keen to impress him, having been absent from of all of his previous battles in both North Africa and Sicily. He had with him a Goth-speaking cavalry commander called Magnus, directed to accompany Ennes, the man selected to lead.

He was a member of the general's close body-guard and a noted warrior; if they were challenged Magnus would seek to fool the defenders, if that failed Ennes would try to fight his way through. Every tenth man was directed to carry an unlit torch and the whole was to be accompanied by a pair of trumpeters.

Timing was critical; he needed those men to be ready to debouch from whatever exit they found just as dawn broke, this while the rest of the army made a feint against that section of the walls close to the aqueduct to distract the garrison.

Thus, from the battlements, in the hours of darkness, the Neapolitan defenders observed many a torchlit group of attackers move into position and the reaction was as expected. The threatened section of the walls was reinforced by the more martial Goths and many a taunt echoed in the darkness to tell these fools what fate they could expect.

Flavius, keen to encourage these exchanges, took another Goth speaker as close as he dared to engage the defenders with offers of gold if they surrendered, their attempts greeted with jeers and catcalls. Hopefully these were loud enough to drown out the noise of that barrier being dismantled and, following on from that, such a body of soldiers struggling in total darkness along a narrow corridor in which they were barred from using their torches, there being too many gaps in the aqueduct brickwork that might leak light.

Some of them found the Stygian darkness and the eerie echoes too much to bear and Flavius found himself called from the walls to consult with Magnus, who had led half the badly shaken attacking party back out into the starlight. Flavius quickly called for two hundred replacements from his *comitatus*, an act that so shamed the Isaurian retirees that they insisted on going back.

There was no time to argue; dawn was not far

off and there was still the need for distraction, perhaps more now that the invasive force numbered six hundred instead of four. The Goth speaker was still where Flavius had left him, now sending insults towards the walls about their manhood and wayward mothers that got a furious and satisfyingly noisy reaction.

For a commander, indeed for the lowest soldier, waiting can be the hardest part of war and Flavius was doubly cursed by not having any notion of how matters were proceeding where it really counted. That changed when the first trumpet blew, soon followed by the sight of numerous waving torches from two of the towers that stood either side of the nearest of the great gates.

The horns of the main force blew to sound the advance and the whole of the besieging army surged towards walls nearly denuded of the previous defenders, who were now too busy trying to retake those towers. The noise now was not of jeering but metal on metal, the yelling of men fighting and the screams of those wounded or dying.

With his men climbing their ladders and coming face-to-face with a poor defence it looked to Flavius as if they might overcome the walls without the aid of those of their comrades within. But Ennes had other ideas and right before his eyes the gates between the towers swung open and their general watched as his troops surged through.

There was no attempt to control them once they were inside, indeed it would have been dangerous to try. Naples had defied the army of Justinian and it would pay the price in both blood and rapine. All Flavius could do was gather

43

to him Solomon, Photius and a large and well-armed body of his *comitatus* to enter the city and seek out the leading citizens, either to cast them in chains or, if they were of the stripe of Stephanus, to keep them alive.

A wealthy trading city and one that had not faced any serious threat for many decades, Naples was ripe for plunder and that was moving forward slowly like a murderous tide, the pace dictated by the rate of pillage. Through every open doorway Flavius could hear the screams of women and children, who would be spared and sold into slavery, as well as the cries for mercy of men who, once they gave up what valuables they possessed, fell silent as their lives were extinguished.

The cobbles beneath his feet were already running with blood, trickling down the slope that led towards the central area and then to the harbour. Bloodlust was being fuelled by ample wine, which required that his bodyguards form a wall of shields before him as gore-spattered men, now becoming insensible through drink, staggered around prepared to kill friend as well as foe.

If such creatures carried severed heads, their more astute comrades had sought out sacks to bear away that which they were busy looting, objects of gold and silver. Others had found money chests and were heading back out of the city to a place where they could be securely left, herding before them the women and children they would subsequently sell. All Flavius could do was let them pass as he struggled to move forward, for he had a more serious purpose.

One time part of Magna Graecia, Naples had

been thoroughly Romanised so Flavius knew to head for what had been the Forum and the Senate House, finding matters easing as he got ahead of his looting soldiery. The area surrounded by the old Roman buildings, as well as the spoke-like thoroughfares and one-time pagan temples now turned into churches, were packed with those who had found time to flee with some of their possessions, the sound of their mass prayers setting up a low hum.

The notables who had defied Flavius had scurried to the Senate House in the hope that they would be defended by what remained of the Goth garrison who had moved out of the fortress to defend the walls and paid a high price in the process. Flavius found what amounted to a small body of men lined up before the oration platform making ready to sell their lives dearly. Before them lay several bloodied and battered bodies, one being that of Asclepiodotus.

Flavius first ordered that the routes to this central precinct be blocked to keep out his own marauding soldiers, then moved forward to parley with the surviving Goths, a mere seventy men now facing hundreds. Stephanus emerged from between the columns of the building, moving through the line of armed men to close with the conqueror and to bow low.

'It falls to me to surrender to you our city and to plead for mercy.'

'Too late for that, Stephanus. I have the right to put every man, woman and child to the sword.'

'Which I hope your Christian conscience will not allow.'

Flavius looked at the body of Asclepiodotus and not just him; the man who had preached defiance was surrounded by what had to have been his supporters as well as the stones by which they had been so cruelly slain. Seeing the direction of the gaze, Stephanus acknowledged an obvious truth: that he and his companions had been killed by his own people.

'And Pastor?'

'His heart gave out when he heard he might have to face you.'

'He struck me as being a fool, perhaps he was not.' Looking past Stephanus, Flavius now gazed on the line of Goths. 'These men do not have to die, perhaps that would be better coming from you than me.'

'What can I offer them, General?'

'Life, no more. I have no desire to fight them twice, therefore they will, if they disarm, be put aboard a ship for Sicily.'

'And slavery?'

'Or they can serve as mercenaries on the eastern frontier of the empire. As I said, life – and if they decline, Stephanus, I bid you look to your own safety and get inside your Senate House, for if fighting breaks out it is never a respecter of persons, however honourable they may be.'

The exchange Stephanus undertook was out of earshot of Flavius or any of his *comitatus,* men whom he suspected were hoping the Goths would refuse to surrender. Their comrades were spilling blood and lining their purse; they too would want that they should have the chance to do likewise. Stephanus obviously had to use persuasion, nothing happening for what seemed an age, until finally, with a clatter of metal on stone, spears and swords were discarded, the Neapolitan notable retracing his steps as Flavius gave his commands.

'Solomon, keep the cordon I have set up in place. A party to take the Goths as prisoners, the rest may relieve those who came here for safety of what valuables they carry, that to be shared out equally.' He then addressed Stephanus again, now standing before him, his face ashen. 'I require you to take me to the city treasury.'

That lay in a separate building, also once a pagan temple and still guarded by Neapolitan troops, who were quickly disarmed. There Flavius was greeted with the sight of large coffers, which once opened were full of gold and silver coin, so much that it was beyond human ability to carry them any distance. A sturdy cart was ordered up so they could be transported back to his encampment, escorted by Photius, to be given into the care of Procopius.

Such booty would help Solomon to feed the army on its march to Rome and there was more. As well as coin, the sheer quantity of gold and valuables was staggering, evidence of a trading city that had long accumulated wealth, and these too would be removed, the most precious shipped to Constantinople to adorn Justinian's palace and to underline the success of his army.

The sack of Naples was diminishing as his men tired of their depredations or felt they had taken from the city as much as it would give up, so Flavius sent his own personal troops fanning out to clear the streets of the residue and get the

47

victors out of the city and back to their camp, a messy task that took until well after noon, this while what remained of the council that had defied him was assembled.

That the remaining notables would plead with him Flavius knew. They would ask for the restoration of their treasury and that what had been stolen from the citizens should be returned – both, and they would suspect this, a waste of breath. Yet he also knew he must throw them some crumb of comfort, for an utterly destitute Naples would look for means of redress and he could only leave a small garrison to hold it.

'I shall give an order that the women and children taken to be sold into slavery be returned to you but you must forfeit your wealth. Let the lesson be sent ahead that any city willing to resist Flavius Belisarius and his army will pay a high price for their arrogance.'

'Excellence,' Stephanus pleaded to a restraining hand.

'The port will once more be open. Resume your trade, repair your losses and understand that from this day on you owe allegiance to the Emperor Justinian. I will leave behind me as well as soldiers the officials necessary to assess what dues you must pay to Constantinople, for the protection of the Eastern Empire will now extend to you.'

Flavius looked past Stephanus to the other members of the Council of Notables, or at least those who had survived. 'And be grateful for your lives.'

There was a temptation to make an exception for Stephanus, who had been honest in his dealings, to restore to him the value of that which he had forfeited, his house having been stripped of its possessions before being set alight. There was a suspicion the man might refuse, which would be embarrassing, but there was another reason to demur.

Stephanus would now surely be the leading citizen of the city and it would fall to him, especially since his advice regarding submission had proved sound, to take a prominent part in the running of Naples and the rebuilding of its prosperity. To favour him with restitution would be to diminish him in the eyes of those he must lead.

The next task was harder: to persuade his own soldiers that it was a sound idea to surrender their prospective slaves and allow the women and children to go back to their destroyed homes. The march on Rome was paramount; there was simply no time to deal with the disposal of such captures, and anyway the army had its plunder, which they were free to keep.

Two days had to be set aside for both persuasion as well as for sore heads to recover, time for Procopius to appoint those of his clerks who would be left behind to help run Naples, both to tax it and to no doubt enrich themselves in the process, as well as for those women and children now released to filter back to the city.

The time came for the surveyors to go ahead and establish the next place they would camp for the night and soon after the army resumed their progress, followed by the heavily laden carts that carried the supplies Solomon had taken from the Neapolitan storerooms, as well as the now more numerous herd of mounts his *domesticus* had gathered in from the surrounding countryside.

There was an obvious and palpable increase in the number of camp followers too; not every captured woman had elected to return to Naples. With their menfolk murdered and their homes stripped and destroyed, something they would have witnessed, the means for them and their children to survive lay with the men who had done the despoiling.

## CHAPTER FOUR

Cumae was the only other fortified city south of Rome but the news of what had happened to their southern neighbour ensured that Flavius Belisarius and his army were welcomed with open arms, the small Goth garrison having fled well before their arrival. Flying columns were sent east to secure the cities in the provinces of Apulia, especially the ports on the Adriatic coast, thus shortening communications with both the Army of Illyria and Justinian.

Meeting no resistance the invaders soon had the whole of Southern Italy under their control, though the need to hold such a vast tract of territory and the towns therein seriously diminished the forces set to continue their march. News from the north seemed to confirm that success had brought serious repercussions: the Goth nobles had met and deposed Theodahad for his failure to act against Belisarius, then elected a new leader called Witigis. Theodahad fled to Ravenna where an envoy sent to bring him back avoided any complications by lopping off his head.

Flavius had to surmise he faced a new and more active opponent, now, he was informed, marching on Rome to reinforce possession of the old imperial capital. Yet Witigis was not free to do as he wished; he had to contend with the same difficulties faced by his now dead predecessor. On his northern borders he had the powerful Franks of Southern Gaul, allied to Justinian and in receipt of imperial gold.

Clovis, the Frankish king, was pressing a claim on what Goth possessions remained within what he saw as their territory, while there was still a strong Roman army on the border with Illyricum; if Witigis denuded the north of men, then that made it vulnerable to either one of those threats.

In response, this new Goth ruler decided to leave Rome with a strong garrison and keep his army in the field as he tried to negotiate to improve his position, first by nullifying the Frankish threat. Basing himself at Ravenna he could react to all three possible pressures as they developed, but he could not account for the perfidy of the citizens of the old imperial capital, who sent an embassy under a divine called Fidelis to the man that posed, as far as they were concerned, the most pressing threat.

'Witigis left behind a garrison of four thousand men.'

Flavius merely nodded; if this envoy from Rome was telling him the truth the number quoted was insufficient to hold Italy's largest city. Fidelis followed with the name of the man who led them, Leuderis, unknown as a fighting quality, with nothing to suggest a reputation that would compensate for his lack of numbers.

'And what of your hostages?'

Fidelis had come as an envoy from Pope Silverius, who held great sway in the city and probably reasoned that, despite the various ongoing ecclesiastical disputes he had with Constantinople, he had less to fear from those who shared a basic religious belief than from the Arianism of the Goths.

His envoy was not one to squirm, being too much the smooth bureaucrat, even if the question was one that should make him uncomfortable. Witigis had taken several leading citizens and senators with him when he departed for Rome to ensure that the citizens remained loyal. There was little doubt as to what would be their fate if Rome opened its gates, which was the offer now being made.

'We must hope for the intercession of Our Lord Jesus Christ. The Goths are barbarians but it is to be hoped that exposure to our ways have tempered their savagery.'

Flavius wanted to reply that the man was wishing for the moon; diplomacy forbade that he say anything but he could not help but reflect on what had happened at Naples and see it in a very positive light, in sharp contrast to the way it had been perceived by him at the time. Never entirely comfortable with the notion of sacking a city Flavius had to admit that what was set in motion at Naples had paid dividends since. Cumae had surrendered to avoid the same fate and now Rome was acting likewise, albeit this Fidelis was wrapping it in righteous embellishment.

'No citizen of Rome, from the *pontifex maximus* to the lowliest street sweeper, could be happy under barbarian rule. How many years have we and indeed all of Italy not hankered after a reunion with our brethren in Constantinople?'

'The Goths have treated you better than others. The mere presence of Pope Silverius in the city, as well as your full churches, testifies to that.'

'What does that count against freedom?' came the suave response.

'Who knows you are here, Fidelis?'

'Only His Holiness and a very few of his closest advisors.'

'Leuderis?'

'Steps have been taken to keep him in ignorance.'

Which sealed the man's fate; just as in Naples, Rome could not be held without the active support of the citizens. Indeed, with its extended walls and eighteen gates even he, with a host over twice the size, would find it a weighty task. As it was, Leuderis made no attempt to hold: the garrison headed north by the Porta Flaminia as Flavius led his men in to the city through the Asinarian Gate. Their commander elected not to go with them; no doubt fearing the wrath of Witigis he handed himself over to Flavius who sent him, as well as the keys to the city, back to Justinian.

Witigis would have no choice but to seek to evict his enemies, so preparations were made for his inevitable assault, the first being the digging of a moat from the Tiber adjacent to the Porta Flaminia all the way round the eastern walls to where the river, flowing south, abutted the southern edge of the fortifications. Gold taken from Naples was used to persuade an initially unwilling crowd of Romans to undertake the task. Repairs were also carried out to the long-neglected walls, while he built and garrisoned a substantial fort on the south side of the Milvian Bridge, which would, he hoped, impede an easy passage to his enemies.

In order to delay the Goth progress, strong bodies of troops under Constantinus and another general called Bessas were despatched to take possession of Tuscany as well as the main towns on the Via Flaminia and points north. This gave Flavius control of the main approaches over the Apennines, while he remained in Rome and, with the aid of Solomon, began to stockpile the quantity of supplies needed to sustain a siege, a task carried out in the face of the pessimism of the citizens, who were certain that the city could not be held against a determined attacker, an opinion based on previous and bloody experience.

The information that trickled in as this work was carried out consisted of the good and the bad; Witigis had surrendered his possessions in Gaul to the Franks and if they had agreed to stand aside from his fight with Constantinople, at least their leader Clovis had declined to provide direct military aid. Yet, with forces released from that frontier, Witigis could now send an army into Illyricum. That initial incursion had met with defeat but relief was at best temporary.

If Clovis had decided to stay neutral, the northern frontier was now open to another tribe of hardy mountain warriors, the Suevics, eager for plunder and willing to act alongside the Goths and no attempt being made by the Franks to impede them. With those as reinforcements, the Goths outnumbered the Illyrian army, forcing them to fall back on and become besieged in the port city of Salona, which left Witigis free to march on Rome.

The plan Flavius first formulated had always anticipated such an advance. His taking of strongholds on the route to Rome was an attempt to bleed the approaching army by forcing them into a series of costly assaults on the towns through which they must pass. Yet with Rome as the key he had as much of a dilemma as his opponent, given he too was constrained in numbers, obliging him to call back to the city most of his troops and leaving behind only token garrisons.

'Witigis has not taken the bait, General.'

Flavius nodded; even if he knew well that no military aim ever survived contact with an enemy he was frustrated. The Goth leader had no interest in occupying the towns his forces held, however tentatively, on the road to Rome. Bessas, the man who had come to tell him of this, also brought the less than welcome information on the size of what he faced, which substantially outnumbered his own army.

'Still not enough to close off the city,' conjectured Constantinus.

'How far ahead of them were you, Bessas?'

Flavius demanded.

That brought a flush to the cheeks of this inferior commander; both Constantinus and Bessas had been ordered back to Rome but the latter had taken too long to obey. Caught by the swiftly moving Goths he had been forced to retreat on Narnia where the fighting men supposed to be within the walls of Rome were now trapped. Bessas had been obliged to ride hard to bring warning of these developments.

'Their forward elements are moving at speed in the hope of gaining surprise.'

'Then we must make sure they do not achieve that. Let us go out and meet them.'

It did not need to be stated where such a flying column might appear. The approach to Rome from the north, given the course of the River Tiber, forced any attacker to head for the Milvian Bridge, which gave an investing force access to the greatest extent of the city walls to the east, over which were cultivated and easily traversed fields. On the western flank, dotted with villages, too much of that was protected by the river itself, leaving only a short section of wall open to assault and one that was, because it was so constrained, relatively easy to defend.

'Who should we send?' asked Constantinus.

Flavius was quick in response. 'I will go myself.'

*'Magister!'* was the anxious response of Procopius.

The secretary got a smile for his obvious apprehension; he was never keen that the man who employed him should expose himself to danger, which he was convinced would have a disastrous effect on the morale of the army should he fall. Seen as a lucky general and a wily one, there was to the mind of Procopius no one to replace him. Added to that was a personal and strong attachment that transcended mere loyalty.

'I must seek to see our enemies for myself, Procopius, or how will I know how to beat them?'

'By allowing others to tell you.'

'No. I need to look this Witigis in the eye, or if not him, the kind of men he commands.'

Not even a general with a superbly well-trained body of personal troops could depart immediately, so it was well into the day when Flavius, Photius at his side, exited the Porta Flaminia and headed towards the Milvian Bridge. This was the site of the battle in which Constantine, the founder of the city to which he gave his name, as well as the ruler who had brought Christianity to the empire, had triumphed. He had defeated his brother-in-law Maxentius to take control of the Roman Empire when it was at its height, to become one body under one emperor.

That was what Flavius had been tasked to recreate, to join under Justinian the two fractured parts of that ancient domain into one whole. If he felt, as a successor to mighty Constantine, the weight of such history, he was also happy to be out of Rome at the head of a thousand-strong body of cavalry. It was not often gifted to a commanding general to be able to act so, his responsibilities as well as the concerns of others placing a bar on such freedoms.

Sure he had moved with commendable speed it came as a shock to find himself facing the vanguard of his enemies and on the Roman side of the bridge, even more so to find many of those from the garrison of the fort he had erected to prevent this had abandoned their post and were now fleeing towards him, quick to tell him that a body of his German mercenaries had defected to the Goths.

The rest of the fort garrison felt they lacked the numbers to fight off the enemy and if that spine-lessness was a cause of fury there was no time to indulge it. Nor was there time to make any tactical dispositions with his own men, given the enemy were making ready to attack. The horns were blown and the call to battle immediately initiated, with Flavius to the fore, a thundering cavalry advance met by a like response, so that both forces clashed into each other, and becoming mingled, were immediately engaged in a mass of individual combats.

It had been a long time since Flavius had been able to test his fighting skills in real action, though he had exercised often with his men to keep them sharp. That he needed such abilities now and at their peak soon became obvious. He had been identified, probably he surmised later by those German defectors, and was thus rendered the prime target.

The Goths' leaders were straining to close with him, well aware that the death of the enemy general was usually the prelude to total victory, and that might include the city itself. Such a manoeuvre was not lost on the men Flavius had personally trained and within a blink he and Photius were surrounded by his bodyguards, who ensured that none of the enemy got close.

In concentrating on him the Goths had lost sight of their main aim, which was, if they could not annihilate them, to drive the Byzantine cavalry back towards the city and hold the Milvian Bridge for their main force. Indeed it was they who lost the initiative and began to fail in both cohesion and forward movement.

The men in command, so busy seeking to kill Flavius and dying in the attempt, left the remainder lacking in leadership and that proved crucial as they broke and streamed back towards the bridge, clattering across the arched stonework with their enemies on their tail.

If success seemed assured, further surprise awaited Flavius on the northern side, proof of how he had underestimated the speed with which Witigis would close in on Rome. On the hills to the north stood lines of infantry drawn up for battle. This was the main Gothic army and with them Witigis had cavalry reinforcements too numerous to contest with.

Once they emerged to mix with their recently defeated comrades there was no option for Flavius but to effect a swift retreat. Given the numbers he faced and the distance he would need to cover for safety, on horses close to being blown by their exertions, he ordered his men to occupy a nearby hill and form up in defence.

These men were Belisarius's own *bucellarii* and if no longer trained personally by their general they formed the very body of troops he had first raised when his mentor, the late Emperor Justin, was still alive. As well as swords and spears they carried bows and arrows and these now came into play, Flavius directing salvo after salvo against the advancing Goths, breaking each attempted attack in turn until their enemies, in receipt of unsustainable losses, broke off the engagement.

With horses no longer winded, Flavius could lead his men back towards Rome, though he chose a different route by which to seek to enter the city, aware that if the enemy had been blooded, it was not beaten and they were bound to follow in pursuit. This would have presented no danger at all if the man in command of the Porta Salaria, two entrances east of the Flaminia, had not refused to open the gates.

'Belisarius is dead,' came the call from the battlements.

That got the furious and shouted rejoinder from Photius. 'Fool of a Roman, you are addressing Flavius Belisarius.'

'The Byzantine general, never! I know you for a barbarian and I will not be a fool for your trickery.'

'Your head will adorn your gate if you do not open up.'

The head disappeared, leaving Flavius no one with whom to argue. On leaving the city he and his men had been trailed by the curious on foot and in dog carts, nothing to remark upon as it was a commonplace. Such creatures would have seen the opening of the fighting, perhaps even the concerted attempts by the Goths to isolate him, and had, once they hot-footed it back to the city, no doubt chastened by the sight of real fighting as against the romance, spread the rumour he had been killed.

If that was bad, it was worse given the Goth pursuit was now too close to ignore. Flavius was trapped with his back to the walls of Rome and left with no room to contemplate making for another more easterly gate. To accept battle is one thing; to be forced to fight is never comfortable and Flavius verbally had to remind his men of what they now faced, either victory or certain death.

With just enough time to prepare he led them forward, this time in a disciplined line, each rider knee to knee with his nearest compatriots, which would on contact present to the enemy an impenetrable wall of spears. Nor did he order a gallop; the pace was a steady if fast canter, which suited the heavy horses his men rode for they would, having discharged a hail of arrows, then hit the enemy with their weight as well as the spear points of those who rode them.

The Goths would never have faced the like; few warriors in these times had, for cavalry once released were usually lost to whoever commanded them. Not the *bucellarii;* this kind of fight was that for which they had been created, the type of warfare for which they practised and now, instead of being to the fore, Flavius, as well as his unit commanders, had fallen back to become part of that continuous line.

The Goths tried to meet them as a body but could not, doing so in a disordered and dog-legged fashion after the assault of archery, which saw their front horsemen die in droves. Within no time at all the rest broke off the contest and retired from the field. Flavius had no intention of

61

pursuing them so he called for the horns to be blown and in an equally disciplined way his men swung their mounts and headed back to the Porta Salaria. As they approached, the gates swung open to allow them entry.

'Find the fool that kept them closed against us,' Flavius ordered.

'And hang him, General?'

'No. But a severe flogging and the stocks will do him no harm. It will alert the other gate wardens to have a care.'

With the Milvian Bridge lost, albeit Flavius had never really expected to hold it, Witigis could now proceed to invest as much of the city as he could with the forces he had and his plan was not hard to discern. He began to construct fortified camps opposite six of the eastern gates, from the Porta Flaminia to the Porta Praenestine. A seventh was built to the west on the Plains of Nero to mask the Porta Cornelia, which meant that Witigis could deploy against the only other exterior crossing of the Tiber, hard by the massive Tomb of Hadrian.

The fourteen aqueducts feeding the city were broken, which had been anticipated, it being a standard ploy, though Flavius made sure that they were well blocked on the city side to avoid any repeat of Naples. The Goths then began the construction of siege towers, the mining of the walls to weaken them, as well as sorties to dam the moat with earthen crossings so that such engines could be got closer to the walls.

Aware now of precisely what he faced, Flavius assigned the threatened gates to his most senior subordinates, Constantinus and Bessas, taking command of the two most vulnerable personally. He ordered that a second stone wall be built within the Porta Flaminia to provide double security and placed in various locations upon the parapet catapults as well as piles of stones, some to be fired by the ballistae, the larger rocks to be dropped on ascending crowns.

One difficulty was the provision of bread; the water from the aqueducts had been used to drive the mills that ground the corn, which had been stockpiled and was plentiful. With those now cut a solution needed to be found so that the city could bake bread and would not starve. It being February the Tiber was flowing fast, fed by the melting snows of the glacial Apennines, so Solomon had boats placed in the river that would drive the mills on the fast current and when the Goths tried to break this with huge floating logs a chain across the Tiber was used to protect them.

Two weeks passed before any real threat seemed imminent, time in which the Goth leader sought to open talks with Flavius, offering him the chance to withdraw unmolested, these being quickly rebuffed. Even as these overtures were being made, work on both the camps and the siege equipment continued, indicating that there had been no expectation that the offer would be accepted.

Witigis prepared to launch his attack on the seventeenth day since that furious encounter at the Milvian Bridge. The grey dawn revealed the Goth forces drawn up before the two gates to the east of the Flaminia, of which Flavius had taken personal command, the Pinciana and the Salaria, these presenting ground suitable for the advance of the Goth assault engines, towers and rams.

Flavius Belisarius had in his hand his own bow, giving orders that no one was to fire a single projectile before him. Out on the flat and fertile fields the Goth horns blew and, pulled by huge teams of oxen and surrounded by dense bodies of men, the siege towers and battering rams began their slow crawl towards the walls. On the parapet the only sound was that of men praying for salvation should they fall.

# CHAPTER FIVE

The very sound of the Goth advance, made up of numerous features, was designed to unnerve the defenders: cracking whips to drive on the lowing oxen, blowing horns splitting the chill morning air while spears and swords were used to batter hard leather shields. The grinding of rough wooden wheels over hard ground was accompanied by the cacophonous yelling of the assaulting warriors, this while those they faced stood in total silence.

Every eye was on the man in command, standing like a statue, his gaze steady and his bow strung with an arrow but not yet raised to fire. If there were those who would see this pose as artificial, as one that implied death held no terrors, they would be wrong. This was what Flavius Belisarius had trained for since he was a boy, under

64

the tutelage of his own father, Decimus, and those the centurion had put in to teach him the art of war.

He had rewarded his sire by being the best of his age, faster on his feet, quicker of eye with a sword, able to outcast his fellows with his spear and superbly adept with the weapon he now held, the kind of bow he had helped to design, given the Hun pattern that had dominated the battlefield for decades did not suit his heavy cavalry.

As to losing his own life, Flavius had long given no consideration to the possibility. Having witnessed his father and three older brothers die through treachery he had felt since that day his own existence had no other value than the service he could provide to the empire of which Decimus Belisarius had been so proud.

In part, too, and so deeply buried as to be far from openly acknowledged, was shame that he had survived. Should he too not have expired alongside them in a fight that perfidy had made death the only possible outcome? He had, as a youngster, taken as his hero the stoic emperor Marcus Aurelius, who held that no man was master of his own destiny and to pretend otherwise was folly. If it had been hard to hold to the tenets of that philosophical soldier as witness to the massacre of his family, he was still imbued with it as a core belief.

He could sense the men he led becoming anxious; surely he was allowing the enemy too much licence in their approach, permitting them to get so close to the walls that the faces of the enemy, or what could be seen under their helmets, was in plain view. There was a collective sigh as his bow was slowly raised to be drawn, and if the chosen target was a mystery it did not remain so for long following the release.

There were warriors atop the nearest siege tower, not many to avoid overburdening the oxen, but enough to present a mark. The first arrow was still in the air as Flavius slotted home a second from his quiver and he was reaching for a third when the man at whom he had originally aimed took the bolt in the neck, two more of his compatriots following before they even guessed they were under attack. Then came the order to fire and suddenly the air was full of flying death as the body of defending archers sent off their first salvo.

That it fell on the enemy soldiers was to be expected; the vehemence of Flavius Belisarius was not. He ordered that they should concentrate on the oxen pulling the battering rams and the siege towers, for to kill them was to render such engines of war useless; there was no human agency able to replace the pulling power of these beasts.

There was as yet little counter fire to worry about, archery not being as predominant in the Gothic force, a point Flavius had noted in that first encounter. Added to that they would be required to fire on a high arc, which obliged them to stop and aim, thus rendering each bowman an easy, static target. The towers and rams slowed as the bleating oxen were first weakened then began to expire, those dying dragging down their fellow beasts, this before they got close enough to present a danger to the curtain wall or the towers that abutted the gates.

Flavius was no longer present to observe; he had chosen these gates to personally defend because if the flat ground used by the citizens of Rome for growing food favoured the Goth engines of war, it also, once they became stuck, allowed him a chance to sally forth and counter-attack. Solomon had been left on the parapet to provide the signal Flavius wanted, one that told him the Goth assault had faltered and was in confusion.

With Photius once more at his side, he ordered the gate before him opened so he and the cavalry he led could debouch onto the open ground, where they gathered into a formidable formation that made standing against them hazardous, especially for men fighting on foot. Witigis had not brought forward his horsemen, which left the field free to his opponent and Flavius took full advantage, rampaging forward to drive back an assault that was already lacking in momentum, the Goths falling back behind those now static siege engines.

To his rear, runners emerged from the open gate carrying flaming torches, others bearing amphorae of oil, this poured over the wooden constructs before the flames were applied. With the Goth foot soldiers stuck, Witigis got his horsemen mounted, no doubt expecting the customary charge from his enemies needed to drive home the reverse.

Flavius failed to oblige; with superb discipline and on command, the *bucellarii* of his *comitatus* reined in their mounts. Once certain the rams and towers were well alight they shepherded the men who had fired them back through the gates, which were quickly shut.

Witigis had launched several simultaneous

assaults, indeed there was good reason to believe that the effort just repulsed had acted as something of a feint to pin the main defence. Once back inside the walls and dismounted, Flavius was brought news from the other places at risk, the most dangerous being on the Porta Cornelia hard by Hadrian's Tomb on the western walls.

There, abundant foliage and the remains of exterior buildings had allowed the enemy to get close to the base without suffering too many casualties and this obliged the archers placed there to lean far out to take aim, this obviously exposing them, which led to losses that soon became too serious to sustain. Also, the catapults placed on the roof of the mausoleum were of no use since they could only fire outwards.

Running out of stones to drop on the heads of their ladder-climbing enemies and with too many wounded bowmen to hold by arrow fire, Constantinus had ordered broken up the numerous classical statues that adorned the rim of the massive tomb. These were then hurled at their enemies in sufficient quantity to drive them back and thus render them vulnerable to the catapults.

Word came that an assault on the Porta Pancratia, also on the west bank of the Tiber but further to the south of Hadrian's Tomb, had likewise been repulsed. Yet as this good news was being delivered, word of real threat came from the Porta Chiusa, three gates to the south of the attack Flavius had just smashed.

He had known from his very first inspections this was a vulnerable spot: due to natural subsidence the original wall had collapsed and a new one had been built on the outer side to shield the damaged section. The Goths, as well as employing siege engines, had been mining under that outer wall, and given they were seemingly successful, there was danger of a collapse. If they followed that up they would press hard and, unaided, his men might not be able to hold.

Such an emergency required the presence of the man in command, the sight of which raised the spirits of those facing the enemy. Here was Flavius Belisarius, who had so often outwitted his opponents. That he did now; the space between the two walls was known as the Vivarium, it being used to graze livestock, but there were none there now and it represented an empty zone, one Flavius saw he could use to advantage.

Instead of seeking to oppose the Goth mining he let it proceed, and soon, as a battering ram was added to effort, the sound of crashing masonry filled the air, followed by a billowing cloud of dust, proof a breach had been created. The first of the attackers who came clambering over the pile of debris could not do so in any real order. What faced them across the greensward Vivarium was not another wall but one where the rubble of the previous collapse had been so raised as to make it defensible.

The sight of such an unexpected obstacle took the verve out of the Goth thrust; it was obvious the man leading the attack was at a loss to know how to proceed against a hindrance he and his men were seeing for the first time. Flavius sent forward his Isaurians to engage them, throwing the Goth ranks into confusion and such disorder that they sought to withdraw through the breach they had just made. Climbing to get clear, the rubble was no easier than their entry and that left them as easy prey to the spears and swords of their enemies.

As soon as the withdrawal turned into flight, Flavius came forward with his cavalry and that ensured a second rout, one that again allowed his men to fire the engines of war the Goths had abandoned and send, in the smoke from all along the east wall, a message to Witigis that his first attempt to retake Rome had failed abysmally.

Even if it was to be the first of many such a reverse, it must provide a dent to their morale, while that of the men Flavius led must likewise soar to see the enemy so comprehensively repulsed. Added to that, it might still the grumbles of those Roman citizens who feared the city was indefensible.

'Your Imperial Eminence must be aware that with the troops I have at my disposal, and having had to detach numerous bodies to act as garrisons in those places which have surrendered to your authority in the southern half of Italy, I can do no more than hold what I have without either reinforcements or some act of others to draw off Witigis and his forces. Lacking that, if I can repel attempts to retake Rome, I cannot break the siege and proceed to fulfil that aim with which you charged me.'

Procopius finished reading the despatch that, once approved, would be sent to Justinian and he looked to his general for authorisation; it had, of course, been discussed prior to composition and included a report on the successful repulse of the first attempt by Witigis to take the city. The information regarding garrisons was accurate; close to a full third of his army was thus engaged and he feared to gather them to him and leave the route south open to rupture.

His secretary and *assessor* was forced to await a response. Flavius was deep in thought, Procopius wondering if those ruminations might include reflections on the nature of the man they both served. It was no secret between them that Procopius reposed less faith in Justinian than the army commander. Flavius talked of him as a friend, Procopius saw him as a fickle weathercock too much influenced by his endemically suspicious wife.

Always seeing plots to depose her husband – that some were real was true but to such a vivid imagination more were pure fantasy – Procopius was as aware as his master that the Empress Theodora saw Flavius Belisarius as a major threat, not only to Justinian but through him to her own person, and her reasoning, to a disinterested mind, was understandable if misplaced.

The man who had won the Battle of Dara on the Persian frontier, the first victory against the Sassanid Empire for several decades, and defeated the Vandals in North Africa was popular in a capital city where those who held the reins of power were not, being seen as honest and straightforward in his dealings, a reputation spread by the very men he led into battle.

The imperial couple stood at the apex of

empire and tended to be blamed for everything seen to be wrong, not least the endemic corruption of the empire's officials with whom the common folk had to deal. Justinian had worked hard since coming to power to curb the depredations as well as the perceived rights the patrician class had abrogated to themselves over centuries: well-paid sinecures and offices in a vast and sprawling empire in which the diversion of monies intended for the imperial treasury was too easy and justice in the courts went to those with the deepest purse.

In trying to promote men of merit regardless of class, Justinian had become locked in a battle of wills with what he called a hydra-headed monster, a nexus of self-interest so tangled it defied full comprehension. The empire must be governed; those qualified to do so and who were incorruptible were too few for the tasks that required execution, all layered into a system: tax-collecting, provincial governance, judicial oversight and military commands.

Added to that there was a relentless campaign of vilification from those who felt threatened by moves to suborn their privileges, while neither Justinian nor Theodora were free from the taint of being born into the wrong class by those who cared deeply for their bloodlines. Justinian's father might have been a patrician but his mother came, like the Emperor Justin and thus his succeeding nephew, from a clan of what were held to be Illyrian peasants.

This was a charge often levelled at Flavius as well by the patricians among his officers, Constantinus included, though never publically. Thanks to Procopius and what he called his confidants it was no secret; there was little that happened or was said in the various villas occupied by his subordinates that the man in command did not know about.

The background of Theodora being even more dubious, it was the subject of endless salacious gossip and graffiti, which had the imperial palace as a hotbed of sexual infamy. This left the imperial couple more feared than loved, especially her because she was known to be capricious. In truth, Theodora was no innocent; she had been mistress to another man before she met and enthralled Justinian.

That coming together had taken place in one of the low taverns down by the capital's docks where the future emperor felt so utterly at home, more so than he did in the homes of the wealthy. There, fathers were keen to present to him, as the nephew of a successful general close to the reigning emperor, their daughters, hypocrisy being no bar to patrician ambitions.

The Empress had been one of the exotic dancers who provided dissolute if enticing entertainment, and if some hinted that she had snared her spouse by sex or sorcery, then Flavius knew more than most what an enthusiastic article he had been, having himself visited these establishments in the company of his now emperor and been amused by his attraction to those of low birth and even lower morals.

Theodora had resented their close connection from the very first time Flavius had met her and that had only grown as she rose to her present eminence. It angered her that Justinian listened to Flavius, but even more the tone that the latter used to address a near divine ruler to whom he should have grovelled; how dare he suppose he had the right to tell his master what he saw as the truth!

The perception of Flavius Belisarius being seen as honest seemed to anger more than temper her animosity, a general who took care to see his soldiers properly fed and promptly paid, which was far from the norm. He had captured the fabulous and priceless treasure of the Vandals, accumulated over centuries of pillage across the whole of the old Western Roman Empire from the Rhine to the Pillars of Hercules in Hispania, yet he rewarded himself with no more than what was his rightful due.

If that was substantial and he was rich because of his military successes and the titles he held, such good fortune made him, to her twisted mind, more not less of a threat. If he succeeded in Italy what would Theodora think of him then? At least that took his mind off matters about which he could do nothing and brought it to those he could.

'We need to find a way to diminish Witigis without waiting for him to mount another major attack on the walls.'

'Does what I have composed for transmission to Constantinople meet with your approval?'

Flavius caught the slightly tetchy tone in his secretary's voice, for he had been too busy mulling over extraneous matters to truly listen and the way it was phrased was of some importance.

Every word would be examined for a hint of duplicity.

'Would it trouble you to read it to me once more?'

The 'No', in addition to the sharp shake of the head gave a lie to the statement; his man was irritated, though there was nothing new in that. Flavius actually preferred Procopius to be as he was, somewhat of the opinion that his master required to be guided for his own good, not that he would ever tell him so. As he was honest with Justinian, Procopius was truthful with him.

At least with all the problems Flavius had his wife was not present; the pair loathed each other, with Antonina convinced that Procopius carried a secret passion for her husband, a notion he refused to believe. There had never been a single incidence since the day they had first encountered each other on the Persian frontier that the man had demonstrated any thoughts that were untoward. Having raised that, it was the next one that was troubling for he could not say the same for his own wife.

Flavius had to force himself to concentrate as Procopius reread the despatch he had composed, aware it was nothing but the bare truth. He needed either more soldiers or some action elsewhere to draw off Witigis, a breakout in Illyricum or a reversal of the truce the Goths had concluded with the Franks, the pity being that such possibilities could not be raised in writing: Theodora would leap on matters that she saw as being outside his responsibilities to tell her husband to beware.

'I have advised you already to send your own embassy to Clovis,' Procopius concluded. 'You are in a position to offer him that which Justinian cannot.'

'No, even what he holds, especially that which Witigis has surrendered to free up his soldiers. Justinian sees such territories as integral to the Roman Empire.'

'Do you believe we can both beat the Goths and fight the Franks?'

'No, but piecemeal, perhaps, and that applies to Hispania as much as Gaul. Anyway, it is of little moment what I believe, what counts is the dreams of our emperor, Procopius, and you know, for I have told you repeatedly, he has harboured those desires since he was a youth.'

'I am aware of your long association.'

That got a wry smile, given the last word had been carefully chosen. Procopius would never allude, as he might, to friendship, given he thought such a connection to be impossible with any ruler and doubly so with the present incumbent. Yet Flavius and Justinian had known each other a very long time, since the day a young Belisarius had come to Constantinople as a near drifter seeking justice for his father and brothers.

If that had been achieved it was down to the man he now served. That redress for the murder of his family had involved a deep conspiracy and one in which he had been as ignorant as those against whom it was truly aimed. Such obfuscation counted for little set against the fact that it was an unqualified success, as the power of his family's nemesis had been utterly destroyed.

Likewise the elevation of his uncle Justinus from Commander of the Imperial Guard to the purple as Justin the First; that would never have happened without the machinations of the nephew, and if it had been contrived by him for a selfish long-term aim it had been another undoubted achievement. Justinian could conspire like no one Flavius had ever met and sometimes, it had been reasoned, he was inclined to get so embroiled in his machinations he acted against his own best interest.

'What a boon it would be,' Procopius said, 'if you could write to the Emperor a letter he would not show to his wife. Perhaps then...'

The wistful hope was left hanging. Justinian, either through fear or blind trust, Flavius was never sure which, shared everything with Theodora. Mind, she was such a termagant if thwarted he doubted her husband had much choice.

'I need to walk the walls, Procopius. Come with me and send for Photius as well.'

They were on the parapet when Flavius posed his question: what are our major difficulties? It was the non-military Procopius who responded.

'Enemy numbers.'

'I said difficulties.' Receiving no immediate reply from either of his companions Flavius added, 'Enemy spirit. A warrior people that elects their king expects that he will be victorious.'

'And if he fails,' Photius interjected unnecessarily, to a sharp rejoinder from Procopius.

'Then they depose him and elect another.'

'Or kill him,' replied the slightly abashed youngster.

'Would it be impious to hope for such an outcome?' Flavius responded. 'It may be, but we can surely sow doubt in their ability to finally win and I cannot wait until Justinian gets that despatch and acts upon it.'

'If indeed he does, *Magister*.'

'Would I be correct, father,' Photius put forward, 'in the notion that you already have a plan?'

'A notion no more, Photius. Do you recall that first encounter we had after we chased away the Goths who had crossed the Milvian Bridge?'

'I recall we were forced to fall back and quickly.'

'True, but we were not routed. We held them at bay and retired when it suited us by the employment of archery. I have a feeling we can do the same outside these walls.'

The slow pace at which they had hitherto walked the parapet quickened suddenly as Flavius made his way back to the senatorial villa he had taken as his residence. There had been no need to commandeer it, the owner being one of those hostages Witigis had taken to Ravenna when he left Leuderis to hold the city. There was no chance the senator would come back either. After the first repulse, Witigis had let it be known who would pay the price for that; he had sent orders that all his hostages should be murdered.

# CHAPTER SIX

The King of the Goths was not inclined to be idle either; he reacted to his reverse by sending a large force to take the Roman harbour at Portus, the place where incoming ships bearing food were unloaded, their cargo being brought upriver by barge, this a signal to Flavius that nothing had happened to dent his determination to retake Rome. Starvation would be added as a weapon, while the carrot was being dangled, inviting the defending forces to redress this ploy, which would bring them into the open in conditions which favoured their enemies.

Witigis still lacked the troops required to completely surround Rome and he had to maintain pressure where he could, yet if it was still not a full-blown siege, the action made matters more difficult for the defenders. A heavily garrisoned Portus under Goth control required that supplies, for both the army and the city, had to be landed at Antium, ten leagues further south. If that as a distance did not sound great, it imposed a huge burden, given it required a minimum two-day journey, the employment of a large number of waggons and oxen as well as a strong escort.

In response, Flavius ordered that the women and children be evacuated to Naples, and if many sought to dodge this edict – the prostitutes and dancing girls flatly refused to budge – the maternal were happy to join, with their depend-ents, a well-supplied column and move to a region where food would be plentiful and the risk of Gothic wrath, which would be terrible if they did retake Rome, was a distant one. As to a military reaction, they had already been con-sidered and the necessary moves put in place.

With them went another reply from Flavius to his wife; Antonina had moved to Naples and was expected by her husband to remain there until Rome was secured. That this did not sit well was evidenced by the stream of complaints that came winging north, insisting her place was at his side. It was no use pointing out the dangers; had she not risked those in North Africa?

Flavius would have liked to remind her that her presence on that campaign had not been his idea, and also that wives accompanying generals of armies engaged in conquest was far from com-mon. To do so he would have had to allude to the truth; it was at the instance of Theodora that her friend Antonina sail for Carthage with her husband, and if at the time Flavius had wondered at the reason for such a request, he was even-tually disabused by Procopius.

Antonina and Theodora were bosom friends from their days working in those taverns so be-loved of Justinian. When the latter had moved into the imperial palace as wife to the then co-emperor, Antonina had been granted an apartment of her own so they could remain close. It was a gloomy thought on which Flavius spent much time in reflection; the way he and she had been brought together, sucking him into a marriage that at the time had seemed to him a gift from God.

Older than him and previously married, Antonina already had a son in Photius who, delightfully, had treated him from the very beginning as if he was his real father. His wife was vastly more experienced in so many ways than her paramour, not least in the bedchamber, a fact in later consideration being not one to dwell on. If Theodora had been no saint it was reasonable, if uncomfortable, to assume the same applied to her close friend.

Scales had covered his eyes and Flavius too often recalled the day they were frayed by his secretary. Procopius had risked his own position to tell him of two truths: that Antonina had a passion for Theodosius and secondly and no less disturbing, she was in constant communication with the Empress. In effect he thought she was spying on him.

'I'd rather have Witigis sharing my Roman villa than you, my dear.'

These whispered sentiments were expressed as he affixed his seal to the latest missive telling Antonina she must stay in Naples. To have her in Rome would mean facing the demons of the knowledge he had, too much of a distraction for an army commander trying to win a desperate battle.

The seven palisaded camps Witigis had set up to invest Rome might seem formidable, and in normal circumstances could have been so. What the Goth could not calculate for was the nature of the man and the army he faced. Even many of those who had not been personally trained by Flavius Belisarius had fought with him for several years now, the junior commanders included, though that did not always apply to his immediate subordinates, men whose views required to be accommodated.

Given he knew his men well and they trusted him, this allowed Flavius a flexibility denied to any contemporary general. Nowhere did that hold more true than within his own *comitatus*, the *bucellarii* component forming a unit he had first brought into being, marrying the abilities of the Sassanid heavily horsed and armoured cataphracts with the fast-riding archery tactics of the Huns.

There were light cavalry too, but men so well taught and their leaders so experienced they acted with a different state of mind to those they generally opposed. If they charged, which they were eager to do, it was with a specific aim in mind, to either rout a fleeing enemy or, more often, to break up any infantry attack. That achieved they would quickly reform and get back to the position from which they set out, to remain a cohesive asset to their general.

With their siege equipment destroyed and seemingly at a loss to conjure up any variation of tactics, Flavius calculated Witigis was not planning any immediate assaults. This presented a window in which the Goths would remain in their camps until their king was ready for another bout, and they were far enough apart to allow for each to be tested in turn.

It was necessary to order the walls to be cleared on the day of his first sortie. A parapet crowded with the now mainly male citizens of Rome would merely alert the enemy to the fact of impeding action. Nor were there trumpets; Flavius sent two centuries of his men out of the Porta Salaria with orders to occupy the crown of one of the many vine-covered hills that dotted the landscape and sat within close proximity to one of the Goth camps.

The reaction was as had been anticipated; the enemy quickly gathered to repel this act of impudence, and since the Byzantines seemed in no way alarmed by this, they formed up five-hundred strong for an assault with time on their side. Just before noon they came, to be greeted by a hail of arrows that decimated their formations and broke apart their unity.

In the slight confusion that followed the Goths had to hastily re-form to repel a mounted assault by the Byzantine light cavalry, men who, once they had inflicted enough casualties, withdrew back to the crown of the hill. Flavius had taken much trouble to scrutinise the Goth approach to fighting, habits they would have evolved over several decades, perhaps even a whole century, his conclusion being they lacked flexibility. Repulsed once, they employed exactly the same tactic when they renewed their advance, usually to suffer exactly the same reverse.

Their battle tactics depended on getting close to their enemies, where their individual skills with sword, spear and axe would allow them to impose themselves and bring about victory. Yet without sufficient archers of their own they could not advance against a body of men overly supplied with that weapon and imbued with the proficiency to employ it.

The cavalry that hit them next did the most telling damage; the *bucellarii* first rode to just out of spear-casting range and, still moving, began to pick off individual targets, most notably the various junior commanders, which did nothing for the cohesion of what men remained. Arrows exhausted, his heavy cavalry made no attempt to drive home the advantage they had gained; they too retired to join with their comrades, arrows also too far depleted, in a well-ordered retreat to the Porta Salaria.

The enraged Goths, now reinforced from their camp, naturally followed as fast as they could, to run straight into a barrage of missiles: stones, from pebbles to head-removing rocks, as well as flaming tar-soaked wads from every catapult the city possessed. For those who survived that and came too close, there was another hail of arrows to drive them off.

Like some omen that manifested itself to celebrate such a success, the next day brought a body of two thousand reinforcements, cavalry and barbarian *foederati*, every one of them an experienced horse archer. These men had been on the way before he wrote to Justinian and they came with assurances that more would follow. The commanders who led them, Martinus and Valerian, fitted seamlessly into the structure of the army yet within their arrival lay the seeds of a problem that Flavius did not appreciate until it became too pronounced to easily counter.

This being hidden for now, it became a regular

occurrence to send out parties of mounted archers to prick the Goths into a reaction and one that always cost them dearly, this while Flavius reckoned his own losses to be calculable on one hand. Witigis tried to respond in a like manner, sending forward through the cultivated fields and vineyards a five-hundred strong force to occupy a hilltop just out of catapult range of the walls.

They barely had time to settle before Flavius sent out a party double their number to contest their possessions, not pressing any attack to drive them by main force from the summit of the mound but hammering them with such a degree of archery that they were compelled to withdraw. Now caught in the open and in retreat the Goths fell to the heavy cavalry, who at first plagued them with more arrows and then got amongst them to do slaughter.

A good half of their number failed to make it back to their camp and the haul in both horses and armour was substantial, so much so that Flavius began to gift many of his foot soldiers their own mount, initiating training in cavalry manoeuvres to ensure they understood his basic tactics, given he suspected that if victory came to him, it would be with the clever employment of cavalry.

'He cannot understand,' opined Photius, with a degree of astonishment. 'Is it not folly to make the same mistake over and over?'

The youngster and his stepfather were watching from the walls a repeat of what had previously occurred; Witigis had once more sent

85

forth a body of troops to tempt the defenders. They had eagerly accepted the bait and delivered another crushing defeat that left the fields and hedgerows dotted with Goth bodies and brought another large equine haul into Rome.

'He must be under pressure from his nobles,' Flavius replied, using words that within days would come back to bite him. 'Sometimes it is impossible for a man in command of an army to be seen to do nothing.'

Four times the Goth leader repeated his mistake, seeking to take the initiative away from the Byzantines and those he led paid the price. Finally he formulated a reaction that did not cost lives, no longer sending forward bodies to be slaughtered but merely to tempt and retire in good order. When Flavius sought to reprise his own previous tactics, the Goths employed a controlled charge by bodies of cavalry waiting for his men to emerge from one of the gates, the aim to drive them back, though never getting close enough to the catapults to be in danger.

Flavius had not deliberately favoured either his own *comitatus* or the newly arrived *foederati* but they had been the soldiers most engaged, such men being simply the best troops available for the hit-and-retire tactics he was employing. Yet it was now obvious that such methods had run their course; Witigis would no longer take the bait and the siege once more descended into stalemate.

Meetings of his senior subordinates were a daily occurrence and usually they passed off with little in the way of disagreement; these experi-

86

enced commanders, now including many who had acted independently prior to serving with Flavius, tended to bow to his reputation and agree to whatever course he suggested. That, as the weeks went by with nothing to show, began to fracture and a resentment not previously noticed began to surface; those he had not used in his expeditions felt left out.

Watching others enjoy the fruits of the Belisarius tactics might have been cheering initially but within the bulk of the army there emerged a degree of grumbling. If it was based on envy it was also underpinned by a confidence that came from the results being achieved by the few. Surely if small bodies of troops could inflict such damage on their enemies the whole army could beat the Goths in proper battle.

'It is as well to recall,' Flavius insisted, when this was raised, 'that even with their losses they still outnumber us by a factor of three to one.'

It was Constantinus who responded. 'It's not just our own men complaining, Flavius Belisarius, we have the citizens of the city clamouring to be part of the fight and they number enough to redress the balance.'

'Quality?' Flavius asked, thick black eyebrows rising.

'Do they have to do any more than stand their ground?'

'I have often seen infantry fail in that regard, Constantinus.'

'With respect, what we face are not open landscapes and highly mobile enemies. We are constrained by walls and rivers, but so are our opponents. I know you as a general who likes to pick your field of battle. Here, outside Rome, you have that choice.'

The response was a murmur of assent from all of those gathered, each one in command of a substantial body of the troops that made up the army. Flavius had always been careful when outlining his plans to make them sound like suggestions rather than orders, for, as a commanding general it was necessary to carry such stalwarts with you and diplomacy was as important.

Up till now that had held but Flavius had ever been aware that, though he was discreet in his feelings, Constantinus chafed at his lack of independence, which he had hitherto enjoyed before joining in the Italian campaign. The relationship between a commander and his immediate inferior can often be a fraught one; should Flavius fall Constantinus would assume command.

They were very different men from vastly dissimilar backgrounds. Flavius with his black hair and beard, naturally dark-skinned, that made more so by exposure to the elements, looked like what he was, the son of a one-time common soldier who had died with the rank of centurion. Decimus Belisarius had been tasked to hold the Danube border with fewer than a hundred men, and if his son had risen swiftly to command armies of many thousands it had been with the aide of Justinian, and that had to be the cause of disquiet in the breast of certain people.

His second in command seemed to have a golden quality to his countenance, with a handsome face topped by blond curled hair going suitably grey. Constantinus was a patrician to his toes and he looked it. Not for him the battered armour of the men he served with; with his slim figure and effortless grace he dressed as what he was. He had been bred to command armies, and if not that, to occupy some important office of state – it went with his bloodline.

Up till now there had been few disagreements. The campaign and subsequent sieges, both those pressed and this one endured, had dictated the way matters worked out, but that murmur was telling; such a reaction from such a body would not have been advanced had there been no need for discussion. That was proved when Valentinus took up the argument. He, like Constantinus, had to be afforded attention; he too was a general in his own right who had once commanded an army in Illyricum.

'We have not lost a fight against the Goths since they came to the walls and the supply situation is far from perfect. A swift end would be suitable.'

'Do not doubt that I wish for such an outcome, Valentinus.'

'Then how can it be achieved if it is not attempted?'

The smile that came with the response took any implied criticism out of the words and soon these men were joined by Bessas, long in the service of Flavius, as well as Martinus and Valerian, newly arrived with their *foederati*. It was in no way a re-volt but a discussion among men whose views were always welcome, albeit one pressed home with more than a normal emphasis until Flavius summed up with the aim of giving himself time to think.

'As of this moment I cannot say yes and I will not say no.'

Standing, he indicated that today's conference was over and most present filed out of the chamber, only Bessas staying behind at the silent request of his general.

'How much of this comes from the soldiers?' Flavius asked, aware that if they were unhappy none had imparted that to him.

'I have never known fighting men not grumble.'

'Me neither, but there are grouses that can turn into mutiny.'

'You have no fear of that, *Magister*, but I would say an army that merely sits behind walls, as does the mass of the men you lead, will not stay content. What Constantinus said about the Roman citizens is true as well. If they do not see our men winning these skirmishes with ease they hear of it and talk, then wonder why the city is still under siege.'

'There's barely a trained man amongst them.'

'There's no shortage of a thirst for a fight from what I can hear.' Bessas suddenly looked sly. 'You're not telling me you have not considered this as a course to adopt?'

'I have, obviously. We cannot beat Witigis by sitting on our arses and you know as well as I that holding Rome is only part of a campaign that must end in Ravenna. We are here to inflict a full defeat on the Goths and that cannot become even possible unless they lose outside Rome. But the timing, Bessas?'

'Thank the Lord it is not for me to decide.'

# CHAPTER SEVEN

The thought of a decisive battle, never in truth far from his thoughts, played strongly on the mind of Flavius over the following days and he deliberately sought the views of the junior officers, those in closer contact with the troops. Thanks to past campaigns he knew many by name, and if few were as frank as they might be, what he heard indicated a degree of frustration: the Goths had ceased attacking the walls and too many were not the kind of soldiers he could employ in his hit-and-run tactics.

Being idle made them restless and that had begun to manifest itself in a spate of criminality, not anything out of control but a series of individual thefts or beatings that went right against the edict regarding respect for the local population, which had been an abiding tenet of Flavius ever since he first exercised command. What was the point of alienating people you may in future depend upon, especially if they were citizens of a city your emperor wished to rule?

Retribution, when a miscreant was apprehended, was swift and brutal; a rapid public hearing at which he presided and if proven guilty an immediate rope or a beheading. In one case, the rape of a young girl who had declined to leave the city, Flavius handed the perpetrator over to the citizens to do with as they wished and the man was brutally quartered, an act he hoped would strike enough fear into his own men as to cap any further transgressions.

In this judicial role he was obliged to have dealings with the important Romans – he had to accept that here in their city he and his men were Byzantines – given it was they who demanded justice. Flavius, always accompanied by Procopius, had been careful to consult with such men from the very first day of the occupation, eager to convey the impression that he was acting in the best interests of both Constantinople and Rome, regular meetings that took place in the building that housed the Roman Senate.

That body still gathered to debate as it had since the days of the Republic, even if it was a sham, as much as its namesake in Constantinople. There the Emperor made the decisions; in Rome it was the heads of the various clans, the leaders of the families who had for many decades controlled the city, oligarchs who sought for themselves the most lucrative offices, sinecures to be fought over in a morass of competing political aims, convenient alliances and endemic duplicity.

The most powerful groups had their less puissant clients, men who knew which way to vote to gain favour and profit. Such clans also employed armed retainers, while exercising control over the criminal cliques that lorded it in the various urban districts, associations that could always be relied on, when the needs of their overlords were unsatisfied by political negotiation, to either riot or intimidate.

The other source of power in the city lay with

Pope Silverius, who in terms of wealth controlled more coin than even the collective senators. Rome had been for two centuries now a destination for pilgrims, many threadbare individuals but a goodly number of wealthy magnates in search of salvation. Every one, high and low, brought their gifts to the city where St Peter had founded their faith.

Was it the Pope who pressed for action, given that in a city under attack those revenues had dried up? A lifetime of observation had told Flavius that divines, whatever creed they ascribed to, cared as much for their coffers as the needs of their flock, too many times the former taking precedence. Had Silverius been whipping up discontent for his own venal ends while staying in the background?

However it had come about, the men he faced now were under pressure from a dissatisfied citizenry, keen to impress on Flavius their willingness to partake in the defence of their city, though not one of them even hinted at any personal involvement. Their volunteer cohorts, they insisted, would be a match for the Goths, a point of view that flew in the face of all previous experience: the same barbarians had encountered little difficulty in ruling the city, both lay and ecclesiastical, with a small garrison, so their claims sounded like vainglorious boasting.

Flavius suspected any untrained levies Rome fielded would be more of a hindrance than a help. Yet employ them he must, if only to keep these puffed-up politicians as well as Silverius on side, they collectively being as capable of causing him difficulties as providing his army with support.

Procopius was sure that some were secretly in touch with Witigis, even if he was himself a man they had once betrayed. Fail to heed their requests and they might undermine the entire defence of the city, though Flavius made a point of originally demurring before allowing himself to be persuaded. That way he flattered them.

'My friends, I find my doubts assuaged and I am humbled by the strength of your feeling for the cause to which we all ascribe.' He made a point of looking at the bishop Silverius had sent as a representative. 'And does not your presence tell us of a divine will that it would be blasphemy to deny?'

The faces before him, hitherto full of eager persuasion, began to relax, while the bishop sought to look suitably virtuous. Glances were exchanged between them to ascertain they had heard right, answered with nods, this as Flavius underlined his point.

'I have long considered when the time would be ripe to seek to fully defeat the Goths and you will be pleased to know I feel it is close at hand. To show that I have confidence in the men on whose behalf you have pleaded, when we move out to confront Witigis, I will employ them as a body and allot to them an important place in my plan of battle.'

Happy murmurs and smiles greeted this statement, which they took to mean an equal share in any plunder of the Goth camps. If they had seemed puffed up prior to what had been said they seemed to fill with even more conceit as the meaning sunk in: their levies were, militarily, to be treated as equals.

'I know you too well,' Procopius whispered as they left the senate chamber. 'You never repose much faith even in our own infantry, never mind these Romans.'

Procopius spoke nothing but the unvarnished truth; if Flavius Belisarius had won many battles there had also been losses, and on those occasions it had been the flight of the infantry in the face of attacking cavalry that had brought on defeat.

He was not alone in suffering from this, it was the bane of every one of his contemporaries, both those who served the empire and its enemies. The army of the day had moved on from the brute foot soldier tactics of the legions. Now the effective arm was cavalry, infantry being raised to provide numbers only when some danger threatened.

This left whoever led them – even if he was inclined, and many were not – short of time to train them to do more than move forward and back as a body, the latter harder than the former, the greater requirement being that they hold their ground when attacked. In addition, they were rarely gifted with the kind of leadership that would meld them into a homogeneous body willing to engage in collective and mutually beneficial action.

Only when he had been given both time and space, as on the way to North Africa, had Flavius been able to pick and instruct their competent officers, while dismissing the inept, for they alone could inspire them to show courage. Lacking proper leadership and perceiving doom about to descend upon their ranks they broke and ran, only to pay the price of their panic as those same horsemen, whom they could not outrun, cut them down.

Flavius waited till he was well away from any risk of being overheard before he felt free to respond. 'Never fear, Procopius, I will take good care to place them where they can do the least harm.'

Which he did, deploying them between the Porta Pancratia and the western walls, packed into a constrained section with the Tiber bridges at the back and stout masonry to their front, where they would remain until the main battle to the north-east of the city had produced a victory.

Yet Witigis had one of his camps on that flank, which needed to be dealt with, so he instructed Valentinus, now in command in that sector, to march out to confront the Goth forces on the Plains of Nero, his task to prevent them from being free to cross the Milvian Bridge, the sole route by which they could reinforce Witigis and participate in the main effort.

'But you are to avoid battle. I will give you the Moorish cavalry to add to your own troops but you are to hold the Goths. Do not engage them closely unless orders come from me to do so and keep a firm grip on the Roman levies.'

The temptation to add 'If possible do not use them at all' had to be resisted lest it get back to the ears of those who had forced his hand; it was a message to impart in private.

Valentinus was not good at hiding his disappointment – he was being asked to act passively, not a command to be welcomed, so Flavius sought to assuage his pride. 'It takes an exceptional general to avoid battle while still holding ground, which is why it falls to you.'

If that was fabrication it sufficed, having been stated before his peers, to satisfy that subordinate. This allowed Flavius to outline the rest of his thoughts, how they would deploy as well as his stated aim to make this a cavalry fight, given the number of horses taken from the Goths meant he could now mount a very high proportion of his army.

'Will the Goths not seek to fight us close to the walls?' asked Bessas.

'I believe we have nothing to fear until we are fully deployed.'

To which Constantinus added, 'Witigis will want this coming contest as much as we do.'

The Isaurians comprised the one major component not mounted; they had come to serve on foot and they would do so now as a body. Yet in terms of battle they were an unknown quantity, having arrived in Sicily as reinforcements. Since landing in Italy they had been given little deployment in the open, though they had the success of that raid through the Naples aqueduct as a laurel.

In the need to move north at speed, followed by the requirement to defend the walls of Rome, Flavius had been afforded no time to act on what he suspected to be their deficiencies. A good number of the men who led them were not of the stamp any general would have chosen, being too careful of their own comfort rather than that of their men.

Added to that they resented any reference to their lack of personal respect, Flavius having been at pains to point out, when he had the time, that men fought not for some great cause but for the fellow next to them and the faith they reposed in the man who was their leader.

His solution was, in part, to replicate the action taken at Naples; he flattered the senior Isaurian officers in whom he had, little faith by giving them the higher status of cavalry and attaching them to the mounted *foederati*. They were replaced with two long-serving members of his own bodyguard, Principius and Tarmutus, the latter the brother of Ennes who had led the Isaurians into the Neapolitan aqueduct.

They would deploy in front of the moat; there the foot soldiers would be close to the city and, if they were broken, would not have far to run to get to a position of safety, while the moat would break the charge of any pursuing cavalry. Neither of the men he appointed questioned the need for such a precaution. If the day favoured Flavius it would be achieved by cavalry, the Isaurians then following up to occupy and pillage the Goth camps.

Yet they had another role and a vital one. Flavius was not the kind of general to assume victory would follow automatically from whichever action he initiated. If suffering previous defeats had been hard, they provided a valuable lesson: with two armies on the field, and on this occasion he would be outnumbered, a steady body of infantry was required to act as a back-stop behind which his mounted forces, if thrown into retreat, could re-form.

The supposition that Witigis would do nothing to impede the movement of his enemies proved correct. He knew from numerous spies what was coming and made no attempt to close with the walls and prevent their exit. Quite the reverse: the Goths lined up before their own camps, further off than anticipated and silent as, with horns blaring and much shouting, their enemies formed up in three detachments of cavalry, each several thousand strong, before moving to within range of where their archery would be effective.

Opposite them in the front centre, the Goths had placed their best protected and heavily armoured infantry, providing security for their less numerous archers deployed to the rear, while Goth cavalry formed the two wings. The difference in reaction to the opening salvoes, compared to previous engagements, was telling; the Goths in the centre suffered less than they had previously by the clever use of their shields. Yet still there were casualties, only this time there was no breaking of their forward line. If a man fell, that merely closed up and the remainder held their ground.

Slowly but inexorably the distance between the two armies shortened as the Byzantines crept forward and with frustration being added to the mix – such a stoic resistance was infuriating – the cavalry began to attack the enemy line, the *bucellarii*, included, given they were running short on arrows. Great loss was inflicted with spears, but they too were diminished and that caused the gap to narrow sufficiently to allow close combat, Flavius's men on horseback against Goths on foot in the centre, cavalry fighting cavalry on the wings.

Witigis had wisely held his centrally placed archers in reserve. But now with their enemies fighting right on their front line and, elevated by being mounted, they presented prime targets, more so the horses than the armoured riders, for without his mount a cavalryman was of little use.

Those who suffered from such tactics and ended up dismounted did not stay to fight on foot; with an abundance of horses held before the moat they streamed back to the city to secure a remount, unwittingly creating an opportunity for their enemies. Such conduct depleted the numbers attacking at a time when there was very little for the Goths to fear from archery and that was the point at which Witigis seized his opportunity.

The charge by the Goth right wing buckled the Byzantine left sufficiently to allow them to turn face-to-face combat into a melee. Now it was Byzantine cohesion that began to crack and as the left-wing cavalry sought to disengage enough to re-form, a near to impossible manoeuvre to carry out while under assault, it began to crumble.

Flavius, seeing what was happening, had the horns blown to order a general retirement, his intention being to re-form the whole behind the Isaurians, who would hold the Goths until he could renew his assault. With commendable discipline his centre and right divisions broke off in good order and successfully disengaged.

The trouble on the left was more acute; there the losses had been greater and the mixture of friend and foe more serious, which had rendered an increasing number horseless. They were straggling to the rear so there was no cohesion in the retirement on that flank, due to lack of numbers and enemy pressure. It broke into a near collapse and the disordered body of men retreated in some confusion, which would not have mattered if the Isaurians had held.

Seeing one-third of the cavalry before them in flight the mass reacted as infantry usually did: safety lay behind the moat and it was that to which they now ran. This meant that without a shelter behind which they could re-form, the rest of the cavalry, albeit in proper formations, had no choice but to aim for the same sanctuary.

The greater mass of the Isaurians were now in a state of utter panic. They did not stop at the moat, instead making for the nearest gates, two placed at a point where they formed a tight angle into which the infantry now crowded, there to clamour at the mass of Roman citizens lining the walls. The gates, despite their pleading, remained closed.

Flavius, Constantinus, Bessas and all the other senior commanders were not idle; with the flat blades of their swords, added to hoarse and repeated shouting, they were busy ensuring that the cavalry formed up behind the moat to repulse their enemies. Only when a modicum of order was restored did it become obvious why they were being gifted the time. Not all of the Isaurians had broken; out in the fields stood two tight squares of infantry who between them had broken up the Goth pursuit.

Led by Principius and Tarmutus, this diminished force was seeking to do that which should have fallen to the whole. That they could not hold was obvious but before he could give them support Flavius had to mount a defence with his back to the walls of the now closed city, any pleas to the citizens to open the gates denied.

'Is there anything more treacherous than a Roman, father?'

'Remember we are Romans, Photius, despite what those swine call us.'

Some order was emerging, infantry being pushed forward to line the inner side of the moat while others were moving to destroy the wooden causeway by which the army had advanced and now retreated. This was stopped by Flavius, who gave permission to Ennes that he should try to rescue those who could be saved, especially his brother, Tarmutus.

Leading three hundred of the heavily armoured *bucellarii*, Ennes thundered over those timbers and initiated a full charge so that their sheer weight would break the Goth encirclement. Their comrades watched as they crashed through the lighter Goth cavalry, to create an avenue by which the remaining Isaurians, and there were now few, could flee, that followed by a fighting retreat.

Ennes personally carried out his brother over his saddle. Principius suffered harsher treatment; being dead, he was dragged back over the moat and once the men who had effected the rescue were safe Flavius ordered the causeway to be hacked down, watching as his triumphant enemy worked to get his forces into the proper formation to finish off what was now a trapped enemy.

'Are we to die here?' Photius asked, with a tremor in his voice.

'If the citizens of Rome will not open the gates all we can do is cost the Goths dear. Now it is time to pray and comport your soul.'

How was it possible that so many thousands of men could be silent; if, like their general, they were praying there was no evidence, while over their heads the residents of the city also seemed to come to a collective holding of breath in anticipation of what was to come, a bloody massacre. Or was it in contemplation of the revenge Witigis would take upon their treacherous city?

Many were later to question the power of prayer, for no attack came; the Goths began to fall back, splitting up to return to their camps, which did nothing to break the silence, even when the fields on the eastern side of the moat were clear of everything but the dead and dying. Then from behind the defeated army came the sound of creaking as the great gates were opened.

That his troops began to cheer sickened Flavius; he had chanced everything to win a decisive victory and he had been beaten and then betrayed. It was a chastened general, his head hanging low, who rode back into the city.

'Why did they not attack, Father?'

'If you can communicate with God, Photius, ask him, for I have no answer. Ride to Valentinus and inform him of what has occurred. Whatever the state of his action he is to retire at once.'

'And the occupants of the city?'

'I cannot do to them what Witigis would have done, Photius.' The voice lost its weary quality and became a hiss. 'Much as it would give me pleasure to do so. Now go, time is pressing.'

On the Plains of Nero the orders issued by Flavius had been studiously obeyed. Valentinus had stood off and used controlled archery to pin the Goths in front of their camp but made no attempt to overcome them. If the men who led the Roman levies had been content to stay where they had been deployed all would have been well but, sure of their prowess and against orders, they marched out of the Porta Pancratia and, making their way through the abandoned building of an exterior suburb, debouched onto the plain.

The sheer number of that body, five thousand men setting up a huge cloud of dust, had to be the cause of what followed. The horns before Valentinus blew and suddenly his enemy melted away, abandoning their camp to occupy the nearest set of hills to the rear where they could mount a defence.

Seeing the enemy retreat, the Roman levies, hitherto in untidy lines, ceased to march in any kind of order. They began to run and did not stop until they were within the wooden rampart that protected the Gothic encampment, where they immediately fell into an orgy of looting. Not to be outdone and in fear of losing out, the Moorish mercenaries likewise set to, seeking to ensure they got their just share, their behaviour immediately copied by the mounted archers.

Valentinus had been in command of a well-disciplined force; within a few grains of sand he was seeking to impose some kind of order on a rabble, while the condition of that which had caused him to flee was not lost on his opposite number. Seeing the chaos before them the Goth cavalry began to advance, which immediately alarmed the Romans.

Attempts by Valentinus to get them to form up fell on deaf ears; men who had been looting now had only one aim, to get back within the walls of the city with everything they could carry. The Moors were now so muddled as to be useless, while the archers, who knew they could not stand alone, took the only course open to them and began to flee as well.

If the well mounted got to safety that was not an opportunity afforded to many of the others. Men on foot running from warriors on horse-back had little chance and the slaughter was great. Nowhere was that more than at the gate itself, open but so crowded with panic-stricken Roman levies that it became a charnel house.

The last command Valentinus could issue, once he and his personal bodyguards had forced their way through the rabble, was to get that gate shut and let everyone still outside it pay for their greed. That was where Photius found him, tears streaming down his cheeks.

## CHAPTER EIGHT

Morale naturally plummeted following such a reverse and the only method by which Flavius could counter that was by a return to his previous stratagem, that of a controlled sortie and then retire. This enjoyed only limited success, due to the higher spirits of the Goths and the way they had learnt to counter his tactics. The fact that preyed on his mind was not the nature of his own failure – in war such things had to be accepted – but the way it had nearly turned into disaster.

If the Goths had put in a final charge it was possible, with the gates of the city shut against him, he would have lost his entire army and the image of those Roman citizens lining the walls in silent contemplation of such an outcome caused a near apoplexy, just as much as the indiscipline of their levies on the Plains of Nero had multiplied his own difficulties on the east bank of the Tiber.

The need to know how such a set of circumstances had come about was a task for Procopius. He agreed with his master that the Roman mob were not capable of such behaviour on some collective natural instinct. Yes, the common people could riot as could any mass of citizens; Flavius had seen that very thing in Constantinople in the so-called Nika riots against Justinian and Theodora, an uprising that had ended in the massacre of thirty thousand citizens in the Hippodrome.

There had been furtive leadership then seeking power for themselves and many had paid the price for mere suspicion of involvement; something of the same must exist in Rome and future security demanded that whoever was responsible be unmasked, a demand easier made than satisfied, as Procopius sadly reported. He lacked the sources among the Romans that he enjoyed within the army.

'It's like walking the sewers, leaving me wading in filth but with no clarity. Hint to one senator that there has been treachery is to invite him to name with certainty his chief rivals and they are just as keen to condemn the source.'

'So it could be any of them?' Flavius asked.

'Or all!' Procopius snapped, before modifying that. 'Not all, but who the culprit might be, I am at a loss to say.'

'Silverius?' Flavius asked. 'He was quick to betray Witigis, perhaps he will be just as swift to do the same to us. I daresay he hoped that with us in possession the Goths would leave Rome be.'

That received a jaundiced look, which obviated the need for Procopius to state the obvious: when it came to wading through ordure the denizens of the Church were worse by a wide margin than their lay brethren. They lied with a facility that flew in the face of their stated occupational godliness. Having seen that look Flavius went to his desk and fetched a scroll, which he handed to his secretary.

'Read this.' His secretary complied, not once, but judging by the cant of his head, twice and both times so slowly as to make his employer impatient. 'Well?'

'It is damning enough, *Magister*, but is it true?'

'You have reason to doubt it?'

'There's a certain crudity to the accusation, it seems too explicit, too lacking in uncertainty. Silverius could very well be engaged in treachery but he would not be such a fool as to leave himself so open to discovery, and I cannot be certain, but I would say this draft of a letter is not in his hand.'

'He will not write his own words any more than I do.'

'No man in his right mind would dictate a missive in which he openly alludes to secret dealings with Witigis. At the very least he would employ a simple code. Added to that, whoever brought you this claims to have read the final missive. Can that too be accurate?'

'You know Theodora has demanded I remove him?'

That gave them both pause; one of the matters that had plagued the empire over several decades had been a dispute on dogma between those who adhered to the creed of Monophysitism. This went against the agreed decision reached by the Synod of Bishops at Chalcedon, all based on an interpretation of scripture. Could Jesus be both man and God? Was there a Holy Trinity of equals? Chalcedon decided yes but many refused to accept the agreed conclusion.

Theodora was strong for the Monophysites while Silverius, who occupied the senior office in their shared religion, was openly opposed to that position. She wanted him removed and replaced with a deacon called Vigilius, who was clearly her creature. So far Flavius had not acted upon the demand, his excuse for delay being that his orders came from the Emperor not his consort, however powerful she thought herself to be.

It was a dangerous game and had his wife been present in Rome it would have been doubly so, for she would have acted not only as an advocate for Theodora but as her partisan, even if he fundamentally disagreed, a fact which was wounding in the extreme. Yet even without her presence, prevarication could only last so long; here was an excuse to act that met with his needs as well as those of Theodora.

'Silverius could be our perpetrator, could he not? Someone – perhaps more than one – gave orders that those gates be kept closed against us and was prepared to see us destroyed. Only Witigis did not finish us off and I still have no idea why, excepting divine intercession.'

'But you must guard against a repeat for we may not be so lucky in future?'

'To the point, Procopius, as always. Send a party of my bodyguards to arrest Silverius–'

'To do with him what?'

'We'll send him to Constantinople. Let the man who rules, not I, decide to please or displease his wife.'

'And Vigilius?'

'He is here in the city, is he not?' Procopius nodded. 'Then he shall become the Bishop of Rome until Justinian says otherwise.'

'Which leaves the senators, *Magister,* and Silverius might be innocent.'

'I doubt he is wholly that, none of them are.' Flavius paused for some time, to think. 'The senators are to be expelled from the city. Let them reside in the country where they can plot to their heart's content, but uselessly.'

At the next meeting of the military council, if that action met with universal approval it was clear that the reputation of the man in command had taken a dent. It was an undercurrent rather than manifest, a feeling not a fact that Flavius's generals had lost a degree of belief in him, the most obvious evidence being in the more forthright way that his second in command felt he had the right to hold forth and act as if he was equal. Not that he proposed any other course than his superior had intended to put forward himself.

Much as Flavius wanted to check his presumption he let Constantinus have his moment; the last thing needed was an open dispute between the two senior commanders, and if disagreements were allowed to break out into the open between the top men, it would lead to the taking of sides, which would be fatal to the enterprise: a divided army could only hope for complete defeat. So it was with a high degree of diplomacy and a frustrating touch of humility that Flavius gave him full agreement.

'We cannot sit idle, so we must do as Constantinus suggests and keep up our raiding. To his claim to take the command of such operations I can only say I fully support it and thank him.'

As ever, when the conference broke up Flavius was left with his secretary, who had on his long, thin face one of those enigmatic smiles that left anyone observing it to wonder if they were caused by amusement or mental superiority.

'Constantinus suggests?'

'He wants to take responsibility for the tactics we have no choice but to employ.'

'And if they begin to work, he can claim the credit–'

'Which,' Flavius interrupted, 'he will further use to undermine my authority.'

'Wise, *Magister?*'

'Necessary,' was the snapped reply.

Being clearly in search of a degree of personal popularity drove Constantinus to seek outright success, but that was not granted to him; if he employed the right commanders and the right troops, some of whom just happened to come from the Belisarian *bucellarii*, he was successful. When he employed other formations and thus avoided the opprobrium heaped on his commanding general for perceived favouritism, the results were less rewarding and sometimes risked being disastrous.

Flavius allowed him to have his head; let the army find out for themselves that only one man knew the right way to fight. It became clear that such pressure told on his second in command. The day came when Constantinus declined to give the task of mounting a raid to another; he proposed to lead it personally, yet he did so at the head of the only other troops who could be said to be fit for the purpose.

No one admired the Hun way of fighting more than Flavius Belisarius; indeed, when creating his own heavy units under Justinian he had modelled much of their mode of fighting on that race. They were the people who had first evolved a way of making war on horseback as mounted archers, albeit on swift and agile ponies instead of heavy steeds and that had given them a fearsome fighting reputation.

There was thus no ill feeling in the breast of Flavius as he watched them exit the western gates and head for the Plains of Nero. His prayers were for success and if he found the behaviour of

111

Constantinus an irritation it was a minor one: the man was ambitious but so he should be. God aid him if he led inferiors who lacked belief in their own abilities.

The Goths came out from their camp to oppose Constantinus, who immediately deployed his Huns to face them. The chosen battlefield was too far off for the whole action to be in plain view, though the general outlines were visible. At first, matters proceeded as they should, the Huns doing that at which they were superbly proficient, riding forward in fast and loose groupings to engage and thin the enemy ranks with arrows.

It was Photius, with his young eyes, who first spotted that matters might not be panning out as well as they should; the twin forces seemed to be getting closer to each other, a concern quickly laid to rest by his stepfather.

'Constantinus knows when to break off, Photius. He saw what happened in the recent battle and will not allow the Goths to get too close to his lines.'

'They are doing that very thing, slowly but successfully.'

'You're sure?'

'I can only relate what my own eyes tell me.'

A cold feeling gripped Flavius then; for all the mixed fortunes of recent forays the balance had been towards success and not failure. When his men had got into difficulties and had been forced to flee it was for gates now under Byzantine control. If they had incurred losses, they had not been serious and as a result the dented morale of his army had begun to repair. Right of this moment the last thing he needed was a major reverse.

The sound of the distant horns did nothing to relieve that feeling, especially as the masses of men began to move and their composition became easier to observe and comprehend. Constantinus had broken off the engagement but it was clear even through the dust that he and his Huns were not headed towards the city gates, while the advancing Goths were hard on their heels, which meant Photius was right.

He looked along the parapet to observe the faces of his other senior commanders and was not reassured; Valentinus was clearly praying, Bessas staring, his expression one of concern, Martinus and Valerian the same. Ennes, now leader of his bodyguard, was looking at him in a way that presaged doom, doubly evidenced by a quick break off from eye contact.

'I cannot support him,' Flavius murmured. 'I dare not.'

Such words were pointless anyway. In order to reinforce Constantinus he would require his own *bucellarii* to be ready to act at once, they being the only troops he could rely upon to effect a good outcome. Having ceded tactical control to his second in command that was far from the case; neither they nor their horses were armed, saddled and ready.

Photius now reported that Constantinus had swung away to the west and he and his Huns were making for an abandoned suburb, then that they had got in amongst the buildings and he could no longer see them. This being a place Flavius had reconnoitred, he knew to call them buildings was overstating their condition. Like every suburb of Rome outside the walls it had been subjected to Goth savagery. Most of the houses that made up what was a farming community had been torched and in many cases their walls had collapsed in on themselves.

'That might give us time,' Flavius cried. 'Ennes, get our men mounted.'

'The light, General,' came the concerned reply. 'By the time they are ready it will be near to dark.'

Ennes had made a calculation that took into account the time it would take to close with Constantinus and in that he was correct. It would be under moon and starlight by the time Flavius and his *bucellarii* would be in a position to fight and that was a bad notion. The feeling that he had to do something faded for the very good reason it would only be to show others he was not being passive in the face of the possible massacre of his Hun mercenaries and their general. Ennes got a nod of agreement, which served to rescind the previous instruction.

The light did fade and in the distance there was a mass of torches, with no one having any clear indication of their locality. Were they in that village or without? Finally they faded to leave only the silver light of the moon and stars as well as anxiety, for the lack of those torches could have two meanings and one was total annihilation.

It was near dawn when Constantinus, at the head of his troops, asked to be allowed to re-enter the city. He and his Huns, covered in dust and exhausted, looked a sorry lot in the light of the torches by which they made their way down

114

the roads that led to their encampment. Constantinus did not accompany them; he was required to report to his commander.

'They crept forward, Flavius Belisarius. It was not an obvious movement, given it was so slow, but by the time we wanted to break off they were too close.'

The temptation to reply 'You should have seen it, fool' had to remain unsaid but the spoken reply was hardly less damning. 'It is a tactic by which we lost in our one major battle. I think we agreed it was one we must guard against in any future engagement.'

'Which I would have done, but the dust the Huns created obscured my view, making it difficult to see what the Goths were about.'

There was some truth in that: horsemen in constant motion, riding forward to sting and then retire on dry ground would have created a murkiness hard to see through. Yet it was still an excuse and a glance round the faces of the others present told Flavius they took it as such as Constantinus continued.

'Those abandoned buildings seemed to provide the only chance of safety and once within them I had my men dismount.'

'Which clearly worked, given the numbers with which you finally returned.'

'The lanes were narrow and the spaces between strewn with rubble, too dangerous for the Goth to seek to fight in. Whoever led them declined to risk that, though he had his men circling the settlement hoping to force us out with nothing but insults.'

Eventually the Goths had retired and would, no doubt and quite rightly, claim a victory; had they not driven their enemies from the field, a defeat which if it had been low on casualties was demoralising? By his actions, Constantinus had allowed a pendulum swinging towards Byzantium to be sent quite markedly the other way.

'You did well to survive, Constantinus.' There was a sting in that remark and the man did not miss it as Flavius added, 'Now I think you must yearn for the baths and some food.'

What followed was a sharp drop of the head from the handsome but dust-covered patrician, an acknowledgement, albeit a reluctant one, that any dent to the authority of Flavius Belisarius was now repaired. It would be he who would now order future sorties and those he chose to lead his men would have to show more in light of today's events.

Witigis was forever probing for weakness and knew that which was the most potent was still aiming to starve out Rome, given the city yet had a huge number of souls within its walls. In order to disrupt the supplies coming from Antium through Ostia he built and heavily manned a fort at Portus that dominated the route, effectively cutting the city off from its main source of food.

Soon there were major shortages and that acted on the mood of the citizenry, who, even under less elevated leadership, demanded that he take them out again to fight and defeat the Goths before they expired of hunger, a request brought to Flavius by the present Bishop of Rome.

'I have been bitten once, Pope Vigilius, I will

not be so again. I require you to calm this furore.'

The newly appointed pontiff replied with studied calm. 'With what, my son?'

'Tell them there are reinforcements on the way in numbers to drive Witigis from their walls.'

'I am bound to ask, Flavius Belisarius, if that is wishful thinking or the truth?'

Flavius had to bite his tongue. His own faith was strong but from his earliest years he had observed the kind of men who officiated within the Christian faith and only rarely had he been impressed. The first bishop ever encountered had been a thoroughly evil man, a thief to his flock as well as an aggressive pederast.

If he had since encountered good and honest men they had been rare and not elevated. No one, as far as he could discern, rose high within the ecclesiastical hierarchy without leaving their soul somewhere on the slippery pole by which they had ascended to prominence. He had no reason to think Vigilius any different.

'You are the Bishop of Rome and they are fearful for their souls. If you say it is so they will believe you and as of this moment that is what is required. I need time to find a way to best the latest moves Witigis has made and get food into the city.'

Flavius was irritated by the amused look on the face of Procopius, who knew only too well what this exchange implied. He too had a low opinion of churchmen and the notion that the one before him was seeking to avoid, not so much a lie as a touch of exaggeration, clearly tickled him.

'You wish me to use my authority to calm the fears of my flock even if I cannot be sure that what I say to them will come to pass? Would that not imperil my soul?'

Such a bald statement rendered Flavius uncomfortable; Vigilius was driving home that if he complied it would be done as a favour. Thankfully, before he was obliged to respond in a positive manner the cleric turned to another subject entirely.

'By the by, the last convoy of supplies brought a message from Constantinople.'

'It brought several.'

'The one to myself and the church was to inform us that Silverius is to be returned to Rome. Justinian wishes that the claims made against him be investigated, which can only mean he is unsure of their veracity.'

Slightly stunned by that news, Flavius could imagine the hoops Justinian must have been obliged to jump through with his wife, who was not one to be easily swayed from any course she had decided to adopt, which probably explained why Vigilius knew of the return before he had been informed. The man before him was her appointee and that position would obviously be under some threat; if Silverius was found to be free of guilt he had the right to reassume his papal office.

The disenfranchisement of Silverius must have caused uproar in Constantinople, a deeply religious city in which imperial interference in church matters was always risky, putting Justinian under so much pressure he felt he had to defy Theodora. The amount of venomous abuse that had exposed him to could only be guessed at. If the thought had its amusing side it also presented to Flavius a difficulty; his emperor was landing the problem right back in his lap and he did not want it.

'That being the case, *Magister*,' Vigilius added, in a silky tone, 'I ask that Silverius be judged for any perceived crimes by those that are qualified to do so. He is a priest and should be examined by the bishops of the Roman Diocese.'

'You feel that will serve?'

'It is not fitting that a lay person should question one who so recently held my office.'

It was a grateful Flavius Belisarius who agreed to that, it being, he felt and for numerous reasons, too hot a stone for him to handle. He only realised that he had done the required favour when Vigilius was quick to hand him his reward, an assurance that he would do his best to calm the passions of the citizens who looked to him for guidance.

'What are you grinning at?' Flavius barked, at a still smiling Procopius, once Vigilius had departed.

'He's a wily bird, General, he must be to have impressed the Empress.'

'So?'

'Beware of what games he might play.'

'That is of little account,' came the snapped reply. 'I must get as many troops from the southern provinces as can be released and you are the only person I can spare to undertake such a task. We need to strip the garrisons and get them where they will be of use. And while you are in the south find out, for the sake of the Lord, if Justinian has sent me any more soldiers, or am I to beat Witigis with defrocked popes!'

# CHAPTER NINE

Sending Procopius south had been the stated object but to get him safely to where he needed to go, armed with all the authority of the man he served, required that he leave the city in darkness and secretly as well as in a manner that reflected his importance. Flavius provided his secretary with a very strong escort, for not only was his mission vital but he was a man the army commander, more than any other, feared to lose, given he fulfilled several functions.

He was the senior and trustworthy bureaucrat who could be relied on to set up the administrative bodies required to control conquered territory. These skills had first been proven in campaigns against the Sassanid empire and doubly so in North Africa, so much so that he had become like an extension of his master's power. Treated by the inferior commanders as an equal, no one dared to condescend to him.

He was also a foil to the Belisarius temperament, which in matters political – and they were as vital as anything military – could sometimes be a touch wayward, too brusque and martial in areas requiring subtle tact. Corresponding with the likes of Justinian through the filtered and able mind of his secretary stopped Flavius from inadvertently causing any dent to the imperial pride.

The other function Procopius fulfilled was just as vital; high command can be lonely and if there was Photius to talk with, he was a youth, not yet well enough versed to act as a sounding board. A man utterly committed to him and one not swayed into indiscretions by flattery, Flavius could talk to Procopius about matters in which discretion was vital.

If he strayed occasionally into areas outside his bureaucratic duties that was acceptable too, for his counsel, though not always correct, was never foolish or based on self-aggrandisement. He was committed to Flavius in a way that was unusual in its totality, which was the reason Antonina insisted it was based on something other than mere loyalty and admiration.

In sending him on what was, in truth, a military mission, there was sound common sense: Procopius would act only on the wishes of his master. Despatch one of his generals and they might see a chance to act, if only for a short time, for themselves. Constantinus, who was certain he had every right to be given the duty, was naturally upset at what he saw as a blow to his prerogatives and self-esteem.

That led to an open and very vocal argument, something Flavius had been very careful to avoid hitherto, and even then he could not say what he wished to, that he lacked trust in a man who was always bound to act independently and seek a little personal glory at a time when Rome was in peril. It was necessary to quite sharply remind him who commanded and who obeyed, with the obvious rider being that if he was unhappy he should take his complaints to Constantinople.

'You heard?' Flavius asked as Photius and Solomon entered his chamber, moments after Constantinus had stormed out; the concerned look on the young man's face made it an unnecessary question.

'Every word, and how could I not? It is unlike you to shout so, even at an ordinary soldier.'

'I don't think I shouted. Spoke firmly, yes.'

'I would reckon Witigis heard you,' Solomon said.

'As long as Constantinus heard is all that counts.' Flavius paused, then, looking pensive, asked Photius a question he would normally have put to Procopius. 'You think me overharsh?'

'Would it wound you, Father, if I said to you that you are rarely harsh enough?'

'Soldiers, especially senior officers, can be touchy.'

There was no humour in what was said next; Photius was deadly serious. 'I was not talking of soldiers.'

Having no desire to talk about his wife, for the second time that night Flavius had cause to raise his voice, which forced Solomon to turn away in order not to be seen smiling.

'Personal matters can wait. Right now I have to find a way to hold onto this city until reinforcements arrive.'

There was more to fret about than a shortage of fighters; the latest Goth tactics had shut down much of the supply to the city and dearth was a precursor to disease as people sought to supplement their diets with foods best left alone, like rotten wheat and vegetables, rats, cats and certain birds. There was also the problem of water now there was a severe shortage of wine.

Never a wise source with which to slake human thirst, when the level of the Tiber fell, as it was bound to do in the summer months, it was increasingly contaminated with human and animal filth, making it foul to drink. But drink it the Romans did, for that same unbearable heat that caused the river to slow acted on people too; they drank and fell ill and despite his best efforts, Flavius knew that his soldiers were no wiser than the citizens.

Once a pestilence took hold it spread like an out-of-control fire. Many of his men died, even more became so weak as to be utterly ineffective. Matters were reaching a crisis, and for the first time Flavius had to consider the need for a plan to abandon Rome. That was before Mundus, the man who had led the escort for Procopius, reported back to his commander that in his journey south and the return there had been not a sign of a Goth, apart from a few parties out foraging, men who had fled at the sight of such a large body of troops.

'There was nothing to trouble us so I undertook a little detour or two.' Seeing the eyebrows begin to rise Mundus was quick to add, 'Without ever taking a risk.'

'So no patrols?' Flavius asked, when Mundus had finished.

'Nary a one. I swept by two of the Goth camps as well as that fort Witigis had built between Antium and Ostia and there was nothing. They are remaining close to their tents and I could have set up camp myself and stayed for the night on the territory they claim to possess.'

Chin on chest, Flavius was set to thinking. He had occupied enough temporary encampments in his own campaigns to know that what might start out adequate would, over time, be rendered unpleasant. Latrines and middens had to be placed further and further off from where the men laid their heads. Also, living in tents through the kind of weather that had existed over the year of siege was far from ideal, steaming summer heat being just as much a trial as wind, rain and the cold of winter.

Was Witigis having trouble keeping up the spirits of his men? Did he not dare to seek to send them out on patrols on the grounds they might decline? If the army and citizens in Rome were falling sick while housed in buildings that fully protected them from the elements, how much more would the Goths be suffering?

'This I must see for myself.'

The ride lasted over three days and took Flavius right round the perimeter that Witigis had set up round the city. In each case what Mundus had told him was correct. The Goths were confining themselves to their camps, allowing him to evolve a strategy to make what was disagreeable positively offensive.

The strong patrols he sent out, several at a time, reversed matters, even if in doing so he risked the entire security of his army; losses in any great scale would be disastrous.

Yet the Goths stayed supine; no longer were the

Byzantines besieged in the city, now it was the Goths who were wary of leaving their camps, and since they were denied the right to easily forage for food, it was they who would begin to suffer from starvation.

'Bring me reinforcements, Procopius,' Flavius whispered to the empty fields to the south of the Porta Ostiensis and the road to Naples, aware of just how much he was stretching his resources. 'Do that and we have our enemies beaten.'

'If they stay as they are, Father, they are defeated already.'

An arm was put about the shoulders of his stepson, the young man being pulled close. 'I fear to say such words too loudly unless God sees it as hubris.'

Procopius was feeling as if he was in the process of taking a beating, locked as he was in an argument with the wife of the man he served. Logic, to which he was dedicated, had no effect at all on the Lady Antonina. No amount of reference to the dangers she might face coming to Rome with him made even the slightest dent in her determination to be, as she put it, 'reunited with my husband!' and he was not able to say that was the last thing his master desired.

How comforting it would have been to contest that with the true reason for her supposed craving. It would not be for pure affection, though Antonina did demonstrate to Flavius a great deal of that when they were in company, quite able to play the loving wife while spying on behalf of Theodora as if it was of no consequence. It was

125

also true that she saw nothing untoward in her being enamoured of Theodosius; in her world, plainly the two, affection for Flavius Belisarius as well as their adopted son, had no connection and was no sin.

'Unless you intend to physically prevent me from getting to Rome then I suggest you say no more.'

'I may have to adopt that course.'

The eyes narrowed and the voice became a hiss. 'Am I competing for my husband's affections?'

'How can you so dishonour that man by such an unwarranted allegation?'

'I see you do not attach dishonour to yourself, Procopius. You may fool Flavius by your behaviour but I can see into your soul and you do not deceive me. Now I need a palanquin in which to travel. Do what those in service are there for and provide one.'

'No doubt you will be happy to see your son as well?'

'That ingrate! I rue the day I bore him.'

She spat that response, her features screwing up to show that her one-time beauty, onto which she had held a remarkably long time, was becoming seriously eroded. The creases on her upper lip were deep now, the crow's feet around the eyes pronounced, and her anger and spite merely exaggerated how much she had ripened. Not for the first time Procopius wondered what she thought she was doing seeking to seduce a man half her age.

'Remember, Procopius, you serve my husband. You do not command him and you do not command me.'

His response conceded a point, in which he had no choice. 'At least you will not lack for protection.'

Given the task of raising reinforcements for Rome, Procopius had thrown himself into it with gusto, issuing orders not only to the garrison commanders of the south to strip out every man they could spare but to the reinforcements that had been sent by Justinian and were languishing in Naples. If they showed the least resentment, the written instructions from Flavius Belisarius were waved under their nose.

He was enjoying himself in an unusual role, utterly unaware of the resentment such behaviour engendered: no military man enjoyed being ordered around by a civilian, however elevated. Had he known, Procopius would not have cared; everything was in place, including supplies set up along the route, and he chose to take a place at the head of what was now a force of some seven thousand men made up of two thousand cavalry, Isaurian infantry and the scrapings of the Apulian and Calabrian garrisons.

His chosen position did nothing to quell any bitterness felt towards him by men who were experienced commanders. Close behind came Antonina in her palanquin, surrounded by her walking attendants, and her background and behaviour were no mystery.

This meant that both were the subject of much unheard ribaldry, he for his pretensions and supposed proclivities, she for her famously lax morals, which were held to be of long duration and included much carnal activity in the company of Theodora, quite a degree of it sapphic, this while their spouses, both emperor and general, were derided for being too weak to deal with their consorts.

Procopius, trailing Antonina, hurried north to advise Flavius that his desired reinforcements were on the move, which required him to pin back the Goths and render them too fearful to move away from Rome in any strength and launch an attack on the column in open country, when he would be unable to support them. That required he go even more on the offensive and the site chosen for the action was the Porta Flaminia, always a defensive position at serious risk, so much so that the interior wall had been constructed behind the main defences to ensure it could not be breached.

It was an avenue of attack just as precious to Witigis, who had to consider that the entire Byzantine army might essay from Rome, in effect abandon the city and get across the Milvian Bridge before he could interfere. Once north of him they would be between the Goths and their capital and base at Ravenna. If it was an unlikely ploy he had to be careful of the man he was up against; he knew just how ingenious Flavius Belisarius could be and was not going to leave anything to chance.

To counter the threat, Witigis had constructed a special forward camp close to what was the main northern entrance to the city and had it not had that double protection, it would have been the gate he chose above all others to attack, given the Tiber provided him a strong protection on his western flank.

He was right to worry about his wily opponent; out of sight and in darkness Flavius had that extra wall slowly and silently dismantled, which meant that what had hitherto been impossible – namely this being a place from which he could sortie out to fight – was no longer so.

When those gates swung open and a thousand cavalry under Martinus emerged, the Goths were taken completely by surprise, yet they rallied quickly to not only fight off these raiders but to drive them back towards the Porta Flaminia in time to get through the gates before they were once more shut, the prize being entry into the city.

That was exactly what Flavius desired; when Martinus and his men began to retreat the Goths pressed doubly hard, at which point Flavius Belisarius himself exited from the next gate along, the Porta Pinciana, leading another thousand men and riding straight for the Goth camp, a place his enemies had no choice but to seek to protect.

Their commander ordered his men to fall back and they moved with speed enough to prevent Flavius from overrunning it, so, thwarted in that aim he rode on slightly before swinging round to attack the Goths and drive them onto the spears of Martinus's cavalry, who had now reversed their retreat and resumed their assault.

Caught between two forces the Goths, too far off from their other camps to be supported, paid the price. They were slaughtered in droves, few getting clear. Flavius retired to the city having sent to Witigis the necessary message: do not dare detach men from the siege of Rome for it will cost you dearly.

The King of the Goths had similar information at that point to his adversary; he knew that there were reinforcements coming from Naples as well as their numbers. Witigis was also aware that sailing up the coast was a strong Byzantine fleet, which made holding on to some of his more extended possessions, especially blocking the ports, untenable.

Disease was stalking his forces too, and his men being almost prisoners in their own camps had left him with a dispirited set of warriors deeply sick of this fight, a mood which would not be aided by the arrival of the Byzantine reinforcements. It was time to talk and Flavius was called to the Porta Salaria to receive envoys asking that he parley.

A meeting was arranged in a special tent set up close to the gate, given Witigis would not enter Rome and Flavius declined to go far from the safety of the city walls. Face to face for the first time the two men naturally sought to assess each other, as no doubt did the inferior officers both had brought along.

Flavius saw a man much taller than he, for Witigis had imposing height. The head was large, the features heavy under thick greying hair and a single impressive eyebrow. The impression could not be avoided that the Goth would have been a hard man to best in single combat, no doubt one of the reasons he had been elected to his position.

What Witigis observed would look slight to a man of his frame but if he knew anything about

Flavius Belisarius he would be aware that he was dealing with a man who could hold his own when wielding weapons. The shoulders were not excessively wide and nor was the body imposing, but the real key to the man lay in the calm expression and steady eyes, under dark curled hair and with a face framed by that thin black beard.

'You have no right to be here, Flavius Belisarius.'

There was no sitting down, no air that this might be a passive exchange between equals. The Latin was guttural and far from perfect in its composition, the tone as harsh as the expression on the face of the Goth King. Flavius decided the anger was genuine, not faked; Witigis believed every word of what he had just said.

'No right? I am in Rome at the express command of the Emperor Justinian, who has title to the whole of the lands of Italy. They are part of the Roman Empire.'

'Long since lost!'

'Theodoric ruled at the behest of the predecessors of Justinian. Since those who succeeded have failed to acknowledge him as their overlord he has sent me to take back that which he owns.'

'Why take what you cannot hold? I demand that you hand back the provinces of South Italy that you have stolen and return them to my authority. If some hollow title is needed by your master, the same arrangement he enjoyed with Theodoric, God rest his soul, then I am willing to let him enjoy it.'

'Even if I was inclined to accede to your demand – which, I may add, I am not – I lack the

131

authority to do so. Only Justinian can decide on such a weighty matter.'

'You are his legate in Italy.'

'I am in command of his armies, that is all.'

Flavius and Procopius had discussed what might come out of this meeting and the kernel of it was needs rather than outcomes. Antonina had tried to do likewise and been brusquely informed it was none of her business, even if her husband knew how such a message, conveyed to Theodora, would be taken.

Winter was coming, the Byzantine army was not in perfect condition and it was possible the Goths were equally afflicted. Witigis could no more win than Flavius. What both men needed was time, to rebuild the health of their men and the potency of the forces they led. It was thus a theatrical gesture that had Procopius lean forward and whisper in his master's ear; the words were already known.

'It may be, King Witigis' – the courtesy of the title got a sharp nod, it being the first acknowledgement of his position – 'that my emperor will be open to what you suggest, I cannot say. All I can do is repeat to you that I will hold what I have until ordered to surrender it. So if you want an answer, one I am not empowered to provide, you must go to where it can be considered.'

'You think I would go to Constantinople?' Witigis sneered. 'Do you see me of so little account that I must go in person to beg?'

'If you choose to go or to send envoys is none of my concern. All I know is that the journey and return will take time and that is without any idea of how long any discussions will last. I am aware that we are both at a stand. You will never retake Rome with the forces you have and I lack the means to drive you away.'

The pause was long before Witigis acknowledged that with a sharp nod; he knew it to be the case but there was no pleasure in admitting it.

'So we need to create time, say three months, when such a journey can be undertaken and our differences can perhaps be resolved at a higher level.'

The locked eyes were more revealing than the words; neither man believed Justinian would agree to surrender anything his general had so far recovered, but Witigis might have something to gain just by talking, perhaps the right to peacefully retain what he still held.

'A three-month truce!'

'Starting at dawn tomorrow,' Flavius responded.

The delay in replying was purely for pride and appearance to convince those who had accompanied him of his solemn consideration; really there was no choice, but Witigis made great play of adopting a pensive pose, his eyes lowered and his hand on his firm, square chin.

'No. I need time to consider. What I will agree to is a cessation of hostilities until I have consulted with my nobles.'

'Agreed.'

# CHAPTER TEN

Witigis, having delayed for the sake of his pride and his standing, finally agreed the truce, giving Flavius good reason to believe the initiative had begun to swing in his favour, something of which he was determined to take advantage. The Byzantine fleet had arrived, escorting to Antium a large convoy of merchant ships, and these were unloaded and their cargoes transported to Rome immediately, relieving the dearth of supply and raising the morale of soldiers and civilians alike.

Within days his reinforcements arrived, the cavalry elements immediately sent to take over certain strategic places that the Goths were obliged to abandon as being too isolated to hold, like the fortress of Portus they had constructed as a lock on Roman provisioning. The presence of that strong fleet and the men that could be deployed from the ships, added to those fresh troops, made continued occupation too risky.

Likewise they had to give up Albanum, which commanded one of the other major supply routes into the capital. The hill city was soon occupied and a camp set up, much to the anger of the Goths, but when the men Witigis had deputed to negotiate with the Byzantines complained, Procopius, handed the day-to-day negotiations, was emollient but firm.

'Flavius Belisarius has issued very strict instructions to all of his men taking over positions previously held by you. They are merely in place to occupy while the truce is in place and are to remain within their encampments and are strictly barred from undertaking any offensive actions unless driven to do so for the purposes of defence.'

Witigis might not like it, but such actions were things he had to accept. Less pleasing to the man making these manoeuvres was the presence of his wife, not least in the way her being in their shared villa altered his life. Not for Antonina quiet solitude and time to ponder on responsibilities and the means of thwarting the Goths; she sought company and now his home was often full of his off-duty officers eating, drinking, carousing and flattering a woman, now long past her prime, who soaked up their insincerities without a trace of modesty.

It was telling who did not attend, either through lack of an invitation or a personal disinclination to accept. Constantinus was an exemplar of that, as were those officers who, like him, came from the patrician class, Antonia's guests being of a less refined hue. Never happy at such gatherings Flavius could at least get away to carry out his nightly rounds. Truce or no truce they were still at war and such fripperies seemed inappropriate.

As had been predicted by Pope Vigilius, his dethroned predecessor Silverius arrived and was handed over, not before he had been obliged to endure a tirade from Antonina in which it was implied that the serene old man seemed to have been responsible for everything since Noah's flood. Finally he was released into the hands of those who would interrogate him with a few kinder words from her husband.

'The charge against me, Flavius Belisarius, is false. I did not betray you.'

The response masked a degree of embarrassment; there had been doubt, both at the time and since, that Silverius was involved. 'I hope and pray that is true.'

'Then I ask that you examine me, given you have the right.'

'I cannot, I have given Vigilius my word.'

Which was as good a way of telling the old silver-haired man that he had no intention of getting embroiled in what was essentially a dispute on dogma. After a short silence, Silverius produced a slight nod.

'I wonder, is God easier to serve than a mere mortal clad in purple?'

Further evidence of the loss of Goth power came with an embassy from Milan, led by their bishop, offering to surrender the city and the whole of Liguria if Flavius would provide the men to hold it. While agreeing to the request, he also sensed it might be a step too far. Goad he might, but he did not want to be the one who broke the truce, so he kept the envoys from Milan talking without acting on that which they desired.

The notion of keeping secret the arrival and presence of such envoys was impossible. Reports began to come in of certain movements by the Goths that raised the danger that they might be preparing to react. The first indication was along one of the broken aqueducts, where the men on guard reported they had seen torches. Flavius and Photius went out personally to investigate, to find the burnt remnants by the wall blocking the aqueduct.

'Naples,' Photius remarked. 'He must have heard of it.'

Flavius ordered more patrols and greater vigilance, as well as extra pickets on all the broken aqueducts: if Witigis was probing for weaknesses it could only be for one purpose, to seek to take Rome by some trick, but in that he was wrong. Ennes, alert to the possibilities of a sudden attack and in command at the Porta Piciana, observed the Goths beginning to deploy in battle formation right in front of his gates.

He sent word to Flavius but did not wait for a response, instead exiting at the head of his cavalry to break up the assault before it could be got into motion. The Goths, caught while the ranks were still disordered, broke and fled but not before they suffered many losses. Flavius had Procopius insist the truce was broken; not so, responded the Goth envoys, the troops Ennes had destroyed had not been assembled to press home an attack, but were merely drilling.

'So what did you say to that, Husband?'

'Maintaining the truce suits me more than Witigis.'

'He might see it as cowardice.'

Looking at his wife, Flavius wondered if he still had any residual regard for her, aware that he could not answer in either a positive or a negative sense. He was tied to Antonina by the insoluble bonds of matrimony, added to which she was the mother of his daughter, now being cared for in Constantinople under the watchful care of Theodora. That put the Empress into the marital equation: how would she react if her friend was maltreated or abandoned?

There were, too, appearances to maintain; it might be the case, as Procopius had more than once hinted, that her indiscretions were no secret amongst his senior officers, but the chatter of such men he discounted. The bulk of his force consisted of middle ranks and common soldiers who, if they cared to look, must see their general confident, even in his domestic life.

The presence of Antonina meant he saw a lot less of Photius, who could neither stand to be in her company nor command his tongue when they did meet. If he was careful of his stepfather's sensibilities he knew how to issue barbed comments that would make sense to his mother, if no one else. As for Procopius, their relationship was pure poison and he took care to keep them apart. Only Solomon, of those close to him, was able to behave with indifference to her presence.

The question she had posed and the manner in which she had spoken irritated him; what happened in negotiations with Witigis had nothing to do with Antonina, not that she behaved as if that was the case. He had to assume she was driven by her need to write to Theodora, and in doing so have matters of importance to impart, either with honesty or otherwise, he could never be sure which. 'Do I not qualify for an answer?' she demanded when his long silence irritated her.

'I am not fool enough to actually believe them.'

'The real question to which I seek an answer, Flavius, is this. Where is this all leading?'

The tone of voice had gone from challenging to silky in a blink, and given she was embroidering that allowed her to look at her work and not hold his eye. She was fishing, of that Flavius had no doubt, seeking to get from him words that would feed the obsessions of her imperial friend, like some indication of personal ambition. He wanted to ask how she could be so treacherous; he could not for the very simple reason Antonina saw where her loyalties lay very differently from those of her husband.

'First the conquest of the whole of Italy.'

'First?'

'Then Hispania and Gaul. That is Justinian's ambition.'

'You're sure it is not more your own?'

'How many times have you posed such a query, Antonina?'

That made her look up, the air of innocence she sought to adopt insincere. 'I don't recall ever having done so.'

'I think the first time was before we ever landed in North Africa and I can remember several occasions since.'

'You're imagining things, Husband, and not for the first time.'

'It is the imaginings of others that cause the problem.'

The weary response came without any of the emphasis that should have accompanied the words, this as Solomon entered to indicate to Flavius he needed to speak with him, a hand held up to ask him to wait.

'What others?' Antonina asked, again all innocence. Did she actually want him to decry Theodora by name just so that she could communicate that to Constantinople?

'You know as well as I do,' was what he said, standing and making for the doorway. 'Better, perhaps.'

'I have not finished,' she snapped at his back.

'Yes you have, Antonina.'

Solomon had retreated to the corridor outside where a quartet of the men on duty were guarding an Isaurian soldier. On seeing the general the fellow knelt in greeting as the commander who had disarmed him, began to explain.

'This soldier is one of the sentinels on the Tiber walls, General. He has come to tell you of a conspiracy to overcome them.'

A brief exchange established the precise location, the point at which the east walls straddled the river and the builders had relied much more on the river itself to provide protection than high masonry. It soon emerged that this man was one of the contingent that had only recently arrived from the south.

'The Goths are at the heart of the plot, I take it?' That got a fearful, nodding acknowledgement, as if the fellow was wondering that he might have been too hasty in coming to Flavius. 'Solomon, please fetch Procopius. You, stand up and look at me.'

The Isaurian could do the first but not the second. He stood head bowed but silent as they waited for Procopius, who, occupying quarters very close to those of Flavius, soon came hurrying into the corridor.

'Now speak.'

'They gave us money–'

'They?' Procopius barked, which got him a jaundiced look from his master.

'To do what?' Flavius asked in a gentle tone.

'The nightly ration of wine, drugged, we was to give it to our mates an' that would allow the Goths to clamber over the walls, them not being as high as elsewhere and our lads slumbering.'

'Who suggested this to you?'

'My close comrade roped me in, said we would be in clover if the Goths took the city with just our help. I didn't want no part of it but I went along so's I could put a stopper in it.'

Flavius pressed for details and if it did not come out clearly there was no doubting the story. Witigis had not given up on his notion of a coup and the bribing of sentries was a gambit that always had to be guarded against. Leave the walls unprotected for even a short period and the Goths could get enough men into the city to overcome the guards at one of the gates and open it.

Enemy warriors had taken advantage of the truce to spend time close to that part of the walls, ostensibly fishing in the river, which allowed for contact. Over several days natural animosity would give way to indifference and curiosity, then banter and even the odd friendly exchange, given soldiers of any hue were so inclined even if strict instructions were given to avoid it. It was something their officers should have seen and come down upon hard.

'What rank is this comrade?'

'Same as me, Your Honour, lowest of the low in the *auxilia*.'

'You will identify him?' A nod as Flavius addressed the guard commander. 'Take him back to his place of duty and fetch the traitor.'

'Am I to bring him here?'

'No, take him to your barracks. I will meet you there.'

Both Flavius and Procopius stood in silence until the Isaurian and his escort had departed, the secretary finally giving an opinion.

'That fellow is not of the rank for such a plot, and by deduction neither is his comrade.'

Flavius slowly shook his head, but it was more in frustration as he agreed with Procopius. Somewhere in this there would be an officer, but how senior? 'There's only one way to find out.'

'Hot irons?'

'And more. We must uncover who it is willing to sell us out. A man once bent on betrayal will not stop.'

A night of extreme pain from one Isaurian ranker revealed nothing; the fellow confessed to the plot but named no other, which left Flavius with the only option open to him. The severely damaged traitor was mounted and lashed onto an ass, that led by halter to the main Goth camp. The message was to Witigis, indicating he was in receipt of a gift as useless as his attempts to take Rome.

With matters progressing so well it seemed to Flavius that problems, long lain dormant, had begun to resurface, not least in the behaviour of

142

his reinforcements, men not attuned to the thinking of their general. Several were executed for transgressions against the citizens they were supposed to be in Italy to protect. Flavius hoped the message had got through when misbehaviour of a greater magnitude was brought before him at one of his now regular audiences during which he heard petitions.

'Where did this take place?'

Flavius asked with a sinking feeling, not relieved when he looked around the chamber and saw how many people were present and listening, including Antonina, who insisted on a raised dais like his own at which to sit at these assemblies, albeit her husband kept it at a discreet distance.

'Spoletum, Excellency.'

Presidius, the petitioner and a Roman citizen, was taken through his tale three times, once by Flavius, twice more by Procopius, as they sought inconstancies but there were none. Resident in Ravenna and fearing Goth revenge against the citizens of Rome, he had fled on the news of the capture of the city, having buried his coffers in his garden. But he took with him two objects of such value as to maintain him for as long as necessary, namely a pair of jewel-encrusted daggers with solid gold hilts.

'They were of inestimable value complete, but for my needs the jewels could be detached and sold separately, Excellency, while the hilt alone–'

'Yes, yes,' Procopius interrupted. 'We understand that, but why were you searched in the first place?'

'Perhaps your General Constantinus thought

anyone passing through from Ravenna to be a spy.'

'Others were searched?' Presidius, fat and sweating, nodded and looked set to gabble on when Flavius cut across him. 'Constantinus did not search you personally?'

The response was a silly giggle, as if to say would a man of such stature stoop to such a task.

'No, it was one of his officers. When he discovered my daggers he took them to show to the general.'

'And they never came back?'

'No. The officer who took them told me they were forfeit.'

Constantinus had been in Spoletum, sent there to delay the Goth approach to Rome, hastily withdrawn when it was obvious they were not going to allow themselves to be held up by unimportant outposts.

'I asked for their return in Spoletum and again when I got to Rome. The general refused on both occasions.'

'Without denying he had possession of them?' Procopius asked.

'He has them, alright,' Presidius protested. 'And while he keeps them I must beg to eat.'

'God grant that every beggar I meet is as larded as you.'

Flavius had snapped at the man sarcastically, but the pleasure of that did nothing to allay what was a serious problem. His second in command had broken a rule for which other men had been hanged. Was this fat and sweating citizen telling the truth? And if he had robbed this fellow, how many more victims might there be, people too afraid to speak out against such an important person?

'Ennes, take a file of my bodyguards and ask that General Constantinus join us.'

A glance around at the faces in the chamber, many shocked, others deeply curious as to what they were about to witness, did nothing to quiet the turmoil of his thoughts; they all knew what 'ask' meant. It was a command not a request, and he was not alone in wondering if force would be required to bring that about: Constantinus had his own personal guards.

He tried to hear other petitions but that was hard, made doubly so as rumours spread and the audience chamber began to fill up, which led to an order that no one else should be admitted other than Constantinus and his escort. If he was not looking forward to what was about to happen, the presence of Antonina, and the slight sneer that told him she knew of his forthcoming dilemma, did nothing to help. She had never tired of telling him his kindness to those conquered was mistaken.

The sound of studded sandals outside the chamber was loud but that was as nothing to the clatter on marble as Ennes entered with Constantinus, he surround by the armed men Ennes had taken with him. The impression given was of a prisoner being escorted and the look of thunder on the handsome face of his second in command indicated to Flavius that he was furious.

'Presidius, step forward,' he shouted, as the party came to a halt before him, the guards falling to the side so that Constantinus was facing him, Ennes, sword drawn, at his side.

'What is the meaning of this?'

'I am obliged to ask you, General,' Flavius said, indicating the citizen now trembling to one side, 'if you know this man?'

The way Constantinus looked at Presidius annoyed Flavius, it being so full of disdain. 'No, I do not and I would appreciate being told why I am being asked and why I have been dragged into your presence like some felon.'

'An unfortunate choice of expression, Constantinus. His name is Presidius.' That brought a flicker of eyelashes from the general. 'He is now going to relate in your presence that complaint which he has brought to me.'

Presidius had to be prompted; faced with a powerful patrician his previous certainties came near to deserting him. But he got his tale out eventually, by which time Flavius had risen from the chair he had been using, descending from his own dais to stand before his fellow soldier, looking right into his eyes.

Constantinus might be listening to Presidius but he knew from where any decisions would come and the blue eyes were steady, the face growing increasingly defiant; if anyone knew the orders regarding respect to the citizens in conquered lands it was he, yet he was searching the black eyes before him for clues as to what would follow. In his attitude he confirmed to his commanding general that what was being related was true.

'You, of all people,' Flavius hissed, as Presidius came to a faltering halt. 'The daggers, you have them?'

'I do!'

Defiance not regret, Flavius reckoned, and that broke his rigidly held demeanour so that he positively barked, 'Presidius would you be satisfied that they be returned?'

A stuttered yes was masked by Constantinus, who spoke in a firm voice. 'You would have been better asking me if I am willing to surrender them, which I must tell you I will not.'

'Damn you,' Flavius shouted, 'do you know what you face? I have executed men for much less. Am I to treat you in different manner because of your rank?'

It was as well Ennes was close; a hand went to the waist of the accused and his dagger came out in a flash of steel, this as he lunged forward. A flat swinging sword blade took him in the chest and checked him, before he was dragged into the arms of the men who had been his escort and his arms pinned.

Flavius, who had not flinched at what was clearly a bid to kill him, stepped forward to take off Constantinus his now useless dagger, his voice so low that only Ennes and those holding their prisoner could hear.

'Surrender them willingly, pay a forfeit. Give me grounds for leniency.'

'Since you're going to kill me anyway, why bother?'

'Killing me, as you just tried to do, was foolish.'

'Better that than I grovel to a man I consider not much more than an Illyrian peasant.'

'Like Justinian?' A nod again, with an added sneer of superiority.

'I do not want to execute you–'
'That would not be out of love or regard.'
'–but I must.'

## CHAPTER ELEVEN

Following the execution Flavius kept a careful eye on the mood of his army, as did Solomon, Photius and Procopius, the last probably to a greater and more telling extent, given his furtive sources, even if he gave a strong impression that he disagreed with the act of execution.

As far as they could discern the lower ranks approved – the law should be blind to eminence and birth – rankers had died for transgressing, so should generals. But it was amongst the echelons of the higher officers, where such things were held in some regard, that matters had to be more carefully assessed; these were men he dare not alienate as a body.

He hoped they, too, would see it as nothing but justice. This was seriously hampered in that quarter by the boasting of his wife, Antonina telling everyone who would listen a different version of the truth. The army second in command had been beheaded, not for a minor peculation but for the way he had insulted her, which was a gross exaggeration. If Constantinus had snubbed her invitations to dine and revel he had always been careful never to condescend to her; he knew her imperial connections as well as her husband.

Patently false as such statements were they could add fuel to a suspicion that Flavius had been motivated as much by class revenge or perceived military jealousies as the need to apply impartiality when it came to treatment of the Italian natives. Listen and observe as he did, there was a limit to the accuracy with which he could discern dissatisfaction in those he met with daily; men seeking advancement in a world of imperial caprice knew too well how to hide their true feelings.

What they did hanker after, openly, was some form of action for a truce that had clearly been broken and in this their general was only too willing to oblige them. With troops to spare now and a city almost certainly immune to capture, flying columns of cavalry were sent out to induce extra discomfort in the breast of an opponent who had always had to keep one eye cast over his shoulder for either a defection or a new zone of conflict.

It was at his back that the real damage was being inflicted; John Vitalianus, known to be one of the most enterprising officers in the imperial army, at the head of two thousand cavalry, had been sent to ravage in Witigis's very backyard, close to his capital of Ravenna. The old Roman province of Picenum was ripe for such a tactic, given it had a higher proportion of Goths within its borders than the rest of Italy.

With the main body of fighting men outside Rome, that left the aged, the infirm, the women and children and these John was busy enslaving, while at the same time sticking closely to the Belisarian creed in the way he cosseted the

149

Italians to win them over to his cause. Naturally that had to be countered and Witigis was being forced to deplete his forces to deal with the threat, a fact reported to him by Procopius.

Flavius never asked him where he got the information he imparted, with such confidence, about what was happening in the Goth encampments. Nor did he question it, his secretary being only too adept at the game of planting or bribing informants.

'Numbers?'

'Three thousand cavalry under a leader called Ulitheus, uncle to Witigis, which shows how seriously he takes the matter. He has staked the family prestige on stopping Vitalianus.'

'John will have to deal with it himself, which I trust him to do, as I cannot reinforce him but so far I cannot fault him.'

The man referred to, part of the most recent batch of reinforcements, had avoided any search for personal glory, a perennial risk with independent commands. He had stuck rigidly to the goal of strategically unnerving the enemy, declining to attack such Goth-garrisoned cities as Auximus and Urbinus, concentrating instead on their anxieties for what they considered their heartlands.

Flavius hoped he had found one senior officer he might be able to trust to be both obedient as well as enterprising for what was now going to be a more mobile and flexible form of warfare where he could not always be present to ensure that which was required in pursuit of the main object was executed as planned.

It seemed so when news came of the defeat of

Ulitheus, indeed his own death at the hand of John Vitalianus, as well as the utter destruction of the forces he had led. With that came an even more encouraging outcome: the Italian citizens of Ariminum, a mere twelve leagues south of Ravenna, had invited the victor to enter and he had obliged, well aware that the occupation of a city so close to the Goth capital must bring on a serious response.

Witigis must have received the bad news at the same time as Flavius got the good. The Byzantine pickets set to watch the Goth camps were able to report that the enemy army was now making serious preparations to depart from a siege in which they had no hope of now succeeding, the aim to move due east to counter Vitalianus.

'Do we let them go?' asked Photius.

'One more blow,' was the response.

Flavius waited with increasing impatience for his enemies to begin to decamp, given he had no intention of facing their main force in a major battle and risking a reverse. He desired to restore the faith of his infantry in their own capability, so his action was planned to inflict maximum damage on a retreating enemy with as little risk as possible to his own men.

In any movement of a host the main cavalry arm took the lead and with the forces who had spent over a year on the Plains of Nero this was the case. Flavius waited until the horsemen were across the Milvian Bridge and on their way to rejoin Witigis, then led his own infantry in a sudden and swift attack on the remainder, to face an outnumbered foot-bound rearguard.

Initially they put up a stiff resistance before being forced to break and run. That sent the rear sections of the retiring main body into a panic, which affected those ahead of them and they began to rush for the bridge. Being a narrow causeway it became a bottleneck for a mass of men either in dread or merely desiring to get swiftly clear of an unwinnable fight. That soon turned to mayhem as terror spread to the entire Goth contingent, who in their sheer volume crowded the western approach, which prevented cavalry reinforcements from the east bank coming to their aid.

A massacre ensued: those that did not fall to the sword and spear either died in the crush on the bridge or drowned as they tried desperately to save their lives by jumping into the fast-flowing Tiber. When the action was over Flavius stood amongst a heap of corpses in total control of anything that might follow. He held the Milvian Bridge in force and even if Witigis had been eager to reverse matters the cost in blood, already great, was too much to risk, given his other concerns.

The siege of Rome was over and the battle for Italy could now resume.

Meeting the wishes of the Milanese delegation, a large force was sent by sea to land at Genoa, before proceeding to Ticinum. The Goth garrison there exited the city to fight them and were soundly defeated. Naturally Witigis, retiring towards Ravenna, was obliged to react by detaching a large body to march on Milan in an attempt to get there before the troops sent by Flavius, a hope in which he failed, meaning his men were committed to another siege and, given the stout walls and full storerooms, one as difficult as Rome.

Not that everything favoured Byzantium: if Flavius had more troops now there were never enough. In order to hold Liguria and the route to the coast fewer than four hundred men were left to enter Milan. They had been obliged to garrison an endless number of towns and cities in order to secure them should the forces of Witigis seek to sever the line of communication. To protect Milan itself, the citizens would need to aid the Byzantines in manning the walls.

Flavius was sure they would do so as long as matters progressed well in other places, most notably Ariminum. This was a stronghold Witigis dare not leave in Byzantine-cum-Roman hands, not that he could do so with all his forces. He too was obliged to denude his army of effectives; unoccupied towns on the road from Rome to Ravenna needed garrisons to stop them defecting to Belisarius, and they had to be of sufficient numbers to drive off any attack that came from the enemy forces that might be following in his wake.

Fortunately for Flavius, with small Byzantine forces still holding strategic places on the direct route to Ravenna, Witigis had been obliged to march his main force by a more circuitous route to avoid them and the check they could place on his progress. This allowed him to reinforce Ariminum with a strong body of Isaurian infantry under Ildiger, prior to the arrival of the main Goth host.

His orders to both the commanders were specific: infantry were secure and effective behind walls, therefore Ildiger should take over the task of holding the city while John and his cavalry operated outside as a mobile force, able to snap at the Goths and disrupt their efforts to sustain the siege of Ariminum. The news that came from there told of dissension, not agreement.

'John Vitalianus refuses to leave the city as ordered. He sends me to say that he has captured it and he will hold it for the empire.'

'Not for his own personal glory?' Flavius replied in a mordant tone.

There was no point in responding to say that this was in direct contradiction of a simple command and one Flavius had taken care should be given by Ildiger in writing, something that had become increasingly necessary. The senior officers who had arrived with his reinforcements were men of high rank and higher ambition who needed to be constrained by unequivocal instructions.

Flavius now had to conclude that the faith he had placed in John was proving to be misplaced and as he looked around at a now more crowded assembly he had to wonder who else would be as likely to act on their own initiative, which brought on a problem he had not yet encountered. Prior to his North African campaign, Flavius had persuaded Justinian to break with tradition and give him sole command of the forces he led and this had carried on once he crossed to Sicily and eventually to the Italian mainland.

For too long the armies of the Eastern Roman Empire had been hampered in battle by the habit of appointing two generals as conjoint commanders of its forces in the field, and that extended to actual battle. Emperors were imbued with a keen sense of history and harked back to Republican times when the joint consuls had led the legions.

Added to that they feared that any one military leader should be too successful because the imperial past was littered with occasions when this had led to rebellion and, on several occasions, to outright usurpation. Dividing the command militated against any notion of individual glory, the unfortunate concomitant of this being division and confusion in situations that demanded clarity and action. Constantinople had lost too many battles because two men faced with the need for quick decisions could not agree.

The other distaff side of command division was that in which John was now engaged, acting on his own initiative and ignoring the greater strategic concern, this being another commonplace in a situation of dual authority in the field. The disobedient transgressor could usually assume that one general would agree with him, if for no other reason than contrariness.

Added to which, if he was of high enough personal rank and well connected within the ranks of the imperial bureaucracy, as was John Vitalianus, he could appeal above the heads of both to the Emperor himself. Control, always difficult and made more so by the execution of Constantinus, was about to get many times more complex.

'I retired south to Ancon,' Ildiger concluded, 'which has been prepared for a stout defence.'

'You have done as well as you could,' was the reply, there being no other that would serve, except the man might have given a more satis-factory response if he had said he stuck his sword through John's vitals. Flavius then addressed his assembled officers with another obvious truth.

'The actions of John Vitalianus we must accom-modate since they cannot be altered. It is vital that Witigis does not retake Ariminum, because if he does we will be required to reverse that prior to any move on Ravenna. Let us hope our miscreant can hold.'

If the man being spoken of was not an obedient subordinate he was a competent one. Vitalianus had arrived in Italy with a reputation for military effectiveness that was known even to his enemies, which made it doubly necessary that Witigis soundly beat him. As Ildiger was reporting to Flavius, the Goth King was surrounding the city and building the siege tower by which he in-tended to capture it, a sight which induced panic in a population now regretting their eagerness to surrender to Byzantium.

A lesser man might have wilted; not Vitalianus who had arrogance and self-belief to spare as well as a physique that could have stood as the tem-plate for the pure warrior. Tall, broad of shoulder while slim of waist, he had an Adonis counten-ance and a captivating manner, these being attributes that had impressed Flavius as much as anyone. His demeanour, with a huge Goth force outside the walls, was to behave as if he had been granted some special purpose from God and that calmed the frayed nerves of those who now needed to rely on him.

156

Yet even the dullest mind knew the city could not be held forever, it required to be reinforced by the main army and John acted accordingly; thwart any quick attempt on the walls and Witigis would be forced to seek to starve him out and that took time. He watched the building of the Goth tower with a sanguine air and that held even as it was realised the machine was not to be dragged to the walls by oxen, as had happened outside Rome, but pushed by human agency. Men inside the structure would therefore be immune to archery so a different method of countering this gambit had to be contrived.

Like all such war-making machines the siege tower suffered from a flaw: once set on a course it could not be manoeuvred to left or right nor advance swiftly, which told the defenders at which point they needed to mass in order to oppose the attack. In an unusual move the Goths dragged it forward, not as was common at first light, but well past the noon meridian, to stop some distance short of the walls to await the following dawn. It was then surrounded with a strong body of guards.

Daylight would bring the expected attack and over a short distance, now the tower was well forward. The sole impediment was a shallow ditch, which lay a short distance from the outer wall. This would be filled with bundled faggots so the tower could be wheeled right abreast of the masonry at a height greater than the parapet on which stood the defenders. It was essential that be stopped.

As darkness fell John led out his men, not for

battle, given they were armed with shovels not swords and spears, there being no intention to take on the strong body of men protecting the tower and induce them into leaving their posts for a fight. If they did, an immediate withdrawal would be necessary for the unarmed men, which led to a nervous period of waiting.

Once he was sure the Goths were going to stick to the task they had been given, John had his men set to work, the task to seriously deepen the ditch – but he had another ploy in mind. The spoil from the excavation was placed at the base of the wall to create an earthwork, one deep enough to prevent the tower from pressing hard upon the stonework even if it could cross the ditch. The sight of those continually moving torches, and no doubt the sounds they heard, eventually made the Goths curious enough to come forward to investigate, albeit cautiously, fearing a trap. It was too late, John had what he wanted and retired unmolested.

The first sight of the morning was of Goth warriors being hung from the front of the tower. It was assumed to be the leaders of the guards that had failed to detect what was happening the night before, now plain for all to see in the dark disturbed earth. Executions complete, the horns were blown and the enemy began their advance, sending forward strong raiding parties who braved the arrow fire from above to throw their tied piles of wooden faggots into the ditch.

John Vitalianus had a strong body of standard Byzantine cavalry but they were not *bucellarii,* which left him short of trained archers and so unable to prevent this taking place. Even with

casualties the ditch was quickly filled to over-
flowing, this as the tower itself crept forward to
the sound of extensive yelling and shield bashing,
the men providing the momentum immune to
fire from catapults or the inexperienced bowmen
on the parapet.

John, still as calm as he had been hitherto, was
smiling as if he knew exactly what was about to
happen. As the front wheels of the tower began to
edge onto those piled faggots the whole assembly
dipped forward, the weight being too great for that
which was supposed to support it. This meant the
warriors on the very top level, the men who were
to launch the first attack, hitherto hidden, became
exposed and they were now close enough to be
assailed by light javelins if not heavy spears.

The archers too had a target; they might not be
fully competent but at the range at which they
were now firing they could barely miss, and such
was the velocity the arrows penetrated the kind of
lamellar armour worn by their enemies. Witigis
brought up a mass of men to push but even as he
got the rear wheels of the tower onto the faggots
he came up against the earth piled up the
previous night. This left a gap too wide to cross
by jumping and now the wooden structure was
being assailed by flaming torches.

Having invested his whole aim in that tower
Witigis had no choice but to begin to withdraw;
he was losing men to no purpose and the frame-
work of his siege engine was beginning to smoul-
der despite the amount of water being used to
suppress the flames. Ropes appeared and slowly
the tower was pulled backwards, which told John

Vitalianus that Witigis obviously wanted to employ it again, no doubt when he had created the means to get it up against the walls.

John was quick to react and lucky that the horses he needed were saddled and ready. Gates opened, he led his mounted men out to engage, using the faggots that had failed to support the tower as a swift means of crossing the ditch. As generally happened with a force moving away from a fight, the Goths evinced little stomach for the battle and paid a high price for their lack of will. Witigis sent more men forward to rescue the tower and they too, having two tasks not one, suffered heavily even if they were successful.

Days passed during which every eye in the city awoke to observe the tower as the sun rose. If it moved the attack was to be renewed – if not, the tactics of starvation would be used to retake Ariminum. It seemed plain that was the outcome and that was underlined when Witigis was seen to be sending away warriors to other duties.

John knew the time had come to communicate with Flavius Belisarius and demand that he be relieved. It did not occur to him that he had ever exceeded his orders and nor did he now feel the need to be humble. As a patrician and a man well connected in Constantinople he felt no requirement to employ excessive deference to his titular commander. The needs of the campaign were obvious to the dullest tactician. This city must be held, so let Flavius do that which was required.

# CHAPTER TWELVE

Unaware of precisely what was happening at Ariminum, Belisarius could at least be sure that Rome was secure, so he left it with a small garrison and marched his main army right across Italy towards the Adriatic. While at the mountain city of Aquila he was informed that Narses the Eunuch, a commander he had known since he was a young officer and at present a steward to Justinian, had arrived on that coast with five thousand men and was camped at Firmum.

Leaving his forces to follow, Flavius made haste to meet with him in order to plan strategy only to find that the problem that had arisen with John Vitalianus was now compounded. A general in his own right as well as the Keeper of the Royal Treasury, and having with him what was in effect the Army of Illyricum, Narses could see no need, and certainly had no intention, of bowing the knee to Flavius Belisarius.

Firstly, here was a fellow he had long ago had as a subordinate. If he had been elevated since to his present position it was as much to do with personal affinities as ability, albeit Flavius was the victor of the Battle of Dara and also the man who had brought about the reconquest of North Africa, so could not be discounted or overborne.

In essence the two, militarily, were equals, which meant that whatever action was undertaken next had to be agreed between them, bringing with it all the problems of dual command: endless discussion in front of officers who obviously took the side of those to whom they were loyal.

Disagreement rose early and at the heart of the dispute was naturally John Vitalianus. He was an associate to Narses and a man who owed much of his advancement to the eunuch; in short he was a client officer and that meant a shared obligation on the part of both. Then there was a memory of Flavius being far from obedient himself, though it was never referred to openly; on the Persian frontier he had disobeyed strict instructions from Narses not to cross into Sassanid territory, only surviving censure due to a degree of devilish subterfuge, added to his high connection to Justinus, then Count of the Imperial Guard at the court of Anastasius, the emperor he succeeded.

Flavius was focused on the capture of the whole of Italy while the new arrival seemed to wish to concentrate on saving his insubordinate client in Ariminum. The time came when the two needed to make a decision because the present dispute threatened the whole operation.

'I have here my instructions from the Emperor, Narses, which if you care to read them appoints me as sole commander of the forces on the Italian campaign.'

'Not instructions made known to me. What may have pertained before does not necessarily apply now.'

'I have no doubt that Justinian intended that I should hold the position he granted me, made plain here in writing and above his imperial seal.'

Narses, older by a decade and an Armenian by birth, had started life, like so many of his race, as a mercenary in the service of Constantinople. Unlike the majority, he had prospered and risen to hold many positions of authority, including important provincial governorships, before being appointed as Chamberlain to the Imperial Treasury.

If not as personally close to Justinian as Flavius he was a man on whom the Emperor relied for advice, added to which Theodora, with a sharp eye on income and expenditure, must trust him as well. He would also enjoy powerful backing within the bureaucracy that surrounded the throne, a body that even in close contact numbered hundreds. If Justinian stood at the apex of that, he was far from the complete master of it: no emperor had ever managed to be that, it being too complex for any one man to control.

Many important offices were held by eunuchs and they formed a band that looked to each other's interests, sometimes above that of the polity they claimed to serve. Not that those deprived of the opportunity to breed were alone in their comradeship; every kind of political grouping a man could envisage was in existence and then there was the fluidity brought on by greed or personal ambition, in which loyalty to ones fellows came a poor second.

Flavius had little love for Constantinople and its endemic intrigues; for all the problems of command in the field they were simple by comparison with the tangled skein of endless conspiracy, one

163

in which Justinian more than held his own and often surpassed his opponents. This was the reason why he could never be wholly relied upon, a point continually alluded to by Procopius. Flavius might have this letter but he could never be sure that his master would not, if it suited his purpose on any given day, repudiate it.

Narses took the parchment handed to him with great reluctance and as he read it he adopted a look that indicated that the words before him mattered little, this as Flavius tried to drive home the point. He kept his voice low in what was, to him, too public a gathering for the making of decisions.

'The wording is quite plain, Narses, and while I do not desire to diminish you in any way, for I respect you and your achievements, I am obliged to insist that the imperial will be respected.'

The older man raised his eyes to cast them round a room that had once formed the senate of this provincial capital of Picenum. Change the armour and colourful accoutrements of the imperial officers for togas and it could have been a gathering in Republican antiquity; two factions vying for power and seeking, in the assembled faces, some clue as to the level of their support. Now, in a louder voice, he addressed the whole chamber instead of Flavius alone.

'It says here that your actions are to be judged as being in the best interests of the state. If I were to say to you that I consider your plan to leave John Vitalianus to hold Ariminum while we attack Auximus to be less than sound, and not in the best interests of the empire, you would see why I cannot agree with you.'

Not to be outdone Flavius applied in an equally carrying voice. 'Do you agree that our ultimate objective should be Ravenna?'

'That does not require to be stated and nor does the fact that Ariminum is between us and the Goth capital. It is on the way to our ultimate goal. By saving it we surely advance our cause.'

'While Auximus lays to the south and even now at our rear, strongly garrisoned, and the men there will, once we are committed to an advance northwards, be able to act to threaten us. I maintain that John can hold and that if we move with our full force on Auximus they will, once they observe our numbers, surrender quickly, removing that threat.'

'And if Ariminum falls?'

'Do you not have faith in a man you have so favoured?'

That angered Narses, it was in his eyes if not his voice; no soldier likes to face an allegation of making tactical arrangements to suit extraneous purposes. 'He cannot fight with my faith.'

'He seems able to act with confidence in his own capabilities.'

'So you wish to punish him for disobeying you?'

Flavius had to work to keep his own voice flat then; Narses had made an outrageous suggestion but if he had to be told so it required maintenance of a diplomatic tone; outcome had to triumph over pique.

'I have been fighting in Italy for a long time now and I have Witigis on the rack. Do you really think, Narses, that I will risk all of that to chastise an insubordinate inferior?'

'We all have our pride.'

'Something a good commander seeks to keep in check, would you not say?'

The great unspoken was that Flavius did not wish to fight any more battles in the open against the Goths if it could be avoided. It was not just Auximus that required to be subdued, there were Goth garrisons forming an arc to the west and they would, in their heartlands especially, always combine to outnumber him, even with these new reinforcements.

He could not say that to Narses; it would sound like excessive caution to the newly arrived component of the assembly. His own officers, who had experienced the same as he, required no telling that care had to be taken and it was wise to fight their enemies only on ground and at a time chosen by themselves.

The ripple of voices that now arose was far from a commotion, but it was sufficient to engage the curiosity of both the principles, Flavius and Narses sitting forward in their chairs to find out what had set so many tongues wagging. The fellow who approached through the assembled ranks was covered in the dust of a long and hard ride, the latter evident in a weariness he could not conceal.

Stepping forward he handed a letter to Flavius who read it in a couple of seconds, it being short, before handing it to Narses.

'The decision is taken?' asked the older man as he read it, a gleam in his eye.

It was with no pleasure at all that Flavius had to concede the point; the words he had just read left him no choice. 'If John says he has run out of food and can only hold for five more days or capitulate, then we must move to aid him at once.'

'Then it would be churlish of me not to meet with your wishes as to how that is to be carried out.'

The acknowledgement that Flavius should plan the next move might look to be one with which to happily agree; it was far from it, given John Vitalianus was once more controlling his actions, a fact made plain to his own commanders once they had assembled at his chosen quarters. His first move was to detach a thousand men to mask Auximus, their task to threaten but on no account to fight.

'Make much noise, as if you are preparing an attack, but retire if threatened.'

Given the fleet that had brought Narses to Italy was available, it seemed foolish not to use it against a city close to the shoreline. Ildiger was put in command of an amphibious force that would threaten Ariminum from the sea. Again they were to avoid battle on their own, forbidden to land unless the forces Flavius would lead had appeared on the landward side of the city.

The main army was split in two, Martinus leading half by the coastal road, while Flavius, accompanied by Narses and his Illyrian forces, would take the remainder on an inland route so as to come upon Ariminum from a different direction. The instructions to Martinus showed some cunning; Flavius did not want his enemies to suspect his chosen path, so the coastal army must light double campfires to fool the Goths into thinking they were the main force. If the garrison then attacked Martinus they would expose their rear to a crushing blow.

It was galling to have to seek approval from Narses, who seemed to Flavius, although he was willing to admit to a heightened sense of grievance, to be taking pleasure in the Belisarian discomfort. It was doubly irritating that the need for harmony demanded he do nothing to acknowledge it. The man who got the backwash of this was Procopius, who understanding the reason did nothing to deflect his master's ire.

'If any of my officers allows a single soldier of that Illyrian rabble to enter Ariminum before we do, I will flay them alive. I want Vitalianus to grovel in gratitude to the army of which he is supposed to be a part.'

'Which, *Magister*, still leaves the problem of Narses.'

'Do you think I do not know that, man?'

'I do not, but I am concerned at how we counter it.' It was then that Flavius realised he was taking his anger out on the wrong person, which occasioned a mumbled apology as well as a nod that Procopius should continue. 'You must send to Justinian for clarification and by a hand that is personal to you.'

'I cannot spare you.'

'But you can Photius. Only Justinian can order Narses to obey you and if that remains a problem unsolved you will face no end of difficulties. Send your stepson to Constantinople with a personal

168

plea to the Emperor, which will allow us to bypass the imperial officials.'

'You mean Theodora?'

The look Procopius gave him then was to tell Flavius to keep his voice down; Antonina was within the same villa and not above eavesdropping on their conversations. A pull of the lips showed that Flavius had got the point and he added softly, 'Even if they rarely meet she will spot he has left.'

'For Rome, shall we say? And will not the young man enjoy fooling his mother?'

'I can think of nothing that would make him happier.'

'Other than fighting alongside you,' Procopius replied, making a valid point; Photius would have to be persuaded to miss the coming campaign, which might involve, at its very best, the taking of Ravenna.

'How do I cover for his absence? I am bound to be asked.'

'Tell the Lady Antonina that he is on some mission for me.'

For once the look on the face of Procopius did not convey the aesthete for Antonina would drink hemlock before asking him anything; as of this moment he had the look of a sated wolf.

What Photius missed, if not the ultimate goal, was a tactical triumph, though as always in war it was not without a degree of luck. Flavius, after marching for three days, encountered and surprised a strong force of Goths marching towards Ariminum and he fell on them at a speed that caused many deaths and even more flight, as a large body of the enemy bolted to a nearby and dense forest, Flavius refusing the request of his men that they should follow.

Narses plainly saw this as wrong and faint-hearted, though it was conveyed by his jaundiced countenance not in words. Why would he question an act that in the eyes of the troops both men led could only diminish his co-commander? But it was not brought on by fear, although high casualties could result in fighting in such a wooded terrain.

Flavius wanted to let them go because with his men covering their escape to the north or west their only hope was to make for their original destination, which was Ariminum. Once there they would alert their comrades to his approach and he had high hopes that would provoke a reaction.

His ploy was justified when within sight of the city they saw the besieging Goths had decided to fight. They were deploying in late afternoon to give the Byzantines battle on the following day. As darkness fell, to the south both armies could see the mass of campfires, which Flavius knew would confuse his enemies, and that was compounded by the rising sun, which revealed, offshore, the Byzantine fleet, Ildiger making sure that it was plainly and visibly manned by warriors and not just sailors.

Faced with the need to fight on three fronts, added to a possible sortie from Ariminum itself, the Goths knew they were beaten. The forward skirmishers, sent to harass them, were called back in when those controlling them reported the enemy was in the process of striking their tents and loading their supply waggons. They were doing so at a deliberate pace until Ildiger began to land his troops on the nearby sandy shore.

Haste then became the order of the day, which meant that when Flavius led his men forward, his enemies having melted away northwards, it was to a field denuded of warriors but covered with much in the way of abandoned supplies, this while Ildiger led his men into the no longer besieged city.

The man who greeted him was less the Adonis than hitherto, having starved alongside the inhabitants and his soldiers. Not a horse was left of what had been a force of two thousand cavalry, every one having been eaten. With hollowed cheeks, much spare flesh and a less than full gait, John Vitalianus, having acknowledged Ildiger, went out to meet Flavius Belisarius, becoming somewhat restored in stature when he espied Narses, the pair quick to embrace.

Nor was it long before he found out about the differing opinions on tactics, which meant his meeting with Flavius alone did not proceed as the man in command thought it should. He felt Vitalianus would do well to grovel for his disobedience; John, never inclined that way, was bolstered by the proximity of Narses and was now, as far as he was concerned, the equal of the man before him.

'Do you doubt it was a direct order?'

If Vitalianus was not physically fully restored, more than one good meal had lifted his spirits and that was evident in his defiant look. 'A general, however clever, who is fifty leagues away, cannot see what is before the man on the spot.'

'The man fifty leagues distant might have a plan that encompasses more than a search for individual glory. And do not forget that I had eyes in Ariminum in the presence of Ildiger, who had the good sense, when you plainly had none, to bring his men to a place where they could be of some use to a campaign. Had he stayed, you would have been starved out.'

'Which I am told you were willing to countenance.'

'Do not think yourself worth it. Remember the two thousand men you led and nearly lost to Goth slavery.'

'They would have died for me.'

'Then they would have died in vain,' Flavius barked. 'Now regardless of that which you owe to me, you are required to thank Ildiger, who entered Ariminum first, as well as publically apologise for overruling him when he brought you my orders.'

The reply was given with cold but suppressed fury. 'I will not.'

'Then you leave me no choice but to send you back to Constantinople.'

'An order I refuse to obey.'

'Is that because of habit?'

Vitalianus stood, his emaciated frame shaking with fury. 'I will not put myself under obligation to Ildiger, and by association to you, and I will remind you that Ariminum was held and the Goths were forced to retire, even if it was not of your doing. If I owe my survival to anyone it is to Narses.'

172

'And if he demands the same?'

'He won't, Flavius Belisarius, for he is not only a better man than you but he is twice the general you will ever be. He knows my worth, and added to that he has the Emperor's ear and has done for many years now. So I doubt you will be sending me anywhere.'

Again it was Procopius who became the sounding board for what was a real dilemma. The secretary was not in the least surprised that Narses had declined to support Flavius in taking action against Vitalianus.

'Narses cannot be seen to abandon John, for to do so would be taken badly by all of his client officers.'

Flavius could appreciate that; did he not himself have men who looked to him for advancement and in return gave him their loyalty? He might reassure himself that he never indulged a poor commander but that did not change matters. The system of clientism had existed since the Republic and nothing he could do would change it.

The response came with a sigh. 'While if I insist, I will split the army.'

'Pray Photius brings back that which you need.'

# CHAPTER THIRTEEN

In a matter of weeks the command situation deteriorated; a far from chastened John Vitalianus engaged in an attempt to undermine Flavius Belisarius and Narses did nothing to squash this, which implied that he would not be averse to the miscreant's aims. As usual, Procopius had his ear to the ground, and through reliable informants quickly established within the ranks of the new arrivals was able to report that Photius would face a counter embassy at the Imperial Court from those who supported a man who had now become a rival.

Flavius was worried Narses might underestimate the Goths, reminding him of the fortresses they held on the Tiber, an arc of eight strongholds with Ravenna to the north and Auximus to the south. Any neutral person studying a map would see the combined Byzantine forces as being surrounded with their backs to the Adriatic, rather than being in the ascendant.

Matters were rendered more complicated because Narses point-blank refused to discuss strategy in private, insisting that any decisions should be arrived at with the aid of the men who would be tasked to carry them out. Flavius suspected he found it easier to decline to cooperate in company than he would if they were alone. His main point was to insist that by remaining in

Ariminum over the winter they were safe, with the sea at their back and a strong fleet in support.

He refused to accept that the security of Rome was vital, that to the people of the Italian peninsula the city had an almost mythical standing as the ancient capital of the Republic as well as the present centre of the Christian faith. Flavius suspected Narses knew as he did of that symbolic importance; it was just another example of his playing to the gallery of his own officers.

'I would wish to march on Milan, Narses, not return to Rome. The siege there is being pressed hard and Mundus has already told us he will struggle to hold for much longer. Besides which, there is a Goth army in the field for us to fight and defeat.'

'And a hundred leagues to march, which will take us away from the security I have just alluded to. That not only renders us exposed, it will risk us losing Ariminum and Ancon, the very cities we must hold. Let your Goths come to us.'

The argument carried on but to little avail and that presented Flavius with a real dilemma. Prior to any attack on Ravenna, which he heartily wished to undertake, he felt the need to ensure his rear was secure. Ever since landing in Italy he had gone to great lengths to guarantee that he could safely withdraw from any forward position without having to forfeit the campaign. There were those even amongst his own officers who saw this as overcautious; he did not, given the alternative might be complete destruction.

He tried to persuade Narses to combine with him on an assault on Auximus to open the route

175

to the south as well as providing an alternative road to Rome. He refused and if the reasons were frustrating they were cogently argued by a man who was no stranger to warfare or generalship; his opinions, even if Flavius disagreed with them, were based on his appreciation of the military situation and could, objectively examined, be just as valid.

As ever a compromise was reached: Flavius would winter in the west, which would relieve the supply situation in an area much ravaged by warfare. But with a few weeks remaining of the campaigning season, Narses would join with him in seeking to take Urbinus. This Goth enclave was the closest to Ariminum and it dominated the Via Flaminia, the direct route to Rome. Milan would be left to fend for itself, which meant an inevitable capitulation.

Even in this, division was quick to show: John Vitalianus advised Narses to camp separately to Belisarius, who had set up his siege lines to the west of Urbinus. Staying to the east of the city it underlined their lack of confidence in a successful outcome, John being particularly of the opinion that the city, well supplied with food and water, would never fall before the onset of winter obliged the Byzantines to move on.

As usual envoys were despatched to offer terms of surrender, these brusquely rejected, which provided enough of an excuse for Narses, urged on by his favoured inferior, to abandon the attempt and retire on Ariminum, this despite the fact that Flavius had begun the construction of the siege engines necessary to achieve a successful assault. Not given to begging Flavius did try, but to no avail.

'And by halving our forces, Narses brings about that which drives him away.'

It was plain Martinus, acting as his senior subordinate, did not know what to say to comfort his general and ended up proposing the wrong alternative, which to him seemed the only one to make sense.

'So we march on to Rome?'

Flavius, normally the calmest of men, positively snarled his response. 'I will take Urbinus without any aid from Narses.'

It required all of his force of personality to drive on the various commanders in an enterprise in which they had little faith – Martinus was not alone in thinking half a host could not carry out such a task. The building of a tower and the construction of a ram required that Flavius harry men who had picked up on the dejection of their officers, a disposition that was doubly evident on the morning chosen for the primary assault.

To quell the pessimism it was necessary that their general very visibly lead from the front, a position of great danger as he was dressed in fine armour and was riding a white horse underneath his very recognisable personal standard. He knew if he fell then any forward movement would cease, not that there was a great deal to begin with, the approach being agonisingly slow given the rumbling tower setting the pace.

The gates opening before him came as jolt enough to stop him dead. A party of Goths emerged to throw aside their arms before approaching the now stationary Flavius Belisarius. Sat astride his fidgeting horse, Flavius had to grip hard with his knees to keep it steady as the embassy came within hailing distance. Their message was brief: Urbinus was his and it was a capitulation, there being no request for terms.

'Pursue Narses, Martinus, and inform him that Urbinus is ours.' The voice went from triumphant to bitter. 'And when you do, ensure that John Vitalianus is with him.'

'Do I say why it fell so easily?'

That was put to Flavius with a grin; Martinus thought he knew what the answer would be and he was not disappointed.

'No details, just be brief and do not forget to gloat.'

Flavius was left, as Martinus departed, to reflect on the way God had favoured his purpose once more. Surely it was divine intervention that had dried up the wells on which Urbinus depended for water, for it had come about from no action of his, the result being that holding out against the siege became impossible.

'They will find out in time, but let them wonder at their caution until they do.'

The response was initially encouraging but ultimately depressing; pricked into action Narses sent John Vitalianus off to take Caesena, the Goth stronghold that controlled the road to Milan. Hurriedly pressed it miscarried with heavy loss of life, though John, determined to match Belisarius with a success, bypassed his failure and drove the Goths out of Forocornelius, which left very exposed the capital of Ravenna.

The news reached Flavius just as he took a second enemy fortress on the Via Cassia to the north of Rome; that arc of Goth pressure that had so concerned him was now very close to being utterly broken. But it had happened at a time when to fully exploit it was impossible. With winter upon the land, cold weather, heavy rains in the lowlands and snow blocking the Apennine passes campaigning became impossible.

It was in these conditions that Photius returned from Constantinople. 'It pains me to say this to you, Father, but my mother may have had more influence on the decision than any representations I made.'

'Did Justinian indicate as much?'

Photius shook his head. 'There was no doubt Theodora knew of the dispute with Narses, it was the talk of the court, and from all you have told me the Emperor would be unlikely to act without including his wife.'

Flavius was perplexed; Theodora did not trust him and as far as he knew she had a high degree of faith in Narses. He had sent Photius in the hope that he would get a private audience with Justinian and extract from him a favourable decision without involving her. This forced him to acknowledge he had been naïve and not for the first time; Antonina was in constant correspondence with her imperial friend so the idea that his differences with Narses were unknown in Constantinople was risible.

He could not avoid searching for motives, given Photius was telling him that Theodora had a hand in the decision to recall Narses, which had

179

him frowning as he racked his brain to try to untangle that which was and would always be concealed: the devious mind of the Empress.

'Does something still trouble you, Father?' asked Photius, reacting to the expression.

'Many things trouble me, my son, but now that Narses has been recalled the major one of those is removed. And the double windfall is I get to keep the men he brought with him from Illyricum.'

It was later, in conversation with Procopius, that a possible solution was arrived at. If Theodora did not trust anyone, Flavius knew she was adept at picking out who to rely on in any given situation. Always alert to threats to her person she would have more than one to guard against and it was possible she needed Narses in close proximity to ward off the machinations of different powerful courtiers.

'There again, Justinian may have just seen the sense of what I have been telling him for years. Two men cannot successfully command an army.'

Procopius was not prepared to believe that, his expression said so.

Two pieces of information came to depress Flavius prior to his departing Rome in the spring. One was the information that the slave girl who had told him of his wife's adulterous behaviour had been murdered shortly after he left Sicily, this while Antonina and Theodosius were still there.

The second piece of information made him feel even worse. Pope Vigilius had not, as he had promised, put Silverius through an ordeal of examination by bishops. Instead he had shipped him to a waterless island and left him there to starve to death, the pity being that the perpetrator was not in Rome when this became known. Perhaps it was for the best Vigilius had decamped to Naples, because Flavius, in a combination of rage and misery, might have committed sacrilege by personally lopping off his head.

'There is no point in asking him if he is responsible, *Magister*,' Procopius counselled, when they discussed the possibility of arraigning him. 'He will deny that he gave any orders to kill Silverius and blame his minions. Besides, do you think he would have dared to act without at least a nod from the Empress? To confront him with the crime is to confront her.'

'The killing of that maid troubles me as much.'

'And again you have had only denial.'

That had been a stormy occasion and one in which Antonina had reacted with fury at the accusation of being behind the death of her maid, described by his wife as a loose creature inclined to seek to satisfy her carnal needs in inappropriate places and with questionable company, that very likely being the cause of her death.

If Flavius did not believe it he had no way to refute accusations aimed at a woman he barely knew. Macedonia had been one of several maids who served his wife, and in any case, such attendants did not tend to last long before something they had done, probably an innocent act, saw them dismissed.

'Even if you had proof, which you do not...'

The response to what was obvious and left unsaid by Procopius came with a sigh. 'Theodora would rush to defend Antonina and I would not get justice.'

'No.'

With so much to do in preparing the next part of the campaign it was not possible to brood on such matters. Flavius did, however, commission a small shrine to the memory of those for whose deaths he felt responsible and that, to the surprise of many, was dedicated not just to Silverius and Macedonia, but also to Constantinus. Asked why by Photius, the reply he gave was true to the way he felt.

'If I had tried to understand him more, included him more in my thinking, trusted him more, he might have had faith in me to be lenient.'

'He despised you, Father. Remember, too, he tried to kill you. He deserved his fate for that and not just the stolen daggers.'

'I was looking into his eyes when he went for his knife, Photius. He was sure I was determined on his execution and for nothing more than his patrician birth. How can it be that I cannot convince a man that I would not hate him for that?'

'Am I allowed to say that you are berating yourself for no purpose? These are but minor matters in that in which you are engaged.'

Flavius shook himself, Photius was right.

If Narses had gone home, John Vitalianus had not and since he had his own numerous *comitatus* the option of not employing him did not exist. For security against his potential malice Flavius sent him north with Martinus as his commander, their task to ensure the forces that had retaken Milan stayed north of the River Po and did not come to the aid of the their comrades as Flavius advanced on Ravenna.

The spies Procopius still had in the retinue of Witigis were able to tell of the Goth King's manoeuvres. Over the winter he had tried to enlist help from the Lombards, a barbarian tribe resident in Pannonia on the northern border of Illyricum, only to discover that Justinian had beaten him to an alliance that would keep them neutral.

His next move was just as dangerous; envoys had been sent to the Sassanids in the hope they would put pressure on the eastern Byzantine border, which threatened would be bound to draw soldiers away from Italy, affairs in that area always taking precedence over other borders. To lose to the Sassanids imperilled the whole Eastern Empire. Such information only confirmed in Flavius the need to bring matters to a conclusion. He had the troops he needed and the inferior commanders he could trust to act as he wished, even John Vitalianus. If that officer did not act for love of his general, his personal ambition was enough to drive him on.

Cautious as ever, the first task was to invest Fisula and free the land route from Rome to Genoa, while simultaneously launching an attack on Auximus and securing the Byzantine rear. This had been anticipated by Witigis, who well understood his enemy. The city was garrisoned with hardened Goth warriors, supplied until its storerooms were bulging and its walls made fully effective to support a fortress that already enjoyed the intrinsic defence provided by its natural features, standing as it did on the peak of a steep-sided hill that dominated the landscape.

Flavius approached Auximus at the head of a ten-thousand-strong army in which he could repose the kind of faith he had enjoyed when he first landed north of Rhegium. His soldiers were healthy, eager for the fight and willing to follow where he led, their spirits raised even more when their general was immediately favoured with some of his famous luck.

His forward elements were able to catch outside the walls a substantial foraging party, entirely unaware of the speed of the Byzantine approach, and engage them. Many of the Goths were killed but an equal number, thanks to their fighting ability, escaped, which told the man come to overwhelm them of the calibre of what he faced and, after he had ridden round the base of the hill, affected his assessment of the tactics to be used, these outlined at his first conference.

'No major assaults will be attempted. We cannot get siege equipment to rest against those walls, the slope makes that impossible. Auximus cannot be taken by storm. We must starve them out, so make the camps you construct solid, given we may be here for a long time, and make sure they cannot forage.'

No assaults did not mean no activity; close attention was paid to seek out any chinks in the Goth defences, ways in which their fighters exposed themselves, that provided by the need they had, in order to preserve their dry feed, to gather pasture on the hillside. A party would emerge daily to scythe the abundant hillside grass. It was natural for the Isaurian infantry camped closest to the walls to sally forth and harass them and their escorts.

This led to a series of small infantry engagements in which not much damage was done to either side. That altered when the Goths set an ambush; hiding unseen in one of the ravines, old and deep watercourses that scarred the mound, a strong group of warriors emerged to pin the exposed Isaurians, able to get between them and safety. Given the Goths were vastly superior in both numbers and close-quarters fighting ability, few of Flavius's men survived.

Doubly galling was the fact that they were able to repeat the tactic on more than one occasion as the too-eager-to-fight and hot-tempered Isaurians repeatedly allowed themselves to become trapped. The commanders further down the slope could see the threat as it emerged – those at which it was aimed were in ignorance – but lacked means to communicate with their men and control their actions.

Conscious of the effect such defeats had on morale and knowing that to forbid any action would be just as depressing, Flavius cast about for a solution, surprised that it was Procopius who came up with an answer. He proposed a method of controlling both the advance and the retreat by using the differing sounds of infantry and cavalry trumpets. One could be employed to initiate an attack on the grass cutters while the other could be used to ensure the infantry withdrew as soon as any threat emerged.

The *magister's* secretary had never been short on self-regard but his thin chest positively bulged when this proved to be a success, allowing the infantry to interfere with the Goths' foraging while suffering no losses themselves. In time that grass cutting wound down; the Goths were eating their horses, not feeding them.

However well supplied, their holding out had always rested on the hope that Witigis would march to their relief but, determined to hold his capital he did not stir from Ravenna. Instead he instructed the Goth garrison of Milan to move out of the city and head south in order to draw off the Byzantines. On their way they would face Martinus and John Vitalianus, now camped on the southern bank of the Po.

The news Flavius received told him that the Goths had reached the river but showed no sign of attempting to cross it and continue on to Auximus. His orders to his juniors were explicit: they too should stay where they were camped; a Goth force north of that wide, fast-flowing river was no threat to him.

If things were proceeding as planned, there was always a devil in warfare and now a real Lucifer emerged. News came that the Franks were moving south with what sounded like a massive host. Even allowing for exaggeration as to their real numbers, it was their intentions that mattered.

In theory the Franks were allied to both competing forces, but did that still hold true? If they combined with the Goths, Flavius would be obliged to beat a hasty retreat for the questionable security of Rome, for against such numbers not even that great fortress could be certain to hold.

# CHAPTER FOURTEEN

To say that the invasion stretched the nerves of
Flavius Belisarius was an understatement; he dare
not raise the siege of Auximus prematurely for to
do so would waste months of efforts and spoil his
whole purpose, doubly galling given the stub-
bornness of a defence that by now should have
crumbled. So he waited anxiously for developments, heartened when he learnt that the new
invaders, having been welcomed by the Goths as
saviours, turned on their supposed allies and
ravaged their territory, enslaving thousands and
killing more.

The Goth army that had decamped from Milan
was assailed likewise, fleeing across the River Po
in disorder, some of their elements actually
riding through the camp of Martinus and John
Vitalianus, who mistaking what was happening
rode north only to encounter the same problem;
the Franks were allied to no one and they too
were forced into a hasty retreat which left them
well back from where they started and nervous as
to what was to follow.

It was a combination of dearth and disease that
saved them from annihilation. The Frankish host
was huge and now occupied lands that had
suffered much from the foraging of previous
armies; there was simply not enough food to sustain them and that brought on the ravages which

always affected an army short on supply – serious and debilitating disorders of the belly being the most common. Such disease restricted movement and being stationary exacerbated the problem, so Theudibert, the most southerly successor to Clovis, decided to cut his losses and retire north.

Just as troubling was a Hun invasion of the Balkans, one part of which nearly reached the walls of Constantinople before the barbarians withdrew, taking a massive quantity of plunder. The second prong of that incursion marched as far south as Delphi and in doing so drew off an army marching towards Italy to aid Flavius. The only saving grace was that if the Byzantine camp knew of these developments; as far as Flavius was aware the Goths holding Auximus did not.

Disillusionment on that point was provided by an Isaurian traitor called Burcentius who, suitably bribed and using the excuse of ill health to absent himself from the siege lines, had undertaken two missions to Witigis on behalf of the garrison, the results of which only became known when he was apprehended and that took place only because a captured Goth informed Flavius of his double mission to Ravenna.

In the first instance Witigis had sent Burcentius back with news of the Frankish incursion, promising to march on Auximus once that was dealt with. When nothing came the traitor was once more bribed to find out the intentions of the Goth King, with an added warning that the time was coming when Auximus would be forced to surrender. This was replied to with soothing words of his imminent arrival.

No amount of hot iron could get from Burcentius a statement as to the veracity of this; the man did not know if Witigis was being truthful or hopeful, and he was finally handed over to his own Isaurian tribesmen do with as they wished. Their decision was to manufacture a wicker cage, raised high on faggots, and burn him alive within sight of the whole Byzantine host, a statement of loyalty as much as an act of revenge.

'If they are short of food let us see if we can cut their water.'

Flavius oversaw the operation to do this personally, seeking to interdict a spring that ran from just outside the city walls into a well-built cistern covered by a thick stone vault and he used the Isaurians, hell-bent on proving their worth. In order to disguise their purpose it was necessary to draw up the whole of his infantry as if they were about to attack and have them move forward as if this was the case.

Those tasked with the real purpose advanced with huge hammers, protected by the held-high shields of their comrades, which allowed the small party to break the cistern to get into the water and begin their work, the aim to so damage the exterior walls that the water would flow downhill instead of into the city. At first the whole endeavour seemed to be going as planned. That changed as the Goths, hitherto unfazed by an assault that stood little chance of success, realised the actual aim. First they rained down every known kind of missile on those trying to protect the cistern breakers: rocks large enough to crush shields, spears heavy enough to penetrate the hard leather and flaming wads, until they broke and ran.

Next a strong party emerged to save their vital water supply, with Flavius ordering the forces under his command forward. With the advantage of higher ground the Goths did great slaughter to the Isaurians, until a section led by a more enterprising leader launched a furious counter-attack that broke through to the now cut-off breakers, forcing the Goths to fall back on their walls, before retreating themselves, taking their hammer-bearing comrades with them.

'The cistern is too well built to be quickly damaged, *Magister*. Those who built it in ancient times knew its worth.'

Aratius, the Isaurian commander who made this report and the man who had driven the Goths back, was crestfallen at their failure, but his general was not.

'Did you not see how hard they fought to protect it, Aratius?'

'We are willing to try again.'

Flavius acknowledged the offer with a pat on the Isaurian's shoulder. 'That would merely spill blood uselessly. There are more ways to spoil a water supply than hammers. Our next visit will be with rotting animal carcasses and lime. Let them drink from their cistern after it has been so poisoned.'

To further depress the defenders the forces that had been besieging Fisula arrived. First seen marching towards Auximus from the elevated walls of the city, it was a sight to raise hopes of relief until they were identified as Byzantine, inducing the precise opposite emotion. Flavius,

190

normally benign with senior captives, drove home the message of hopelessness by parading the leaders of that now surrendered garrison before the walls in halters as if they were cattle and humiliating them.

The sight was enough to finally break the defenders' resolve; the leaders came out to parley, their initial offer being that they would exit with their weapons and possessions then march north to Ravenna. Given that city was the next object on the Byzantine campaign it was wise to dismiss such a suggestion, as to let go men – and proven fighters at that – whom they would have to fight once more was imprudent.

In addition, after so many months of siege, the army Flavius led was looking to some kind of reward for what had been a debilitating effort, grumbles which soon reached their general's ears and had him resolve to be a great deal more firm in his demands. High-value warriors, well provided over many years with much in the way of booty, the Goths of Auximus were far from poor and that fact was known to the men who had been besieging them.

The compromise, brokered by Procopius, was a just one for both parties, especially since, for the garrison, one of the less pleasant options was a resumption of the siege followed by wholesale slaughter. Yet they would face that rather than penury, so it was agreed they would surrender half their wealth to their opponents and they would not join Witigis but go east to fight in the service of Byzantium.

With winter once more approaching haste was

required. One general, Magnus, was sent on a forced march to the north of Ravenna to patrol the south bank of the River Po and ensure neither men nor supplies could cross. He was aided in this by the army of Vitalius who, having been held up by the invasion of the Huns, was now free, given they had retired with their plunder, to cross the Timavo from Illyricum and close off the northern bank.

There he came across a fleet of barges loaded with grain destined to make their way through the marshlands that surrounded Ravenna and supply a city in much need of their cargo, held up because the water level was too low to allow passage. As it rose with autumn rains that same grain was used to supply Flavius Belisarius.

Witigis was now on the horns of a real dilemma: he faced starvation in a siege he could not break, with so many of his fortresses lost and too many of his warriors either captive, sent east as mercenaries or locked up in places that he had to hold, such as the passes in the Cottian Alps between Gaul and Italy, secured to prevent a second Frankish invasion.

There they were being pressed daily in a fight where their numbers could never suffice, and Theudibert, well aware that the Ravenna garrison was short of food and faced with a formidable general leading a buoyant army, offered to support Witigis for a half-share of Italy. That reached the ears of Flavius, who sent Ennes to Witigis to remind him of the recent way the Franks had behaved, the obvious concomitant being that they could not be trusted.

Matters went from bad to worse for the besieged. First the forces on the Alpine passes surrendered. Meanwhile Vitalius was ravaging Venetia, the sole region from which Ravenna could be supplied, and Flavius had sent strong forces to take possession of those now abandoned passes and to demand the surrender of any Goth garrisons still remaining in the region.

Not that such a mission was without difficulty; the men who had left Milan to succour Auximus and had been scattered by the Franks, had partially re-formed and the man who commanded them, originally on his way to Ravenna, changed tack and marched against them. Luckily, Martinus and John Vitalianus were still in the region and able to combine and create a force strong enough to bring about a victory without a battle.

Flavius made sure that Witigis heard of this development and understood that he was now cut off from any possibility of aid. As if once more, the hand of God intervened: the grain storerooms that held the last of the Goth supplies caught fire, either by accident or sabotage, which took with it the food that might have sustained the city, albeit on very short rations, throughout the winter. It was time for Witigis to talk.

If Flavius Belisarius was now in complete control of Italy he had no control over extraneous matters and here his emperor intervened. The envoys sent by Witigis to Constantinople had done better than he could have hoped, aided by the stirrings on the eastern border. There the Sassanid Empire and Byzantium were engaged in a low-level conflict that threatened at any moment to erupt into all-out war. Faced with such a hazard Italy would become a sideshow.

Domnicus, the chief negotiator sent by Justinian, was empowered to offer Witigis a treaty, his terms being for half the wealth of the Goth treasury and all of Italy south of the River Po. Given his situation Witigis was eager to accept, his only problem being that Flavius Belisarius, on the spot in a situation of which his imperial master was ignorant, refused to allow the proposal to be implemented.

The imperial envoy was quick to tell him he did not have the right to act so; Flavius merely asked him how many men he could put in the field to stop him. But he did offer Domnicus one sop: he could appeal to a conference of the senior officers of the Army of Italy and if they agreed, then Flavius would bow to their judgement. Having made that offer he was not fool enough to allow it to happen without he had a prior chance to put his case.

'I would remind you all, that it is not you that is questioning the imperial will but me.' A glance around the assembled faces showed a mixture of caution and in one or two cases outright defiance, but it was as well to remind them all that to defy Justinian carried with it a risk to their careers. 'I hope you trust me not to shirk the accusation, if it is put to me, and seek to spread responsibility.'

'Then why have you assembled us?' demanded John Vitalianus, still far from reconciled to the man who had led them to their present overwhelming superiority.

'If you collectively counsel that we allow Witigis his treaty, then I will not oppose your wishes. It is my hope you do not.'

'Which flies in the face of what you have just said, Flavius Belisarius.'

Vitalianus again and he was smirking to have pointed out what he saw as an anomaly: if he was asking their opinion he was obviously spreading responsibility.

'No, John, I am saying that if you stop me I will respect your wishes. Any who have no opinion are free to remain silent.'

'Well I for one will not,' barked Martinus, glaring at Vitalianus, with whom he had reportedly enjoyed a stormy relationship these last months. 'The Goths are beaten. Surely if Justinian was here to see that, the offer would be withdrawn.'

That set up a rumble of agreement to which Flavius responded. 'I agree. We have within our grasp outright victory and the time to press for such an outcome. To my mind it would be folly to throw away years of campaigning for a bastard peace.'

Looking at the faces and sensing he had carried the room, he asked a servant to send to Domnicus so he could join them. Not that he called for his officers to speak, but only to listen. Once the imperial envoy had concluded his view that Justinian should be obeyed it was Flavius, and Flavius alone, who replied in the negative. What he had achieved, and those among his subordinates with the wit to see it would discern the fact, was security for himself.

None in the future, Vitalianus especially, would

be able to say at some hearing on his conduct, that he had total victory in his grasp and had failed to press it home. Flavius knew that such was the nature of the world in which he lived, and the malice that could be created by jealousy, he could one day be accused and sanctioned for obedience to the orders of Justinian or find himself on trial for the very opposite.

'It is depressing that even in an army the need to think like a politician is necessary.'

Procopius, who never ceased to think that way, merely gave his master a wry look. 'You may need all the wiles of that profession, given there is a secret embassy waiting to see you.'

'From Witigis?'

'No, but the men waiting are from the highest Goth nobility.'

'And what is it they wish to say?'

'That they would hardly impart to me, *Magister*. I am but your servant.'

'When you say secret...?'

'The approach was made to me. I made sure no one knows of their presence. If anyone asks, I will say they are Roman citizens who reside in Ravenna and are naturally concerned at what is about to become of their home city once the Goths are deposed.'

It was all very well for Procopius to be devious, indeed it was often essential, but at this moment Flavius had a feeling he was not being gifted the truth in the matter of secretarial ignorance. Odd that with all the power at his command there was no point in asking if that feeling was true.

'Will you see them?' That got a raised eyebrow,

to which Procopius added. 'In my opinion you must.'

'Then bid them enter.'

'I ask your permission to post guards on the doors with instructions to use force to ensure you are not disturbed, this a request put to me by these visitors.'

Flavius smiled at the word 'visitors', but he nodded and went to stand close to the flaming brazier that heated the chamber, on the opposite side to the doorway. He felt for his dagger and eased it in its scabbard while making sure there was a sword close by. These men would have been searched, of that he was sure, but a three-to-one advantage did not debar them from attempting to assassinate him with their bare hands.

The trio who entered did so in the manner of conspirators, slowly, their eyes darting around the chamber from one oil lamp to the next before finally settling on the logs burning before the man they had come to see. They were dressed in clothing of high quality, wore objects of gold and silver and had on their shoulders soft fur skin cloaks. In their eyes and their bearing, once they had relaxed somewhat, it was possible to see these were warriors and accustomed to respect.

'Who is it I am being asked to greet?'

'No names,' protested one, who stood slightly ahead of his companions, which marked him out as the leader. He had unblinking blue eyes and a wide, hooked nose large enough to dominate every other feature on his face. The look was serious, added to which his Latin seemed perfect. 'At least, not yet.'

'Procopius, some chairs for our visitors.' Once these had been set out Flavius added, 'I wish my secretary to remain, which I trust will cause you no concern.'

A sharp nod from the same hook-nosed fellow; his companions stared straight ahead and added nothing and Flavius took a chair of his own.

'Then I am awaiting what it is you have come to see me about.'

'As you know, Flavius Belisarius, we elect our rulers.'

An amused smile and a shrug. 'It is not beyond the habits of Constantinople to occasionally act in a similar fashion.'

'And you will not be surprised to learn that we have tempered our faith in Witigis to lead us.'

'It would ill suit me to slight a man who has fought me, and well.'

'But he is also a man who has lost.'

'It is rare in war that one side does not win while another loses. But Witigis has been both shrewd and resourceful, therefore I would be un-happy that anything said should diminish that.'

'And what does the man who has won wish to gain?'

Flavius shrugged. 'The approbation of his peers, the respect of his officers and, in my case, the gratitude of his emperor.'

'And if he could be granted more?'

'Such as?' Flavius asked, even if he knew what was coming.

'Italy.'

'I have already conquered Italy, which given you're here can hardly have escaped your notice.'

'We have come to offer you the kingship of the Goths.' It was hard to keep a straight face, even if Flavius had got there ahead of the actual words, even more difficult with that which was suggested next. 'And if you aspire to the title of Emperor of the Western Roman Empire, then we, the Goths, will support you in taking that title. We're sure that you will carry the majority of your army with you as well.'

'Not even Theodoric the Great aspired to that, or if he did, he had the sense not to provoke Constantinople by calling himself "emperor".'

'He chose not to, you may decide otherwise.'

Flavius looked at Procopius, whose face, lit by the oil lamps and the flaring logs, looked avaricious. It was as if the offer was being made to him.

'This proposal is being made without the knowledge of Witigis?'

'It is. Should you accept, we will tell him.'

Flavius spread his hands in a gesture of concern. 'If I was to even consider your proposal, and that is yet to be decided, it would only be on the understanding that he concurred. You Goths, as you say, elect your rulers, but too often the man deposed also forfeits his life.'

The elaborate shrug was far from reassuring, which had Flavius adding an insistence that the offer had to come from Witigis before it could even be deliberated upon.

'So I bid you return to the city and speak with him, but of course I offer you refreshment should you so desire it.'

'No. But I ask that we be able to return on the morrow?'

'That you must arrange with my secretary, who seems to know how to get you in to my presence without the knowledge of anyone else.'

'And your inclination, Flavius Belisarius?'

'There is as yet no such thing.'

'But there might be?'

The reply came as Flavius stood. 'What there will be is serious contemplation.'

Interview plainly over, the trio likewise stood and with direct looks departed, escorted by Procopius. Left to think for several minutes, Flavius was still in deep meditation when his secretary returned, to give him a meaningful glance that presaged a question, and one Flavius had no desire to answer.

'Not a word, Procopius, if you please. Let us see what the morrow brings.'


# CHAPTER FIFTEEN

It was fanciful to think that his secretary would stay silent; no great depth of perception was required to recognise that he had a hand deep in the whole approach. Those Goth noblemen had come to Flavius through him and there was a nagging doubt as to who had initiated the notion. Had Procopius sought them out or was it, as had been implied, the other way round? The former was the most troubling and a restless night did nothing to help settle the mind.

Despite their fraught relationship, Flavius still

breakfasted and dined with Antonina – appearances had to be maintained and they did share a villa. Over that meal she began to question him as to what was to happen next, which also served to make her husband uncomfortable. How much did she know? His wife was a very acute observer of both mood and movement, who was not beyond listening at doors. She had spent time with Domnicus and would know in detail what were his instructions from Justinian and how they had been overborne.

Hints that refusing to bend to the imperial will was a dangerous game were mixed with sly enquiries as to what he might hope to gain from such an attitude. Did they hint at knowledge and if so where could it have come from? Procopius would never give her any information, but Antonina was well able to browbeat servants into indiscretions and very often that was unnecessary.

As a group they were numerous and ever the enemy of secrecy, being all around, silent and often having their presence ignored, a point made to Procopius when he and his master were once more alone. For the sake of security this took place in the open air, walking through lines in which the tents were empty, the soldiers being at their daily exercises.

'Nothing was said that would be overheard by my servants and I ensured none of your own, or those of your wife, were able to witness the arrival of that embassy.'

'Embassy?' asked Flavius, it being an odd word to use, implying that he was already a ruler. 'Do I qualify for such a thing?'

Procopius let that pointed observation go by. 'As long as you maintain the fiction I presented, that these envoys are Romans, that should keep matters secure. As you will have observed, their leader spoke excellent Latin and the others, who have heavy Goth accents, did not utter a word from their arrival to their departure.'

'Present, I assume, only to ensure their spokesman did not betray their cause?'

'Probably.'

'What a polity they wish me to oversee.'

'Perhaps it is one that in the right hands could be improved and I doubt it is any worse than pertains in the imperial court. The men who came to see you have certain fears that would be laid to rest by acceptance of what they offer.' The look that got was an instruction to be specific. 'What will they lose if they merely surrender? Their wealth, certainly, both individually and as a tribe, just as did the Vandals when you took their treasure.'

'What else?'

'They fear to be sent to the east as captives, with no chance of ever being able to return. They would thus be split from everything they hold as precious.' The pause that followed, covering several paces and accompanied by a studied countenance, had an overdramatic quality. 'I am bound to enquire, *Magister*, which way your mind is working?'

'As of this moment, Procopius, it is not working at all.'

As an attempt to deflect further question that was a complete failure, and now Procopius adopted a grave expression as he made what had to be to him a point of some importance. 'Am I at liberty to say that whatever you decide has some bearing on my station?'

'I have never known you shirk such a liberty.'

The laugh that accompanied those words, again an attempt at deflection, also fell flat. Procopius had to swiftly adjust what had become an angry expression brought on by the way his concerns were being dismissed.

'Then I ask to be allowed to outline the options you face.'

'Which makes it sound to me as if you are in favour of acceptance.'

'There are arguments on both sides. All I ask is that I be allowed to express matters as I see them in order to aid you, which is a function I have previously enjoyed and one I hope you have found useful.'

'It is unlike you to go fishing for praise.'

His secretary took that as permission to proceed, which if it annoyed Flavius, left him unable to stop the flow of words that followed.

'It would be impossible to deny that you deserve the offer made to you. Recall with what numbers we arrived in Italy. How many gave the force under your command any chance of success? Few, and perhaps with myself as one of them.' That engendered a dismissive and slightly embarrassed wave. 'I hope you do not doubt my loyalty to you personally.'

'How could I, since it is daily demonstrated? If I have campaigned successfully, Procopius, I have done so only because of men like you. It takes more than soldiers to win a war and you have matched my very best fighters.'

'I have seen it as an honour, *Magister*, though your kind words encourage me to continue to air my thoughts.'

If Procopius noted the weary quality of the response it had no bearing on the way he spoke; he was earnest, occasionally passionate, and not beyond insults aimed at the imperial couple.

'Theodora hates you and is jealous. No matter how well you behave she will see in your every action betrayal – and does Justinian, whom you call a friend, put a stop to this? No! He allows his wife to traduce the man who helped to save both their lives and their thrones.'

'I was not alone in that.'

'But if you had not acted, would others have been so keen to protect them from the Nika mob?'

'It is a mistake to underestimate Theodora, Procopius. Justinian was all for flight, a ship was waiting in the palace harbour. It was she who was prepared to stay and die rather than run away.'

'And you admire her for that?'

'How could I not?'

'Did you also have reason to admire Justinian?' Flavius had stopped at the horse lines and, having brought with him a small sack of carrots, the next part of the conversation was accompanied by the crunching of equine teeth. 'I have never made a secret of my opinion of our emperor, have I, *Magister*?'

'No.'

'And you have served him faithfully.'

'I have done my duty as a soldier of the empire.'

'Not without frustrations.'

The last carrot gone, Flavius turned to face

Procopius. 'I tire of this, so please come to the point. You know I value your advice and it is obvious to me you want to give it to me. So no more hints, Procopius, speak out.'

'Even if what I say might be treason?'

'We are alone, no one can overhear you and I will never use against you anything you now say, on that you have my word.'

'Do I detect from that you are minded to consider the offer the Goths have made?'

It was now the turn of Flavius to be irritated and his response was severe. 'That is a question I have already answered!'

Another long pause followed as Procopius marshalled his thoughts, and he even, again Flavius thought dramatically, took a deep breath before continuing.

'If I was to make a case for acceptance it would be on these points and I ask for your indulgence beforehand if in talking I stray into areas of a personal nature. First, it is my opinion that you serve an emperor who does not know your worth and that is made worse by the suspicions of a woman whose opinion should count for nothing.'

'But they do.'

'Theodora has reason in her own mind to fear you. The success you have enjoyed leading our armies, the way you are popular with the people and your patent honesty make you a candidate to succeed Justinian should the Emperor die, and where would the power of Theodora be then?'

'I am glad you say "succeed".'

'I know you too well to suggest otherwise, even if I find your loyalty to that throne misplaced, yet that is not the subject on which I wish to pronounce. What do you gain by accepting the offer made to you? Equality with the Emperor instead of subservience to a man so fickle no person can know his mood from one moment to the next, as well as a ruler so weak in his bedchamber he will allow his spouse to conspire against the most upright of his generals.'

'It is probably wise to leave bedchambers out of this.'

'And what of his public behaviour? When you were given the consulship it was done in a manner designed to say that if you had enjoyed great victories, then it was under his hand and his guidance.'

'It was still a great honour, Procopius.'

'It was shabbily given and how much was Theodora's hand in that, a woman who has trapped you into marriage that has within it more misery than regard and will do all in her power to keep it so.'

'Photius thinks I should kill them both.'

'Without pausing to consider what would happen to you?'

'That is not the reason I do not act upon his counsel.'

'Honour again?'

'Sacrilege!' came the near shouted reply. 'How could I face my maker with such an act on my conscience, as if I do not have enough already?'

'Would you not, as a ruler in your own right, be able to put Antonina aside? Perhaps you could find a warmer bed mate, for it aids a man to be so comforted.'

'But not you?'

'There are needs I do not require, as other men do, inclinations that render them weak.' That got a snort from Flavius. 'In ploughing my own furrow I am free to act effectively.'

'And advise me to accept the kingship of the Goths.' There was no response so Flavius was obliged to ask the next obvious question. 'And what about Emperor of the West?'

'It would be impolitic to assume such a title immediately, but if you ruled Italy, Justinian would be obliged to treat with you.'

'Or send an army to defeat me.'

'One he would struggle to raise with trouble brewing on the Persian border.'

'So there I am treating with Justinian, for what?'

'Peace, security, recognition of the kind once enjoyed by Theodoric the Great.'

'And if it came to war?'

'You command the best army the empire can field and you are its best general. How many of the citizens love Justinian? Even fewer have any regard for Theodora. If he does not grant you peace he risks that you march on Constantinople, and I would wager that if you were to do that the citizens of the city would overthrow Justinian in favour of you.'

'I marched on Constantinople once before, Procopius, and was full of hope till I saw its walls.'

'While I maintain it would fall from within if you were the man to besiege it. Recall when you walked or rode unescorted through the streets how people hailed you. Neither Justinian nor Theodora dare move without a large number of guards. I would also add, *Magister*, that the object of unification of the twin parts of the empire, to which both you and Justinian are wedded, would be just as valid, perhaps even more so, under an Emperor Flavius Belisarius.'

'How many necks would I have to sever to realise that vision?'

'How many deserve to have their heads removed?'

'You and I perhaps, Procopius, for even discussing this.'

Seeing the secretary about to speak Flavius held up a hand to stop him, not least because their promenade had brought them full circle to where they were now approaching the building that acted as the Byzantine headquarters. Within the walls would be assembled his senior officers for the conference that took place every day, and those men would be eager to hear what was to happen regarding the capture of Ravenna.

'I have enough to consider, perhaps too much, but I have one question to pose to you. If this dream of yours came to fruition, where would you see yourself?'

'In your service, as I am now.'

'But richer?'

'A matter in which I have little interest.'

That was true, as far as Flavius knew. Procopius was not one to turn away a chance to make money. He never sought to hide the bribes he was offered to open doors to an audience with his master, who, ever since he began campaigning in North Africa, had a horde of folk pleading for him to intercede and solve their problems. Much of that sort of problem never even reached his ears; Procopius had dealt with them and in the nature of things had been given many presents for his actions, all of these declared and shared.

'More powerful?'

'When I look at the empire, *Magister*, I see many things that I would be desirous of changing. So the power to effect such would be satisfying, yes.'

During the conference Flavius made no mention of the Goth offer. Instead he and his fellow leaders discussed how Ravenna might be taken by assault, though no one thought it to be easy. The city had been chosen as the capital by the Emperor Honorius for several reasons, not least that being on the Adriatic favoured communication with Constantinople and made imperial rule less arduous.

Yet the main motivation, in a time of barbarian incursions into the north of Italy, was its natural defensibility. Ravenna was surrounded by marshes, which made it impossible to truly invest. The city, with such watery barriers had no need of high walls and it would even now be impossible to overcome if the Goths had enjoyed access to the sea, presently denied to them by a Byzantine fleet.

Flavius found it difficult to concentrate as he listened to the various proposals, some of them sound in purpose if difficult in conclusion, as well as one or two bordering on a mad desire for personal glory. The words he had exchanged with Procopius as well as the points made by his secretary rattled around in his head, made troubling by the fact that much of what had been said was nothing but the plain truth.

Those same envoys would come again tonight and he had to provide them with an answer, but he resolved to do more; to draw out from them what other concerns they had so they could be dealt with. He brought the conference to a conclusion by suggesting that if no word came from Witigis by the following day, a message should be sent inviting him to surrender.

'And in case you think it is only that, surrender will mean the impoverishment of the nobles as well as the citizens of Ravenna.'

That satisfied the most gory-minded of his commanders; blood they loved to spill but what might accrue to their coffers was just as important, even if it had to be paraded through the streets of Constantinople to be gawped at by the mob. As had happened with the treasure of the Vandals, a hoard plundered from the whole of Roman Europe over two centuries, the Emperor was obliged, once the crowd had been afforded their glimpse of such fabulous wealth, to share the spoils of war with those who fought and won his battles.

The prospect of the forthcoming meeting was not aided by the information that Antonina was planning one of her entertainments and her refusal to put it off. She had invited dozens of officers, many of them young and junior, as well as some of the more refined women who had become camp followers: Roman and Goth war widows, often from places taken by Flavius Belisarius and his armies, who traded their bodies for food, comfort and, it had to be admitted, sometimes for love.

'You are a dullard,' was her response when Flavius declined to attend, even for a short while.

'You dazzle enough for both of us,' was the diplomatic reply as his wife flounced out in a huff.

The sounds of that entertainment lay in the background as Procopius led the trio of Goth nobles into his private chamber once more, this a more bustling entrance than hitherto. The first words imparted told Flavius that Witigis was in full agreement to the proposal and would relinquish his power in favour of his enemy as long as certain conditions were met.

Flavius allowed them to be stated, the primary condition germane as to whether he accepted the kingship or not and that related to their treasury. How could he take that from them when it would be partly his own? Likewise, if he left the service of Justinian he would be a fool indeed to surrender to the Emperor any of the men he might need to hold on to his claim.

That stated, the time had come for an answer to the most important question of all. Would he agree to become King of the Goths? The eyes of four men were upon him, unblinking, and Flavius had the impression he was the only person breathing.

'I am minded to accept, but not here and not in this room. Such a commitment can only be made when Witigis is present and able to formally announce, before his nobles, that he is standing aside. It is to that same body I must make my pledges.'

'On the treasure and us and our fellow nobles retaining our freedom?'

211

'Those would naturally be granted at the same time.'

For a man who could address a whole army, that last remark was so softly pronounced as to risk the need for repetition. The faces of the Goths, once their Latin speaker had repeated them, relaxed enough to allow them to nod, while Procopius could not stop the slight smile which adorned his face.

'I bid you return to Ravenna and convey this to those to whom you must report. I must myself go to join my wife who is, as you can no doubt hear, entertaining our guests. It would be impolitic to stay away too long and perhaps set minds thinking when we still have a need for concealment.'

The envoys seemed to understand and accept this; they had limited knowledge of his private life. It was Procopius who had the strange expression, no longer smiling, he was looking at his master with troubled curiosity.

'A word, *Magister*, after I have seen these men safely out of our lines?'

'In the morning, Procopius, unless you would care to join Antonina and I.'

## CHAPTER SIXTEEN

The time had come to send away those of his generals who may cause him trouble. Flavius despatched John Vitalianus and several of the commanders who had come with Narses, their

212

task to take over with their contingents various Goth fortresses dotted over northern Italy. His reasons being sound this was readily accepted; such a move would nullify the risk of any attempt to relieve Ravenna as well as ease what might become a drain on supplies.

Not stated by either party was the motive for the way his orders were eagerly welcomed. With the Goths virtually beaten, these men would be free to plunder at will and in a polity that would willingly give up its possessions to avoid being ravaged. To the likes of John Vitalianus, Ravenna, though a wealthier prize, might turn into a siege of months, if not years. Better a bird in the hand when it came to full coffers.

If moving problem generals proved easy to accomplish, there was as yet many a dilemma to solve, not least the probing curiosity of Procopius. To avoid his secretary was impossible; they worked in close harmony on a daily basis on such matters as feeding the army, the state of the men's health and corresponding with the various other commands and functionaries all over the Italian peninsula and Illyria, as well as communicating with Constantinople.

If Procopius probed to little avail that was as nothing to Antonina, who had a nose that could smell conspiracy a league away. In addition to her curiosity she added another problem to the life of her husband, for Flavius had sent Photius back to the capital once more. His wife had then sent for Theodosius, a man too fearful of Antonina's natural son and possible violence to ever be in the same place.

Her husband was too preoccupied to give it the attention it deserved; having challenged Antonina in Sicily, following on from the revelations made by her maid, and having received an outright denial of any impropriety, he had to accept that even with what he had been told by Photius he had no actual proof that she had transgressed.

He had a plan to implement and for once it was held within himself, not even discussed with Procopius, not yet confided to his generals and certainly kept well secret from his wife. He had supplies moved closer to Ravenna, so that the besieged city could be fed, and then called a conference to gain support for his aims.

'Though I will not yet refer to the conditions under which this has been made, the Goths have sent envoys offering to surrender their capital and bring an end to the war in Italy.'

That set them talking, as each mind calculated what this would mean to them; war brought rewards, but so did peace. Flavius let it rumble on until it began to naturally diminish, eyes turning from neighbourly exchanges regarding what offices might fall to the successful and back onto the man who would control them.

'I've good reason to believe that Witigis'll stand down as their leader, or failing that be deposed by the same kind of vote that gave him the crown. The question we must settle is this: is such an outcome best for the empire? As you will know from my difference with Narses, my instructions from our emperor set that as a tie to any action I take.'

'And the alternative?' asked Martinus, exercising his right of seniority to enquire, even if the answer was obvious.

'To take Ravenna by storm?'

'In doing so we would lose many of our soldiers,' Martinus replied, to a ripple of agreement. 'They are as likely to drown in the marshes as fall to an arrow or sword.'

'I agree it will not be easy.'

'Given it would take time, we would have the problem of supply,' added Ildiger.

'All of this is true, but what I require from you is open support for my own inclinations, which is to accept the Goth offer.'

Flavius let that sink in; he was being open and if any had doubted why he had sent so many men and their commanders away they could be in no doubt now. It was also unnecessary to explain the politics of what he was seeking, nothing less than a full agreement to a course of action on which he had set his mind, as a means of protecting himself against future censure.

The history of the empire was replete with instances of men being successful in war being brought low at some later stage for real or perceived corruption on campaign and that was a many-headed beast that rarely had much to do with the theft of treasure. Victory always raised a man's profile, which made him an automatic target for anyone either jealous or fearful that their present situation could be rendered insecure. Even if they could not bring him down they could dent his reputation.

He had made a foe of Narses, for one, and he was a man with too many connections to treat lightly. The old eunuch would not be alone in a city where Flavius knew he already had enemies, even if such people never revealed themselves. A smile and warm greeting in the corridors of the imperial palace was not to be taken at face value; it could just be the prelude to an accusation of malfeasance.

'I see the Goths as humbled. To fight on and seek to destroy them is not in the best interests of both the empire and the Emperor. So I propose to accept the offer of surrender and enter Ravenna under truce, sparing the Goths any blood as I spare the men I lead. If any here think that unwise or contrary to my instructions say so now.'

There were any number of exchanged looks before the nodding began, that followed by vocal acceptance.

'Good, I will ask my secretary to prepare a document to which we will all append our signatures and our seals. If that offends anyone's sense of honour I ask your forgiveness, but hope that you will see the need.'

Once that was prepared and signed Flavius sent word to Witigis, still the Goth leader, saying that he would accept the surrender of the city and enter at the head of his army within two days. That completed, the barges full of grain seized by Vitalius, which had been held back by the low water in the river, would be allowed into the city to feed a near starving population, this ensuring that the Byzantines would be welcome by the populace if not the warriors.

Given time to prepare, the Byzantine army worked hard to shine in what all saw as a victory parade, one not dissimilar to that which might one day follow down the Triumphal Way in Constantinople. Every bit of finery owned by every soldier would be on display and that went too for their general, who wore his finest armour and rode his most handsome horse.

His place was ahead of the open-sided palanquin in which sat a superbly attired Antonina, insisting on her right to give precedence only to her husband and not his officers or men. It was a sorrow to Flavius if not to her that Photius was absent from this moment, galling that behind his wife rode Theodosius, who had put not one jot of effort into the campaign but seemingly spent his time both in North Africa and Italy fleecing the locals and filling his coffers, albeit in a quasi-legal fashion.

The Goth nobles had gathered before the Roman palace built by the Emperor Honorius to greet their conqueror and, for many included in the conspiracy, they hoped their future ruler. In the latter they were to be disappointed: following on from the formal handing over of the keys of the city, the first thing they were told was that his loyalty to his own ruler and the empire transcended anything else that could be gifted to him.

That declaration set up loud objections; had Flavius not promised their envoys of his intention to accede to their offer of the kingship? Equally of interest was the expression this engendered on the faces of his senior commanders, all finding out for the first time that such a proposal had even been advanced. The most telling was that of Procopius, who could not keep off his face a thunderous look, there to indicate his feeling of a personal betrayal.

There were Goths present prepared to react with violence and they had to be restrained by their more sober comrades. The men Flavius led had already set about disarming their foes and here, within the audience chamber of the old palace, the man who had repudiated what they thought had been a commitment was surrounded by his personal bodyguards in numbers that would do nothing other than produce a massacre.

'There were fears that your assembled would be sent to Constantinople as captives. That, I assure you, will not happen.'

'Are your assurances worth anything, Flavius Belisarius?'

'Yes, Witigis, they are, but I require that those who've homes elsewhere disperse. If they do not, I must confine them as I am obliged to do to you.'

'Is that what I am now?' Witigis asked. 'A prisoner?'

'An honoured one who will be treated with respect.'

'Our treasury, which you led us to believe would be safe?'

'How many talents of gold do you think Justinian has expended in Italy? Is it not the misfortune of war that the loser must forfeit what they own to offset that? If I left it in your hands I would as well leave my head along with it. I would soon be accused of harbouring it for myself.'

Ennes stepped forward to take charge of Witigis, who was escorted to a set of the old imperial apartments. The guard commander already had his instructions to treat the Goth leader with respect and to ensure that whatever comfort could be provided for him be made available. Flavius, once his audience had dispersed, made his way to the part of the palace once occupied by Theodoric.

If he was not a Goth king he was yet the ruler of that leader's old patrimony and one of his duties would be to visit the great mausoleum built to hold the great man's remains, this being a personal inclination to honour Theodoric's memory as well as a politic act to impress the inhabitants.

Behind the army came the instrument that would control the fate of the city: Procopius and his numerous clerks, along with priests who would rededicate churches that had been used in the Arian rite back to an observance of proper Roman Christianity, albeit instructions had been issued that they be tolerant of religious differences.

If Flavius had faced the Goths without any conscience, that did not extend to his secretary, who plainly felt betrayed though he held in his feelings until a whole raft of matters had been dealt with, orders issued to military commanders and various officials regarding the governance of the city. Knowing what was coming, once they were alone, Flavius got his reasoning in quickly.

'I did not swear to accept.'

'Then why give the impression that you had?'

'You can ask that in the one-time residence of a Roman emperor? I have Ravenna without having to fight to gain it. My soldiers are, as we speak, taking control of the provinces to the north without spilling a single drop of blood. I have brought to an end nearly five years of conflict.'

'So it was a deliberate falsehood?'

219

'It was a stratagem and a successful one and at no time did I ever issue a binding oath. I cannot fathom why you are so troubled.'

'No, and there is the pity. I find I have dedicated my life to a man who cannot see what is in his own interest and is blinded by a faith that I do not share. Do you think this will end the malice of Theodora? Do you think that Justinian will treat you as he should? Did you ever truly consider what it was the Goths were offering and where it could lead?'

'I did, Procopius. I gave it much thought.'

'And chose the wrong course.'

'To your mind, not mine,' Flavius insisted. 'Do you not know me after all these years? Do you not know where I would seek reasons on how I should act?'

The response had about it a quality of defeat. 'Your father.'

'My whole family, Procopius, may God rest their souls. I was brought up to be a Roman and so were my brothers. Our father saw it as the highest duty of our lives to live and, if need be, die for the empire and that is the fate that fell to them even if it was a tainted one. It is my hope that one day, I may meet them in some celestial paradise, especially the man I revered most in all my life. Would you have me face him when I betrayed that which he held dear?'

'You were afforded the chance to enhance the empire by being its ruler.'

'At the cost of rebellion. That is too high a price chalice from which I do not wish to sup.'

'Beware there is not a cup of poison awaiting

you anyway.'

'You would have me act the creature Theodora suspects me to be. Even without the memory of my father that is something to which I could never ascribe.'

Over the weeks that followed Flavius saw his policy bear fruit as one after another the Goth leaders who had not been trapped in Ravenna came to the city to offer obeisance to this new dispensation. Yet as always there was a gremlin waiting to fracture what should have been a satisfactory whole, a single leader called Ildibadus, who held Verona. Initially willing to surrender, he withdrew that when he heard that the Goth treasury was to be forfeit to Justinian.

Added to that, his fellow nobles were deeply unhappy that Flavius had spurned their offer of either regal or imperial estate and Ildibadus became the focus of that dissent. He had an ally in the nephew of Witigis who still held Milan, and, combined, the pair formed a bloc that tore a hole in the peaceful fabric Flavius was seeking to construct. He had to watch from the sidelines as moves were made to elect a new king, the crown finally being settled on the head of Ildibadus, though not before, at his instigation, it had once more been offered to and declined by Flavius Belisarius.

Given their losses and his strength this did not worry the man who had taken Ravenna; he was sure that very little campaigning would be required to put paid to any attempt by this truncated force to effect matters. It was an irritant, not a difficulty, that was till matters elsewhere intervened, this in the form of an order from Justinian.

'Recalled?'

'To take command in the east, *Magister.*'

There was a look on the face of Procopius and Cabasilis, the descendant of a famous imperial general and the messenger from Constantinople, as if to imply such orders were only an excuse to get him to the capital where reasons would be found to arraign him for some invented offence, and there was one obvious risk. Could the news of the Goth offer have got to Constantinople and back again in such a short time?

That it would not remain a secret was obvious, there were too many people now involved and Flavius had to assume his own inferior commanders would have picked up more than just rumours, though nothing had been said in his presence. Antonina, if she had found out, would be as indiscreet as always and she was perfectly capable, it seemed, of ascribing to him motives the opposite of those he displayed.

Then there was Procopius, clearly unhappy; relations between the two had palpably soured in the month since the occupation of the Goth capital. There were no more private conversations and certainly no discussion of policy. Now everything was done in a way that spoke of estrangement; formal and being businesslike it was also impossible to fault.

Flavius had known that matters were far from peaceful on the eastern frontier long before Cabasilis arrived. The so-called Endless Peace which had been concluded between Justinian and King

Kavadh, the late ruler of the Sassanid Empire, was always fragile, having been bought, Justinian paying the princely sum of eleven thousand pounds in gold to keep him within the borders of his own empire, more being supplied annually.

That it had held for eight years was remarkable; Kavadh had agreed to peace many times, only to break it when he needed to bleed Constantinople for funds to pacify the many tribes that formed his fractious subjects. He ruled over communities that were forever fighting each other or seeking to combine to bring him down. If the tribes were not rebelling the Sassanid nobles were conspiring, and they had in the past been too powerful an entity for their king to tame.

With Kavadh gone, his son Khusrow had proved to be a more astute ruler. He made better use of the Byzantine gold, employing it to bolster his positon, most tellingly to break the power of those high nobles who led large bodies of soldiers and could thus, in alliance with tribal leaders, threaten his position.

Khusrow had also re-formed the Sassanid army so that it was no longer under the control of numerous satraps but the king himself, and more formidable for it, and he had once more begun to ravage the domains of the Eastern Empire. He would be back next year when the rivers were flowing fast enough to water thousands of horses and the fields full of ripening crops with which to feed an invading army.

'Cabasilis, does he not know that another year here will see matters settled for good?'

That was a foolish question, born out of frustration, to put to a mere messenger and it got the only possible reply. 'I can only convey his instructions, *Magister,* and they were plain.'

'I ask you to leave us, Cabasilis. Solomon, my *domesticus* will provide you with food and wine, and feel free to use the baths.'

'My instructions were to see you board the vessel in which I came and to sail home immediately.'

Flavius laughed at the absurdity – it was typical of the man he knew to issue such a command without any thought to the ramifications. Flavius could not just leave as if he was going for a stroll, there were still responsibilities to exercise. He had to make sure that everything was in place and that his successor had a proper grasp of that which needed to be done.

The Goth treasure would go with him, ensuring a welcome in Constantinople, for riches delivered to an emperor always partly fed down to the citizens as well as the victorious soldiers. Added to that, after a successful five-year campaign, he would be leaving without the results of his efforts: chests of gifts and coffers full of what was his just due in rewards. And then there was Antonina and their combined retinue of servants.

'Leave immediately, without gathering my possessions? Surely not even Justinian would have me arrive back in his city naked and a beggar?'

The messenger was young and even if very well connected he was in the presence of the conqueror of Italy. It would be impolitic to argue so he did as he was bid and left the chamber. A sign from Flavius had his guards and attendants do likewise.

'I am minded to send for Justinian and ask him

224

to delay this move.'

'Are you seeking my advice, *Magister?*'

There was no mistaking the coldness of the tone, which brought Flavius no pleasure and he responded with deliberate calm. 'I am.'

'And if I no longer feel qualified to provide it?'

'I have offended you, I know, Procopius, but our association is one of many years' duration, I hope prolonged enough to allow that you fulfil a function I have always found of value. Justinian has presented me with a dilemma and I am at a loss to be sure of how to respond.'

'Since you trumpet your loyalty to the empire and he rules it you do not have a choice. He commands, you obey.'

'So we go back to the east and leave the final act here to another?'

'We, *Magister?*' The slow shake of the head preceded the blow. 'I fear there is much to do still in Italy that I feel required to oversee. It is also true that you might prefer to depend on another to carry out those functions which you have entrusted to me in the past.'

If Flavius was at a loss as to how to respond he was never going to plead, nor would he refer to what had remained unspoken: what Procopius would have gained if he had taken the Goth crown and the imperial title of Western Emperor. His secretary was ambitious, which was fitting, and if they had never discussed where his association with Flavius might lead, it had never been much of a mystery.

Despite his reservations about the motives of Justinian, Procopius knew that the Emperor reposed a certain faith in the man he served. Not enough, he would maintain, to imperil his position or even slap down his wife but sufficient, barring some terrible failure, to ensure that his favourite general would always hold lucrative and powerful commands and the concomitant of that was a position of importance would likewise fall to his secretary-cum-legal advisor.

How far that could lead was again never openly alluded to, but surely at some point Flavius Belisarius would move on from being a field commander to some great office in the imperial bureaucracy, despite the malice of Theodora. Again Procopius would rise with him, yet such an elevation always lay on the edge of a cliff; close to the actual seat of power it was possible to fall much more rapidly, so it never held the true promise of security.

There was little doubt now that Procopius had engineered the offer of the Goth crown. That, to him, solved all the possible future problems he could envisage. No longer a mere legate of Justinian, Flavius would treat with him as an equal and perhaps even threaten his diadem and behind that would sit his trusted factotum, free to dream that one day he himself might even hold the highest office of state, not just in Ravenna, but in Constantinople.

'If I cannot feed your ambitions, Procopius,' Flavius concluded sadly, 'I can only assert my allegiance. Oblige me by calling Vitalius to my presence, so I can begin the handover of my command. I hope you serve him as well as you have served me.'

# CHAPTER SEVENTEEN

It was not a single vessel that set sail for the east but a substantial flotilla, carrying Flavius, Antonina and also the general's *comitatus*, his personal fighting retinue who went wherever he was active, their care delegated to Solomon. To ease his mind and temper, his wife had been accommodated with her retinue of servants on a vessel of her own, while Theodosius and his coffers had been allotted a separate galley to keep them apart.

Cabasilis he kept close partly to probe for any hint that his recall had to do with the offer of Goth kingship, not that he had any fear of the consequences, his conscience being clear. Yet he had enemies in Constantinople, rivals for military position, like Narses. Then there were the relatives and associates of the executed Constantinus. Such voices would seek to dismiss any claims to probity.

On balance he had to accept the reasons given for his recall were true. With Justinian preoccupied with what was happening in Italy, Khusrow would be well aware that the troops and commanders needed to stop his depredations simply did not exist in Asia Minor. He had cut through great swathes of territory, almost unopposed, to invest several cities, this at a time when envoys from Constantinople were present and negotiating with him.

It was also obvious that Khusrow was fired by a high level of greed rather than a desire to take and hold ground. Cities invested had been obliged to buy their way out of being sacked with a levy of several hundreds of pounds of gold. Those places that refused and Khusrow did assault provided him with hordes of slaves he was eager to ransom. Not that Khusrow was satisfied; a demand had been sent to Justinian seeking more gold as a bribe not to repeat his success.

There did not seem, either, to be any intelligence of what he planned to do next year, a question to which Flavius would have loved an answer. Cabasilis had neither information nor an opinion, which left Flavius, for the first time in many years, with nothing to plan for; he was in the dark and would remain so until he heard from Justinian.

It was a strange feeling to be unoccupied; there were no commands to issue, nothing to reconnoitre, no despatches to be sent to inferiors. He was thus reduced to the level of a sightseer, walking the deck and observing the shore from which fleets rarely parted the sight of even in summer. At this time of year, with the possibility of equinoxal tempests, the sailing master kept a sharp eye on the clouds and the sea state, ever ready to run for one of the many sheltering bays that dotted the coastline of Greece.

Introspection had previously been held at bay by the daily requirement for activity. Now, on a slow and broken voyage, Flavius had the freedom to assess his actions and if he had previously thought about the battles fought prior to this watery interlude, and his competence as a commander, he had never done so with so much absorption.

The balance was in his favour, of course; he was leaving behind a well-beaten enemy but that did not stop critical analysis of the mistakes he knew he had made. In this Procopius came constantly to mind, he being ever ready to find excuses for any setback suffered by his master, always able to find a scapegoat on which to pin the blame.

The loss outside the walls of Rome Flavius saw as his worst defeat and the excuse Procopius conjured up then would not hold in a mind bent on honest and critical examination. He had not been driven to it by more ambitious minds bent on glory or a quick result: even if he had been persuaded and allowed his own judgement to be compromised, even if blame could be attached to the broken infantry and their incompetent commanders, there was no question as to ultimate responsibility.

Added to that was the thought as to how it might have ended in disaster, with his forces locked out of the city by the refusal of the Romans to open the gates. In talking with Witigis, whom he had treated with honour, Flavius had found out why, when they had the Byzantine forces at their complete mercy, the Goths had not attacked.

'The crowds of men on the walls, thousands of them.'

'And?' Flavius had enquired, confused.

'We feared a trap and with good cause, given the number of times you sprang one on us.'

'But those lining the walls were not fighters.'

'They looked as if they might be to me and

those who I looked to for counsel. We concluded that once engaged we would be so locked into battle as to prevent any safe withdrawal, and once those men emerged we could be overwhelmed.'

'I am told I am lucky,' Flavius sighed. 'Perhaps, after what you have told me, Witigis, there is truth in that.'

'It gives me no joy to say to you, Flavius Belisarius, that it takes more than luck to win on the field of battle.'

'You were a worthy opponent,' was the reply, a fitting one and true, given to a man with whom he had become less of an enemy.

'Not worthy enough.'

At night, as the galley ploughed through the Mediterranean swell, the wind whistling in the rigging and, when that fell away, the row master's mallet beating out a slow tattoo, Flavius was too often subject to the recurring nightmare that had plagued him since the day his family had perished, their deaths played out in an ever-shifting vision of blood, pleading and his own uselessness.

Added to that there was the parlous state of his marriage. He was torn between believing Antonina to be innocent of infidelity and the wild imagining of her in that very act, neither of which gave him any indication of what to do about it. In other dreams they lived in harmonious bliss, but they always morphed into scenes of murderous rage in which she lay hacked to pieces while the cohorts of Satan tore at his flesh in retribution.

If dawn was welcome, after weeks of travel, so was the sight of the spires of Constantinople, never before a vista to provide much pleasure. The main fleet was ordered to proceed to Galatea while the command galley altered course and headed for the private imperial dock.

On his return from the Vandal war the imperial couple had been on the quayside to greet their victorious commander; nothing of that sort was to be afforded to Flavius now, even if he had with him a valuable treasure, one admittedly not of the size he had brought from North Africa, the fruits of two centuries of theft from the old Roman provinces of Gaul and Hispania. The Goths had plundered but none had done so as successfully as the Vandals, whose mere name had become a byword for pointless destruction.

He had transferred Antonina to his vessel in expectation and both had dressed as if to be received by Justinian and Theodora. Long before the galley tied up it was clear from the absence of activity on the quayside that there was no such greeting awaiting them. Instead there was a second messenger of no higher calibre than Cabasilis with instructions that Flavius was to proceed immediately to Justinian's audience chamber, while his wife was requested to attend on the Empress in her apartments.

Never one for display and neither willing to respond to a clear insult, Flavius felt keenly the need to send to his emperor a message that he, if only on behalf of the men he had led to victory as well as the offer he had refused, was entitled to more. Sending Antonina ahead, then arranging for the Goth treasure to be taken to the imperial treasury, he changed into a simple set of clothing, one more suited to a general on campaign than the courtier Justinian would expect.

Walking the seemingly endless corridors of the palace he was reminded of the sheer number of functionaries necessary to run such a dispersed patrimony. That took no account of the thousands of servants and the guards of the Regiment of the Excubitors, placed at intervals to protect against any possibility of an attempt on the lives of their rulers. Having served in that unit as a young officer, Flavius could not avoid sly inspections to ensure they had maintained the standards he thought necessary to the imperial bodyguard.

As usual there were the high officials making their way from one set of chambers to another, attended by fawning inferiors, their arms full of scrolls. Such men, catching sight of him, were quick to arrange their features in a form of greeting but there was no friendliness in the looks Flavius received; this was not a building in which to indulge in such luxuries.

On entering the audience chamber he was further discomfited by the fact that the place was full of those men gathered to advise the Emperor, which sent to him the message that he was to be treated as just one of their number and not, as he had become accustomed to in previous meetings, as a privileged companion allowed private audience.

The crowd parted to allow him to approach the dais on which sat a gorgeously dressed Justinian, a sceptre in his hand and a crown of laurels on his head. In doing so he passed a clutch of officials, such as John the Cappadocian and Narses, who did not favour him with even a hint of welcome. Indeed the eunuch's failed attempt to hide a glare was almost amusing and would have been fully so if it had not indicated to Flavius that his standing in the imperial firmament must be, regardless of his successes, somewhat open to question. The likes of Narses and John reflected the imperial mood; they never challenged it!

'You seem a touch tardy in attendance, General Belisarius. Is it that your head has been turned by events?'

Not Flavius, nor *magister*. It was the lack of those words of respect as much as the tone that killed the half smile, as having bowed low, he raised himself to look steadily into the eyes of the man he had so faithfully served, the thought in his head inadvertent but impossible to ignore that perhaps Procopius had been right.

'Your Excellency would not have wished me to leave the treasure I brought from Italy unattended to so I could answer your summons.'

The Emperor looked him up and down, taking in the plain smock and unadorned belt, as well as the metal-studded sandals that had made such an echoing noise on the marble flooring. 'And you are required to dress like some common soldier in order to oversee such a task?'

'I dress like a soldier, which is what I am and I aspire to be nothing else.'

Which was as good a way as any of telling his emperor that he was not like the other men in the chamber; who amongst them would have turned down what he had? Looking at Justinian, Flavius was struck by the changes in a man he had not seen for over five years. The reddish hair was still as untidy as uncontrollable locks could be, but it was tinged with grey. The face, never handsome, had deep lines that had not before been present and bags under eyes that at least had the same look Flavius knew so well, ones in which there was always the impression of something hidden.

The head canted to one side, again a well-known habit, as Justinian replied, looking his general up and down as he did so. 'You speak freely and without apology for keeping us waiting, not just from the point of landing but in the time it has taken you to obey my order to depart from Italy.'

'Speaking freely has always been a privilege I was granted in times past.'

Narses spoke then, having come close to the throne to witness the first exchange, this as Justinian looked peaked at being so challenged. 'It would do you well to show greater respect now, Belisarius.'

'Just as it would behove you, Eunuch, to recall that you and I are equals and that affords you no right to make any comment on how I behave or to address me in a disrespectful manner.'

There was a sound behind Flavius then, of a sort of shuffling; in so calling Narses a eunuch he had returned the insult in full measure. The sound had to be ignored, he needed to hold the imperial eye. Justinian lifted his head to cast a look around the assembly before coming back to gaze at Flavius, who did not blink at such an examination.

Many years before, at a time when the man before him had been no more than an aide and relative to his uncle, and on many occasions since, he had sworn to be honest in their dealings, never to flatter where truth was required and never to praise actions that were questionable. They had known each other for a quarter of a century now and it was no time for that to change.

He would serve Justinian, yes, but he would never grovel to him, as would so many of the courtiers present. The other thing such creatures might do was conspire against him for their own ends, some even to the point of potential usurpation. Given he would never stoop to such behaviour, Flavius expected to be treated differently, even if what he had turned down in Ravenna was obviously no mystery.

In the silence that followed, as the pair locked eyes, Flavius was seeking the reason for such a cold greeting. Certainly Narses, on his return, would have done all in his power to diminish him, almost certainly playing down the fighting ability of the Goths, which would simultaneously dent the reputation of the man who had been beating them for years.

Flavius suspected powerful satraps such as John the Cappadocian would be extremely jealous of his success and thus also be a man to traduce him, odd since their opinions on certain matters coincided. Not all: John had been employed by Justinian on his ascension to bring more order to both the law courts and the collection of taxes. That he lined his own pockets in the process was tolerated by the Emperor on the grounds of his own increased revenues: besides, to find another who would not be equally corrupted by the opportunities this presented was close to impossible.

His other task, and here Flavius was a full supporter, was to help break the power of the patricians by bringing into the imperial bureaucracy men from more humble backgrounds yet with the talent to carry out the functions of government. If this earned him the hatred of the old ruling class it also allowed the Cappadocian to build a body of support committed to him personally. Never a shrinking violet, the man had now become intolerably self-regarding.

Flavius had to accept that his reception could be cold for another reason: habit. Occupying the imperial throne left any emperor at the mercy of advice ever leavened with flattery as to his own innate wisdom. Having occupied the position for over a dozen years now Justinian would have become accustomed to such sycophancy. Perhaps he had lost sight of what had been his abiding opinion of such courtiers, a not very elevated one prior to taking the diadem.

The men who surrounded the Emperor were politicians, still too many of them patricians, greedy for advancement in both sinecures for themselves and income and employment for their relatives. They counselled a person who enjoyed untrammelled power against any individual and as a defence against arbitrary judgement they formed self-protective cliques to temper that power.

Justinian stood abruptly. 'Come with me.'

There being no doubt as to whom he was addressing, Flavius could again hear a sound, this time made up of sighs and grunts. Narses got a black look before he obeyed, following Just-

236

inian out of the audience chamber and tailing him to his private apartments where, once past the guards, his servants, no doubt well able to read the imperial mood, quickly left them alone.

'You seem not to fear angering me.'

'I admit to my guilt.'

'And if I said I am tempted to send you to the dungeons so that you may see the folly of that?'

A swift and shallow bow of the head was appropriate; Justinian was just capricious enough to follow up on such a suggestion. 'You have that right, Excellency, though I cannot think it would raise respect for you anywhere should you exercise it.'

'That sounds very much like a threat.'

'It was not intended as one.'

'I sense an overmighty subject, one who thinks himself my equal.'

'Since I cannot be both I will settle to be a subject.'

If it was unstated both knew what they were talking about: Ravenna.

'Can you not see how you have diminished me by the way you have just behaved?'

'I see that I have treated you as I have always done, honouring your office while remembering how you always welcomed that I told you the truth.'

'Are you so sure I welcomed it?'

'I am very sure that you should, as did your uncle.'

'Do not quote him to me.'

'I do so only to remind you that you once reposed the same faith in me that he did.'

'While you have no notion of how many voices I hear that tell me such trust is misplaced.'

'Which you have good grounds to ignore since I am standing before you.'

'I am assailed by strident declarations that your actions in Italy, not least in the way you have lined your purse and dragged out the campaign, need serious enquiry.'

'Narses will be behind that.'

'He is not alone. Do not forget that Constantinus had a powerful family and you had him executed like a common thief.'

'The memory of that affords me no pleasure but I had to act with equity for the sake of the army.'

'I am pressed from other places, Flavius.'

The given name at last, and that had the one so blessed wondering if part of what Justinian was up to was an act. Surely he did not believe that his most faithful and successful general would divert money to his personal coffers or extend a campaign unnecessarily to add lustre to his name, those being the twin and all too common allegations made against the effective by the envious?

Exposed to a drip feed of accusation, had the Emperor reacted in public merely to display a level of displeasure that would satisfy the many Belisarius enemies, which would include not just the likes of Narses but any one of his counsellors troubled or made to feel insecure by his success?

How many had been jockeying for the command that Flavius had come to take on even if, as *magister militum per Orientem* it was his by right. Field generalship brought rewards of its own, but to the avaricious it also presented great opportunities for personal enrichment. If Narses and the Constantinus family had sent hares running against him, there were many who would be willing to join in the chase if only to advance their own prospects.

The spectre of Theodora could also lie at the back of this but that was, as a defence, unmentionable. Flavius might be truthful with Justinian but he knew what areas not to stray into, matters too sensitive to be alluded to and she was the primary one. If he could not comprehend the bond that united them, Flavius knew it to be so unbreakable that not even the most intimate companion could refer to its negative aspects.

'If I am to be examined I can hardly proceed to the duty for which I have been recalled.'

Justinian had never been good at disguising a sly thought: the head canted and there was no eye contact so that Flavius, who possibly knew him too well, was given the impression of a sudden idea entering the imperial mind and what followed did not do anything to dent that impression.

'The eastern border is paramount. I am prepared to pay Khusrow for peace, but only to a certain level, and I am also willing to protect you, Flavius, from the accusations made against you.'

This was a point at which other generals, eager for glory, might have suggested it would be better to crush Khusrow than bribe him. It being a subject often discussed between them, as it had been when Justinian's uncle wore the purple, it was not one Flavius would advance, for it had long been held by wiser heads that to subdue and occupy the whole of Persia was a recipe for ultimate disaster.

If the Roman Empire struggled to hold onto what it already had, and could contemplate expansion back into once held provinces where the population could be counted on to provide some sort of welcome, territorial conquests in the east were too big a mouthful to chew on. Quite apart from the sheer amount of land needed to be conquered then controlled, success would bring the empire up against the formidable forces that troubled the eastern Sassanid frontier and in many senses stopped its kings from too many adventures beyond the Euphrates.

The sly thought? Justinian would not set in train an enquiry into any behaviour in Italy, but he would not kill off the notion entirely. Why give up a point of pressure that could be applied without being mentioned? If Flavius failed against Khusrow, such an accusation could be allowed to resurface in order that the Emperor could defend his own standing.

'The sooner I am gone the better,' Flavius said.

That got eager nodded agreement, but Justinian did not pick upon the deeper meaning in what seemed like eagerness to get back to a theatre of war. More pressing to Flavius was to get away from what he saw as a sink of iniquity and one in which being present was much more threatening than any of the many battlefields on which he had risked his life.

Soon the pair were bowed over maps, examining the various possibilities that Khusrow might engage in. The eastern border was a twisting line of over five hundred leagues, peopled by fickle tribes that were well used to taking advantage if Rome seemed to be winning over Persia and vice versa. He had several routes in which he could launch an invasion and all had to be guarded against. If Flavius was to have the top command he was in need of competent subordinates.

There were imperial troops on the frontier but not enough; allies would be needed and part of the task of the *magister per Orientem* was to first engage them and then properly employ their levies. Justinian too had a responsibility, and that was to provide prompt and regular pay for those in his service, not always forthcoming at the times in which it should and that, gently alluded to, pointed up one of the limits of imperial power.

The Emperor could propose but it was up to the bureaucracy to dispose and gold meant to pay soldiers had a way of being delayed in its true purpose so that such men, by lending it out at interest, could enrich themselves with no thought to the ultimate consequence of their peculation.

'Do not fail, Flavius,' Justinian said in conclusion, the grave look on his face somewhat manufactured. 'There are too many here in the palace who would take pleasure from such an outcome.'

'I will do what is required of me, Excellency.'

The tone of that, Flavius deliberately employed; it was not rousing words of assurance, it was a warning that his emperor also must do as was required. If there were pinches in the distribution of supplies, he must either root them out or find a way to bypass them.

# CHAPTER EIGHTEEN

There was no way to avoid the Empress Theodora even in such a sprawling palace. Given the way she fawned over Antonina and made a point of visiting their shared apartments on a daily basis made it doubly impossible. Seeing them together it was hard to know who was the ruler and who the subject, so close were they in their thinking and interactions.

Instead of behaving like grown women they acted like a pair of prepubescent girls and their jokes at his expense, usually built around the notion that it took more than good intentions to make a good ruler, became repetitively wearing and many times he had to bite his tongue to avoid blurting out that Antonina would have made an atrocious queen.

In one sense life had become less complicated. Theodosius had seemingly decided that Antonina's behaviour, never even remotely discreet, was too life-threatening and had departed for Ephesus, the story being that he was intent on becoming a monk, which got from Photius the response that pigs might fly.

Originally cast down by what she called the loss of her dearest (and platonic) companion, Antonina was always able revive her spirits in the company of the Empress and did so. Their shared history gave them much to talk and laugh about and the only relief for Flavius, not eager to hear even a hint of their previous adventures in their long past places of employment, or to being told how lucky he was to have such a wonderful wife, was to make his excuses and leave and get on with the business of preparing for the forthcoming campaign.

In this he had engaged his stepson, now mature and responsible, as a replacement for Procopius and if Photius lacked that functionary's natural skill he made up for it in his enthusiasm and sheer application, not that the task of supply was ever straightforward. Too many people had a lock on such things as weapons and armour from the imperial manufactories, and if they demanded a bribe to provide the equipment needed – Flavius Belisarius could appeal directly to Justinian – they would not let anything pass out of their possession without it being plain how much they were being put out by such demands.

When it came to forward supplies of food and feed for the thousands of horses required to successfully campaign, indeed for the mounts themselves, that fell within the remit of John the Cappadocian. There Flavius found a level of avarice that provided an almost insurmountable bar to his needs in both the quantity and quality of that which was required. The threat of imperial intervention he casually dismissed and it was odd that the person most incensed by his inaction was the Empress.

'Ask Antonina,' was her response when he queried why she was so openly furious at John's behaviour. There was also the question of how she knew of his intransigence: Flavius had never complained to her, she being the last person he felt he could look to for aid.

'Theodora hates him,' was his wife's answer as they dined together. The temptation to respond that John was in abundant company had to be bitten back. 'And he and I could well cross swords if he continues to behave as he does.'

'Not literally, I hope. He might have the girth of a pregnant sow but I doubt you would best him.'

The smirk that accompanied the joke made Antonina angry and she spat back at him over the table on which they were dining. 'He diminishes you at every opportunity. Would you have me listen to him insult you and let it pass?'

'Me?'

'Don't sound surprised, Husband. You know he hates you.'

'I know he resents my success. I would be indifferent to that if he did not control the supply of what my army requires.'

'You should not be,' Antonina replied in that exasperated tone often adopted by wives who despair of their husband's apparent passivity. 'The way you let people talk of you sometimes—'

'I have two choices, Antonina, which is either to ignore it or take a weapon to the miscreant. Given I suspect John is not alone in his envy, that might result in the palace corridors running with blood.'

'It may come to that if the Cappadocian's ambitions are not checked.'

'What ambitions?'

'So you are blind as well as a fool.'

That was too close to the bone for Flavius; even

if she was referring to another matter entirely, the spectre of Theodosius had been raised. Right now that particular grit in the oyster of his marriage had absented himself, Flavius thought because Photius was present.

'I am neither, which you well know.'

Antonina entirely missed the allusion, locked up as she was in her thoughts on the Cappadocian. Not wishing to dip his toe in that particular septic well, Flavius avoided a direct reference to her possible infidelities and returned to generalities.

'It surprises me that you care so much.'

'Why should that be?'

Antonina was good at showing offence, just as in many times past she had shown a real facility for affection. Her whole body now seemed to react as if there was some inner spring animating her anger, and as she responded her tone of voice went through at least three different, all equally dramatic, phases: fury, bellicosity, then an icy form of triumph.

'You think I would let that fat slug insult the man to whom I am married and just let it pass? I will give him a piece of my mind. He'll slink away when I am finished with him, I can tell you.' She fixed him with a glare. 'But, of course, you don't care, do you?'

'Is there a particular reason why Theodora so hates him?'

The slow shake of his wife's head, allied to the look of despairing wonder, spoke volumes. 'Do you not see him for what he is?'

'Fat, wealthy, full of conceit and, as I have found, impervious to censure. Justinian will not

245

listen when I complain of him.'

'Which makes Theodora despair, for he is as blind as you seem to be.' Her eating knife was waving now and she was addressing him as if he was indeed short on brains. 'The Cappadocian has spent the last ten years filling offices with men that owe everything to him. Why would he do that?'

'He's doing it on behalf of Justinian, who put him in place to change the nature of the bureaucracy and break the power of the patricians.'

'Good for him, then, that in the process he has amassed a cohort of men who will support him.'

'In what?'

The eyes went to the roof above her head in exasperation. 'He wants the throne for himself, and the man sat on it is too blind to see. Thank God he has a wife with a sharper eye.'

'John for emperor,' Flavius chuckled. 'The notion is absurd.'

'Is it, Flavius? He is the richest man in the empire.'

'It takes more than money to rise to the purple.'

'Then how did Justinus manage it? Have you not told me the tale a hundred times of the coffers full of gold that were given to the officers of the Excubitors?'

The memory nearly brought her husband to the blush; he did indeed recall the way Justinian – he had been Petrus Sabbatius then – had conspired to get his uncle, who held the office of *comes Excubitorum*, elevated to the recently vacated throne by diverting money provided by another courtier for a different candidate to gain the prize.

Flavius had been involved in the conspiracy but

his discomfort was brought on by the memory of his lack of an ability to see in what he was being embroiled. If others had been duped, not least the man elevated by the intrigue, so too had he.

'The Excubitors were supporting one of their own and a man in whom they had faith, and quite rightly. Recall that the Hippodrome hailed their choice.'

That was dismissed with an airy wave. 'Oh, I know. You never tire of telling me how sainted was Justinus, the true paragon and surrogate father to whom you owe everything. I just hope you are not so forthcoming with his nephew.'

'I have never thought it too wise to overpraise his uncle to Justinian, but I have had occasion to remind him that when we talk of him, we speak of a man of some virtue.'

'Words that cannot be applied to the Cappadocian.'

'He will never rise to the purple. First of all he would have to kill Justinian, which, given he is one of the most suspicious men in creation, will be near to impossible. From what I can observe too, his Excubitor bodyguard are fiercely loyal.'

'And if he were to die naturally, what then?'

Flavius crossed himself then, but as he did so the underlying concerns of his wife surfaced for they would be those of her great friend. Theodora, bereft of Justinian, would be exposed and perhaps John would have a chance, and the obvious conclusion to such a line of reasoning was obvious. The Empress was not one to wait to be thrown to the wolves, which rendered John's position one of some danger.

It made him glad he was about to go on campaign, this being the thing he had always hated about the capital, the endless plotting of one faction against another, and at the peak of such schemes there were too many souls who saw themselves as better able to rule than the incumbent emperor. It had been true when Anastatius was alive, was so when Justinus ruled and would be rife, too, under his nephew.

'It is near blasphemous to even consider such a thing, Antonina. Now I beg you, let us leave John to his peculations and change the subject.'

'Promise me you will challenge him if he insults you in person.'

'So that I can kill him? Fat and wobbly John, who has never been a soldier, never fought in a battle and as far as I know would be lost in how to use a sword?'

'He knows how to employ his tongue.'

'Just as I know what would shame me, Antonina. If I fight, it will be with a man who can match me, not some useless tub of lard.'

Which was as good a way as he could think of telling his wife he was not going to stick a sword in the Cappadocian's belly just to please her friend the Empress.

'I had no idea how much I would miss Antonina while she campaigned with you, but I do now and I desire to keep her close.'

'Your Highness could have sent for her at any time and I am sure my wife would have sped back to your side.'

It was fascinating watching Theodora, who

seemed to have the ability to believe whatever she was saying whenever she was saying it. It was she who had insisted that Antonina accompany him to North Africa and subsequently, to Italy so that his wife could act as her spy. If her behaviour with Theodosius, whom she insisted was an innocent companion, was a great unmentionable in their marriage, the act of her betrayal in corresponding with the Empress was a greater one. Nor could he, tempted as he was to be honest, mention it to Theodora.

Like her husband and indeed his wife she had aged, so that the dark beauty which had at one time impressed him was now faded. Her face was sagging and no amount of powder or unction could disguise that the skin that had once been as smooth as milk was now lined and broken.

In fairness, while harbouring these thoughts, Flavius had to admit that time had changed him also. His beard was no longer jet black but tinged at the extremities with grey and he wondered if he shaved it off what he would discover underneath. If the bags under his eyes were any indication, then he would be in for a shock.

Yet he was bound to wonder what lay behind this request that Antonina stay with her in Constantinople and the spectre of Theodosius came immediately to mind. Theodora would no doubt happily facilitate such a liaison, given her own behaviour within the palace was a constant source of both speculation and jibes.

Try as he might, Flavius was once more reminded that he had never quite got to grips regarding her relationship with Justinian. He knew, from his time spent in the company of the young Petrus, when he himself had been an innocent youth willing to be corrupted by the much more experienced debauchee, that his proclivities were not straightforward.

Justinian took great pleasure in being the voyeur and it was rumoured that Theodora was only too willing to indulge that particular taste, even with multiple partners. Against that was one simple fact: every ruler or consort was the subject of scurrilous accusations and they always seemed to centre on their sexual preferences. There was not one disgusting act he knew of that had not at some time been attached to their names.

'I find myself on the horns of dilemma, Highness.'

It was amusing to observe Theodora's confusion, for his response had thrown her and there was some pleasure in that, even more in playing out a game in which he would gain no more; as empress and consort she had power of her own – more vitally, she had a hold over her husband.

'I have become accustomed to have Antonina by my side. Will I be the successful soldier still if I am denied her support?'

Theodora was no fool; she knew he was toying with her but she too was forced to indulge in pretence. Not even an empress could always be open and now she found no trouble in arranging her features to convey sadness.

'It pains me to deprive you of that, Flavius. But I hope and pray you will see my need for companionship, just as I appreciate yours and have in the past done much to facilitate it.'

250

'You have been most gracious.'

That made her purse her lips, which made very apparent the small vertical wrinkles between that and her nose. Flavius knew he was sailing close to a dangerous shore in baiting her and so was quick to add, 'Of course, I would not dream of denying you that company in which I take so much pleasure.'

Theodora could not keep a trace of a hiss out of her reply. 'Then it falls to me to thank you for – what did you say – "being gracious".'

'Now if you will forgive me, Highness, I have to attend upon the Emperor and outline to him how I plan to thwart the designs of Khusrow.'

There was no doubt in anyone's mind that the Sassanids would cross the border once more. Khusrow had again demanded a huge sum of money from Justinian as well as an annual stipend to keep the peace, an ultimatum that had originally been agreed to. Using the excuse that the Sassanids had broken various pledges, the offer had been withdrawn. If only to save face Khusrow must react.

The question was not just how to counter the threat but to comprehensively defeat the enemy. Cheering news had just come that Martinus, sent ahead to Dara with the Belisarian *comitatus,* had with the help of the garrison repulsed an attempt by the Sassanids to take the great fortress on which any defence of the frontier must rest. With the season for campaigning well over, Khusrow had retired back into his own territory.

'The border is too long and the opportunities for

251

an incursion too spread for any one man to counter. I suggest that I have overall control based on Dara and that there should be two junior generals who will be free to act independently to the north.'

'You have men you prefer?' Justinian asked.

'Bouzes is already in place and I would send Valerian to take command in Armenia.'

'Excellency,' protested Narses, this being no private meeting; he had no need to elaborate on that single word of protest.

'No, Narses, I need you here in Constantinople.'

The eunuch had no idea that this had been a subject discussed between Flavius and Justinian when they were alone, as had the suggestion that feeding money to Khusrow was indulging an appetite for Byzantine gold that would never be satisfied. Flavius wanted to employ another plan and had been given at least a nod to proceed, and the last thing needed was that bugbear of split command.

Narses would not be the only soldier seeking opportunities in the field and if there were good candidates he was too senior a figure to be one. Flavius had insisted on sole authority once more, and when his demand caused a regal frown he had driven home his point by reminding his emperor that his successes had all been when he had enjoyed sole command. That publically conceded he moved on to more troubling matters.

'Now I must ask that John fulfil those commitments he has made to ensure that the army in the east can operate effectively.'

'Has he not done so?'

Justinian asked this with an air of faux innocence as the substantial bulk of the Cappadocian swelled at the perceived slight on his not properly carrying out his duties. Flavius had been badgering his emperor for weeks to intervene and get the man to release supplies that he knew were already in warehouses on the city's docks, there to be pilfered and sold off by the men supposed to be guarding them.

Such prevarication provided many with a reason to act in a sympathetic manner and for all his attempts to avoid intrigue, Flavius could not wholly avoid being embroiled in conversations with the higher functionaries of empire as he went about his daily business in the palace or attended the near endless gatherings that Antonina adored and he more often found trying.

Always attended by the imperial couple, these assemblies tended to stiffness until they retired, when those who served them could relax and get back to their intrigues and jockeying. Then there were the daily Masses, held in what Justinian was sure to be his most proud achievement as emperor and one cast in stone that would stand as his legacy.

The century-old wooden Church of St Sophia, on the eastern edge of the imperial palace, had suffered in the Nika riots, having been set alight by the insurgents and burnt to the ground. To replace it Justinian had employed not only the greatest scientific minds of the age, he had scoured the empire for the materials and artefacts to build and furnish the paramount holy church in Christendom, creating a dome so wide and high that his more superstitious subjects feared to enter lest it collapse on their heads.

It was instructive to be within the confines of St Sophia in his company, he being like a child with a favourite toy. Deeply religious – many said Justinian was such a sinner he needed to be in order to procure forgiveness from God – it revealed a side to the Emperor that Flavius knew from past association but few others experienced.

It seemed as if within its walls, with its stained windows and great columns, he was at some kind of peace, the tension that was these days a constant normality evaporating as he took pleasure in describing the details of the design and the problems he and his advisors had overcome in construction.

There were times, at social gatherings and even following on from the Masses that Flavius enjoyed; meeting and reminiscing with men with whom he had happily campaigned, while some of the long-serving imperial courtiers were people of a wit he found difficult to match, not that he tried to.

Yet too often what began as an engaging conversation strayed into areas of which he was determined to stay clear. Gentle enquiries as to his opinion of Justinian's abilities or his military strategy; the odd aside, usually humorously delivered, that was yet a sly dig at Theodora and either her pretensions or her perceived proclivities. Each he was sure, were hooks designed to draw out from him a point of view that would then lead to an invitation to greater intimacy and possible collusion.

Even when he had been resident in the palace, and he had been as a young Excubitor officer, Flavius had never managed to discern the currents and groupings that to Justinian appeared as an open book. The Emperor, both in power and prior to assuming his position, always seemed to know who was allied to whom in what was an ever-shifting set of temporary coalitions, rarely, it had to be said, directly aimed at the throne, more often the goal being a desire for support into a more lucrative office.

It was therefore with some joy that he was able to announce his departure for Dara. The campaigning season was nearly upon him and he required time to set in train the various stratagems he hoped would frustrate the designs of an enemy already on the move.

He spent his last night, attended upon by Solomon, close to the capital at the villa he had bought as a home for himself and Antonina not long after their marriage. Overlooking the Bosphorus it was a place of sad reflection, since he and his wife had never spent a single night together under its roof.

Dawn found Photius at the gate at the head of his personal bodyguards, as well as a strong body of Goth mercenaries who had come east to fight with a man they admired and one who might bring them much plunder. In such company it was possible to put aside the ghosts of what might have been and look ahead to the only situation in which Flavius knew himself to be contented.

Command of an army left little room for personal introspection.

# CHAPTER NINETEEN

On his way to take over command, picking up mercenary contingents *en route*, Flavius found the troops he would be required to lead into battle to be demoralised, lacking in equipment and patently frightened of facing an enemy who always outnumbered them and seemed, under Khusrow's military reforms, to be invincible.

Many a commander would have despaired at this but Flavius had been in such a situation before and was therefore untroubled, eschewing modesty to remind them the army was now led by the Victor of Dara. That alone lifted their spirits and their general knew that fully supplied with weapons, given proper training and under good officers, even the most fearful body could be brought to the peak of fighting ability and these were the matters he set out to address.

His spies reported back that Khusrow was not bent on a second incursion into central Mesopotamia. He had gone north to fight the Huns, a tribe forever raiding his borderlands and that presented Flavius with a golden opportunity: he had time to exercise his men, and that complete he could invade Sassanid territory with no fear of meeting the main enemy force.

At a gathering of his officers only one pair demurred at this plan, the two imperial *duces* of Phoenice Libanensis, who ruled jointly from

Damascus and Palmyra. In that region they faced the pagan Lahkmids, long-time allies of the Sassanids. If they denuded their territories of troops to join Flavius it would leave them exposed to a Lahkmid invasion.

It was Arethas, the leader of the Ghassanids, neighbours and co-religionists to the Lahkmids, albeit less observant of ritual, who pointed out that at this time of year committed pagans were forbidden to go to war and would be so constrained for two whole months, during which they must worship their gods. Flavius was then able to promise the *duces* that he would release them within sixty days so they could return to their fiefs and defend them.

He did not have to travel far in order to make contact with an enemy. The Sassanid twin to the Byzantine fortress of Dara was Nisibis, a mere three leagues distant and just as powerful a stronghold, certainly one holding a garrison large enough to pose a danger if just bypassed. Flavius dismayed many of his officers, men now thirsting for action, by ordering his surveyors to stay well away from the walls and to lay out the Byzantine camp at a distance, which required him to explain his thinking to his inferior in order to put a cap on much vocal muttering.

'It is a poor commander who does not learn from his errors. When I fought Witigis outside Rome I paid no heed to the fact that he deployed his forces further away from the walls than seemed, at the time, necessary. Yet he had a clear reason to do so and it is one I now wish to adopt.'

A look around the assembly showed many an

eager listener but also some expressions that hinted at either doubt, indifference or mystification.

'The Sassanid *spahed* in Nisibis is Nabedes. He has substantial forces under his command and we have to assume him to be capable. Khusrow would not have entrusted to him such an important strategic asset as his major border stronghold if he was not a trusted subordinate. It is my belief that if we give him room he will come out from behind his walls to fight and drive us off, rather than accept to be put under siege.'

'It is what you did at Dara,' Photius added, now in a position to speak in support at such gatherings.

'I did not venture so far, but then I had no intention of a pursuit. This time I wish to anticipate the possibility as Witigis did at Rome. Let Nabedes come to us, and if we can force him into a retreat, the gap between his army and safety could be so great that we might ruin the defence of Nisibis. If we succeed, the city will fall to us without the need to mount an assault.'

Obeyed by the majority, there were two men who thought they knew better than their general, the prime mover being a junior called Peter, like the late Constantinus a well-connected patrician who saw no reason to defer to a man of the character and breeding of Flavius Belisarius. The other commander, swayed by Peter even if he admired Flavius, was known as John the Glutton, given he was not a man to be any distance behind at mealtimes.

Declining to stop within the limit set, they

marched on until not much more than a *milia* separated them from the enemy, a full half of the distance Flavius had decided upon. There was no time to recall them and besides, Flavius half wondered if Peter had inadvertently provided a temptation that the Sassanids would not be able to resist. With that in mind he sent word to the miscreant to stay where he was but to post a strong and alert guard against a night assault.

Dawn brought news that Nabedes had taken the bait. He was deploying his forces outside the walls, no doubt full of confidence based, Flavius suspected, on the way the Sassanids had routed every Byzantine force they encountered the previous year. Hubris in an enemy is ever a positive.

Orders were issued that the normal time of breaking to eat was to be postponed past noon, Flavius sure that would be the time the enemy, who knew well the habits of Eastern Roman armies, would launch their assault. It was as well he was ready, his forces drawn up to fight, for in the distance a huge cloud of dust told him that troops were moving in mass formations. By the time the message came from Peter that he was under attack – it had come while his men were, in another act of defiance, eating their midday rations – the main force was moving, with the Goth mercenaries well to the fore, eager to show their mettle.

They found the men led by Peter and the Glutton in dire straits, indeed they passed some of them fleeing the field. But so ferocious was the Goth assault they drove back the forward Sassanid elements and those troops recoiled on the supporting elements. Seeing the main Byzantine force closing at speed and with his army in some disarray, Nabedes ordered the retreat, the very outcome that Flavius had sought.

Yet thanks to Peter, the fight and flight was taking place too close to the walls of Nisibis and if the Sassanids lost substantial numbers, it was nothing like the amount that would have fallen had they had further to run. The main force got back through the gates not far off intact, which rendered impossible any chance of taking the city by a coup.

In dressing down his two errant commanders it was plain who had initiated the disobedience. Peter was sent back to Constantinople in disgrace and John the Glutton, the lesser offender, warned that any further insubordination would see him thrown into Justinian's dungeons with no food, a warning he extended to his whole command when they met again to discuss what would happen now.

'If we try to take Nisibis, Nabedes can hold out for the whole summer, so we must march on or our incursion is a waste.'

'And leave him along our lines of communication, *Magister?*' asked an inferior commander called Trajan. He had once been part of the Belisarian *comitatus* and was well trusted by the general who had promoted him.

'We will achieve nothing here and it is to be hoped that Nabedes has been chastened by that which he has just experienced. He dare not lose Nisibis, given it would likely cost him his head, so I would have him cautious now and prepared to stay behind those walls.'

'Do we not need supplies of food to come through Dara?'

The amusement that caused, the question being posed by the Glutton, made him blush, while everyone else added comments on his obvious girth until Flavius, with a raised hand brought it to an end.

'The territory into which we are going to advance is fertile enough to support us. We need no supplies from our own possessions. The city of Sisauranon is no more than a day's march to our front. That is our next objective.'

If the army marched on, Flavius did not; he kept a sharp eye on the gates of Nisibis for any sign that Nabedes might emerge, in which case he would swing his forces round to confront them. It was with a mixture of relief and disappointment that the *spahed* acted as predicted, the gates staying firmly closed, leaving him to ride hard to catch up with his strong rearguard.

There was no manoeuvring outside Sisauranon; as soon as they were properly deployed and their demand for surrender had been rebuffed, the Byzantines assaulted the walls with ladders, only to find them strongly held. Mounting losses caused that to be called off, which meant a siege; Flavius knew he would have to employ such a tactic: to leave two fortresses in his rear, who might combine their forces, was too dangerous.

Yet this place was not Nisibis, being nothing like as formidable, with walls in a poor state of repair and a smaller garrison. Sure it would succumb at some point, it did not require to be invested by his

261

whole army so he detached the forces led by Arethas, as well as over a thousand of his *bucellarii* under John the Glutton, to raid across the Tigris.

Their task was to ravage at will in a region of Persia that had not seen conflict for decades and, being well watered and fertile, was rich because of it. To ensure John was not once more tempted to exceed his orders he was accompanied by Trajan. Once Sisauranon was captured and provided the information sent back by his raiders promised good rewards, Flavius would advance with the whole army to join them.

The first indication that he might take Sisauranon quickly came with the capture of a party of deserters, their reason for flight the fact that the city was so short of food they had been put on starvation rations. They also informed him it was full of Byzantine captives taken on the previous Sassanid incursion, it being the numbers of those, and the ransoms they might fetch, that had left the fortress lacking in sustenance for the defenders.

An envoy was despatched to negotiate with promises that surrender would mean life and a degree of liberty for the citizens, or death for all if they forced a continued assault. The fighting men were mercenaries and would be sent back to Constantinople, with a recommendation from Flavius that Justinian employ them far away in Italy. The terms were accepted and Flavius marched in as the one-time defenders, and the Byzantine captives, marched west under escort.

Waiting for news of his raid across the Tigris, the army was troubled by a serious outbreak of plague in the ranks, brought on by contact with the inhabitants of Sisauranon. Many were dying, which had him move his men to a series of camps out of the newly captured city, yet reconnaissance parties sent east brought back no news of Arethas or the Glutton, this while their commander had a problem in that time was running out: the sixty days he had promised to the *duces* of Phoenice Libanensis was nearly up and that would severely cut a force already short on effectives due to disease, so it was time for another conference.

'I cannot ask the contingents from Damascus and Palmyra to remain and you can all see how our effectives are diminished by sickness. Men are dying every day and our only hope is to get away from here so that at least some may recover their health in more benign locations.'

As always he looked around the assembled officers to seek to discern if there was disagreement, not that he anticipated any. They would have to give up Sisauranon but that was a necessary price to pay because it could not be held; any garrison left behind would be beyond succour should the Sassanids seek to retake it, and besides, it would act as a magnet for the Byzantine garrison at Dara, perhaps drawing them into a fight on terms chosen by the Sassanids.

'We have the city treasury and we will destroy the walls prior to departure, so rendering it useless to Khusrow.' The option to advance was posed as a rhetorical question and one he answered himself. 'We have no idea as to what lies across the Tigris, and given our numbers it is my opinion it would be a risky venture to probe further into Persia without knowing it to be clear of our enemies.'

A murmur of agreement followed the summation. 'So, I will send messages to our forward elements that I intend to withdraw and that they should do likewise. We will send the sick ahead to the coast and form up to their rear to protect them. Best to think of fighting another day than to risk being caught away from our own lands when we are weakened.'

John the Glutton and Trajan caught up with Flavius before he reached Dara, not hard given he was retiring at a snail's pace so as not to tire his soldiers, while also seeking to deceive the enemy in Nisibis and leave them confused as to his intentions. The number of laden carts they returned with testified to the success of their mission, carrying enough booty to gladden the hearts of the most avaricious of plunderers, spoils that would be distributed throughout the army.

'Arethas?'

'He parted company from us when we decided to retire,' John responded. 'Which was forced upon us even before we received your orders.'

A questioning look demanded he continue. 'Arethas sent hunting parties out to bring in food and also to warn against any enemy approaching from the east, which was just as well. They spotted a strong force of Persians that massively outnumbered us, so flight was our only option. With so much plunder, which might slow us down, Arethas suggested we divide it before retiring–'

'To which you agreed?' Flavius asked.

'Yes. He undertook to bring his half back directly and we would bring the rest by a different route.'

'Photius, send out scouts to the east to look for Arethas.'

'I thought he would get here ahead of us,' said Trajan, the look on his face one of confusion. 'He did ask us to delay a day and give him a head start.'

'Well, let us hope for all our sakes he is not far off. If he brings in anything like that which you fetched, Khusrow might drop dead from apoplexy.'

Slow as the army moved no sign came of Arethas or any of his Ghassanids. Questioned more, both John and Trajan admitted they had seen no sign themselves of any Persian forces and once back at Dara, and still no sign, the *solidus* finally dropped.

The cunning Ghassanid leader had taken half of the plunder, but not to share with his Byzantine allies; he would keep it to himself and his people. Word came eventually that he was indeed back in his own territory and so were the spoils. He would stay there too, for to venture out and risk being caught by Flavius would have cost him his head.

News also came about the activities of Khusrow and it proved the spies wrong; the information that he was attacking the Huns turned out to be false. He had instead led his forces into the province of Lazica, which bordered the eastern edge of the Euxine Sea, an important region for that alone, doubly so since it bordered the Caucasus Mountains and the passes that led into Scythia, home to any number of barbarian tribes, most troublingly the numerous and murderous Alans.

The reasons, hard to fathom originally, emerged

over time and it all fell to the depredations of those who had been given the rule over Lazica by Justinian, though they did turn out to be clients of John the Cappadocian. By levying excessive taxation, manipulating the courts and the setting up of monopolies of food, oil and wine they had, to enrich themselves, bled Lazica dry.

This so alienated the local tribes that their ruler had sent to Khusrow and offered him suzerainty over their kingdom in place of obeisance to Constantinople. Petra, Justinian's stronghold in the region, had fallen and the old Greek province of Colchis was now firmly in the hands of the Sassanids.

Flavius was left to lament that the policy of his was the right one, to always treat the indigenes, whoever they were, as if they were your own citizens and never to seek to fleece them for private gain. That said, anger at what had occurred had to be suborned to what was happening now; Khusrow had his victories and would now be marching south, hopefully taking too long about it so that, with winter approaching, he would not have to be faced until the following year.

An equally troubling problem was the presence at Dara of Antonina, newly arrived from Constantinople. Flavius had been told of her intention to travel to Dara outside Sisauranon, with an added plea that her husband should send to Theodosius, skulking according to her in Ephesus, to make his way to Dara also, a plea he ignored and was careful to keep from the ears of Photius since the mere mention of the name sent his stepson into a fury.

As usual she arrived as if there could be nothing amiss, which produced from her husband a degree of bitter respect for her sheer effrontery. Added to that, Antonina felt she had reason to be proud seeing she brought with her news of the downfall of John the Cappadocian, whom she had embroiled in a plot to replace Justinian. Cock-a-hoop about her success, she was unable to understand why, when she had finished relating her adventures, her husband did not equally relish the tale.

She had befriended John's daughter, flattering a young innocent in order to get to the father. Initially guarded, the Cappadocian had fallen for her blandishments, in which Antonina had invoked the name of Flavius to insist that there was no real enmity between them. She assured him they shared a creeping despair over the way the empire was being run as a dual franchise by a useless emperor and his devious consort, to whom John was a mortal enemy.

'I told him he was at risk and must act to save himself, also that you regretted turning down the offer the Goths made and would be ready to back him if he chose to overthrow Justinian and Theodora to ensure better rule.'

'You used my name?'

Antonina cackled then. 'Such is the old fool's vanity that he actually believed me.'

'You said I would support him?'

'Don't look so upset. It was only to seduce him into indiscretions. You were never in any danger because of it.'

'And what did he think he was going to get

from me?'

'Military support, of course. You would pledge the loyalty of the armies in Asia Minor and appeal to the citizens in the Hippodrome to proclaim him. Against both of you Justinian would be lucky to escape with his life, which was not something the Cappadocian was prepared to extend to Theodora.'

'Proclaim him from the imperial box.'

'Where else?'

'For which I would have to have been in the city.'

'Are you being deliberately dense, Flavius? It was never intended that you should act, only that the Cappadocian would reveal himself. What I would have given to see his face when Narses had the palace guards arrest him.'

'For being drawn into a conspiracy that he had no part in starting.'

'You sound as though you feel sorry for the fat old goat. He was conspiring, all right, all he needed was a bit of a push to act and show his hand.' Her face changed, to take on a sly look. 'He was not beyond hinting, by the way, that any bargain could be sealed on my body.'

'An offer I am sure you encouraged him to think likely.'

Suppressed it might be, but there was no doubting the fury in Flavius's voice.

'Why are you so angry? You hated the man.'

'Because, Antonina, I recall our previous conversation about John, whom you were encouraging me to challenge and then to kill. If you acted against him it was to please Theodora, so I have to suspect that your attempts to embroil me in murder were on her behalf as well.'

'Nonsense.'

'Is it, Antonina?' Flavius had to steel himself then to say what came next, to get out into the open what still disturbed him in the dead of night. 'Is it nonsense that Theodosius is nothing to you but a platonic friend?'

'I have told you–'

'You have lied, just as you lied with such ease to the Cappadocian, and I have been as much a fool as John. Theodosius is such a platonic friend, I am told he fled to Ephesus to avoid your attention to him, so embarrassing had it become–'

'A lie,' she spat, 'and one no doubt related to you by that ingrate son of mine.'

'No, Antonina,' came the weary response. 'It is the truth and one of which I am sick. You have no idea of how much I wanted to believe you were being truthful, and I would guess no notion of how much of a fool I feel at this moment.'

'Flavius,' she protested, in a way that indicated this was no great matter and would soon be solved.

The shout was so startling and loud, echoing off the stone walls, that she physically recoiled. 'Solomon!' His *domesticus*, in the company of several armed men rushed into the chamber, to be given orders in a near whisper. 'Take the Lady Antonina and confine her to some part of the fortress, I need not know where.'

'Husband,' she squealed, but to no avail; all that lay before her was a face made of stone.

'Do not speak, for if you do you will keep lying,

and I tell you, that so troubles me I know not what I would do, for I am not immune to rage. Best you are out of my sight and for some of the time out of my mind. Be satisfied that I cannot do that which would be recommended to me by one who has known that which I have refused to accept.'

'Photius! You choose to believe him in place of your own wife?'

'Wife? You were once that but as of now, you are not. I should take you down to the cistern, Antonina, and drown you. But I cannot, so I grant you life but know that is all you will ever have from me in future.'

'I am innocent.'

'Solomon, take her out of my sight.'

## CHAPTER TWENTY

The fact that Flavius Belisarius had imprisoned his wife could not stay secret for long and in no time messages were flying back to Constantinople with the news. There was no need to tell Theodora of the cause, she knew only too well, and nor was it possible to stop her putting pressure on her husband to recall a general who was, after all, not engaged in fighting, it being winter.

Those who served Flavius knew their man well, none more so than Solomon, who ensured that if Antonina was confined it was not in the dungeons but in a set of apartments which, if not as regal as those from which she had been removed, were quite comfortable. Not that such consideration was acknowledged, she being loud in her complaint of being treated worse than a heretic beggar.

Her husband did not enquire after her well-being and there was a tacit acceptance by those close to him that it was not a subject to be alluded to in even the most oblique way. Not that Flavius was unaware of the stares he attracted as people sought to discern the effect such a bold step was having on their leader. Others, less intimate, looked at him differently, some sneering at the cause of the dispute, that was until they caught his eye.

In trying to appear unruffled and to carry on with the tasks that occupied him, ensuring the sick were cared for, sending away contingents to winter in less diseased locations on the Mediterranean shore, purchasing and storing supplies for the coming year, Flavius was yet aware of those surreptitious glances. The realisation of familiarity was what made him uncomfortable; he now grasped that many of the silent exchanges in the imperial palace had been of a similar type.

It should not have bothered him but it did, the palace, indeed the whole of Constantinople being a hotbed of debauchery, easily recalled from his own forays into the dock area with the yet to become emperor, Justinian, and he had himself been far from chaste, indeed that was where he had first come across Antonina, though they had not shared any intimacy until Theodora, finally wedded to the heir, brought her friend into the imperial wing.

The vows he took when marrying had put a stop

on any such excursions, for to Flavius they were sacrosanct. How wounding was it that the same did not apply to his wife and how could the son they had adopted not see that his behaviour was an outrage against God? Was Photius right when he insisted that such sins were enough to justify killing them both? If he was, it could not, for the sake of his soul, fall to him to be the executioner.

'The command is plain, *Magister*. You are to return to Constantinople at once and in the company of your wife.'

The imperial messenger was coated in the dust of travel and no great imagination was required to calculate the time it had taken for the imprisonment of Antonina to reach the ears of Theodora and for her to react. The information must have flown to the capital, and judging by the state of the man before him, the order had come back with the kind of haste normally afforded to news of a barbarian incursion. There was no choice but to obey, with one caveat imparted to Solomon.

'The Lady Antonina and I will travel separately. She is to be brought to our villa south of Galatea and she will enter the capital from there while we will proceed directly. Also send word to Photius that he too is to make his way to Constantinople.'

Solomon was good at hiding reactions but even he could not keep the wonder from his face, a look to which Flavius responded. 'What could be more damning than the word of her own natural son?'

'You feel you require that, *Magister*?'

'Solomon, I have no idea what I will require. All

I do know is that within the imperial palace my wife holds more sway in certain quarters than I do.'

'The Emperor–'

'May act, but too many times I have known him sit on his hands when it means confronting Theodora.'

The journey was made in no great haste, it not being a confrontation to which Flavius was looking forward. He imagined that Antonina, in her separate caravan, would be wild with frustration and there was some satisfaction that he could inflict such an emotion upon her, but it was nevertheless an uncomfortable two and a half weeks in which he was left to contemplate what he might face. Not death, he had no fear of such an outcome, but disgrace, even if it was manufactured, was another matter.

Had he known what his stepson was up to, Flavius would have been even more concerned but that he did not find out until he was in the capital. Photius, who harboured no illusions about the behaviour of his mother or the transgressions of her paramour, had gone to Ephesus with a party of soldiers and abducted Theodosius before taking him to the winter quarters of the *bucellarii* where he was thrown into a prison cell.

His other act was to strip the miscreant of the monies he had so assiduously collected, a fortune distributed amongst the troops as a present not from him but from their general. That accomplished, he then followed his orders and travelled to Constantinople.

'I am at a loss to know how you can treat your wife so, Flavius Belisarius. Your actions are those more suited to a barbarian than the Roman you soundly profess yourself to be.'

'I would wish to hear from you what you think of her behaviour, Highness?'

Theodora bristled at his tone, but Flavius was determined that in matters matrimonial she had limited rights of interference. She had received him in a room normally the preserve of the most intimate discussions involving her husband and his closest advisors, exchanges of the kind that never went beyond these four walls.

Flavius had been here many times before but never alone with the Empress and he surmised that the location was part of the message she wished to send to him: that whatever she decided would be approved of by Justinian.

Despite several requests, his emperor had refused to receive him, startling behaviour given he was denying audience to his most senior military commander, which left Flavius to conclude that if Justinian was adept at embroiling himself in conspiracies he was equally adroit at staying out of those he considered too challenging, and the marital problems of his general would fall into that category.

'As a woman I have perhaps a better understanding of Antonina than you.'

'While I will openly admit to having very little understanding at all.'

Sensing her about to respond Flavius spoke quickly to cut her off; he had no desire to hear excuses from her lips, any more than he wanted to be once more exposed to the lies of his wife.

'I also feel, Highness, that these are matters of which no other person need concern themselves.'

'You deny me the right to support my friend?'

'Support her by all means, but not to me.'

He had the sense that Theodora was slightly thrown by the vehemence of his contention. Just like her husband, she was so accustomed to deference that for anyone to take a high tone against her caused discomfort and it would be doubly the case with him, given he had ever been careful of her self-regard. Discomfited she might be but that did not last; with a flare of her nostrils and a loud explosion of air she soon reasserted herself.

'Have a care how you talk to me, *Magister!* There are people in the dungeons below our feet who have cause to regret such an error.'

'If you feel incarceration is what I deserve, then I invite you to call for your guards.'

Theodora was a quick thinker; she could not have ensnared Justinian without her sharp wits and certainly she would never have maintained her imperial estate without a keen nose for pitfalls. For the first time since her marriage Flavius was daring her to act in a way towards him that could only rebound badly, and the pause before her response was evidence that she got the point he was making.

Power she had, but so, because of his popularity amongst the citizenry and especially the soldiery, had he. Was he not famed for his loyalty and honesty? It was common knowledge now that he turned down a chance of independent power. If that provided only a measure of protection, in this case it was enough.

Imprison him on a whim and there would be grumbling in the streets, catcalls from the crowd in the Hippodrome, and for all both of them knew, much more. She had enough experience of the febrile politics of the metropolis not to set hares running without any idea where they would go.

'I have too much regard for Antonina to send the man to whom she is wedded to prison.'

The Empress turned her back to him then, he surmised to avoid him seeing the fact that she thought the excuse as feeble as did he. Added to that, Theodora needed to compose herself and get back her regal posture, which required several deep breaths before she again faced him.

'Do not assume I have no sympathy for the problem you face, Flavius.'

If the given name was meant to relax him it had the opposite effect, but it seemed politic to say nothing.

'I have already alluded to my sex and that grants me insights denied even to the most astute of men. Antonina has reached an age in which the sentiments that have sustained her and made her the person she is are cast into doubt. If I was to say I have had cause to share the same, I would hope you would understand.'

'I will readily admit to being mystified by the working of the female mind.'

That got a nod from Theodora, being for the first time a tactful response, followed by the kind of slight smile that to a man is part sympathy and part despair at what women see as blindness. Flavius recognised it because he had been exposed to it so many times. It was often employed by Antonina.

'I think you would acknowledge that your wife was once very beautiful.'

'As were you, Highness.'

That changed her expression once more to a frown; was it a compliment or a barb to a woman equally past her prime? But Theodora was intent on making a point and nothing Flavius said was going to deflect her.

'We look in the polished silver and see the ravages of time, Flavius, and that induces a concern that never affects men. The vision of what we see, allied to the feelings that causes, makes us ask questions of ourselves. Are we still the object of admiration or do those who might have once flattered us look through to lay eyes on a younger, more comely countenance?'

'I have never given Antonina cause to think that.'

'There, you show your lack of understanding. It is not what you say or do that matters.' She tapped her head very gently. 'Everything to do with these concerns is in here, where you cannot see.'

'God can see,' Flavius snapped.

Her response was equally sharp. 'Yes, he can, and do not doubt his forgiveness. We are all sinners, Flavius, you included, and it shows an arrogance I scarcely credited I could apply to you that you do not share such grace.'

'I would consider it presumptuous to do so.'

'Then perhaps allow yourself to be advised by one closer to the celestial than you.'

The temptation to say that Theodora was bordering on blasphemy was acute, but then Flavius had to remind himself that those who occupied the imperial throne might think of themselves as semi-divine. Certainly they were treated as such by their courtiers and servants, even sometimes by the mob that hailed them when they entered their box in the Hippodrome.

'Yet there is another consideration,' she added, adopting a look of deep concern. 'The happiness of my good companion.'

There was no point in alluding to his happiness or misery, Theodora would care naught for that.

'In addition, we cannot have the man tasked with defending our polity publically at odds with his wife. It is not only unseemly, it is dangerous to the throne.'

'Are you suggesting I condone her behaviour to save the blushes of you and your husband?'

Taint by association was the point of that remark but it was an unsayable one to make too plain. No matter, she knew what he meant. Talk of imperial debauchery was the stuff of much gossip and that would only be fanned if the Belisarius marriage was added to the mix.

'What you suppose to be her misdemeanours.'

'If you doubt the truth, let me examine our adopted son, a gathering in which I would want to include Photius.'

'I cannot imagine Antonina welcoming his presence, and besides, he is not in Constantinople.'

'He is, on my orders, on his way.'

That changed the imperial mood abruptly; her nostrils flared again and the expression on her face seriously deepened the lines of her age. 'Flavius, I have tried persuasion and I tire of it.

278

You seem blind to the needs of my friend as well as those of the empire, which shows to me a selfishness of which I thought you incapable.'

'Selfishness!'

That outburst was ignored, and the voice as she continued was emphatic.

'I speak not as a person who was once her companion but in my capacity as Empress, and in this I also speak for the Emperor. He wishes that you be reconciled with Antonina as much as I do and for the very same reasons, added to which there might be doubts about your ability to lead our armies with such a burden gnawing at your soul.'

'You and the Emperor have discussed my private affairs?'

'As an imperial servant you have no private affairs.' Her hands came up to produce a sharp slap and that summoned a servant who, on a nod from Theodora, departed without speaking.

'I have just summoned Antonina to join us, Flavius, and this is a demand from those to whom you owe everything you have and all that you might achieve in the future. Greet her fondly or–'

She did not complete the sentence, which was a clever way of allowing him to range over all the possible consequences without the need for a direct threat. Flavius was about to openly allude to warnings about mobs and the unpopularity of the imperial couple when the door opened once more to admit Antonina, who barefoot, skipped lightly across the marble floor in a manner more suitable to a young girl than a mature matron.

She had dressed simply for this occasion, in a

white garment of billowing soft material that showed the contours of her still impressive figure as she moved and Flavius was fleetingly reminded of the attraction he had felt for her on first acquaintance. Then in a display so contrived it nearly made him shout, she dropped to her knees at his feet and, grabbing both his hands, brought them together to repeatedly kiss them.

'If I have behaved less than well I beg your forgiveness, Husband. I admit to being a weak creature who is barely worthy of you.'

Again the tone was unbecoming for a woman her age, pitched too high as if her years had fallen away and she was yet to reach puberty. He was not looking at her, but at the agate eyes of Theodora, who had a forbidding smile on her face.

'What a heart of stone you must have, Flavius, if you can ignore such a plea.'

'Surely, Father, you did not forgive her?'

Rarely discomfited in the company of anyone, Flavius was that now and the incredulity in the voice of his stepson only made that more acute and that robbed his response of any veracity.

'If a person pleads, am I not allowed to grant such a thing?'

'Absolution for a whole raft of sins?'

'Had you been present, Photius, you too might have melted.'

'No, and for one very profound reason. My mother prevailed upon Theodora to command that Theodosius return to Constantinople.'

'You cannot know that.'

'I do because the culprit himself told me so.'

280

'You have seen Theodosius?'

Photius ignored the surprise on his stepfather's face, his own taking on a gloat that matched the tone of his voice. 'More than seen him, I have taken him prisoner. He could not run from me this time and I swear when he found me and my men outside his door he soiled himself.'

'Prisoner?'

'Yes. Right now he is in a cell which he shares with the rats, and all that money he stole I have given away. All I require now is an order from you and I will return and slit his gullet.'

Photius mistook the silence, not aware that Flavius was too shocked to speak, and he began to pace as he told a tale that clearly excited him, speaking quickly in short, near breathless bursts.

'I alerted him to his impending fate. He grabbed my knees and wept like a mewling baby. It was only luck that I caught him before he departed. The instruction from Theodora was in writing so he could not deny it. He did try, saying he intended to ignore it, as if he would. The man is not only an ingrate he is a cowardly weakling who lacks the will to die like a man.'

'Photius, stop. What you have done was not wise.'

'I have done that which is necessary. I will not see you humiliated any more.'

'Rather I was humiliated than that you should cross Theodora.'

'Damn Theodora!'

'No, Photius,' was the sad reply. 'More likely you have damned us both.'

The tale of what he had done was not long in

281

spreading; Theodora had sent a second demand to Ephesus that Theodosius should obey her summons only to have the messenger return with the story of what had occurred, Photius having shown no discretion in his actions; the taking of Antonina's paramour had been noisy and well witnessed.

Photius was arrested as soon as that messenger related his tale, while a body of Excubitors was sent to the *bucellarii* encampment to take up those who had aided him in the enterprise. They were brought back to Constantinople in chains and sent straight to the torture chamber where they revealed every detail, not that they could add much to what had already been extracted from Photius.

Flavius did not have to think too hard to discern what it was these torturers were after, a question that would have been put to them by Theodora. Had he ordered his stepson to act, or had it been done without his knowledge? To compound his discomfort, Theodosius was also back in the capital city having been rescued, and on the horns of a dilemma – he would himself be questioned – he had no one in the palace to whom he could confide the problem.

# CHAPTER TWENTY-ONE

There was no call to face either Justinian or Theodora. The act of enquiry was left to Narses and was carried out in an informal manner designed to put him at his ease. In that it failed: he was as nervous and alert as a cat.

'It is necessary to know the answer, Flavius Belisarius, a simple yes or no. Did you order your stepson to imprison your adopted son with the eventual aim of murdering him?'

If only I knew which one to give, Flavius thought. Say it was all the doing of Photius might put his life in danger but there was no way of knowing if that was true. Say he had ordered his stepson to act, as a means of saving him, was equally fraught for both of them. The game was a deadly one and he knew he was not well equipped to play it.

'Would I be allowed to ask what Photius faces?'

'You would if it had any bearing, but it does not.'

He had to assume that his stepson had taken all the blame upon himself, otherwise this interview would have been conducted in a different manner. It was the truth, yet if he agreed with that he might be condemning a young man whom he loved to an execution.

'Perhaps, Narses, given your circumstance, you might fail to appreciate the passions that can be aroused by what has taken place. Both Photius

283

and I have been shamed.'

'Did you order Photius to kill Theodosius?'

'Is that a question you would answer?'

'I am not being examined.'

Flavius made a point of looking around the empty chamber, his eyebrows raised. 'So it seems, neither am I. Where are the judges?'

'Allow that I will suffice.'

'I cannot do that without knowing what the outcome will be.'

'Strange justice when you require the sentence before the trial.'

'If there is to be a trial, then I will answer any question put to me. But you will forgive me, Narses, if I decline to tell a courtier, however powerful, that which I might impart in confidence to my emperor.'

'A person with too much to consider to be saddled with this.'

'I demand an audience.'

'Which will be denied.'

'Am I to return to my post without a consultation with the man who commands me?'

'Be assured he reads your despatches with great care.'

Which was as good a way of any of indicating to him he would indeed be returning to Dara. Was that a slip up from Narses or a pointer to what he was seeking? Would Justinian want a scandal, the same applying to Theodora? It was not impossible to execute Photius secretly, though there would be rumour and gossip, which must include his mother, and her friendship with the Empress being no secret, she might be tarred by it.

Secret retribution was not an outcome that could be applied to him; if he was to be punished it would have to be in full view of the populace and with all the reasons known. This private questioning indicated the imperial couple did not relish the affair becoming public and on that assumption he could give an answer. If he was wrong they could both suffer.

'I have many times threatened to kill Theodosius with my own hands, but I have spoken in a passion. To proceed from that to the act is a different matter, but I am willing to confess that had I been within striking distance of him I am not sure I could have restrained myself.'

'And Photius?'

'Acted as he saw it on my behalf, made as angry as I by the behaviour of his mother, while being equally wounded by the callousness of Theodosius.'

'So he determined to kill him.'

'He wished to do so, but he did not. He imprisoned him–'

'And impoverished him,' Narses interrupted.

'Then he came to me.'

'To ask for your approval of an action he has admitted he wished to carry out.'

'Approval which I declined to give him. And I say this, Narses. I know Photius. He would not have acted unless I gave him express permission to do so and I daresay when the hot irons were pressed to his flesh that is what he confessed to.'

'No order?'

'The reverse, Narses.'

Flavius nearly went on to say that he had

instructed Photius to free Theodosius but he stopped himself; he had not and he doubted if his stepson would have invented such a story, even under torture.

'You accept that your stepson committed a heinous crime?'

'I accept he acted foolishly but from laudable motives.'

'Theodosius says that Photius relished telling him that he was about to be killed on your orders.'

'A lie that would have no trouble passing such treacherous lips.'

The eunuch put a hand to his chin, to worry the flesh, and in doing so he dropped his eyes and remained in contemplation for some time, this while Flavius questioned his motives for being present. Had Justinian instructed him to it or was it an attempt to render the command on the eastern border untenable for a rival? If it was, Narses would be the natural replacement and Flavius knew from past experience he was militarily ambitious.

He was not given a clue; the eunuch stood up abruptly and left the chamber. In the following days no action was taken and finally he was summoned into the presence of Justinian, but not on his own. There were a number of his counsellors present and the subject was confined to the forthcoming campaign against Khusrow, should the Sassanid King invade again, as he was expected to do to both take plunder and put pressure on Constantinople to pay more gold.

Only at the very conclusion could Flavius ask for the release of Photius, and that in a whisper.

The response was a sharp head shake and a black look.

There were two factors mitigating against any attempt by Flavius to help Photius: his own public renown and time. In the latter case the kind of delays the bureaucracy imposed on him as he sought equipment was an aid not a hindrance; instead of an immediate return to the east he could move freely in the palace complex as he apparently sought to chivvy various officials into action when, in their presence, he seemed full of understanding for their difficulties.

The former was more troublesome, added to the possibility that Theodora, known to employ spies, was having him watched. Never had fame seemed to him so much of a burden. Flavius had never much cared for the kind of public approbation with which he was regularly assailed in the streets of the city on being recognised.

To walk the Triumphal Way as a successful soldier, a conqueror and newly appointed consul was one thing; in such a circumstance a cheering crowd was to be expected. To be applauded for merely passing by seemed crass, he being unware that it was the very fact of his walking amongst the citizenry without pomp or protection that added lustre to his reputation for humility and probity.

He was at least relieved of the presence of Antonina, who preferred the royal apartments close to the Empress against residence at the seaside villa, not for reasons of comfort but because Theodosius was once more in Constantinople. Her behaviour was once more a standing rebuke to his soft nature, as if the imprisoned stepson was not an even greater running sore.

To do anything himself was impossible; even to plead for clemency was likely to produce an effect directly contrary to that aimed at, and in this he had to face the combination of the Empress and his wife. Antonina in particular was determined that Photius should be punished for his attitude to her over many years. She had openly advocated, he had been told, thankfully to no avail, that the torture he had suffered should be continued.

His only hope was old comrades. The city was full of men who had served with him, the kind of middle-ranking officers that he had always taken care to look after so that they too would attend to the needs of those they led. Anyone of high rank he could not approach, they being inclined to put their career way ahead of any perceived debt they owed to their one-time general, an understandable response, if one he found frustrating.

To meet the men he needed to talk with required the kind of subterfuge at which he might be a master on the battlefield but was anathema in normal life. He was obliged to leave the villa not only in darkness but in a covered wagon, this while the house behind him was fully illuminated by burning oil lamps, with busy servants much in evidence.

Under the canvas canopy Flavius was dressed in a heavy, hooded cloak as a double precaution, his exit swift and taken just as the wagon turned a corner so that anyone following would be unsighted. This found him in a familiar setting, if one he had not visited for a decade.

The streets in the dock area were narrow, dark and stinking, the only light, and a gloomy one at that, coming from the sconces above the various tavern and brothel doorways. His choice of destination had been advised by Solomon, who knew more of the habits of the men Flavius sought than did their one-time commander. His experience of this area had been in the company of the pre-imperial Justinian and the elevated types with whom he associated, their pleasures taken in the most salubrious of the establishments.

Once he had found the basement he was seeking, care had to continue to be exercised. The tavern was crowded, it being a haunt for soldiers, not dock workers or itinerant sailors, and the fug set up by the burning of cheap oil did much to add gloom to the light such lamps were supposed to emit. This made finding a table at which to sit difficult, compounded by the need to examine those who would be his neighbours before he could park his backside on a bench.

Still hooded he was on the receiving end of many a stare, for what was common outside on a winter night was not the same within, which meant the cowl had to be removed, but not before the low-beamed room had been the subject of a ranging examination. The act of throwing it off was a calculated risk, given his face was known to many, but most customers were too engrossed in their own affairs to even look in his direction.

The tavern was small and made to seem more so by the fact of being busy. The tables were packed close and at one end lay a tiny clear area in which there would probably be dancing and maybe more lewd demonstrations. There was a rickety staircase leading, he surmised, to cubicles, for this place would act too as a brothel. It was impossible to avoid reflecting that if both the Empress and his wife had come from a better class of establishment, this was the kind of life they had lived prior to the good fortune brought on by Theodora's marriage.

The sudden burst of loud singing, being in Latin, had him spin to place it, the tune itself being one he recognised, having heard it many times as he walked the lines of his encamped soldiery. The words were filthy, raucous and ultimately blasphemous but that mattered less than the nature of the source. Flavius waited until he had been provided with a pitcher of wine before he moved towards the now silent singers, picking up the tones of their rough exchanges, traded insults that created much amusement.

The table was too crowded to allow him to sit, each bench fully occupied by a set of scarred individuals, all in some kind of apparel that identified them as military: tunics, a breastplate or two and the odd removed helmet. Experience told Flavius that there would be a hierarchy, if not in rank then in personality; there always was in any group of soldiers and the man with the loudest voice, sat at the head of the table, seemed to be that and was thus the object of his stare.

At first the reaction to that was a look of fury, for the gape would seem like a challenge. That only lasted a second before the eyes began to narrow and the man leant forward slightly to add a keen look. Those same eyes soon went wide and so did the fellow's mouth, whatever he was about to emit silenced by the finger at the mouth of Flavius Belisarius.

The reaction had been observed by his companions, which brought a small oasis of silence in the noisy room, one that allowed Flavius to ask for permission to sit, which was quickly ordered by the man at the table head and obeyed by his companions, several of whom were now staring open-mouthed at their new companion, who placed his pitcher of wine on the bare wood and spoke in Latin.

'It is a poor guest who does not come with gifts.'

'A Greek habit, Excellence,' intoned the leader, 'from ancient times.'

There was wit as well as shrewdness in that response; the man was saying to Flavius that his presence in such a place, added to the manner of approach, smacked of dangerous subterfuge.

'You would honour me more by not using titles or names.' That got a sharp nod followed by a glare that encompassed the whole group of eight men. 'You would also honour me by naming yourselves, since to my shame, though I seem to recognise several faces, I cannot put a tag on them.'

They tumbled out, each spoken in a near whisper. Colonus, Euphrastes, a pair called Brennus, and the rest he missed. It was Colonus who had the air of leadership Flavius sought, and with politely phrased requests he moved until they were sat close.

'I heard you sing in Latin.'

'It is our tongue, General.'

291

'Do I sense Illyricum in your accent?'

'It takes a sharp ear to detect that.'

'Not to one raised by Illyrian parents, Colonus.'

The whole table had gone quiet, which was inclined to attract more attention than any amount of noise. Again Colonus showed a shrewd appreciation, making a loud toast, taken up by his fellows, that followed by a bark to keep talking. Then he brought his head close to that of his one-time general.

'I am bound to ask why you are here.'

'As I must ask what is known of my troubles.'

The pause was of no great length, but it was significant and made more so by what followed. 'Word is you sent your lad Photius to murder a fellow who was...'

'Dallying with my wife,' Flavius said, finishing a sentence with the words Colonus was clearly too embarrassed or cautious to utter. 'So it is common gossip?'

'Aye.'

'And?'

'Not a man at this table would not do likewise, though they would strike the blow themselves.'

The tone of that alerted Flavius to the undercurrent of what was being implied: that if he was being cuckolded, then it was a matter he should have sorted out himself and not given over to another.

'If I was to swear, Colonus, that no such order was given, would you believe me? I would not imperil my soul by cold-blooded murder.'

'It would be a fool who doubted the word of–' The sharp headshake stopped the indiscretion;

292

even whispered, Flavius saw the use of his name as dangerous, which allowed Colonus to finish with, 'a man such as yourself.'

'You served me in Italy, I think.'

'The whole table did, though we came with Narses.'

It seemed politic to enquire more, and to include his companions in a recollection of their service. There was also a possibility that these men formed part of the Narses *comitatus*, and if they did their loyalty to the eunuch would be absolute. That fear was laid to rest by some of the choice insults aimed at the man who had brought them to Italy from Illyricum and to comparisons with their better treatment once he had gone home.

They had been withdrawn not long after Flavius himself departed Ravenna and now formed some of the garrison of the capital, none too happy since there were no spoils in such a duty. Such general information flowed for a while, but Flavius was aware that Colonus was no longer taking part, and in a lull the man who had been identified as the senior centurion posed the obvious question.

'I need help, Colonus, and I am prepared to pay a sum you would never chance upon even if you took Croesus himself prisoner.'

'Then it is help that comes with great risk.' Flavius nodded and Colonus fell silent for a while. When he did speak he again showed that he had a brain. 'This duty has to be about your stepson.'

'He is in prison – I want him freed and I cannot do that by mere pleading.'

'By violence?'

'That would be to invite certain death. He is

beneath the palace and even if I know you to be hardy fighters you cannot take on the whole regiment of Excubitors.'

'Then it has to be bribes.'

'I would say so.'

Colonus fell silent again, though he again waved his hands to have his companions keep up their faux enjoyment. To concentrate his mind Flavius produced a soft leather pouch, which when he laid it on the table, testified to the weight of its contents by the telling thud.

'We could take that and do nothing.'

'You could, Colonus, and that also tells you I am short on alternatives.'

'And how do I convince you that is not a waste?'

The glance at the purse meant no further explanation was required.

'Are you free to visit the barracks at Galatea?'

'I am when off duty.'

'Tomorrow?' A nod. 'I will be there visiting the wounded I sent back from Dara. I will not be hard to find for a centurion wishing to pay his respects to a man who once led him in battle. There we can talk freely and I can advise you on how you can do that which is barred to me. If you are not there, then I will know this was a waste. If you are, what you see is but a down payment on a far greater sum.'

Flavius was halfway to standing, and aware of the combined stares of men who had once more fallen silent. Still he addressed Colonus, and softly, his hand over the leather pouch.

'One piece of advice from a fellow soldier. It'd be wise to share your good fortune with some of your companions. This is no task for one man.'

There was no need to add more and the look in the other man's eyes said plainly he understood.

Flavius Belisarius had no need to explain his presence in a military camp, least of all the near permanent base at Galatea. It was there Colonus found him, to be introduced to Solomon who would from now on be the Illyrian centurion's point of contact, and that at arm's length. He was given a sketch plan of lower floors of the palace and it was established that the way to get Photius free would require a combination of money, guile and perhaps some physical force.

'The thought of that does not daunt you?' Flavius asked.

'If it did, General, I would never take part in a battle, would I?'

'How many of last night's companions have you included?'

'The whole table.' Seeing the raised eyebrow and the implied point that excessive numbers could be dangerous, Colonus was quick to add, 'Might need every one.'

Once Colonus had departed Flavius was left alone with Solomon, who even if he said nothing, showed in his expression severe doubts as to the chance of success. Flavius had a different opinion.

'I have often had cause to thank God for my luck, but never more so than now. It must have been his hand that guided me so quickly to these men. With that, I am sure his grace will attend to what must be achieved.'

Solomon crossed himself.

# CHAPTER TWENTY-TWO

Whatever concerns Flavius had travelled east with him, but the duty he found there put the problem of Photius into the background, to only surface when he received a coded message from Solomon to say that the first attempt at freeing him had failed. Lacking details that induced frustration, there was at least some reassurance that the men Flavius had engaged seemed determined to keep trying.

His first task was to reassert control over generals who had lost the habit of obedience over the months of winter. Thus he declined to agree to a request by Bouzes and his co-commander Justus, an imperial nephew, that he come to them, they having retired to Hierapolis well away from any possible zone of battle. They were quickly ordered to concentrate on the location he chose, one well placed to contest ground with the enemy.

The main problem, as before, lay with the intentions of Khusrow; his movements dictated those of the Byzantine army, which was not organised to invade Sassanid territory, this due to the continued prevalence of the plague, a situation which had deteriorated since the previous year. It now seemed to affect much of the area of his military responsibilities all the way to the Mediterranean shore, though his army seemed relatively healthy.

Even so, Flavius split his troops into small packets to contain the risk of the disease spreading – which once caught was too often fatal – his aim to bring them together only when he was sure he would face an enemy. This blight, equally visited upon the Sassanids, was in his favour and with Khusrow moving his army within areas of infection that must expose his soldiers to greater risk.

As well as manoeuvring, the Sassanid King was busy complaining, sending messages to Flavius that he had anticipated ambassadors with which to treat. If he hinted at peace he was really interested in the amount of gold he could extract for abandoning Byzantine possessions. Flavius wanted him out, but he had no desire to bribe him to depart.

Having extracted an agreement from Justinian that no ambassadors would be despatched, he had undertaken to deal with Khusrow at no charge on the overstretched imperial coffers, though he had no faith that the Emperor would not bow to pressure from those on his council who saw bribery as the only answer to border incursions, wherever they took place.

Khusrow was advancing along the Euphrates again, using the river, fast flowing during late spring, to protect his right flank. Then he swung south to invest the city of Sergiopolis. As reported to Flavius, it transpired that the priest of that city, a divine called Candidus, had the previous year agreed to pay ransom for Sergiopolis but had reneged, which was enough to enrage a king who loved nothing more than money.

Being in no position to satisfy the renewed

297

demand, Candidus had gone to the Sassanid King to plead poverty, only to be much tortured for his transgressions. When, with hot irons applied, he finally offered to pay he was abruptly informed that the amount required was twice that originally promised, a sum he had finally promised to procure from the treasures of Sergiopolis.

'If anyone should be able to hold out under torture it is a priest.'

This opinion advanced by Bouzes was one with which Flavius was disinclined to support: too many of the divines he had encountered would sell their soul to avoid discomfort, never mind pain. In any case, Candidus had promised more than the city could deliver and that led to a siege, one only lifted when the Sassanids' supply of water became so depleted – all the wells were within the walls – they could no longer keep fit their horses and Khusrow was obliged to retire to the banks of the Euphrates.

He was now moving into the region of Commagene, on a southerly route that would eventually lead him to Jerusalem, a city so long at peace and so much a source of pilgrimage that it presented a fabulously rich prize. To counter this Flavius moved his army to a point that threatened the Sassanid road back to their own possessions, one they would be obliged to take even if their incursion was a success, though he made no attempt to follow them.

His deployment was enough to stop the Sassanid advance as Khusrow pondered how to counter this move, with the added problem, passed to Flavius by his spies, that plague was seriously affecting his forces. Flavius decided to ask him to send an envoy who would agree a way of getting his disease-ridden army home, a tactic not universally approved of, the compliant being aired by the imperial nephew when the senior commanders came together.

'The best way to achieve such an aim is to defeat them.'

'I promised your uncle to remove Khusrow from his domains. How I do that has been left to my judgement.'

Bouzes, equal in rank to Justus but much more experienced, spoke to back up Flavius. 'Remember the plague, Justus. To fight we must concentrate our own forces and then do battle with foes who are racked with the disease. That brings with it the risk of contamination. We could lose half the army.'

'A risk I am willing to accept.'

'Generous of you to do so on behalf of those you lead,' was the less than tactful response.

'Glory is all very well, Justus,' Flavius added in a more emollient tone. 'But take it from one who knows, success is sweeter, however you come by it.'

Regardless of sickness, Khusrow had to be wary of moving deeper into Byzantine territory with an army across his line of retreat. A message came to announce an envoy was on his way and while that was happening he undertook not to move. The question troubling Flavius was simple: if he wanted to avoid a battle, what could he do to convince the Sassanid invader that he would be best back in the safety of his own domains?

In terms of force numbers the two armies were fairly evenly matched, but the problem of disease dominated his thinking and that same difficulty must prey on the mind of his opponent. However, if Khusrow could be convinced his enemies were fit and free from the plague he would be doubly cautious about meeting them.

'I need the very best physical specimens you have. The tallest, the stockiest and the most martial-looking and none of them showing any signs of sickness.'

'To fight?' asked Justus hopefully.

'No, we are going to hunt.' There was pleasure to be had in the confusion this caused as Flavius added, 'No armour is to be worn, just leathers for the chase. Make sure the horses they have are the fleetest of animals too, not heavy cavalry mounts.'

The pavilion Flavius had erected, bordering a forest and set of hills known to be full of game, was magnificent and decorated with numerous colourful standards. He filled the interior with tables at which the men hunting could consume that which they caught, the food prepared by a positive army of cooks, necessary since by the time all the men Flavius wanted had been gathered they numbered over a thousand – a risk, but one it seemed reasonable to take.

The proportion of barbarians was high: Flavius's Goth levies from Italy, Vandals and Moors from North Africa, Heruls from the north Balkans, Gepids and Gautoi from across the Rhine, they the best of the physical specimens on show. There were large wooden tuns of wine and the assembled men were encouraged to drink it, though in quantities that would not affect their ability to ride. Their general wanted them cheerful!

Flavius had scouts out to alert him to the approach of the Sassanid envoy; this was a show and one that must be in progress as soon as the man came into view. What he would observe first would be the sheer quantity of tents. Closer to he would see parties of huntsmen coming and going, while from the scaffolds they had set up hung the carcasses of the most recent catch: deer, antelopes and the odd bear. He was lucky with the wind too, which blew into the face of the approaching party, carrying the smell of meat cooking over charcoal into their nostrils.

The man who greeted the envoy was himself in hunting clothes and full of good humour, speaking in Greek, not his favoured Latin, which was in sharp contrast to the man he addressed. He was named Abandanes, known to be a close advisor to Khusrow and a fellow in whose wisdom the King reposed great faith. Invited to enter the pavilion, Flavius led him to a private chamber shut off from the main space, a room filled with fine furniture and fabulous hangings depicting scenes of the chase from classical times.

'Do you hunt, Abandanes?'

'No,' came the astonished response; that was not a question he was expecting and nor was he of a build that indicated he had ever been sporting. He had the look of an indoor man, with his pale skin, loose jowls and bulk.

'Pity, I have rarely seen a forest so teeming with opportunities as the one close by.'

'I have not come upon such a frivolous purpose.'

'It is good that soldiers have pleasure as well as duties. They fight better when they are merry.'

Flavius invited the envoy to sit, which Abandanes, being older and clearly quite unsuited to the ride he had been obliged to make, sank into gratefully. He had hardly made contact with the chair before he was off on his king's favourite mantra, which was how easy it would have been to avoid conflict if only Justinian had sent the men needed to negotiate.

'I bear the rank of *magister*, Abandanes, and I am empowered to treat with you on behalf of the Emperor.'

'With respect, Flavius Belisarius,' came the smooth and condescending reply, 'this is not a matter for the military. I mean no disrespect when I say that more subtle minds are required.'

'But peace is easy, Abandanes. All your master has to do is to lead his armies back into his own domains.'

The older man produced one of those smiles that hinted at intricacies too obscure for a mere soldier. 'You do not consider he has grounds to be where he is?'

'Clearly you do.'

'Promises have been made—'

It was not tactful to interrupt but given he was accused of being a mere soldier Flavius had no hesitation in doing so, added to which his voice was not as gentle as this fellow felt he had a right to expect.

'Not promises, Abandanes! Proposals, at best.'

'I fail to detect a difference. Or is it the intention of the Emperor to dangle mere carrots.'

302

'We generally reserve those for our horses.'

That the older was offended by the jest pleased Flavius; he wanted him to be, though the impression of success was fleeting. The man was a diplomat and high in the counsels of his ruler, so he knew well how to respond with grace.

'You are not known for being a player with words, Flavius Belisarius. It will please me to report back to my king that you have that gift.'

The thundering of horses' hooves took the attention of both men, with Flavius abruptly standing. 'Join me, Abandanes, let us see what the latest hunting party has brought in.'

'I prefer to keep talking.'

'I must insist. My men would want no less than my admiration for their exploits and yours will only add to their joy.'

Unhappily obliged to concede, Abandanes followed Flavius out to where a party of Vandals, sat astride foam-flecked horses, were proudly showing the carcass of a lion as well as the still bleeding wound by which it had been slain.

'A single thrust by one hunter,' Flavius explained when the event had been described to him. 'A Vandal used to hunting the beasts in their own lands. I am blessed with so many good men but they may be the best.'

The envoy was near to surrounded and whichever way he looked he could see fit and strong soldiers, some dark-skinned like the Moors, others with the flaxen hair and reddened skin of the very far north, and added to that there was everything in between from within and beyond the bounds of empire.

'You have travelled a great distance today, Abandanes. I suggest that you eat with me, then rest. The light will be gone soon and you will witness how my barbarians entertain themselves. As for parleying, that can wait until the morrow.'

The planting of the information had been prepared in advance. Flavius was sure that a man like Abandanes would despatch his attendants into the encampment to seek out a friendly eye in the hope that it was conjoined with a loose tongue. An eager retainer came back to the guest tents and soon Abandanes himself was on the move. No attempt was made to stop him and Flavius was gratified to observe that on his return he looked very unhappy indeed.

'Time to invite him to dine, I think, Bouzes.'

'He has heard?'

'By his miserable face, I would say yes.'

'Is he soldier enough to understand?'

'There is no need for military knowledge to know that Khusrow's options have been severely amended.'

The Sassanid King had only two routes back to safety and one of them he had already traversed, leaving it, as his army lived off the land, barren of supply. If the ploy had played out properly, Abandanes had been told that Flavius had put a strong force of cavalry across the only other path and at a place where, with the need to traverse a narrow ravine, superior numbers would count for nothing.

That left the choice of a full battle, always risky, doubly so against the only general that seemed able to beat the Sassanids. It was that or a negotiated way past a force that was sufficient to pin him in a bad place, one made precarious as Flavius could come upon his rear. It was telling that the subject of negotiation did not arise as they ate, yet despite his best efforts to hide it, Abandanes was clearly worried.

Flavius was the very opposite; he was jovial and a good host as he enquired of the family of the man he was entertaining, at the same time lamenting the problems Khusrow had with all the tribes that bordered his lands to the east and north, these being difficulties shared in many cases by Byzantium.

He felt he had every right to be merry; even if Khusrow chose battle he would do so on Byzantine soil, and outside a catastrophe Flavius could suffer a reverse and still retire on any number of fortresses. His opponent risked much more: if he was defeated or even obliged just to surrender the field he would have to retreat over many leagues at the head of a beaten army, short of morale, and with his enemy on his tail.

A whole day went by in fruitless talking as Abandanes and Flavius went through the motions of diplomatic exchange that both knew had no purpose. There was talk but no guarantees that Khusrow would retire in peace, merely suggestions, and should he do so the Sassanids could expect that Justinian might finally appoint ambassadors to talk of what price the empire would be willing to pay for an end to conflict.

Flavius agreed that this was possible but was adamant he could not commit Justinian to anything, for to do so would step on the imperial prerogative. It truth, both men knew matters would be decided when Khusrow was apprised of his situation and not before. Naturally Abandanes was sent home with gifts, fresh skins from every beast the forests nearby contained, as well as a valuable statue that had once been the property of Khusrow's father, Kavadh. It was one of the spoils of the Battle of Dara.

'Not very subtle,' Bouzes observed as they watched the envoy's caravan depart.

'It's not meant to be. It does no harm to remind our foes I once beat them.'

The scouts sent to observe the movements of the enemy reported that, after only a few days, they were heading east and their direction would bring them into conflict with Justus. Flavius issued orders to the imperial nephew to get out of Khusrow's path, with an additional threat to send him back to Justinian in chains if he disobeyed. Then he brought together his own forces but made no move to advance and impede the enemy.

Those same watchers observed the Sassanids throw a bridge across the Euphrates and only then did Flavius move, to make his presence felt on their rear and chivvy them on. He too crossed the river to maintain the pressure. A message came from Khusrow claiming to have met his part of a bargain never agreed, to which Flavius responded by requesting he keep moving east.

Once out of Byzantine territory he then undertook to send the news to Justinian with a request that the ambassadorial demand be met, as long as no Byzantine property was damaged by the retiring army. To save face, Khusrow demanded a hostage; Flavius was happy to oblige for he had achieved his entire aim, and that long before the campaigning season was complete.

He had chased Justinian's enemies out of the imperial lands and it had cost not a drop of blood or a speck of gold. Task complete, Flavius retired with his army to Edessa in Mesopotamia, central to his area of responsibility, sure that his enemy would retire to Persia.

Khusrow, no doubt to save face, took advantage of the lack of Byzantine pressure to sack the city of Callinicum, this before he announced his intention to observe the peace, which brought from his opponent a rare outburst of fulmination at the perfidy of the Sassanid dynasty.

The sight of Solomon approaching the gubernatorial palace of Edessa, a sorely missed man, had Flavius examining his expression long before they were close to each other. Not wanting to betray even a clue as to what had happened, his master was surrounded by high-ranking officers as well as his bodyguard, the *domesticus* merely nodded in a manner which was enough to tell his master that Photius was free, a whispered explanation later explaining it had taken four attempts before it had been successful.

'His health?' he asked once they were alone.

'Damaged, *Magister*. The tormentors worked on him hard.'

The excuse of another more private hunt was contrived and both men set out with a small group of Flavius's personal followers at dawn so their general could rendezvous with his stepson, not that they were given a chance to observe the meeting, being halted well away from the church in which he was hiding.

What Solomon had said did not do any justice to the truth. Photius was gaunt and if his face was much scarred it could only be guessed at how wracked had been his body, less fulsome than it had been, obvious when they embraced, indicating skin and bone. Even his voice was different, no longer strong but hoarse, that matched by a tearful Flavius who knew what he must say and had no joy in the delivery.

'I cannot take you back into my service, Photius.'

That got a wan smile. 'I would scarce be of use to you and know I must continue my journey, Father.'

'To where?'

'Jerusalem, where I will seek sanctuary in a monastery in the hope that my mother and her evil twin will leave me in peace.'

'Never have I wanted to harm her more.'

'Yet I know you. You will leave her punishment to God.'

'I beg you write to me. No name but I will know it to be you.'

Solomon had removed himself and father and beloved stepson spent a full glass of sand quietly talking, recalling better times until finally it was time to pray for a better future. Photius would wait until Flavius and his party were well away from the tiny chapel before moving on, all his stepfather could do as a last gesture being to make sure he did not lack for funds.

'My needs will be little now. No weapons or armour, or even a horse. A donkey at best, that and a plain garment.'

A final embrace, a parting without looking back and no doubt an escort wondering why their normally buoyant general was silent and seemingly cast down in despair, which lasted even when the sun went down and they made their way by the moon and stars. Flavius arrived back in Edessa well after midnight to find the palace a blaze of light and, given the varying guards assembled outside, full of his senior officers.

Bouzes was outside and he spoke as soon as Flavius dismounted before the stairway. 'Word from Constantinople, *Magister*. The plague has reached the city and is raging.'

That did not surprise Flavius, but the concerned expression on the face of Bouzes hinted at more. 'One of the afflicted is Justinian.'

## CHAPTER TWENTY-THREE

The implications of that did not require explanation; both men had seen too much death at the hands of that affliction to be aware of the potential consequences. From the first signs of lassitude they had seen men develop the swellings that presaged a serious illness rather than minor distress. Then came the shaking as even on a hot day a man could complain of being chilled, followed by pain in fingers, nose and toes as they turned black, another sign only too familiar to a fighting soldier who had seen his comrades require limbs to be removed after a battle to save their lives.

Strong men cried in agony at the pain they were subjected to from limbs that grew increasingly stiff. Those close by them, men in their ten-man *decharchia* or their camp wives, knew the disease to be entering the fatal stage when they began to cough up black blood or dark spots appeared on their yellowing skin. Sometimes those close by, fearful for their own lives, tossed such victims into the specially dug plague pits before the final signs of life were extinguished.

The other obvious worry was time; if the Emperor had fallen victim to the plague, the time taken to get the news to Edessa might mean he was already dead and the implications again required little discussion: the imperial throne was empty and there was only one person well placed to act upon that.

'In your absence I called a conference of senior officers and we agreed that the Empress Theodora should not be allowed to promote a candidate.'

'It sounds like Zeno and Anastatius all over again,' Flavius said, with a slow shake of the head.

'Can you not see it bodes ill for you, *Magister*?'

'Worry less about me and more about the empire, Bouzes.' Then he lifted his eyes and looked at his leading general. 'Where does Justus stand in this?'

'With all of us. He knows the Hippodrome will never acclaim him. He is too young and lacks

310

support. But you...?'

That got a wry smile. 'Whoever thought it could become a habit, turning down imperial titles?'

'We cannot let Theodora choose Justinian's successor.'

Again the point was driven home; without her husband Theodora had little bordering on no power, added to a raft of enemies who would be only too eager to extract retribution for the way she had used her influence to impoverish and isolate them. Her fate would not be mere removal from authority – she was too much loathed by the mob for that – so it would take little for those who hated her to whip up the kind of multitude that would see her torn apart.

That she would naturally stop at nothing to avoid, added to which the path to safety was no mystery. When the Emperor Zeno died his consort felt equally at risk, although she had fewer high officials antagonistic towards her. With no obvious candidate to succeed Zeno she had married handsome Anastatius and had him commended then accepted in the Hippodrome.

Theodora would do likewise but more tellingly, without Justinian to restrain her, she would be swift to kill off anyone she thought threatened her ability to continue to rule. If imperial authority ever seemed arbitrary there were checks on a monarch's power making it dangerous to alienate too many potential adversaries.

Justinian had known that, which is why his reforms, though effective, had moved at the pace of a snail. His wife would not be so restrained and that had the potential to throw the whole polity into something akin to a civil war. Quite apart from the obvious bloodletting of internal dissension, Khusrow would be quick to take advantage and he might, in an interregnum, be granted the chance to conquer at will.

'It was unanimous, Flavius. In the case of an imperial vacancy the Army of the East will support your candidacy.'

'Officers of the Army of the East,' Flavius responded, his caution plain.

'We do not need to ask the soldiers. They will acclaim you as soon as they hear that Justinian is no more. And who do you think can stand in Constantinople against the only high-ranking person who can walk the street unescorted and be cheered by the populace for doing so?'

'The devil is in your very words, Bouzes. If Justinian is no more?'

'How many survive the plague?'

'Some do and he will have the best attention a man can be granted. Perhaps he will even have divine aid.'

That got a jaundiced look from Bouzes; to him, Justinian was more likely to seek that from Satan than God. 'I ask that you enter the tent now, Flavius, so that you can see the temper of those you lead.'

'I am weary, Bouzes, and for reasons other than merely too much time spent on horseback.'

'Your officers are waiting to acclaim you as their emperor.'

Bouzes was clearly frustrated but he was up against the immovable force of one who was not inclined to act when uncertain, either as a general or a man. 'A night of sleep and contemplation will alter little.'

'Can I say to them that the notion is not one you entirely reject?'

It was Ravenna all over again to Flavius and he knew Bouzes was right. On the assumption Justinian had died, Theodora would have to be thwarted and he was the man best placed to do it. Once more he had to find an answer that satisfied without making a commitment.

'Should that come to pass which we fear, I will not shirk my duty, wherever that takes me. Tell our comrades that.'

Solomon had proceeded straight to Flavius's own quarters and got ready a deep tub of hot water in which his master could bathe off the grime of his day's travels, this after several cups of wine chilled by mountain ice. Sat in that, with more water being added at intervals, he had much to contemplate and it was doubly depressing that he lacked the company of Photius, with whom he could at least speculate out loud. Not that his stepson would urge caution; quite the reverse, he would be hot in favour even if it came to bloody usurpation.

Of course, if Justinian was dead and he was acclaimed as emperor – not an outcome he entirely thought of as welcome – then Photius could be brought back to Constantinople as a free man, his crimes forgiven. That led to thoughts of Antonina; how would she react to her husband being elevated and how would that test her loyalty to Theodora? Would their positions be reversed?

'*Magister!*'

The gentle shake from Solomon brought him out of a deep slumber and a lubricious dream in which he had assumed the purple and surrounded himself with a whole tribe of comely young concubines eager to satisfy his every whim. The erection he had was not induced by fantasies of sexual gratification but by the need to relieve himself, so naked and hardly dried, he went on to the balcony to piss under a canopy of stars as well as a low moon.

Inevitably he looked to the heavens as if seeking guidance, and what hit home then was the weight of responsibility that might be placed on his shoulders. If Justinian had found it difficult to rule with ease, how much more so would he? That he had no desire for the office meant little, for if he shied away from his responsibilities to the empire that could bring on chaos as factions fought for power.

If his whole life had been dedicated to serving the empire and its ruler he would be a coward indeed if he shirked this most onerous of obligations. There in the inky sky, to his troubled mind, lay the soul of Decimus Belisarius looking down on his son and his dilemma, but of guidance there was none. Realising he had been stood for a long time after he had completed the reason for being out in the open, Flavius addressed a heartfelt plea to the place where he assumed the deity he worshipped resided.

'Dear God, if you can find it in your compassion to save Justinian, I beg you do so.'

Such a plea did not obviate the need to face his officers once they assembled the next morning, and as he entered the audience chamber it seemed to him that they stiffened with a greater degree of respect than they had hitherto shown, as if they already thought they were looking at their sovereign. Even Justus, who as an imperial nephew might harbour resentments, was gazing on him with open respect, this as Bouzes stepped forward and, on receipt of a nod from Flavius, began to speak.

'It is our belief, *Magister*, that a message be sent immediately to Constantinople and to the Empress Theodora to say that no candidate of hers will be acceptable to us. To also say that if she has already acted, whatever has been decided will be annulled.'

'You do not fear that to be premature?'

'How can it be?' Bouzes barked. He had always been of a bellicose nature and had the physical attributes that went with it: stocky build, a square face of reddened skin and eyes that could actually flash with anger. 'Can you not see that one of her first acts will be to kill you?'

'You cannot know that.'

'If she wishes to live herself, then she will feel she must.'

A murmur of agreement followed that statement, which had Flavius holding up his hand. 'Let me speak, my friends, please?'

That was sophistry; they had assembled for the sole purpose of hearing him and Bouzes was not the only one seemingly frustrated at what was seen to be prevarication. They wanted Flavius to declare himself, not for his sake but for their own. Like all men, they craved certainty and added to

315

that there would be no lack of ambition; an Emperor Flavius would elevate those he trusted.

'We know that Justinian is afflicted just as I know, that like me, in your nightly prayers, you begged that he should recover.'

It was hard not to be amused at the differing reactions that engendered; there would be those present who had entered such pleas on the mere grounds of Christian convention, perhaps even one or two who wholeheartedly meant it. At the opposite end of the spectrum would be the men who saw the elevation of their general as a chance for personal advancement. A recovery of his full health by Justinian was not one to entice them to genuine prayer. What Flavius had to disguise was his own reaction to their confusion.

'But know this. Should God not grant such a dispensation, I will not stand by to see the office of emperor filled by convenience.'

'You will act?' Bouzes demanded, on behalf of them all.

'For the sake of the empire. Now, first we must send a carefully worded despatch back to the capital and the Empress, with a plea for the recovered health of her husband but also with the counsel that no precipitate act should be contemplated.'

'Tell them you will put yourself forward, *Magister*,' cried Justus loudly.

Was that too eager, an attempt to deflect any suspicion of personal ambition? Flavius thought not; the look that accompanied the words was too genuine.

'There is no need to state the obvious, Justus.

Theodora does not lack for brains. She will know that the consequences of seeking to retain power might end badly for her and will value her life above everything.'

'I know you, Flavius,' Bouzes called, again with an angry face and so fired by passion as to eschew his title in place of familiarity. 'You will spare the sorceress.'

'Again, there is no need to state the obvious.'

He was trying to tell them another palpable fact: that if Justinian did recover what had been discussed in this tent would not be seen in a kindly light, which is why he spent the whole day writing and rewriting his despatch until he was sure it would do as required. It was from him to the palace and under his seal and he gave it to the man charged to carry it personally.

The messengers would have passed each other, perhaps they had even spent the same night in one of the imperial posthouses along the route. Yet they would not have exchanged notice of what they carried, that being a stricture religiously observed. The fellow that entered the portals of Edessa brought what to Flavius was good news.

Justinian had survived the worst of his affliction and was now on the way to recovery. Even in his wildest flights of fancy he could not have imagined how different was the response to the communication to which he had appended his seal. The Emperor was still too ill to transact business of any kind; the despatch went to Theodora and, as Flavius had pointed out, she was no fool, added to which she had lost nothing.

Narses arrived within two weeks, his instructions to both Bouzes and Flavius were abrupt: they were to return to Constantinople without delay and explain to the imperial estate the meaning of their presumption. The word 'estate' told both men that if they were to be examined it would not be by an advocate appointed by Justinian but by his furious consort.

That she would know of the meetings held in the Palace of Edessa was obvious and no doubt, too, she would be aware of what had been discussed down to the very words used. If she did not have spies with the army, highly likely given her previous behaviour, then there were enough people writing to their relatives who would have picked up information while the matter lay in doubt to give her chapter and verse.

'You will go back under individual escort,' Narses pronounced with harsh glee, 'so there will be no chance to collude and concoct some tale to save your skins.'

'You are so sure they require saving, Narses?'

'*Magister?*' asked Bouzes, his red face for once pallid.

Flavius knew for what he was asking. Bouzes wanted him to arrest Narses then pronounce a rebellion, something he could not even contemplate. In declining he was condemning himself and Bouzes to an uncertain fate. How could he convey by a mere look that what Bouzes was asking for was impossible, and not just for him?

The army might well have acclaimed him and backed his cause with Justinian dead but it would not do the same if he still lived. There was a huge

318

difference between a just act to prevent an out-rage and outright rebellion, and he would never ask for such a pledge.

To do so would turn the whole empire against them and initiate the civil war he had feared if Theodora had acted precipitously. Men who might have stood aside and allowed his candidacy to proceed would not be so inclined if he rebelled. Like Vitalian, the insurrectionist general he had first followed as a youth, he might find himself outside the mighty walls of Constantinople with the entire establishment of the empire, military and civilian, ranged against him. Others might claim a citizenry willing to offer support; they did not count, and anyway only a fool would place reliance on such a fickle entity.

'It is an imperial command, Bouzes, and one we are bound to obey.'

The look Narses gave him then was one that chilled his blood.

'There were those who said I was taking a risk coming here as I have. I was able to tell them, Flavius Belisarius, that I know you too well to be fearful of you. You lack the stomach for hazard.'

'Perhaps when they make you consul you can pronounce that from the oration platform.' That dig struck home; no eunuch had ever been afforded that honorary rank and he doubted any one of their number ever would. 'And then there is the other pity, Narses: you will be unable to tell your children and grandchildren what a genius you are.'

'I look forward to you having to eat those words.'

'Do so. Now, if you will excuse me I must request that my *domesticus* make arrangements for us to travel.'

As he passed Bouzes, Flavius spoke softly. 'We did nothing of which we can be ashamed.'

The growl he got back was louder. 'In your mind perhaps, Flavius, but you will not be the one judging them.'

Narses must have made the necessary arrangements on the way; in the grounds of each imperial *mansio*, residences specifically set aside for travelling high officials, a separate tent had been erected into which each general was put, only Narses being accommodated in the building.

Some indication of the depth of what awaited him came to Flavius when, at one stop, he found his old comrade Martinus, passing in the other direction to take over his vacated command. He had previously been recalled when the *magister militum per Orientem* arrived in Dara to resume his rightful place.

Despite the objections of the escorting officers Martinus insisted on talking to Flavius, not least to get an appreciation of what he might face on the border, reassured when he was told that the very sickness that had brought on this present impasse would give him time to organise his defences, given the Sassanids were equally troubled by it.

Naturally talk turned to what Flavius and his comrade might face. Justinian, according to Martinus, was as weak as a mewling infant and surrounded by physicians who were adamant that exertions of any kind would kill him, this reinforced by his wife's insistence that he take care. In short, Theodora and those who formed her partisans were in control.

'Bouzes is seen as the instigator. Justus will escape with nothing more than an admonishment, for blood will save him. You? Theodora is reputed to be incandescent with rage against your name and you will readily appreciate the number of voices whispering in her ear to add to her anger.'

'Does anyone know how hard I have tried not to make enemies?'

'No one else but you would think it possible, Flavius. I can only imagine the bile my appointment to replace you has engendered.'

'I must ask you, Martinus, if matters had turned out otherwise what–?'

Flavius stopped, but he did not have to finish the sentence. Martinus smiled in a way that implied that to ask was plain foolish.

'I might have been obliged on meeting to prostrate myself.'

'A stupid and demeaning Persian habit.'

'One Theodora seeks for Justinian.'

'Thank God he resists.'

'It will come in time, perhaps not ours but in future. We adopt too many customs from our eastern neighbours.'

'While there are always some willing to grovel.'

The smile was still there. 'Not you, Flavius.'

'No doubt Theodora cannot wait to test that assertion.'

'Would you have put yourself forward if Justinian had expired?'

'According to my officers I had no choice.'

'Then it might please you to know that when news of his illness became known, yours was the

321

name on everyone's lips from the corridors of the palace to the marketplace.'

'With obvious exceptions.'

'Do you fear Theodora?'

'I would be a fool not to.'

'And she, my friend, would be a fool not to be in dread of you. She knows she is hated in the city as much as you are loved.'

Martinus actually laughed when, even under sun-darkened skin, he saw Flavius blush.

## CHAPTER TWENTY-FOUR

Bouzes went straight to the dungeons accused of treason but Flavius was allowed to reside in his own villa while a commission was prepared to examine him for his alleged transgressions. Nor was he confined, and that allowed him to walk the corridors of the imperial palace where he tried to gauge the mood of those with whom he came into contact, not that such a thing was simple; he was under a cloud and no one wanted to be seen deep in conversation – exchanges were brief, hopes that all would be well for him whispered, the speed at which the interlocutor hurried off common.

The difference lay, as Martinus had pointed out, in the streets of the capital. There his greetings were heartfelt and loud and Flavius was more aware than ever of a fact he had always been reluctant to acknowledge since his consular year. He was seen as a champion of the people, a man of high rank and proven ability who never-theless was honest. If he disliked the sound of the notion that he was a block on arbitrary imperial power it was one impossible to ignore, just as it was also untrue.

Odd that John the Cappadocian was one of the few people of influence to seek him out. He had suffered arrest as well as interrogation, had seen his fortune sequestered and all of his official appointments stripped away so that, on the face of it, he was now a man without power. After a period of disgrace, Justinian had restored part of his wealth and all of his physical property, though he still lacked office.

Yet John retained the loyalty of some of those non-patrician fellows he had brought into the imperial bureaucracy and so he could claim his sources inside government were sound. The mes-senger inviting Flavius to meet with him had to wait a long time for a reply, as the recipient pondered the wisdom of being observed in such company and how it would affect his forthcoming hearing.

'You were right to be cautious. Theodora will know of your every move.'

'The actions of my wife–'

John held up a flabby hand – he had lost none of his bulk in confiscation – to indicate that his visitor should stop. 'Your wife is Theodora's crea-ture, Flavius Belisarius.'

'For which I have been rendered a laughing stock.'

'There are many who choose to be sympa-thetic,' came the less than convincing reply, 'but 'that is not why I asked you to call upon me.'

'I admit to being surprised by the invitation and I worried that it might be part of some conspiracy, which given where I presently stand could be foolish.'

'I see it as being mutually beneficial.' That Flavius was confused did not show on his face, but then to such a practised politician it did not need to. 'By coming here we have both sent a message to the Empress that you do not stand alone.'

'I have not sought your support.'

'And nor, under normal circumstances, would you, quite the opposite I suspect.' He shifted his substantial body in his chair and fixed Flavius with a direct stare. 'I have been stripped of power by the machinations of Theodora and I suspect that she wishes to do that to you.'

John expected him to respond; to Flavius it seemed to make more sense to say nothing.

'The prospect does not concern you?'

'I have faith that my past service will count for something.'

'Why do you think I was brought down, Flavius Belisarius?'

'If Antonina is to be believed, it was through your own hubris.'

'I admit to being foolishly tempted and it hurts to admit that even I, who would have claimed to know the workings of the imperial administration inside out, who would have told you had you asked that there were no undercurrents of place-seeking and power-grabbing to which I was un-familiar, was so enamoured of the idea of ultimate control as to allow myself to be played like a newborn child.'

The Cappadocian looked into his lap then, slowly shaking his head at his own folly before speaking again. 'Even I could not see just how much Theodora manipulates Justinian.'

'And you do now?'

'Threats.' The need to explain was in his visitor's enquiring look. 'Justinian is always on guard for conspiracies to oust him and that existed before he ever succeeded his uncle. He sees a secret knife wherever he looks.'

'He has always had a suspicious cast of mind.'

'On which Theodora feeds.' John smiled ruefully. 'You have been close to him, there are rumours that he would not have seen his uncle elevated to the purple without your hand in it, yet even that does not shield you from mistrust.'

John waited for Flavius to be open about the truth of that assertion, even if, as Flavius saw it, his aid had been peripheral; the Cappadocian waited in vain and that, no doubt brought on by a degree of frustration, opened him up to an annoyingly magisterial lecture on the way the world worked.

Neither of the imperial couple ever felt secure, Justinian because of his nature and Theodora for her dependence on her husband. Thus the Empress saw the need to form a separate source of power, yet such was the mistrust she engendered that such hopes were regularly dashed, Flavius's wife being exceptional in her attachment. Theodora's response was to seek to create a permanent state of crisis, to play on her husband's fear of usurpation with a continual run of intrigues

325

designed to bring them both down.

'Not that every one of such conspiracies is of her imagining. Put enough patricians together when their privileges are being atrophied and talk of a better emperor is habitual. And you, Flavius Belisarius, by what was proposed in Edessa, have played into her hands, which I am sure you can see.'

There was sophistry in this; in his previous pomp the Cappadocian had probably been every bit as eager to feed Justinian's obsessions as Theodora, and they probably worked in tandem prior to his becoming too much of a hazard to her, for Flavius did not doubt that had been the driver of her actions.

Why had he been invited here? Was it to make a useful connection for what was coming to him or was John the one seeking to send a message to Theodora – that by openly associating with him, if he was diminished in stature, he was far from being toothless? It smacked of all that he hated about Constantinople, where everything was seen through a fog much greater than the natural one created by a cold wind on the warm waters of the Bosphorus.

'It is my intention, Flavius Belisarius, to use what little influence I still retain to act as your guide in how to thwart Theodora's designs upon you, for do not doubt that of all the fears she perceives to her position, you are the greatest. To deflect her you will need the skills I have acquired over many years. To do that I need you to be fully open with me about what took place.'

John's face had taken on a look designed to

326

imply reticence; his words inferred the exact opposite. 'Bouzes has been questioned and is adamant that the decision to check Theodora was taken when you were absent from Edessa. Also that your officers pressed you to accept their offer of support, which you acceded to only on condition that Justinian was no more.'

'You know this?' was the guarded reply.

'Allow I have my sources. If true, it provides you with a sound defence.'

The worrying thought arose unbidden; that perhaps this was all show. Could it be that Theodora had put him up to this in order to extract statements that could subsequently be used against him, such as an admission of complicity? Yet John was a purported enemy of Theodora or he had been! Such a thing would be easily altered for a man eager to regain his lost power, and as of this moment she was in a position to grant him favours. If it appeared at first to be fanciful it was merely another indication of the miasma into which he had been thrust.

'It is true, John, and because of that I am happy to answer for my actions.'

'You rely on justice to save you?'

There was no doubting the innate cynicism in that response. Determined not to be drawn, Flavius replied. 'What else is there?'

The chamber of the senate was full and those attending had gone to some trouble to get out their finery so as to create an impression that this examination was theirs and important. Flavius, who had every right to be present in his own capacity as a member, could not avoid looking up to the gallery from which, unobserved, he suspected Theodora would be monitoring proceedings; these proud men counted for nothing, despite their pretensions.

The man chosen to examine him, sat in a position where he could easily take the floor, was a stranger, but that applied to many of the attendees, those who held no important office in the palace but fulfilled less elevated tasks of governance away from the centre of power. Flavius rarely came to this place when in the capital, and that applied to many here now.

Why would they bother? For centuries it had been no more than a talking shop. Even the post of consul had been abolished in the year '41, to be added to the imperial titles. If he had not still been unwell, Justinian would possibly have presided, though there was the possibility of an excuse, given Flavius knew him so well.

In his place sat the ex-consul Flavius Decius, who had held the title fourteen years previous. He appeared nervous of his role and even if he looked the part with his bald dome and serious mien, his voice held a tremor as he opened proceedings by introducing the person chosen to prosecute the case.

'I call Ancinius Probus Vicinus.'

The name came as a shock, the last part bringing back unpleasant memories. Vicinus was the family name of the man responsible for the murder of his father and brothers, and Flavius peered hard at him to see if there was any likeness. The senator appeared many years younger than him, but he had seen years of hard military service while Vicinus had the pale and smooth countenance of the scribe.

He was far from slim and there was something in the face which reminded him of the man he had brought down so spectacularly, which took him back to the day he had fired the Vicinus villa, this after it had been stripped of everything of value. There had been two children, a boy and girl, sent away in penury, for there was no intention to make war on the innocent. Could this be the boy?

'Flavius Belisarius, the charge against you is that you did conspire to usurp the power and position of your rightful emperor, Flavius Justinian Augustus. How do you answer?'

'With a clear conscience.'

Vicinus turned to the clerk sat close by and hissed that a plea of innocence be entered. He then went through a list of Flavius's titles up to and including that of *magister*, before moving on to the events at Edessa. Whatever had been the intentions of John the Cappadocian he felt sure he had been afforded the truth: that Bouzes had not sought to save himself by implicating his commander. If they had had their differences in the past, Bouzes had served him faithfully and was not the type to hide behind a falsehood.

'At a meeting of your officers you put yourself forward as a candidate to replace the Emperor, did you not?'

'No.'

'You are required to explain,' came the sour response, 'not just to deny.'

Flavius made a point then of glancing up at the

329

balcony as he outlined what had happened. A person, several in fact, could, by sitting well back, be in occupation without being seen. He went on to explain that in his absence his officers had been told of Justinian contracting the plague, and experience within the army indicated that the affliction was more often fatal than survivable, which had naturally raised concerns about a succession. 'Especially,' Flavius said, in a very loud voice, 'when the imperial couple had no children.'

If he had doubted Theodora was listening, the murmur that set up, as well as the looks that went skywards to the balcony, laid them to rest.

'My view of what should be done was contained in the despatch I sent back to the capital in which, under my seal, all my officers and men professed their loyalty to the Emperor and the empire, as well conveying the information on the depths of our prayers for his recovery.'

'This enquiry is concerned by what you decided should that not come to pass.'

'Thanks to God's grace it has.'

'Which is of no matter when we are seeking to uncover a conspiracy.'

'What conspiracy?'

'The despatch you sent contained threats.'

'If that is so, I beg you read it out to the senators present and they can for themselves judge if that is true. By my recollection, following on from our hopes of a recovery, was a mere request that the Army of the East should be consulted about who would succeed, should the worst occur.'

'A threat.'

'A request! I would assume the same sentiment

would animate those men who command the imperial armies in Italy, North Africa and Hispania.'

'You put yourself forward, did you not?'

Flavius's eyes ranged round the senate chamber. 'I would not presume to take prerogatives to myself that properly belong to this august assembly.'

'We have evidence that you saw yourself as Augustus.'

'Then I demand you produce it. What I did pledge was to act in the best interests of the empire in any capacity I was called upon to perform.'

'Which included the diadem.'

If he had been tense, Flavius felt he could relax. The care taken in that despatch he had sent back to Constantinople was paying off handsomely. As he had said at the time, Theodora had the wit to read what was not stated and it had been carefully composed to fit that need. She would discern a warning if she acted precipitously but anyone else could read and see nothing but innocent intent and genuine concern.

Vicinus tried by repeated questioning to extract from him something incriminating, but for once, in this city and so close to the palace, Flavius felt in real control.

'I am bound to ask where you claim to have been when your officers, and this has been admitted, chose to put you forward as a candidate for emperor.'

Bouzes would not have been so foolish. 'I think they decided to consult me on my return. I doubt they were so bold as to make what could only be a possibility a statement of fact.'

'Your absence was convenient, perhaps too

much so.'

'I was away hunting,' Flavius added, 'having just successfully foiled the aims of the Sassanids and driven their army back into their own territory. Since you have never, I suspect, commanded soldiers in battle – and certainly not an army – you will be unaware of the strain such office imposes, nor will you know of the need to take time to replace responsibility with pleasure.'

'Or intrigue.'

'I challenge you again, as is my right as a senator. Produce the letter sent from Edessa and let my august colleagues pronounce upon it. If they can see guilt, then I am willing to abide by whatever judgement they make, albeit, as I said at the outset, my conscience is clear.'

Vicinus turned to the ex-consul Decius. 'There are matters here that require to be pondered on. I request a suspension of the examination until the morrow.'

'Granted.'

The session broke up noisily, the chatter of the senators echoing off the marble columns and stone walls as they filed out. Few even looked at Flavius and only two deigned to speak, one John the Cappadocian, who still held his senatorial rank. But he came second after Ancinius Probus Vicinus, whose look was one of pure disdain.

'You do not know me, Flavius Belisarius, do you?'

'Perhaps I do, if not to recognise, know of you.'

'I am the son of Senuthius Vicinus.'

'That occurred to me and all I can offer you is my sympathy for such a tainted bloodline. It cannot be easy to have a murderer for a parent.'

'You destroyed my family,' Vicinus hissed, 'and left my sister and me as near beggars.'

He was about to add more but Flavius cut across him, his tone one of truly suppressed anger. 'Damn you, how dare you even allude to loss after what your father did to mine? At least I let you live, which should have you kiss my feet in gratitude.'

'The only thing I wish to kiss is your gravestone.'

'Then if you are the true son of your father you will be looking for someone able to use a knife on a dark night. For, like him, you are more likely a coward than a fighter. I do, however, offer you this. Meet me any time you choose with any weapon you choose and I will happily give you a chance for the revenge you have no right to expect.'

Vicinus held up the bundle of papers that had formed the case. 'I have my weapons in my hand and they are such that you will be unable to fight them. If I have my way, the knife will be visible just before it takes out your eyes. You will end up begging in the street and when I spit on you be assured I will name myself!'

Flavius wanted to hit him and was about to, when the bustle from the balcony distracted him and that allowed Vicinus to slip by and leave the chamber. John, who had been witness to the exchange now came forward.

'He begged to be your examiner.'

'One day I will tell you why.'

That was responded to by a smile from thick wet lips. 'The rumours of how you aided Justinian's uncle to the purple are not the only ones that float about. It is said that Justinian contrived your revenge and in doing so brought down one of the most powerful senators to serve Anastatius, a man who might have strong say in the succession.'

'Such stories are old and from a long time past.'

'Do you think you have seen off Theodora?'

'I have dented the case.'

'True, which would be of use if it was the only one against you.'

'What else could there be?'

Again a smile, but neither friendly nor humorous. 'I sensed when we met you do not trust me, for which I can see sound reasons. But know this, Flavius Belisarius, survival in this world is not like the field of battle. Here there are no friends or enemies to see and recognise, merely people with whom to associate or not and time bears on that. Yesterday's problem can be today's solution.'

'So?'

'When you appear tomorrow there will be other charges laid against you.'

'What charges?'

'Come to my villa later and I will tell you.'

His absolute assurance irritated Flavius, who had not fully calmed down from his brush with Vicinus. It was only later that he wondered if it had been wise to so abruptly decline any aid from the Cappadocian by saying, as he strode away, 'My conscience is clear!'

# CHAPTER TWENTY-FIVE

Thinking the following day would be a repeat of its predecessor, Flavius was thrown when the object of the questioning went nowhere near the meeting at Edessa. Vicinus, who should have been chastened, looked supremely confident when he stood to speak to a hushed chamber. Now it was he who with some deliberation threw a glance at the balcony.

'The senate has decided to call into question, Flavius Belisarius, certain of your decisions in your campaigns on the Persian border. I will put certain points to you and ask for an interpretation. I remind you that when you answer you do so before not only the senate of the Roman Empire but the Augustus whom we see fit to elevate to a position of guidance.'

Flavius, as Vicinus produced a dramatic pause, was thinking the word 'guidance' to be farcical; the assembly never dared challenge any decision made by Justinian or any of his predecessors all the way back to Octavian. The graveyards of the empire both east and west were full of the bones of those who had gambled and lost.

'Added to that, you are answerable to God Almighty for the replies you provide.'

'I have never doubted that the Almighty can see into the very depths of our souls and that sins committed in this life are paid for in the next.'

Meant to check Vicinus it failed; he flushed angrily. 'You will confine yourself to answering what questions the senate puts to you. Your observations are not welcome.'

'To some more than others,' Flavius added pointedly. Such blatant defiance had Vicinus turn to the presiding officer, Decius, who responded with a sonorous rebuke.

'Ancinius Probus Vicinus speaks for this house, Flavius Belisarius. When you defy him you likewise defy the senate, which will hardly bend us to whatever defence you produce.'

'I ask that the charges be read out to me.'

'A task I will happily undertake.'

Vicinus aimed his words at Decius who told him to proceed with a nod. His prosecutor then picked up a sheaf of papers and made his way to the well of the chamber there to wave them, though he obviously knew the contents off by heart as he made no reference to them as he spoke.

'Item. That in the campaign of the Year of Our Lord, five-forty-one, you prematurely broke off fighting the enemy King Khusrow in order to rendezvous with your wife Antonina Belisarius at the fortress of Dara. In short, you placed your private desires ahead of the needs of your responsibilities.'

Flavius actually laughed, which brought a flush of anger to the cheeks of Vicinus. But he did not add any words to state how absurd such a notion was, given he had no desire that she should be at his side at all. That was dirty washing, not to be aired in public.

'I hear no reply?'

'While I suspect that given the inane nature of such an accusation you have more stupidities with which to accuse me.'

That got a look around the chamber from Vicinus. He was enjoying playing to the crowd, his face now wearing a smile that spoke of a deeper knowledge than his peers.

'We are, my fellow senators, in the eyes of the accused, stupid.'

The voices of protest did not come from all the attendees, Flavius supposed it only emanated from the throats of those seeking to impress Theodora, and their desire to do so could be graded by their level of shouted rebuke.

'By your actions you left isolated a substantial body of your own command. Your precipitate withdrawal handed back to Khusrow not only the recently captured city of Sisauranon, but in bypassing the fortress of Nisibis you failed to counter a thorn in the side of the empire. In what way do you plead?'

'I retired because of plague in the army. Sisauranon was too far into Sassanid territory to be defended and there was no threat to our territory from Nisibis.'

'No threat from Nisibis,' Vicinus sneered. 'Such a small matter that Anastatius Augustus, may God rest his soul, doled out a fortune in gold to build the fortress of Dara so that what you call "no threat" could be countered.'

'There are many august people here in atten-dance, but few are soldiers, even less are com-manders and none, I can say with confidence, have beaten the Sassanids in battle. I bow the knee to no man in that.'

Again Flavius was acutely aware of the way his words were received; that some of the senators were embarrassed when reminded of his famous victory, it was not enough to give him the impression that his statement altered the mood of the entire chamber.

'Past splendours are not germane to this examination of your conduct, for what happened in forty-one was only a precursor to an even more telling dereliction shortly before you were called back to face this house. You are called upon to answer as to how it was possible that the Sassanid King could, at will, sack the city of Callinicum and enslave the entire population while you had an army in the field with the express purpose of opposing him. I might add he is now demanding we ransom these unfortunate captives.'

'We agreed a truce, he broke it and it would not be the first time a ruler of the lands of Persia had broken a solemn undertaking.'

'Solemn undertaking,' Vicinus intoned, as if it were a disease as deadly as the plague. 'And to whom was this "solemn undertaking" given?'

'To me, as *magister militium per Orientem.*'

'How convenient that you can produce this notion that is unknown to anyone else. Perhaps you would care to show where in writing this agreement exists.'

'It was verbal and witnessed by my officers–'

'Who would be the same men,' Vicinus interrupted, 'who saw you as a potential emperor? I doubt we can look to them for an honest assessment.'

'You could if you were willing to try, which I sense is not your intention.'

Flavius was thinking of John the Cappadocian and his hints of the previous day. He had been foolish not to listen; at least he would have been prepared for this travesty of a trial, though he knew the outcome to have already been decided. Vicinus was not finished, as for the first time he consulted his papers and the list of further accusations poured out.

'There is the matter of misappropriation of part of the Vandal treasure of North Africa, the tardiness of campaigning in Italy and questions regarding whether pay due to the army was instead diverted to your own coffers.'

On and on he went, there seeming to be no part of the past decades' service in which Flavius had not either lined his own purse or, as a general, acted in a way inimical to the needs of the empire. It was odd to be so described and hear the disbelieving sighs of a group of men who were, unlike him, usually guilty of such crimes. It raised the nature of the word hypocrisy to heights never before achieved.

'How do you plead?' Vicinus demanded, holding up the list of supposed transgressions.

'My conscience is clear,' Flavius replied with slow deliberation, 'but your own, Ancinius Probus Vicinus, is as clouded as that of the man from whose loins you sprang.'

'Fellow senators,' was the shouted response, those papers waved with fury this time. 'Am I to be so traduced, and you with me, by such an ingrate? What honours has the empire bestowed on him only to find their faith misplaced?'

It was necessary for Flavius to detach himself from the proceedings as they continued, he refusing to grace the accusations with a reply, which carried on until the point where the ex-consul Decius asked that he remove himself while the chamber deliberated on how to respond. That he prayed was hardly surprising but it was not for forgiveness, if you discounted his own known sins, or for his life or eyesight, because he had to believe that not even Theodora would dare to be so vindictive with a man who was such a hero to the citizenry.

'I beg not to be dishonoured.'

He begged for that in vain; the first act, sonorously pronounced by Decius but surely previously decided by the Empress, was to strip him of his title of *magister*. Next came the sequestration of nearly everything he possessed in terms of money and goods, though he was allowed to keep his villa south of Galatea. Lastly he was stripped of his *comitatus,* the best soldiers in the empire, they to be put up for auction to anyone seeking a military command and who had the means to fund their pay.

'Finally, Flavius Belisarius, you are to attend daily the imperial palace so that at his own convenience the Emperor may call upon you to explain your manifest crimes and failures.'

If Flavius could not fathom the need for the last it soon became plain as, wandering the corridors with no real purpose, he was exposed to endless ridicule from anyone who chose to employ it; he was a pariah now and he would not be allowed to forget it, yet he harked back to Marcus Aurelius and the stoicism he had preached, so that when insulted he could smile in response, which did much to discomfit those seeking to diminish him.

The real problem was that he was barred from the audience chamber and had no contact by which he could apply pressure to Justinian to reverse the malice of his wife.

Of Antonina there was no sight; she made no attempt to contact him and he responded in kind. It was deeply wounding that part of the case presented by Vicinus must have been formed by her malevolence; no doubt she blamed him for the death of Theodosius, as if he could have fought off the disease that killed him. Or was it that she was such a dupe as to provide testimony coloured by her own twisted logic without a thought to the consequences?

Even ignored he was able to garner news of the state of fighting in the various theatres of war. In the east it was stalemate, which was of credit to Martinus, who had continued the Belisarian policy of containment. Matters were going well in Hispania, but in Italy the Goths had revived under a new king called Totila and his successes, allied to Byzantine losses, made for grim telling.

On leaving Ravenna his replacement, a patrician imperial administrator called Alexander had been appointed to rule Italy as a province of empire. He had turned out to be rapacious to an alarming degree, even going so far, it was reported, as to debase the coinage, the gold thus removed from the edges being split between himself and the imperial treasury, which kept quiet those stealing from that same sum of money in Constantinople.

His other acts, also condoned, were equally grasping. Alexander levied fines for the smallest perceived infringement and added to this was his accusation that the troops for whom Flavius had been responsible had been overpaid and thus must make restitution. He accused the Italians of underpaying Goth taxes going back to their invasion a century before and demanded such sums be made good, which infuriated the native citizens. In short, Alexander had undone all the good work Flavius had achieved in keeping the local population as supporters of Byzantine rule.

Worse, Alexander's inferior commanders took their cue from him so that all over Italy there was now discontent at Byzantine rule and that had allowed the Goths to revive their military fortunes. The king who had taken the sceptre from Witigis, Ildibadus, had immediately sought to reverse the gains made by Flavius but with little success and part of that was brought on by an endemic Goth problem of internal dissension.

The ramifications of their disputes were tedious to relate and almost too tangled to comprehend but one fact was plain: Ildibadus had so alienated some of his close followers that one of them had taken advantage of his position to stab him to death and he was replaced by a tribal chieftain called Eraric.

In that leader they had seemingly found a fitting replacement for Theodahad, though his manoeuvres were aided by the inactivity of those who should have contained him, the numerous military commanders who now seemed more interested in fleecing the citizens of the towns over which they had control than fighting the Goths.

Even a pariah picked up gossip, although a good source of information was John the Cappadocian, who seemed willing to risk the displeasure of Theodora to openly communicate with him. Thus he knew of Eraric's open request that he be granted the peace offered to Witigis, which involved the Goths surrendering all the lands south of the River Po.

'I swear,' John had informed him, 'that these Goths make us look like saints. This Eraric has secretly offered to sell Justinian the whole of Italy.'

'I can imagine the price to be high,' had been Flavius's jaundiced reply.

The price had proved too high for the Goths as well; Eraric should have known such an offer could not be kept from gossip and that proved to be the case. Murdered by his own troops the kingship had devolved onto Totila and in that king they had found a leader worthy of the title.

The moribund military commanders in Italy, prompted it was said by a furious Justinian, had finally roused themselves to react. Gathering in Ravenna they had set out to confront Totila who held Ticinum, the Goth city in which their rulers were chosen. Verona was on the way and it seemed sensible to take it first, but what the army in Italy now suffered from was the curse of divided command and it was not just two generals but several.

What followed, as passed to Flavius by John, had been an unmitigated disaster, yet at first the matter seemed easily settled. An imperial sup-

343

porter resident in Verona had offered to surrender one of the gates and after much discussion and seeming reluctance to be responsible for taking advantage, one man had taken up the gauntlet. He was Artabazes, the former Governor of Sisauranon, who had entered Byzantine service with the men Flavius had sent back to Constantinople.

The reports indicated he had succeeded in taking control of the surrendered gate with as few as a hundred fighters, at which point he called for support from an army that was encamped too far away to speedily provide it. It was also a force in which endless discussion must proceed any action, so by the time it began to advance it was too late. When they finally arrived outside Verona, Artabazes and his men were in dire straits.

They held the curtain wall but the Goths, having seen how tardy was the Byzantine response, had retaken the actual gate, which left Artabazes and his men isolated. Pleas that an attack should be launched to aid them to withdraw fell to another lengthy and ultimately destructive dispute amongst the various generals and that left those still fighting no choice but to get away as best they could.

A few, including their leader, managed to get off the walls by rope; most were obliged to jump with the obvious consequence that those not killed in the attempt suffered such damage to their bones that they fell as easy prey to the enemies. With a failed attack the Byzantines moved on Ticinum unaware that Totila had decided to give them battle and was also moving on the river.

In sole command he proved to be a better opponent than the divided foes he faced. As Flavius had always insisted, division in the counsels of command could not but be observed by the men they led. That meant a lack of faith in proper leadership, which made the mood of the army fragile. This was proved by what followed.

By the simple ploy of fixing the Byzantine front and giving battle, then bringing up a force unknown in number that he had sent across the river previously to attack their rear, Totila induced the kind of panic inclined to affect any badly led force. Almost without having to fight, he watched as the Byzantines disintegrated and fled the field.

That had ended the year's campaign but when fighting was renewed in the spring Totila held the initiative and he was rampaging at will through the peninsula. In order to bring some cohesion to the Byzantine forces Justinian despatched a general with the rank of *praetorian prefect,* which gave him full authority to act in the Emperor's name. But despite having men at his disposal the *prefect* was both timid in his actions and quite unable to command those he had been sent to lead.

Totila had bypassed Rome and captured city after city to the south, few of which had walls to resist him, and given those that did contained enemies that would not move from their protection, he was able to range all over Apulia and Calabria, depriving Justinian of the revenues of those provinces needed to sustain a badly paid army. The result was a raft of defections.

The prize for Totila was Naples, well garrisoned and with a strong fleet on the way from Rome to reinforce that. It was to no avail; Totila knew they were coming and intercepted them with a fleet of his own, inflicting a stunning defeat and capturing their commander, who was obliged, when paraded before the walls of the city, to tell the citizens of Naples it could not look forward to relief, and after a truce of three months the city surrendered.

'Flavius, how good it is to see you.'

These words from Antonina, who had appeared in a ghost-like fashion from behind one of the great columns of St Sophia, who had found her husband in prayer. He was, as usual, asking that those for whom he cared, alive or dead, had the Lord's blessing, a point he made to his wife when she was informed of his entreaties.

'Am I included in such supplications?'

This was asked with that air of faux innocence that Antonina had ever been able to contrive and the look on her face was one that held no hint of guilt for what had happened, either in his trial or since.

'Would you consider you deserve to be?' he replied, getting up from his knees.

'I would hope that you think of me kindly. I am after all your wedded wife.'

'And an example to all in the depth of your attachment.'

Intended to dent her carapace it failed utterly, as does water off the back of a duck, which reminded Flavius that he was, in many ways, no match for her, the fact of that reinforced by what came next.

'I was much distressed by what happened to you.'

'And so quick to show sympathy. I am touched.'

'In fact,' she continued as if he had not spoken, 'I was saying to the Empress that I reckoned your punishment to be too harsh.'

'I am sure she was moved by your opinion.'

'Theodora takes heed of what I say. I have told her you would readily seek her forgiveness.'

Her sudden appearance was suspicious in itself, after many months in which she had been distant. But Flavius had now become so inured to monarchical manoeuvring that he felt he could discern the undercurrent of what was happening.

'She has nothing to forgive me for.'

The response came with something close to a sneer. 'It is a poor sinner who prays yet cannot see his faults.'

'Why are you here, Antonina?'

'In church? What an odd question.'

That failed to satisfy; he knew from long past that while she paid lip service to religion and could be called upon for a bit of chest beating if there was an audience to impress, her faith did not run deep. She was wedded to earthbound power not the celestial.

'I have thought about you a great deal since...' That got a pulled and anxious expression; she did not want to refer to his downfall too openly. 'Your difficulty. I have racked my mind to find ways to help you.'

'Don't tell me. You have pleaded with Theodora

to meet with me.'

The eyes shot wide. 'How did you know?'

'I decided, since I had nothing else to occupy me, to study how to be a courtier in this sin pit of a palace, a place in which you seem so much at home.'

That finally got through her defences. 'You have no idea of the effort I have put in to intercede on your behalf.'

'No, I have not,' was the mordant reply.

'And after much begging I have got Theodora to agree to meet with you.'

'How kind.'

'Indeed, if you were to accompany me now, she is alone in her apartments and I know, if I ask, she will receive you into her presence.'

He wanted to refuse, to tell his wife and through her Theodora, to go to perdition, but against that was his present state of limbo, which was driving Flavius mad. Also, he had to believe that this was in truth a summons and that meant there had to be a reason behind it. Was his pariah status about to be withdrawn?

'I can hardly wait,' he said, indicating that she should lead the way.

That did not encompass a far journey; St Sophia was attached to the imperial palace by a private passageway and soon Flavius found himself in the presence of Theodora, alone as had been promised.

'Highness,' he said with a bow.

'Do I observe humility, Flavius?'

'Who could not be humble in the presence of such prominence and piety?'

The look that got, for she could see the barb, was one that indicated he could still irritate her and easily, which pleased him. More important was the fact of her muted reaction; there was promise here and if he had prayed for the souls of others in church, he now uttered a silent one for himself.

## CHAPTER TWENTY-SIX

What was Theodora really saying when she claimed that the pleading of Antonina had led to a softening of the imperial position? That due to such intercession and her own application to Justinian, who, rumour had it was now recovered, had it in mind to end his present isolation and reinstate him in imperial favour. If anything underlined the falsity of that senatorial judgement it was this: the notion that on a whim any verdict arrived at could be overturned, though that hardly came as a surprise since the charges, wholly specious, had been inspired from the same source.

There was one obvious undercurrent: any relaxation would only be considered and maintained if he showed a true appreciation of the manifest attributes of his wife. Tempted to list them as disloyalty, deceit and infidelity, added to a conceit that allowed for no self-appraisal, Flavius held his tongue and if part of him knew that to be craven he sensed he was close to a prize worth his silence.

'In order that you know I bear you no ill will,

and in appreciation of my good friend your wife, I have agreed that your daughter Ioannina should be betrothed to a member of the imperial family.'

That caused Flavius to look at Antonina; Theodora was talking of a girl he had barely seen since birth, both through being away at war and his marital estrangement. It made him feel ashamed that he had no real knowledge of her and given his wife looked so pleased by the pronouncement all he could do was offer a feeble thanks.

'My husband has demanded to see you.'

'I am, as always, his to entirely command.'

Despite the sincerity with which that was imparted, Theodora could not help but look at him with suspicion to see if he was once more mocking her.

'I would point out to you, Flavius, that whatever privileges you allotted to yourself previously when addressing the Emperor no longer hold. He will talk, you will listen and if you speak, confine yourself to the mere answering of his enquiries.'

'And when am I to attend upon him?'

'You may wait outside his private chamber and you will be summoned.'

It pleased Flavius that Justinian did not intend to haul him before an open meeting of his counsel in the audience chamber. This would, he was sure, have led to a humiliating listing of his supposed crimes, just so the Emperor could then appear wise, benign and merciful. Much of such gatherings were constrained by ritual and theatricality as the Emperor sought to demonstrate his sagacity, this while being fawned on by people who privately, if the rumours were true, thought him of little worth.

Attendance had been blessedly rare, Flavius being too often on campaign to be included in meetings in which too little was ever resolved and time was wasted by the courtiers in making statements, either self-aggrandising or in defamation of their rivals. The only joy was when two men in conflict for some well remunerated service were simultaneously present; neither could be open in either ambition or condemnation and for an uninvolved observer their manoeuvrings and sophistries had some value as entertainment.

The anteroom, apart from the two Excubitors guarding the inner chambers, was empty. It was also lacking in anywhere to sit, which obliged Flavius to pace back and forth, the only interruption being when the door was opened to allow one of Justinian's more intimate advisors to depart. Finally the *magister officiorum* exited, to favour Flavius with a surprised look. Moments after his departure a servant emerged to beckon him in, staying without himself.

The interior was lit by dozens of candles and if the room had windows they were so heavily draped as to be of no account. Was the form of light to flatter a man who wished to disguise the ravages of both his recent disease and increasing age? The way Justinian was pacing back and forth, very few steps back and forth at a hurried pace, took Flavius back to a time when both were young; even then he had been a restless soul who gave the impression of a mind in permanent turmoil.

'You may sit,' was the rasping introduction,

'though God knows I should have you branded with red-hot irons.'

'Would that be to satisfy your conscience or to trouble mine?'

That stopped the pacing and got the still standing Flavius a glare, made more hostile due to the light and the shadows it cast. Outside Flavius had been afforded time to think and he had concluded that to grovel to Justinian would be useless. Was it possible, given the information he had been fed by his wife, that the Emperor believed a man who named him a friend had set out to usurp him?

There was no point in seeking to guess at such a problem; he needed to convince Justinian that such accusations were false and the one thing that might bend his mind to even a hint of truth was for someone who had always challenged him to miss an opportunity of doing so now. Whatever else he must face, Justinian had to be presented with the Flavius Belisarius he knew.

'You deny your transgressions?'

'I deny wishing for your passing. Had God seen fit to reject my prayers for your recovery I would have acted as I always have.'

'Don't tell me, Flavius,' came the mocking response. 'For the good of the empire.'

'A duty which falls daily to both of us.'

'I see your tongue has not been stilled by your recent travails.'

'I have learnt to be more skilful with certain people but I cannot change the way I address you. If I am required to do that I would rather you dismiss me from your presence and allow me to return to being ignored.'

'For the love of God, Flavius, sit down!'

'Why am I here?'

'You are here because I want you here.'

'Want or need? Did you really believe I would betray you?'

'Why not?' came the weary response. 'Everyone else seems bent on doing so. Not a week goes by when I do not hear of some attempt to topple me.'

Conspiracies all brought to you by your wife, Flavius thought; it was not a politic thought to express. There was also something in the way Justinian had responded that indicated that he knew the notion of his rebelling had to be nonsense; the man who had turned down the crown of the Goths? He had been ill, probably near death's door, which had left Theodora in total control. Would Justinian have believed a word of the accusations if he had been hale?

When Flavius finally sat down, Justinian came close enough to allow the features to be studied and the ravages of what he had gone through were there to see: hollow cheeks, eyes that were embedded in deep sockets, and given he was wearing a silken cowl, it had to be assumed he had suffered the kind of severe hair loss Flavius had witnessed in his surviving soldiers. That explained the candlelight in the middle of the day.

'Admit you needed to be reminded of your place?' All that got was a nod; there would never be a verbal admission of guilt but it seemed enough to satisfy Justinian who laid a hand on his shoulder and pronounced. 'Your sequestration is over, Flavius. I require you to go to Italy.'

'If you intend to reinstate me, let me go back to

Dara and with everything I enjoyed in terms of rank.'

'Italy is where you are needed and as to reinstatement, well...' The pause was followed by a sigh. 'Martinus has only recently been named as *magister militum per Orientem*. Can you not see it impossible to strip him of that or to recall him when he is properly carrying out his duties and is fully engaged in manoeuvring against Khusrow?'

'You have the power to do as you wish.'

That changed the imperial tone markedly. 'It seems I do not have the power to command you!'

There was no choice but to succumb and what followed was a description of how dire matters were in the Italian Peninsula where the various Byzantine generals seemed content to remain in whatever towns and cities they held, making no effort to combine against Totila. Flavius was to be restored to a senior military command and had the promise that his wealth, now in the possession of Theodora, would be returned, a promise only kept in part, since she subsequently gave part of it to Justinian and he saw no reason to decline such a gift.

Equally disquieting was the insistence by Theodora that Antonina once more accompany him, no doubt to fulfil the same purpose she had previously performed: namely to keep the Empress fully informed of her husband's actions and statements, which, in the case of the latter, with Flavius now being very guarded, she would probably have to invent.

What he could not have was his previous title or his old *comitatus*, now in the service of other

354

commanders, men who had paid large sums for their service. When he asked for soldiers, especially *bucellarii*, that too was hardly forthcoming in any great number. Unknown to Flavius as he set out from Constantinople, along the Via Egnatia, at the head of no more than a thousand men, was that he was heading for years of frustration, mainly due to the lack of effective fighting men, but also because he had, in Totila, an opponent who had learnt from him.

The Goth King had adopted the Belisarian policy with the natives; even in Naples, which by the laws of war he had the right to sack, Totila had avoided punishing them for holding out against him. He did the very opposite to a population near to starvation, bringing in food with which to feed them and even controlling the distribution to avoid the kind of sudden overeating which could kill. He had shown clemency to the Byzantine garrison by allowing them to march out with their equipment for Rome, and given many were now locally recruited this spread the word to the Italians of a wise and temperate ruler.

By the time Flavius reached Salona on the coast of Illyria, recruitment by bounty in that province had quadrupled his forces but that counted for little in a situation in which matters had deteriorated. If he was to be successful, it rested on the men he had been appointed to command and they, even those who had served with him previously, were no longer the homogeneous body he required.

Declining to cross the Adriatic by sea he decided to take the land route to Ravenna but before he moved pressure on several Italian garrisons obliged him to send supplies to avoid unnecessary surrenders. That did not stop the rot; certain places were not only opening their gates, they were going over to an enemy who seemed to gain in strength as Flavius struggled.

On reaching Ravenna he found it hard to persuade the non-Totila Goths to take service under his banner, and even worse the Byzantine soldiers stationed there also declined, a blow that no amount of reassurance from his *domesticus* could soften.

'You are still held in high regard.'

'Am I, Solomon?'

'The men here who once served under you remember your care for their welfare and they are more than willing to attest to it for those who did not, Goths included.'

'Yet not a single man saw fit to attach themselves to my standard,' Flavius muttered.

'It is their present leaders they do not trust. They are certain that at some time in the future you will be recalled and they will once more fall under the command of generals who do not act as you do. These are men whom they have also refused to serve. It is not you alone.'

'Then,' Flavius sighed, 'we must show to them that there is gain in fighting with me.'

That was an aim easier enunciated than achieved and really it was as much an answer to inactivity as any desire to impress. All that could be despatched were small parties of troops, never more than a thousand at a time, to seek to apply pressure on Totila that would have him move to counter it, thus relieving stress on strongholds like Rome.

Even if he was not personally present, some of the magic which had attached to his name seemed still to prevail. Vitalius, the *magister* who had aided him in raising troops in Illyricum, was sent with those levies into the province of Amelia to tie down the garrison in Bononia, which allowed him to exert control over the surrounding, supremely fertile area. This forced Totila to send a superior force to dislodge them.

Appraised of the Goth approach, Vitalius set up a series of ambushes that nullified their numbers, which led to repeated encounters in which the Goths were decimated, till over time their strength was utterly diminished. Just at the moment of ultimate success, the levies from Illyricum decided to go home, being in receipt of news that the Huns were ravaging their homelands. Vitalius had no choice but to withdraw in haste.

The next move saw a thousand men sent out under the command of Thurimuth, the leader of Flavius's bodyguards. They were despatched to the hilltop town of Auximus, under siege by Totila and held by Flavius's old comrade Magnus. Having succeeded in getting into the town it was decided to mount a series of sorties to assess the full strength of the enemy. Enjoying mixed success, such raids did establish that even reinforced Magnus had insufficient numbers to break the siege.

Those same reinforcements imposed a strain on the supplies needed to hold out and avoid surrender due to starvation, so it was decided

357

they would be of more use outside the walls. Unware that some spy had told the Goths of the plan, they left by night and ran straight into an ambush in which they lost a full tenth of their effectives as well as all their supplies, the survivors forced to flee for Arminium.

Flavius, meanwhile, had been restoring two fortresses long ago destroyed by Witigis, rebuilding the walls and installing new and stout gates. This again was a ploy Totila could not ignore and he set out to reverse the move by an all-out assault, only to be repulsed and obliged to pull back. If that was a positive there was another side to the coin: Flavius had used up all his men and was now in a position to do no more.

His only act was to send to Rome and order Bessas, in command there, to remain entirely on the defensive and to avoid entanglements outside the walls, but it was plain to the simplest eye that he was stymied. Totila held the initiative and until Flavius was reinforced that would remain the case.

John Vitalianus was still in Italy. He might be prone to insubordination but he had strong connections at court, especially with Narses, so he was despatched back to Constantinople to beg for men and weapons. That took time and in the interim, despite the fact that it was right on the cusp of winter, the pendulum swum decisively against Byzantium.

The fortresses so carefully restored by Flavius could not be supplied and were, when besieged a second time, forced to surrender, Flavius lacking the manpower to intervene. These losses were closely followed by two more with only Perusia holding out and that despite the death of the man in command; yet there was even worse news to follow: Totila was marching on Rome.

Aware he did not have the means to counter this, Flavius recrossed the Adriatic in order to both recruit and seek his requested reinforcements from Constantinople. There he was informed that Vitalianus, too long about the task set for him, had taken time to marry the daughter of one of Justinian's nephews, his anger only assuaged when it became plain that with trouble on every border the men just did not exist to aid his cause.

When the time came to return to Italy, with most of the campaigning season already gone, that had eased enough to bring him soldiers, if not enough. Flavius knew he must somehow succour Rome and keep it in imperial control, yet the same applied to Apulia and Calabria. Much as he did not want to split his limited forces he had no choice but to send a substantial body under John Vitalianus, who was at least an enterprising and active officer, to secure the southern provinces.

The tactics used by Witigis, Totila had replicated. Camps were built opposite the eastern gates of Rome, the Milvian Bridge was strongly held and once more there was a Goth presence on the Plains of Nero. Like his predecessor, but with more alacrity, he took control of the route to Portus, as well as taking other steps to cut Rome off from any chance of supply, which would eventually mean starvation for the densely populated city.

Before long, within the walls, the citizenry were pleading with Bessas to release the massive amount of food he had stockpiled for his troops. This he declined to do but he did nothing to stop his soldiers selling part of their rations at inflated prices to those in dire need, creating an atmosphere of distrust that could only have one outcome, a crisis made worse by the approach, once more, of winter.

Flavius had possession of Portus itself, but there was that bar across the route, known to be lightly held and needing to be broken. He despatched a body of men, five hundred in number, led by Phocas, another member of his bodyguard, to join troops already holding the town. Word was sent to Bessas of their intention to attack the Goth camp and when, with a request that he sally out to combine with them.

The assault was set in motion before any reply was forthcoming, Phocas and his men making deep inroads into the Goth position, but in time resistance hardened as it became plain they were not supported: Bessas had declined to move, even if the commotion caused by the fighting must have been audible in the city. This left no option but to withdraw.

Word was once more sent: a second attempt would be made and again Bessas was begged to provide the aid that would be needed. It never got going; Totila had been informed of the intention and ambushed the whole force, killing the leaders along with most of those they led.

The only other route by which food could be brought into the city was by rowing barges up the

Tiber and here Totila had built two wooden forts at a point, not far from the walls and hard by the road to Portus, where the river narrowed, with a bridge of joined timbers stretched between them. The plan formulated by Flavius to counter this showed he had lost none of his flair for innovation.

Lashing a pair of barges together and planking their decks he had a wooden structure constructed that in height would overreach the Totila forts. On the very top of the flimsy-looking edifice he had placed a boat filled with pitch-treated timber and brimstone. This floating surprise was to be followed upriver by every barge and boat that could be mustered in a convoy containing enough food to keep Rome going for a year, each one given built-up sides with slits that could protect his archers while giving them the ability to discharge their weapons.

At the same time a commander called Isaac the Armenian was given care of Antonina and took charge in Portus but it was made plain he must remain static and on no account risk losing the quays; his task was diversion, this as an unequivocal command was sent to Bessas; he in turn must now sally forth and attack the Goths to keep them occupied.

Flavius took the lead barge with his bodyguards and set in motion the troops he had ordered to march up the inland riverbank. The discovery of a metal chain downriver of the Totila forts imposed a check, but not for long as the men guarding it fled and it was quickly dislodged. The guards who ran alerted those holding the forts and given there was little distance between them

361

and the Goth encampment masking Portus, and a signalling system in place to warn of trouble, the soldiers there began to rush to aid in the defence.

Still too far off to intervene they could nevertheless see the wily ploy of their enemy. Forcing the vessel that held his flimsy structure against the bridge, Flavius had the boat atop it set alight and the whole tipped over to crash into the base of one of the Goth forts, the dry timber immediately catching fire. To the screams of those hundreds of men trapped inside, condemned to burn to death, his men attacked and overcame the second fort and could then begin the task of destroying the bridge.

If only Isaac the Armenian had obeyed his orders all would have been well. But he had seen many of the Goths departing to confront Flavius and the temptation of engaging with a weakened enemy proved too much. Essaying forth at the head of a mere hundred fighters he immediately launched his own attack, and by severely wounding the camp commander, which broke the morale of his followers, was able to drive the Goths right out of their camp.

Isaac was not of the stamp needed to take advantage of this minor success; his men lacked the discipline required and he the commanding presence to stop them resorting to the plunder of a camp full of the possessions of an army that had enjoyed several years of success, men unaware that what had driven the Goths back was a degree of panic. Those busy ransacking for spoils were in a serious minority and as soon as the Goths re-formed they took back their camp with ease and great slaughter, Isaac being taken prisoner, a fact relayed to Flavius without any detail as to how it had come about.

Fearful that Totila had taken Portus and fearing for the consequences for Rome and the whole campaign – there would be the need to pay ransom for Antonina too – Flavius immediately set out to confront them, hoping to come on them while they would be in a state of some disorder. This meant, partly also due to the fact that Bessas had not obeyed his orders, abandoning the attempt at resupply.

That it was a mistake only became apparent when he knew Portus was still in Byzantine hands, though that provided small compensation for what had been a highly unsuccessful manoeuvre on the Tiber. When he heard that Totila, in retribution for the death of the leader wounded in Isaac's attack, had the Armenian beheaded, he could not summon up even a pinch of sympathy. He was even heard to say that if the Goth King wanted to remove the head of Bessas, then he would be happy to hand him over.

Rarely cast down for long by reverses, Flavius was now, and a health that had always been robust failed him too, rendering him unable to initiate further actions. All he knew was that if Rome had been at risk before, it was doubly so now.

# CHAPTER TWENTY-SEVEN

If the behaviour of Bessas had been well short of that required up till now, the failure of the attempt to resupply Rome did nothing to improve it. From denying food to the citizens he extended that to his soldiers, who now found they were required to acquire their rations from rich senators who had bought them from their commanding general. Needless to say the prices Bessas charged his middlemen was high – he was having new coffers made to hold his burgeoning fortune – and so ever higher was that paid by the desperate.

Badly fed soldiers no longer bothered to carry out their responsibilities and it was a brave officer, himself forced to barter for his supplies, who even hinted at any punishment for a dereliction of duty. The mass of the citizens of Rome, becoming skeletal, cared nothing for who ruled the city only for who might feed them. Only the corpses that began to fill the streets were indifferent.

The Isaurians had ever been a bane to Flavius Belisarius: numerous and usually infantry, rarely cavalry, they were badly led and with leaders averse to doing any training to alter such deficiencies, only ever effective when he had taken a personal hand in how they were led. The story emerged, as so many did in this troubled campaign, long after the events themselves. Four junior Isaurian officers had lowered themselves from the walls and gone to Totila to offer him a way into the city by the Asinarian Gate, for which they were responsible.

The Goth King had seen the hand of wily Flavius in this – a trap that would cost lives, diminish his standing and dent the morale of his army – so he declined to accept. Undeterred, those same Isaurians had returned to him twice more to renew their offer until he finally accepted they might be telling the truth. Even then he took the precaution of sending two of his own trusted bodyguards to ensure the traitors were telling the truth. They reported back that the walls were barely manned.

In darkness and silence Totila deployed his army, but it fell to no more than a handful of his axe-bearing Goths to climb the ropes let down by the Isaurians and be the first to breach the defences. The axes were employed to smash the bars holding shut the great gate, and that opened, allowed Totila to lead his men into a city where there was no will to mount an internal defence.

Those who did not seek sanctuary in one of the dozens of churches fled out of every gate the city possessed that provided a chance of escape. Bessas was to the fore of that, leaving so hurriedly that his dozens of bulging coffers were left behind for Totila, who was to reward the Isaurian defectors not only with much of the gold but with offices rich in spoils to run the city of Rome.

Totila punished the wealthy and powerful who had traded with Bessas by giving his men a free hand to plunder their villas and warehouses, but he showed a better appreciation of his priorities by feeding the needy citizens. The Goths were afforded another advantage: Rome fell to Totila in December and he would thus winter within its walls and not in the camps surrounding the city, rapidly becoming fetid. His next act was to despatch a body of Roman divines to offer Justinian peace.

Bessas, at present nowhere to be seen, was not the only insubordinate inferior Flavius had to deal with. All his attempts to oblige John Vitalianus to march north and combine with him failed. John could claim that he faced his own threats – Totila had sent a token force south to contain him – but it was insufficient in number to justify the excuse.

Now holding the capital, Totila could release more men to take back control of the fertile south of the peninsula. That they failed brought on an unexpected response: he decided to raze the walls of Rome and render it indefensible. In addition he set out a plan to fire all the important buildings, including structures that dated from the time of Augustus Caesar, an act that would diminish Rome's importance.

The desperate appeal from Flavius Belisarius to desist bore fruit; the sender pleaded for preservation of ancient glories and also pointed out that Totila, holding the city, would be fouling the value of his own possessions. Added to that Justinian would be unlikely to grant peace to such a despoiler. The Goth relented but with a good third of the defences torn down he felt he could leave Rome without even a token garrison for, even if the Byzantines retook the city, they would be unable to hold it.

Sending a strong force south to contest Apulia, Calabria and Lucania with John Vitalianus, and that included many senatorial hostages from Rome, he left a robust force camped at Tibur five leagues to the east of the city – a day's forced march – this to deter the Byzantines holding Portus, while personally retiring on Ravenna.

Betrayal was not confined to the likes of Bessas; the loyalties of the Italian Peninsula had become so fractured that treachery had become a commonplace and Totila was as subject to that as Flavius. Spoletum and Perusia were brought back to Byzantium by treachery but it was really the capital city that mattered, both for its size and emotional appeal.

Sure Totila was gone, Flavius set forth at the head of a much diminished *comitatus*, men he had recruited on his being given the Italian command and now numbering no more than a thousand effectives, to reconnoitre what had been left behind. Betrayed by an informer they rode straight into an ambush by the Tibur Goths, who had marched from the east to confront him. The Byzantines were outnumbered and it was only the generalship of Flavius added to the discipline of his personal troops that saved what should have been a rout.

The Goths attacked expecting panic but as had happened before they found their enemies quick to form up for battle, with a speed that reversed the prospects of an easy victory. Flavius led his fighters into the melee with no care for his person, slashing to left and right at mounted opponents and ignoring the blows that got past his shield and were landed on his armour. As had also happened in previous engagements, he needed to be rescued by his bodyguards but not before he was the victim of several minor wounds.

The Goths lost more than Flavius, yet he was forced to retire to Portus once more, to bathe and have such gashes and abrasions treated, to be made aware – and not for the first time, as he examined old scars and recalled other areas of his body rendered black and blue by combat – of how lucky he had been in so many years of battle to still be whole.

'You are a fool to risk yourself. You're a general, you should behave like one.'

This was the constant lament from Antonina, who could not be barred from observance of his latest lacerations and bruises. It would have seemed like sympathy if he had not wondered, instead, if her concern was prompted by fear for her own needs should he expire. Only Flavius alive made her of use to Theodora.

Justinian responded to the peace offer from Totila by advising the Goth to treat with his representative in Italy. Flavius knew as much as the Goth that he was in receipt of a refusal. The war had to go on, but with little faith from the general in command that he could repeat his previous success; he had neither the men to do so nor, in the likes of Bessas and John Vitalianus, inferior commanders who would unquestion-ingly obey his orders, the former because of his greed, John through the connection he had to Theodora through his marriage.

Not a man to rest, even with odds so heavily stacked against him, and sure he had both luck and God with him, Flavius left Portus with nothing but token protection and marched with all the men he could muster on Rome, which he entered into unopposed to find much destruction. Time was not on his side and he needed new gates made, added to which there was a huge stretch of wall to be repaired.

Bluff was needed; ramparts were erected that would not withstand much in the way of assault or mining but he made sure that was hidden on the outer face by adding a smooth coating of lime. Employing the ditch he had dug prior to the previous siege Flavius had stakes placed in the base to make it more of an obstacle. Most important of all were the supplies he brought in to the city, which could not rely as it usually did on the ravaged countryside that surrounded it.

Totila did not make it to Ravenna; the news of the Belisarius move obliged him to reverse his course and make for Rome, where he expected a quick return to the status in which he had left it. Yet the Goth army moved at no great pace, giving Flavius over three weeks to effect repairs, so what the enemy was faced with, a lack of gates notwithstanding, looked formidable; it was not, but show was as good as strength when that was the only choice.

Totila did not hesitate to attack, he threw his men forward with no preparation at the open spaces where the gates once stood, these now filled with the best troops Flavius could deploy. They held because the Goths, in such a constrained killing zone, could not deploy sufficient numbers to overpower the defence and, pressing forward, they were at the mercy of murderous archery and rocks thrown from the parapets to either side.

Exhaustion and the approach of nightfall brought the fighting to an end but it was renewed at first light, only this time Flavius had decided not to stay on the defensive and that threw the Goths into such confusion that, when assaulted, they fell back. The danger for Flavius now was a too eager pursuit and it was only by riding out at the head of his fastest cavalry that he could get ahead of his own fighting men and, having ordered a withdrawal, could cover their retreat.

On the third day he again varied his tactics, leading his whole force out of Rome to confront Totila on open ground. That it was luck that carried the day rather than better soldiering was later accepted. The man bearing the standard of his king fell and the banner with him, which indicated to the Goths their leader had perished and that caused a degree of panic. In some disarray they did recover the standard but the heart had gone from their purpose and, since he held the ground, Flavius could claim to have been victorious.

Whatever decided Totila to abandon his attempt to take Rome – it was suspected to be arguments amongst his nobles – the Goth King withdrew to the east to winter, this while Flavius set about the task of once more making the city the formidable obstacle it had been on his first campaign. When the next season arrived, Rome had warehouses bulging with food, a strong garrison, solid walls and new gates.

Copies of the keys to the city had been sent to Justinian.

What drew Totila off were the activities of John Vitalianus. The Goth decided he was a thorn he had to excise and he marched south with a large part of his army to effect this. By avoiding the roads and using mountain tracks he avoided John's scouts and managed to surprise him in his encampment, which he attacked after the sun went down. While that was a success in the sense that the Byzantines fled, it failed, due to the darkness, in his main aim, which was destruction.

Unbeknown to the Goths, reinforcements were beginning to arrive from Justinian, the largest contingent from Armenia, but they were immediately reduced in number by being caught in an ambush by Totila, the price paid for their commander refusing to put himself under the orders of John Vitalianus and thus caught unprepared and exposed.

An even larger contingent was coming with Valerian, *magister militum per Armeniam*, but he took the view that it was too late in the year to begin campaigning and settled down to winter in Illyricum. It took a direct order from Justinian and the arrival of spring to get Valerian to move across the Adriatic.

There he combined with John Vitalianus and Flavius, who had left Rome under the command of a general called Conon. Totila was not idle; he knew where his enemies were and brought all the forces he could muster south to fight them in what became a to and fro set of engagements that were far from decisive for either side.

Rome came close to being lost again due to the behaviour of Conon; he had, no doubt, heard of the kind of monies Bessas had made when he held the city and he set out to copy his behaviour, selling food at inflated prices and controlling what came into the city. This time the citizens rebelled and the soldiers, unpaid for a year, declined to intervene.

Conon was murdered in the Senate House and, realising how far that put them beyond the approval of Constantinople, they sent a message to Justinian threatening to hand the city over to Totila if their crimes were not pardoned and the troops supposed to protect them paid, both demands rapidly acceded to.

Flavius calculated that he did not have the men to beat the Goths, and thanks to his subordinates the mood of the natives was no longer one of welcoming the men from the east as liberators. With a war seemingly endless, in which their homes and crops were either destroyed or seized and their wealth expropriated by both sides, the circumstances did not exist for a repeat of the previous conquest without the deployment of overwhelming force.

Sending piecemeal packets would not serve, the fighting would go on but to no conclusion. That message required to be sent back to the capital, and since he assumed that all his previous pleas for more men had to bypass the suspicions of

Theodora, he decided that the appeal should be made to the Empress, and there was only one envoy he could think of who might persuade her.

'My place is here by you.'

'Your place is like mine, Antonina, where the empire needs you. I require you to go to Theodora–'

'Require!' was the huffy response.

'I need more soldiers and a lot of them. I need you to persuade the Empress to cease to worry about what ambitions I might have and think of the good of the empire as well. I can write to her, I can send someone else, but I have no one in my entourage or among my officers who can do that which you will find easy. Not only to get to see her immediately but to have her listen.'

She was far from convinced and there was also the possibility of Antonina seeing the disadvantage of giving up the role Theodora had allotted to her.

'Do you too think I hanker after the diadem?' That got no answer. 'What can I do to convince you? I could have had the title of Western Emperor and I said no. That would have made you Theodora's equal.'

Sounding genuine took some effort; he had not been entirely against the notion Procopius had advanced, that in such a role he could cast his less than wholehearted companion aside. Even thinking about it now, he was not sure he would not have been tempted, despite the threat to his soul. Procopius had countered that fear by hinting at a papal dispensation.

'I could never be her equal,' Antonina insisted,

not entirely convincingly.

'And you are all the better for it.' Given he rarely even came close to flattery with his wife, that had some effect. 'You have often hinted that I do not treat you with the respect you deserve.'

'Like a chattel most of the time, and when was the last time you came to my bed?'

Flavius did not react with his usual excuse of being either too busy or in recovery from some fight or other; he was long past feeling much passion for Antonina. Yet he had never said so, having, through a natural kindness that had appalled both Procopius and Photius, declined to employ words that would wound her, feelings. There was also the residual thought, which was far from flattering to him, that insulting her would not be wise.

'There is no more important mission to be undertaken. The only person of greater standing than you Antonina, is me, and I cannot leave my command without being suspected of rebellion, the very thing I choose to utterly deny. Must I plead with you?'

A soft probing response. 'You would make it known that I am important?'

'Not important, vital.'

A pout now. 'You know that some of your officers feel free to insult me at any time of their choosing.'

They don't, Flavius thought, but you, my dear, see an insult in a want of adulation.

'I have not observed it,' was the feeble response.

'Then, Flavius,' she hissed, 'as I have always contended, you are blind.'

The way she paced a bit, her arms hugging her

374

body, he knew to be role playing. When she stopped and looked at him he felt certain she was about to agree to his request.

'I want you to call a meeting of all your senior officers.'

'Why?'

'If you are going to announce the need for an embassy to Constantinople and if you are so insistent that I am the only one you can trust to carry it out, that is something I would wish to be stated in public.' The voice hardened. 'I want to see the faces of those who feel free to slight me when you announce that.'

'Of course,' came the reply; it was small price to pay so she could gloat.

'And as soon as that has been arranged you must go aboard a fast galley to Dyrrachium and on my authority employ every means at your disposal to make the fastest journey possible.'

That clearly appealed: to be able to order every posthouse resident to provide her with transport. Antonina loved ordering her maids around; now she would be able to command men to obey. To watch her swell as her mission was announced, to a gathering of officers who could not fathom why they had been summoned, had amusing elements to Antonina's husband. In her it produced obvious and rather unbecoming conceit.

Antonina never returned to Italy. She made a fast journey and what came back, sent by her and brought to Flavius by imperial messenger, was much more telling. Theodora was no more; she had died after a short illness and by the tone of

Antonina's letter, the fate of the Army of Italy was of secondary concern. What would she do now her patron was gone?

The message from Justinian arrived right on the heels of that from his wife; it was a categorical order that *Comes* Flavius Belisarius relinquish his command in the peninsula and return with all speed to Constantinople.

# CHAPTER TWENTY-EIGHT

This was no homecoming in triumph; if not quite the reverse Flavius had no reason to expect any kind of grand welcome and nor was one provided. There was to be no docking at the private imperial harbour, the landing was in the main dock area. Yet Antonina, alerted to the vessel bearing his standard was in the offing, was on the quayside to greet him. As soon as he landed she rushed forward to kneel at his feet and having grabbed his hand, kiss it.

'My prayers have been answered.'

The welcome threw Flavius; overt displays of affection had been rare in their marriage for quite a long time but it did not take much thought to discern Antonina's reasoning: with Theodora gone she was without high-level protection and she would have reasoned, as had he, that Justinian had not recalled him at such a time to inflict on him any kind of punishment.

'Whatever fears you had Antonina, let them rest.'

Up came the face, with damp eyes. 'I feared only for your person. You were surrounded in Italy by many who would be jealous of what position you could be elevated to. And then there is the sea itself, never still and always dangerous.'

That she was deliberately avoiding the real reason he had to expect, which annoyed Flavius. Surely for once she could be truthful and say she needed him and his protection. In amongst all his speculations on the voyage – and they had ranged far and wide – what to do about his errant wife had barely surfaced. Had he become so immune to her endemic underhandedness as to just take it as part of the life he had to live?

'I sent word to the palace as soon as I heard your galley had been sighted.'

'Then I best make my way there.'

The response was swift. 'Is it not better to wait? Is not best to let Justinian summon you rather than appear too ardent to kneel at his feet.'

'I don't kneel at his feet,' Flavius replied with real anger. 'Others may give way to Persian follies, not me!'

To accompany that rebuke he hauled Antonina to her feet to see confusion in her expression, which was part a frown yet mixed with uncertainty: she probably wanted to chide him but was cautious of doing so.

'If you go to the palace I shall not accompany you.'

'Because you don't want to or you cannot?'

The old Antonina emerged then, her eyes flashing. 'Do you need to be so deliberately cruel?'

'I wasn't aware of being so, but it is obvious

that with Theodora dead you are no longer such a welcome visitor to the parts of the palace she once occupied. Which makes me wonder where you have been laying your head.'

'At our villa, where else?'

'Then go back there, Antonina.'

'You will come there?'

'Of course. Where else would I go?'

It came as no surprise that Justinian kept him waiting. For all the peremptory nature of his command to return, he would still be conscious of his rank; emperors did not inconvenience themselves for anyone. That accepted, the time he took to send for Flavius rankled, so it was a far from benign *comes sacri stabuli* who, having gone through many more layers of bodyguards and Excubitors than had ever previously protected Justinian, was ushered into his presence.

At least there was daylight; the drapes were open, albeit there were two broad-shouldered guards outside to ensure no one could cast a spear into the room and kill him. He looked better than the last time Flavius had clapped eyes on him, fuller of face and body, though he had never been large. The two men appraised each other for several seconds before Justinian spoke.

'You have gone grey, Count Belisarius.'

'Who would not in your service, Excellency?'

'Are you going to make things difficult?'

'I am obliged to ask what things.'

'Do you know how few people are ever allowed to sit in my presence, Flavius?'

'And I am supposed to grovel for being allowed to occasionally do so?'

Flavius knew he was pushing and perhaps too hard. As Justinian slowly shook his head, as if he was being faced by something preposterous, Flavius could not help but examine the motives for his own contrariness, almost as if he wished to cause discord between them. If this was his aim, he failed, given Justinian smiled, his head canting in that familiar way as he did so.

'It is refreshing, if exasperating, Flavius that you do not change.'

'For which I have always hoped, too often in vain, that you would respect me.'

'Does it not show respect that I want you by my side?'

Flavius was about to ask for what, but that would have bordered on the foolish. He had reasoned over the weeks of travel that with Theodora gone Justinian might lack a trustworthy companion, for whatever had been her fantasies and intrigues she had been his faithful helpmeet and there was a need for a replacement. Justinian had more or less stated by what he had just said that was what he desired.

Was the prospect one to savour for a man who had never been at home in the imperial palace? Flavius thought not but he also knew that if commanded to fulfil such a role he had no choice but to obey.

'Would it displease you if I said I am a soldier and I would be happier employed as such?'

The reply was coldly pragmatic. 'What I need takes precedence over any desires you may have.'

'You know I am no good at,' Flavius waved, unable to think of the right words, 'what goes on

379

within these walls.'

'Never fear, Flavius. I have rediscovered since my sad loss that I still am.'

What transpired felt at first like some kind of limbo. He was accommodated in the imperial palace, given a set of apartments close to those of Justinian, and it was made plain to all who counselled him that Flavius Belisarius was amongst their number and important, a fact driven home by the number of private conversations he had with the Emperor as well as the fact that he and Antonina would accompany Justinian twice daily to pray at the Church of the Holy Apostles where Theodora was buried.

From his wife, now happily back in the palace too, he heard of the death of the Empress, caused by a mammary malignancy, which she had kept hidden for some time until it could no longer be kept from view. Justinian had been distraught at the loss and that was emphasised by the way, when he spoke alone with Flavius and a difficulty was aired, he was often to say what his late wife would have done.

She had been heavily involved in religious arguments and it was in an act of faithfulness – apparently he had sworn at her deathbed – that Justinian put much effort into seeking an accommodation between the Monophysites of Asia Minor and Egypt and the European proponents of Chalcedon. It was not a circumstance to make Flavius happy: he was used in this as an honest broker between what he knew to be a pair of irreconcilable positions.

'They will never agree, *Autokrator*.'

The use of that Greek term of address, employed by everyone else close to the Emperor now, had been a small concession of Flavius and the first time he had employed it Justinian had given him an odd look, until he got the underlying meaning that his *comes* had finally accepted his role as a courtier.

Naturally his elevation to such a position caused resentment among men who saw him as a rival and as Flavius set his mind to understanding how the structures of power operated in the empire his appreciation of the burden Justinian carried grew. It had never been a mystery to him that the polity was too large for one man to govern, yet the complexity, once he began to get a grip on it, staggered him.

His first lesson was in rank. It was easy to assume that certain titles meant a man was more powerful than those of lesser station, yet that was untrue. In a system that had been based on clientism since the days of the Republic, it soon became apparent that a title meant little; it was to whom you were attached, either a superior or a whole host of inferiors, that granted power and there was one very obvious fact: Flavius Belisarius was sadly lacking in such support.

Many sought to ensnare him and that was tempting, more to Antonina than to her husband, and she would comment frequently upon the opportunities. It was, of course for her a subject to which she was committed and he was not: money. Corruption was rife but it seemed to trouble his emperor little.

'It does not concern you that men line their own purses at great cost to the empire?'

Justinian sighed, as if the subject was one of which he was weary. 'The better ones fetch in more than they steal and in my place you soon learn that many attempts have been made to find another system of governance and most have proved disastrous.'

'The Cappadocian, how much did he steal?'

To Flavius this was a cause close to his heart; his armies had suffered particularly from the depredation of that man.

'He did what all office holders do, but look at the courts and the manner in which they were re-formed. How many of our judiciary are no longer patricians looking after the interest of their class?'

'I seem to recall John replaced them in venality. He was adept at selling verdicts.'

'Less adept at seeking power.'

Say nothing Flavius; he had learnt quickly that any criticism of Theodora was most unwelcome and to mention her entrapment of John would never serve. The hardest occasion to remain silent was when Justinian thanked him for his gift of part of his fortune. Theodora had told her husband Flavius had insisted upon it, when he had never even been consulted. He could have asked for it back, but why would he when he was now in receipt of so much imperial bounty?

Slowly but surely lines were being drawn within the bureaucracy between those who resented Flavius and wanted to actively work to diminish him and the others who sought to recruit him into backing whatever cause they were presently pursuing. Narses soon showed he was an enemy, while the likes of John the Cappadocian, partly restored, made moves to appear an ally.

A quickly rising Ancinius Probus Vicinus was solidly placed in the lower ranks of officials, he having attached himself to a powerful patrician clan who had once supported his father and uncle. Both were seen as victims of Belisarian malice, his hatred fuelling their attitude. He discussed the matter with Justinian, given the Emperor knew as much about the case of Senuthius Vicinus as did he.

He had also come closer to understanding the bond that had existed between the imperial couple. There had been a sexual element, of course, though he never even hinted at wishing to have that defined. Being an emperor was a position of utter loneliness if you had no one at all to confide in. If it had within it elements of genuine affection, the pair had a bond that rested on mutual survival. Justinian was as aware as his wife of what would happen to her if he lost his throne or expired. He therefore knew without equivocation that she would always act on his behalf.

His own marriage had settled into what seemed a convenience; Antonina enjoyed what she saw as the glory reflected on her by her husband's position. Naturally, given her vanity and inability to see the wood for the trees, she assumed to herself inappropriate airs and graces and was quick to complain to Flavius if she felt slighted. For the sake of peace he assured her the supposed miscreant would hear of it; they never did, for he was as opposed to wasting his breath as he

383

had been to wasting his soldiers' lives.

Yet in one area he found himself powerless against her. The betrothal of his daughter Ioannina, arranged by Theodora, no longer found favour with Antonina; how quickly had her old companion gone from saint to sinner, to be lambasted for matters in which Antonina had previously been her stout supporter. The betrothal was to be called off, which had Ioannina come to her father, whom she barely knew, asking him to intercede, given she had formed a genuine affection for the imperial nephew. Here she was before him, a sweet child of tender years, in tears and her apparently so powerful parent was in no position to help her.

'It was your fortune Theodora was after, don't you see? Ioannina is your sole heir. The whole thing was arranged when she gave it back to you. That woman, when I think of some of the things she did!'

'The child is unhappy,' Flavius pleaded.

'For now,' Antonina scoffed. 'Take it from one who knows, when you clearly do not. She will get over it.'

If there were matters of religion to occupy him, Flavius did not forget the military, and Justinian always consulted him when such matters were raised. The enmity with Narses was barely disguised and it proved to be something Justinian could not settle, even if he made his displeasure known. The old eunuch would counter any proposal advanced by Flavius and that applied to the continuing running sore of Italy.

'Narses is ever badgering me for a military

command and I weary of you two fighting like cats in a sack.'

'Not as much as I do, *Autokrator.*'

'I am minded to send him to take command in Italy now that Germanus is gone.'

An imperial nephew, Germanus had been proposed by Flavius as a fitting man to take command in Italy. On his way he was obliged to divert and repel a large incursion by the Slavs. That achieved and on his way to Italy once more, Germanus had fallen ill and died. A replacement was urgently required.

'He could be a good choice.'

'Flavius, he's your sworn foe.'

'What bearing does that have?'

'Of course, he would be out of your hair.'

'What's left of it,' came the reply, which got an imperial frown. Justinian was well ahead of Flavius in hair loss. 'But that has nothing to do with my opinion, though I will say this. It matters less who you send to Italy than that they are given the means to ensure success.'

'The cost, Flavius,' Justinian moaned.

'Not to spend now is foolish. And if anyone can conquer Italy completely think of the taxes that will produce. Besides, Narses is your Treasury Chamberlain. If anyone can find the money he can, perhaps in the coffers in his cellar.'

Did the eunuch ever learn that his subsequent successes had come from the arguments advanced by Flavius Belisarius? Did he know that when he made such slow progress – it took him a whole year to get from Illyria to Italy proper – that the same man calmed Justinian and prevented his recall? Narses arrived in the peninsula with that which Flavius had never had, a huge army and over the three years of his campaign he utterly destroyed Goth power.

The war was going well in Hispania too, with the Visigoths being driven back from places they had held for two hundred years. On the eastern frontier Martinus was repaying the faith placed in him. After a long campaign he took Petra and beat a huge Sassanid army to finally bring peace to the frontier, albeit not without a huge payment of gold from the imperial treasury.

At the side of Justinian, advising him was the man most of the citizens of Constantinople still considered to be the empire's best general. Flavius Belisarius could still walk the streets without an escort, was still greeted and applauded for his known probity. In the imperial bureaucracy and the courtiers surrounding the Emperor he was hailed as the only one not engaged in endemic theft.

The man who refused to see himself as such, went about those duties that his emperor demanded of him, was honest as he had always been, never shrinking from telling Justinian when he thought him mistaken, always with his mantra that if he spoke offensively it was for the good of the empire.

He was the envoy of choice in any dispute, and that extended to dealing with Pope Vigilius, a man he would happily have sliced in two. Without Theodora to protect him Vigilius found himself at odds with Justinian and that was a battle he could not win. He was finally deposed and sent into exile on an island that at least had food and water, which Flavius was not sure he deserved.

To say there was peace never could be true with such long borders. There were incursions all the time as various barbarian tribes sought to plunder the wealth of Byzantium.

Narses had been obliged to put aside Italy to repel a Hun invasion and it was ever the case that the most porous frontier was in the area of land within which Flavius had grown up.

The Danube could never be anything other than porous; the number of points at which it could be crossed made utter security impossible. It had been like that when Flavius was a youngster and it was still like that now, held by a thin screen of small detachments based on the various riverbank cities. They were not strong enough to prevent serious incursions and had no choice if they faced one but to withdraw into their strongholds and wait for succour from the capital.

As long as the numbers of invaders could be counted in the hundreds all was well. When they came in thousands that left the borderlands at their mercy. Concern was mitigated by their limited aims: plunder until checked and then a swift withdrawal across the river with their booty, knowing they would not be pursued.

'The leader is a Kutrigur Hun called Zabergan, *Autokrator*, and he leads a force calculated at twenty thousand men.'

'Cut that in half,' Flavius advised.

'Half is still a great number,' was Justinian's

response, before he turned back to the fellow who had brought the unwelcome news. 'Do we have any notion of his intentions?'

'All we know is that Zabergan is heading for Thrace, while another part of his force has taken a path that will bring them to Greece.'

Maps were produced, instructions despatched to Narses, still in command of a huge army, to tell him of what was happening in his rear, but the problem lay in Constantinople. The size of the army was not as it had been on Justinian's accession. Everything that could be mustered was on the various fighting fronts so there was no readily available force to send into Moesia against Zabergan. It was a case of wait and see what this Hun would do.

He came on; there was no retiring back to the Danube with his spoils and if the city itself was safe – nowhere had walls like Constantinople – that did not apply to the hinterland. Intelligence came hinting that Zabergan was intent on crossing to Asia Minor, tempted by a land that had not been plundered for centuries and was dripping with possibilities.

To get there he would ignore the capital of the empire; all he had to do was get across the narrows of the Hellespont and the men to stop him did not exist. The various companies that were quartered in the city had become the domain of the rich and idle, men who looked very martial in their fine liveries but would be of no use in a real fight.

Given all of his experienced generals were away fighting, when Zabergan reached Melantias, a mere sixty leagues from the capital, Justinian had only one man to turn to. If he had few soldiers he at least had a brilliant man to command what could be cobbled together.

'A poisoned chalice,' was Antonina's vociferous opinion. 'So the mob will stop howling at him.'

'Yet one I cannot refuse.'

'You'll get yourself killed. Do you intend to face these devils on your own?'

'Perhaps,' Flavius replied, as he made his way out of the palace to join Solomon and the bodyguards he had managed to retain, 'I should send you to frown at them.'

'Don't die,' was her wailing cry.

She would not have heard Flavius's reply, it being too soft. 'We all die, God wills it so.'

## CHAPTER TWENTY-NINE

A hundred-strong *bucellarii* consisting of some of his old *comitatus,* leavened by Goths and Vandals who had taken service with him, was never going to be enough to confront and stop Zabergan, so Flavius sent his most trusted men to those places in the city and surrounding countryside where old soldiers gathered, with enough in the way of rewards to tempt them from whatever life they had chosen, and by the time he had departed the city he had a force numbering some six hundred effectives.

Everyone was superbly equipped, for their general had raided the quarters of the useless units, such as the *Scholae Palatinae* and deprived them of their weapons, armour and horses. As a leader who had always valued experience over numbers he was not content – how could he be, facing a host of the size reputed? – yet he was lifted in spirit by the way the various contingents gelled within days into a proper formation.

The lack was in any infantry and that was impossible to address, so again using Justinian's gold he bribed the peasantry on his way to depart their fields and hamlets and take service in what would, and this was driven home, be a case of them protecting their hearths from a marauding horde heading their way.

Watching them move up the road he was reminded of the host led by Vitalian over forty years previously, of which he had been a part. Fired by religion, that march on Constantinople had consisted of very much the same sort of people – farmers, artisans, day labourers – and they carried the same variety of weapons. Old swords and spears had been dug out, axes were more numerous and sharp enough to shave a chin. It was the other tools that amused: scythes, pitchforks and one he recalled had once probably saved his life, a long-handled pollarding tool with a serrated billhook at its end.

Solomon rode at his side, a man who, if he bore the title of *domesticus* and was responsible for the organisation of the life of his general, was much more useful than any mere domestic servant. First, he was brilliant at supply so that the marching army, now numbering thousands, never lacked for food or warmth. Added to that, he had proved both in North Africa and Italy to be a clever commander of men, indeed against the Vandals Flavius had stood off and let Solomon successfully complete a battle he had been the first to engage in.

Progress was attended by a great dwell of noise, this due to the enthusiasm of the peasants he had recruited who, never having been in battle, were convinced of their innate ability to beat any foe they came across. God was with them – so were their priests – and he would not let them fail against pagans.

'How I pray that they are right,' Flavius said, when Solomon alluded to the almost constant bursts of cheering that emanated from their rear, as well as that which animated it. 'I hope, too, some of them make it home.'

'We have been in some bad places together, *Comes*, but I can't think of one worse than this.'

'Do not be insulted if I say that any man who has no desire to be here has to remain.'

'Where else would I go?' Solomon barked, clearly irritated.

Flavius smiled to take the sting out of the exchange. 'I don't know about you but I could think of a hundred places.'

'Home?'

'Where would that be, Armenia?'

'Where else, with a sound roof, good horses and women and all the time in the world to hunt.'

'My father's *domesticus* was an Armenian and an irascible old mentor he was. I would not be here without him having saved me on more than one occasion, but when you talk so fondly of home I fear I have none.'

Solomon knew better than to allude to the villa they had so recently departed, rarely occupied since Flavius had been accommodated in the palace and still not seen by him as a domicile for a family. He was also aware that in years of serving alongside his general he had never alluded to the past beyond his arrival in Constantinople.

'There had to be a home once, *Comes*.'

'There was – and a happy one. I had good friends, a strong family and I can even remember fondly the pedagogue whom I teased so mercilessly up until the day it was all taken from me. We are now retracing steps that I took in the aftermath. I have wondered since we set out if being on this road is taking me towards my destiny.'

'That is a gloomy reflection.'

'True,' Flavius said emphatically, 'and that is a mood that will not serve. We must act as if victory is foretold.'

'Don't let the priests hear you say that, they will think it blasphemous.'

It took a week of marching to get into a position that would oblige the Huns to react, Flavius having no doubt his approach would be known. He hoped Zabergan would have no idea of the composition of his army for, if he did, there could only be one result. At every stop for the night, he had lit ten times more campfires than were truly required, hoping to fool the Huns as to his numbers.

Out ahead of his forces, indeed even in front of his cavalry screen, hard by a settlement called Cherson, Flavius found the kind of battlefield he sought, a long narrow valley, not too steep-sided but heavily wooded and one that would require Zabergan to take a wide detour to avoid him.

'Not that I think he will want to.' This was addressed to the trio of leaders he had chosen to act with a degree of independence. There was not a general amongst them and for that Flavius was grateful. Instead of persuasion he had men who listened carefully and accepted without question that what he proposed must be followed. 'We will be heavily outnumbered. The task is to take from our enemies the advantage they draw from that.'

Less sober were the peasant levies; if they had been full of braggadocio when setting out, a week of free food and mutual dares had raised their enthusiasm to a dangerous level and the risk from that was that they would become uncontrollable. On what he hoped would be their last night of camping, and before they were fed, Flavius had them gather so he could lecture them on what he required.

'My fellow citizens,' he bellowed, arms out-stretched, raising a murmur of approbation, hardly surprising given these folk were more accustomed to insults from men of the Belisarius stamp. 'Upon us rests the security of the whole state. We, and only we, stand between the barbarians and the gates of Constantinople.'

The response started as a couple of yells but ended up as a roar of bellicose defiance.

'Do you know of me?' he demanded when that died down. 'I am Flavius Belisarius and I have beaten every enemy the empire has faced these last forty years. Persians, Vandals, Goths and even some Italians.'

That got a cheer; mostly Greek, these levies hated that race. Flavius then listed his victories; Dara, Carthage, Naples, Rome, Ravenna, even if most before him would never have heard the names and could certainly not place them in their narrow world.

'But!' Up went a hand that indicated restraint. 'I have only been successful because I have been obeyed. No general can win a battle. Only the men he leads can achieve that. Do you before me wish to beat the Huns?'

That naturally produced an even greater roar as Flavius dropped his voice just enough to force those before him to lean forward to listen. 'Do as I tell you, keep your eye on my standard and do not go far from it, and we will prevail. Now, I call upon you to fill your bellies, to see to your weapons and pray, for I believe it cannot be long before the Huns come to chase us away. What a fright we shall visit upon them.'

'I don't think I have ever heard you boast before.'

'It makes me uncomfortable, Solomon, but the times require it.'

The only sign of the Huns the following day was scouts reconnoitring their camp. For all his attempts to fool them in darkness Flavius knew he could not do so in daylight, nor could he avoid it being seen that he was preparing a defensive ditch all around his position. Those scouts would be counting his numbers and from that Zabergan would draw a very obvious conclusion: an easy victory awaited him.

It was necessary to anticipate that he would

move on the next day, so Flavius, in the pre-dawn, made his deployments. Two-thirds of his cavalry were despatched to hide in the woods either side of the valley while the remainder, under his personal command, stood at the head where it opened up into a wide area of pasture cut by a dry river bed. Part in and part out of that were his peasant levies under Solomon.

His hopes were rewarded by the sight of the glinting on armour and the men he had set out to watch for the enemy came back with the first bit of good news: the Huns' numbers were guessed at around two thousand, which meant that Zabergan had not brought to the field his entire host.

As soon as they began to advance Solomon blew a horn that had those peasants yell at the top of their voices while brandishing with fury whatever it was they carried.

The next move had to place a question in Zabergan's mind, even as he began his advance. Flavius led his small force forward, passing over the defensive ditch and filling the valley floor from side to side.

The Huns were eager for battle and in Zabergan they had a leader fully confident of victory, to Flavius a dangerous combination and he watched as his enemies acted exactly as he hoped. What had been a steady progress broke into a fast canter and for some a full-out charge as the Huns sought to close with the thin crust of fighting men they faced, not checked by the fact that the enemies did likewise, though in a flat and continuous line.

The *bucellarii* checked the leading elements of the Huns by arrow fire before they hooked their bows over the saddle horn and took hold of their spears. Behind them the peasants had set up such a cacophony of noise that it drowned out the sound of thudding hooves and yelling combatants and by stamping their feet they also sent into the air a huge cloud of dust which, on the wind, drifted down the valley.

As soon as the two opposing lines met, with the Hun advance momentarily checked, the men Flavius had placed in the woods emerged at full tilt to hit both the flanks of their enemies, which drove the Huns in on themselves creating a dense mass of horsemen most of whom could not get at the men attacking them for their own comrades. It was obvious that both in front and to the sides the experienced fighting men Flavius had deployed, better armoured and mounted than the Huns, were killing at will.

Flavius was in the heart of the central battle and he was rarely engaged against just one enemy. A sword stroke cut through his thigh but that had to be ignored. Another swinging blade hit his helmet and so dazed him he had to spin his mount away to clear enough space to recover, finding himself enclosed by his own bodyguards as he re-entered the fray.

A low blow from an axe got under his shield to dent his chest armour and he knew he had suffered a wound but that too had to be disregarded as the battle reached its climax. The Huns were penned in, milling around and mostly useless. The sound of horns struggled to be heard over the still yelling peasant levies and now the dust was among the fighting, making it hard to see anything.

That must have affected Zabergan, who would be unable to observe if those screaming peasants, who Flavius knew would look formidable at a distance, were about to push forward and get in among his horsemen. If they did the result could be a catastrophe and slowly at first, then with increasing pace, the rear elements of the Huns began to withdraw, soon followed by their comrades desperately trying to disengage from their personal contests.

Solomon had his orders and as soon as the fact was relayed to him – he could not see for the dust either – he ordered the peasants forward. If they were barely visible the rising sound of their stridency must have conveyed to Zabergan that he was in danger of being overwhelmed. Within a blink, all those at the front could see was the retreating flanks of the Hun horses.

Flavius had not felt pain until that point but it came upon him now, both from the wounds he had suffered as well as blows inflicting less damage. Yet he could not relax for he feared his own levies, if they got out of control and went after the Huns, would be massacred; such peasants could not face proper fighters in an open battle and he was now riding before them accompanied by his horsemen to block their desire to run after the enemy.

That it succeeded was only by a narrow margin, added to the fact that having shouted for so long many of the host were hoarse and only too eager to desist. Their general was thus able to convey that they had won a great victory and so replace the desire for pursuit with celebration.

'One battle, Solomon.' Flavius gasped as the mendicant monks worked to repair his wounds. The gash in his thigh had gone deep and he had several broken ribs, from armour so dented it had been a task to get it off without causing further harm. 'If he comes again we will not beat him twice.'

He was still comatose when the news came of the Hun withdrawal. Zabergan had suffered just enough to make him worry about progressing further, so he offered to sell his thousands of Thracian captives to Justinian, which was readily accepted, at which point he headed north, back to the Danube and home.

Flavius required a litter with which to re-enter the capital but the cheering was just as vociferous as it had been when, on his return from North Africa, he rode along the Triumphal Way on horseback. It pleased him that those Vandals in his service, and the Goths too, were hailed with equal passion.

Justinian provided the best physicians but it was weeks stretching into months before Flavius was fully ambulant, albeit with a pronounced limp, while the black bruise on his chest seemed permanent, which had the people attending him shaking their heads. His popularity soared as that of Justinian fell; the Emperor castigated for buying Zabergan off instead of pursuing him and destroying his army, this by a citizenry that had no idea such a thing was impossible.

Being a rod for discontent had an effect on their relationship; Justinian hated to be booed in the Hippodrome when Flavius Belisarius, limping and clearly in pain, was loudly cheered.

The day three months later when the Excubitors came to arrest Flavius was one of brilliant sunshine and he was in a good mood, overseeing a better laying out of his garden, this while Antonina entertained a whole host of neighbours only too willing to listen to her boasting – she had a hand in winning all of her husband's battles of course – for the chance of proximity to the wife of such a hero; they scattered quick enough when the fact of his arrest became known.

'The charge is that you have engaged in conspiracy to displace the Emperor.'

'Again?' Flavius sighed.

By the time he reached the palace dungeons, he had once more been stripped of offices and wealth. The source of the charge was none other than Ancinius Probus Vicinus and it was relayed to him that proof existed of the crime. Two of his *comitatus* had been arraigned for plotting the downfall of Justinian and under torture had implicated their general, which obliged him once more to face the senate and interrogation by a man he knew wanted him disgraced.

'You deny the charge?' Vicinus crowed.

'Of course.'

'The senate has evidence.'

'Obtained under torture,' Flavius replied, his hand on a chest that now contained a permanent pain.

'Which is valid. Hot irons will produce a truth that would otherwise be concealed.'

'My fellow senators,' Flavius cried, wincing as

he did so.

'You are not at liberty to address the house.'

'I am and I defy anyone to prevent me. Step forward, Vicinus, if you wish and you will experience the difference between serving the empire and serving your malice.'

Looking past his prosecutor Flavius raised his voice, ignoring the stabbing it produced. 'I have served the empire and its emperors for near fifty years and been faithful all that time. You know the offers made to me and declined, and I suspect you are also aware that none of you may walk the streets of the city as freely as I do.'

That set up a low hum. 'Could I depose my emperor? Maybe, but it requires me to break a vow to a man I hold in higher esteem even than the *Autokrator*. That is my father, Decimus Belisarius who, along with my three elder brothers, was murdered by the father of the man now accusing me of seeking the diadem.'

'A lie!' Vicinus yelled.

'You are so steeped in treachery, it is so in your blood, Vicinus, that you cannot even conceive of honesty. Who overheard my men talking of revolt?' Pain notwithstanding he pointed at a number of senators to be favoured with shaking heads. 'You? You? On whose orders were they tortured until they confessed?'

'Know this,' he cried, a digit now aimed straight at Vicinus. 'I destroyed this man's father and impoverished his heirs. I did so with the secret assistance of our Emperor Justinian when he was no more than secretary to his uncle.'

That set up a whole raft of whispers as heads

400

came together to cogitate on what they were being told. 'If you do not believe me, I demand you call Justinian before this house and question him on the truth of what I have said.'

It would have been amusing if it had not been so serious. No senate would dare call an emperor to face them; it was a good way to see the inside of the dungeons.

'I am sick of this kind of accusation levelled at me more than once. I, as one of your equals and an ex-consul, demand that you vote now on whether this charge is valid or part of a conspiracy that may well be aimed at disguising the ambition of others. You have nothing but torture evidence. Torture me if you must but it will be to no avail. And then I invite you to face the citizens of Constantinople and convince them of my guilt.'

The slow handclap from the balcony took every eye in that direction. It had to be Justinian and he was telling the house which way to vote.

'Why did you not intervene earlier? You must have known it was nonsense.'

'Do I know that,' Justinian said, canting his head and pulling at his few remaining strands of grey hair, 'when nearly every voice I hear tells me you are conspiring against me?'

'I see I am a victim of my own absence from your council, which has allowed others to work on wits surely becoming addled.'

'You dare not address me so.'

'I do and I will.' Flavius responded, stopping a hand that was halfway to the pain in his chest. 'Those who spoke of this, hate my success. They wish to see me a beggar.'

'All your offices and your monies have been restored.'

'What was it, jealousy?' Justinian actually went white but Flavius would not let him speak. 'Do you so hate the cheers that greet me in the Hippodrome that you seek ways to clip my pride?'

'Don't deny you are proud, Flavius.'

'I am proud of the service I have given you and your uncle. I am proud that when the time comes to meet my Maker I will have nothing of which I am ashamed.'

'Are you so free from sin?'

'No man is and no ruler either. I hope that God and the saints are so impressed with the Church of St Sophia that they will forgive you, for you are but a man.'

Flavius hit a nerve then and it was deliberate; others might seek to imply that his imperial estate was semi-divine, but neither man believed it to be true. If Justinian feared anything it was the prospect of answering for the way he had lived his life and the manifest sins therein, hence his devotion to prayer.

'Know that I wish you no ill,' Flavius added, 'but I must tell you that I will provide you with no more of my service.'

'You will do as I command.'

'What, and me to appeal to the mob you so fear?'

Flavius turned then, and despite being angrily called back, limped out of the imperial presence. It was only out of sight that he found the need to lean against a pillar and allow the marble to cool a heated brow. He felt his time was coming: the latest wounds had tapped his resolve and left him feeling weak. He was no longer fit to do battle and had no desire to still advise. That Antonina was furious he took as inevitable but he lacked the strength to argue with her.

Less than a year after his success against the Huns the moment came when the effect of that chest wound could no longer be held at bay and Count Flavius Belisarius went to meet his maker. The last image in his mind as he slipped out of life was of himself crossing a field next to the River Danube inhabiting a body sixteen once more rather than sixty. Standing waiting to greet him and smiling were his father and three elder brothers eager to tell him that he had nothing to fear.

# AUTHOR'S NOTE

The Emperor Justinian survived his greatest general by a mere eight months and the conquests undertaken during his reign did not hold. Under his successors, North Africa fell to Islam and they, crossing the Straits of Gibraltar, took most of Spain as well. Between Rome and the Alps, despite the success of Narses and his huge army, a level of force never granted to Belisarius, it remained an area of conflict between Franks, Burgundians and Lombards until it became part of Charlemagne's Holy Roman Empire.

Only in the south did the conquests hold. Byzantium continued to rule the lower half of Italy, despite Saracen and Lombard pressure, for five centuries. The race that subdued the Lombards and finally evicted from Italy a polity that still thought of itself as the Roman Empire, were the Normans, a story told by the author in a trilogy beginning with *Mercenaries*.

The publishers hope that this book has given you enjoyable reading. Large Print Books are especially designed to be as easy to see and hold as possible. If you wish a complete list of our books please ask at your local library or write directly to:

**Magna Large Print Books**
Magna House, Long Preston,
Skipton, North Yorkshire.
BD23 4ND

This Large Print Book for the partially sighted, who cannot read normal print, is published under the auspices of

## THE ULVERSCROFT FOUNDATION